OF SHADOW & SEA

Will Wight

Books by Will Wight

THE TRAVELER'S GATE TRILOGY

House of Blades

The Crimson Vault

City of Light

The Traveler's Gate Chronicles

THE ELDER EMPIRE

Of Sea & Shadow

Of Shadow & Sea

Of Darkness & Dawn•

*Of Dawn & Darkness**

**forthcoming*

THE ELDER EMPIRE : FIRST SHADOW

OF SHADOW & SEA

WILL WIGHT

Of Shadow and Sea

Book and cover design by Patrick Foster Design/Amanda Key
Cover illustration by Melanie de Carvalho

ISBN 978-0-9896717-3-6 *(print edition)*

www.WillWight.com
will@willwight.com
twitter.com/willwight

To NegaMom, who always supports my parallel self in Earth-1.

Welcome, Reader.

Right now, you're reading the first book in The Elder Empire series.

But it's not the ***only*** *first book.*

Of Shadow and Sea *was written in parallel to* ***Of Sea and Shadow****, which takes place at the same time from a different perspective.*

You can begin with either book, and you will find that they each tell a complete story. Upon finishing ***Of Shadow and Sea****, you will be fully prepared for its sequel,* ***Of Dawn and Darkness.***

But I wrote these first two books together, and their stories intertwine in a way that I think you'll enjoy. I invite you, when you're through with this book, to check out ***Of Sea and Shadow.***

Until then…

Welcome to the Elder Empire.

CHAPTER ONE

FIFTEEN YEARS AGO

When they had to kill a grown man, the children worked in pairs.

The Bait, usually a girl, would lure the target in by faking some sort of crisis and begging for help. When the target isolated himself, the Knife would drive their blade home.

By mutual agreement, Mari was always the Bait. She had long, curly hair and big eyes that looked like she was always ready to cry. Sometimes adults would stop her on the street and ask her what was wrong, even when she wasn't trying to lure anybody.

Shera was the Knife.

The two of them dressed poor, but not too poor. They couldn't look like homeless beggars, or the target would never stop. Maxwell had provided a faded dress and cheap blue ribbon for Mari, and a boy's pants, shirt, and cap for Shera. No shoes.

Some of Maxwell's older children complained about how they hated waiting; the long, boring stretch of hours between the time you set up your ambush and the time the target wandered through. Sometimes the target would *never* show, and you wasted your whole afternoon.

Not Shera. This was her favorite part.

As Mari sat on one side of the street with her chin in her hands, waiting for the target to pass by, Shera leaned against the wall of an alley, eating chunks of meat from a stolen skewer. The noise of the Capital blurred into a soothing lullaby, and she found herself drifting off as she watched the people pass her alleyway: a tourist couple carrying their luggage; a shirtless Izyrian hunter with a musket over one shoulder and a rabbit in his hand; an alchemist with her mask hanging down around her neck, biting her lip and scribbling on a clipboard.

Shera could watch the crowds all day. You saw all kinds of people in the Empire's Capital.

The familiar sights and the droning music of the city lulled her to sleep, tugging her eyelids down. She curled up against the alley wall, hugging the skewer to prevent its one remaining piece of meat from falling to the ground.

She so rarely got the chance for a nap. And now they could be here for hours…

Shera opened her eyes again at the sound of Mari's voice. "Please, I don't know what's wrong with her," the girl choked out, through her sniffles. "She's fallen asleep and won't wake up!"

Why can't she let it go? Last time, Mari had brought the target around the corner and found Shera fast asleep, knife still clutched in her hand. That had required some fast talking—and some fast work with a blade.

The sun had all but set while Shera napped, leaving her blanketed in the shadows of the alley. Perfect. The target wouldn't be suspicious when he failed to see her.

Shera rolled up to a crouch, hiding behind a crate of empty bottles. She tore the last piece of meat—now cold—from the skewer and tossed the empty stick away. Still chewing, she pulled the knife from the back of her pants.

"I am no physician, girl," Kamba Nomen said, his voice shrill and precise. "I can promise nothing for your sister."

Maxwell made sure that his gang of children knew their targets better than they knew their own reflections. Before Shera could see Kamba, she knew him: a short, dark-skinned man with a limp, walking with the aid of a cane. He was a Reader, but not the sort who cleansed battlefields of lingering resentment and invested scythes so that they cut wheat more efficiently.

"He's a different breed of Elder-spawned filth," Maxwell had assured them. *"He lays curses for hire, and as the whim strikes him. A woman sold him a bad piece of fruit, and within the day her cart collapsed. Sent her to the physicians with two broken legs and a cut neck. Last week, a neighbor of his burned up in an unexplained fire. The Empire has no use for this man, children. He deserves his fate."*

The silver-capped tip of Kamba's cane appeared around the edge of Shera's crate, and she tensed her grip on the knife. He wasn't supposed to see her before she struck. She was going to have to fight.

Ice grew in her heart, cold spreading inside her like frost on a winter field. If she had to fight Kamba, so what? Either he would die, or she would. Her hand steadied on the knife, and her body loosened.

But Mari hastily ran up and grabbed Kamba's other hand, directing him to the other wall of the alley.

"Not there! Over here."

Kamba leaned over, looking into the shadows where Shera and Mari had placed another bundle of clothes. In the darkness of the alley, it should look enough like a little girl crouched under a blanket.

The Reader nudged the bundle with his cane. "This doesn't look like—" he began, but he never got to finish the sentence.

The Bait had done her job. Now it was time for the Knife.

Shera leaped, kicking off the nearby crate and latching onto Kamba's back like a monkey.

Maxwell had warned them about the dangers of confronting a Reader. "*His jacket might be invested. It could turn your knife, so don't risk it.*" Shera didn't. She stabbed him in the throat, where his jacket couldn't cover. Blood sprayed onto the alley wall and trickled over her fingers.

She dropped back to the ground as Kamba staggered around, flailing his arms. One of his spasms jerked his cane back, catching Mari on the shin.

Mari muffled a shout and fell backwards as Kamba finally quieted, twitching and bleeding on the alley stones. Shera quickly dragged him behind the crate—no one on the street would look twice at a suspicious stain on an alley wall, but even the Capital's indifferent citizens might come investigate a body in a rich man's jacket and pants.

Then she walked over and knelt, examining Mari's leg. "Is it cracked, do you think?"

"It hurts," Mari said, real tears welling up in her eyes. "And he almost found out. If you had taken one more second..." She shuddered. "I'm still shaking. Aren't you?"

Shera wiped her knife off on the dead man's coat and stuck it back down the waistband of her pants. "Shaking? It's not cold."

Mari sniffled, wiping tears from her eyes. "Not from the *cold*. Weren't you scared?"

"Of what?"

Shera glanced around the alley, in case she'd missed the sight of an Imperial Guard or some monstrous Elderspawn. Something to be scared of. Surely Mari couldn't have meant she was frightened of Kamba. The man had walked into an alley, and they'd stabbed him. Where was the threat?

Through her tears, Mari let out a long-suffering sigh. "Sometimes I want to be more like you. Other times, I think you'd get yourself killed in a week without me to take care of you."

This spoken by a girl who might have been ten years old. Shera wasn't sure about her own age, but she knew Mari couldn't be that much older. But for some reason, the other girl liked to think of herself as the mother.

Shera looped an arm around Mari's shoulder, helping her to her feet. "Who's taking care of who?"

Together, the pair made their way back to Maxwell's safe house, leaving a corpse behind them.

The safe house for Maxwell and his brood of adopted children rested underneath an *actual* house, a residence across from Gladstone Imperial Park that his family had owned for generations. The two stories above street level were furnished the way a single man living alone might keep them: dishes piled up on the table; a whiskey cabinet perpetually open; only two chairs in the sitting room.

But if you pushed the piano aside and rolled up a cheap Vandenyan rug, you found a trap door.

The three floors beneath formed the home where Shera and the others spent most of their time. Now that Mari and Shera had arrived, with Shera helping Mari down the ladder, they found the safe house in a state of panic.

A girl ran up to Shera, hauling a pillowcase stuffed with odds and ends. "*There* you are! Maxwell says he won't leave without you."

Shera exchanged confused glances with Mari. "Where is he going?"

The girl almost dropped her pillowcase in her excitement. "You haven't heard? Oh, that's right, you've been away. Well, Benji and Keina didn't report in at sunset. When Maxwell went to look for them, he found them *missing*. So he checked the traps in the upstairs house, and they've all been disarmed!"

Shera still felt like she was looking at a puzzle with half the pieces gone. "So...Benji disarmed the traps and ran away?"

A few children ran every few months. Sometimes Maxwell brought them back and dealt with them himself, as examples. Other times, he came back empty-handed. He called the losses, "acceptable costs of doing business."

"You don't get it?" the girl said. "We're under attack! Somebody found us!

They might be here right now!"

She seemed more excited than terrified, hurrying down the hall with her pillowcase over her shoulder.

This time, Shera didn't need to look at Mari's face to know what she was thinking. They hurried downstairs together, Shera helping the hobbling Mari along.

As they shuffled down the hall, Shera heard a clatter and glanced back over her shoulder. There was no one else in the hallway. Only a fallen pillowcase, spilling its treasures all over the ground.

Of the girl, there was no sign.

The safe house was simple, and simply decorated. White walls, bare stone floor, and functional rooms with the bare minimum of cheap wooden furniture. The children slept in beds packed one against the other, sharing straw-stuffed pillows and scratchy woolen blankets.

Shera considered it the most comfortable home she'd ever had. With her real mother, she'd be lucky to have a single blanket in a filthy alley.

The pair hurried through the safe house, passing a steady stream of boys and girls bustling around and clutching their meager belongings. After Mari asked directions three times, they finally found their way to Maxwell: waiting for them in the discipline room.

The discipline room was lined with metal cages, where Maxwell's unruly students found themselves locked for days at a time.

He'd given up using that punishment on Shera after the first time, when she'd simply curled into a ball and slept from sunrise to sunrise.

Maxwell himself stood at the far end of the room, his sleeves rolled up, carrying a cage away from the brick wall. When he heard them enter, he staggered a few steps to the right, dropping the cage in a clatter of iron.

Some students saw Maxwell as their father and called him such, but he never insisted. Personally, Shera had never seen him as family at all.

He always wore black pants and a black shirt, with a white rose tucked into his shirt pocket above the heart. Some of the older girls giggled about how handsome he looked, with his curly brown hair down to his shoulders and his compact, muscular figure. Again, Shera found it difficult to think of him in that way.

He was just Maxwell.

When he turned and saw Shera, he gave a relieved sigh. "Shera. At last.

I was worried that they would...never mind. Did you see anyone in the upstairs house?"

Mari moved away from Shera' support, stepping gingerly on her good leg, and answered. "We saw no evidence of any intruders, Maxwell."

"Of course you didn't see anyone. They're too good for that." He rubbed his hands together, invigorated, but his face still looked drawn and tight. It was the same look he wore in the first day or two after a child ran away and he couldn't bring them back.

He raised his boot and kicked another cage out of the way, and Shera finally saw what he was doing. A low metal grate rested in the middle of the wall, leading into a dark tunnel.

Maxwell nodded to the tunnel. "The other children are trying other means of escape, but this is where we'll be going. Rebel soldiers used this to move from base to base in the Kings' War."

"Should we gather anything from the house, sir?" Mari asked.

He didn't look at her. "Shera, what have I taught you about weapons?"

"A warrior is never unarmed," she said.

Maxwell gave her a proud smile. "Good girl. The others know where to rendezvous, but I didn't want to risk you getting lost. Come on, now."

Mari hesitantly raised her hand, as though asking for permission to speak. "What about—"

"Yes, yes, both of you. Into the tunnel, quickly. If they're who I think they are, we don't have much time."

Shera grabbed Mari by the shoulder again and began helping her toward the tunnel, but Maxwell held a hand out. His eyes sharpened. "What happened to Mari's leg?"

He directed the question at Shera, but she waited for Mari to answer. "I...the target hit me with his cane, Maxwell. It isn't bad."

Their leader shook his head. "Mari. There's too much at stake this time, girl. The Empire is sick, and we are the cure. But if these *hirelings* have their way, we'll never get to spread our good work."

He turned from Mari, picking up a crowbar to pry away at the grate. "Ordinarily I'd wait for you to recover, but we don't have time for that now. You'll slow us down."

Shera had completed the assassination of Kamba Nomen without a single instant of fear, but now a worm of doubt and uncertainty crawled its way into her heart. Instinctively, she stepped between Mari and Maxwell.

"Shera," Maxwell said, without turning around. "When do we kill?"

"When the target has earned his fate. When the target serves no useful function."

He gestured in Mari's direction with his crowbar. "Today, Mari serves no useful function. Quite the opposite. Finish your work."

Mari turned to Shera, eyes wide, tears streaming silently down her cheeks. "Shera..."

Shera looked between Mari and Maxwell. In the back of her waistband, the knife felt freezing cold.

She didn't want to kill Mari. *Why not? Because she's my friend? That doesn't matter. If she's useless, she's useless.*

But Mari was the one to shake Shera awake when she overslept. Mari made fun of Shera for being lazy. Mari told her when she should be afraid, even if Shera didn't feel it.

"She does serve a useful function," Shera said. Mari stared at her, hopeful.

Maxwell turned fully around, gripping his crowbar like a sword. "Then what is it?"

"I can't...I don't have the words for it. But I have a use for her."

Their leader blew out a breath, running his empty hand through his hair. "Children. I sometimes forget that they're children." Gently, he placed the crowbar on top of a nearby cage.

Then he pulled out a pistol and shot Mari in the chest.

Gun smoke filled the tiny room, the shot echoing like a collapsed wall. Shera couldn't take her eyes from Mari, who staggered backwards in her red-stained dress, clutching at a nearby cage for support. She finally collapsed, her mouth working for a few more seconds before she stopped trying to suck in a breath that wouldn't come.

Maxwell tossed his pistol aside. "What have I taught you about mercy, Shera?"

There is no such thing as mercy. There is only hesitation.

But this time, she didn't say it. She remained silent, thinking about Mari.

Her friend was dead. Shera confronted death every day, but she rarely thought about it. Death wasn't personal...except, this time, it was. It hurt like a knife to the chest, and she couldn't quite understand why.

And with the pain, her thoughts grew cold.

Maxwell had grabbed his crowbar again and resumed his work on the grate, prying it away from the brick wall. "No one else has learned my lessons better than you have, Shera. The Consultants think they have the best, but they won't be able to compete with you."

Shera stood behind Maxwell, her knife in her hand, thinking of Mari.

She cocked her head, aware of something she had never thought of before. Maxwell engineered the deaths of dozens, perhaps hundreds of people. He *deserved his fate.* And as for his 'useful function'...

"I have no use for you," she said.

He was starting to turn around when she drew her knife across his calves. He fell to his knees, screaming, and she plunged her knife into his back. Five times, to be safe.

The other children soon arrived, drawn by the sound of the gunshot. From the doorway, they each saw Maxwell, facedown in a pool of his own blood, as well as Mari's body slumped against a cage.

Some of them cried. Others screamed, and still others remained silent. A few looked as though they'd finally been released from prison.

But when they saw Shera, sitting on top of a cage with a bloody knife, none of them entered the room.

Kerian stood in the hallway of Maxwell's safe house, watching her fellow Consultants work. Or rather, watching the *results* of their work.

It was rare, even for her, to catch a Consultant in action.

A twelve-year-old boy raised a shaking pistol with both hands, pointing the barrel at Kerian—the only target in sight. She didn't bother moving.

A black shape passed across the boy and he was gone, pistol and all. A nine-year-old girl, who happened to be turning the corner at that exact moment, gasped and dropped a bundle of clothing. Before she could run off, a pair of black-clad arms reached down from the ceiling and pulled her up through the trap door.

Idly, Kerian fiddled with the leather satchel that hung from her shoulder. She had prepared for any number of contingencies, and thus far none of them had materialized. She couldn't help the boredom. Gardener missions were many things, but they were rarely boring; even if you had to lie perfectly still under a flowing river for six hours, breathing through a reed, assassinations had a thrill all their own.

She was the only Gardener on this mission, for which she was glad. Certain instincts could be hard to suppress, and they wanted these children back alive. The clients had specified as much, for understandable reasons.

The clients were the parents of these missing children. And they had finally offered such an obscene sum of money that the Consultant's Guild could not turn them away.

As glad as she was that she didn't have to rein in a team of Gardeners, she could never get used to working with Shepherds and Masons. The Masons weren't suited for *real* stealth work: they relied on their disguises to see them through, and they couldn't see that disguises served them nothing. A Mason hustled into view now, dressed as an old lady in an apron, chasing a girl down the hallway.

It doesn't matter if you look harmless. If you're a stranger, these children will run. It seemed, sometimes, that Masons left common sense on the island with their Consultant blacks.

Shepherds were a little better; at least they wore black. They were so *skittish.* Kerian had personally witnessed a Shepherd running from an eight-year-old boy with an undersized saber. Shepherds had been trained for so many years to minimize risk that they didn't recognize a harmless target when they saw one.

These children, on the other hand, had been raised like Gardeners. Or as close as Maxwell could come to it, having never seen the Garden himself.

Kerian strolled down the hall, searching through her satchel with one hand as she walked. *An extra pair of knives...useless. Climbing gear...unnecessary. An invested hammer in case we have to break through a wall...well, that one might come in handy.*

She still hoped someone would attack her. A mission didn't feel right without the risk of danger.

When she heard the pistol-shot ring out through the safe house, Kerian's spirits soared. Here, at last, something was happening.

She made her way downstairs, catching snatches of the reports from Shepherds who had—*of course*—already checked out the noise and returned.

"...Maxwell dead."

"...shot one of the girls. Don't know..."

"...looked like he was trying to escape."

A crowd of children clustered around the door to the room full of cages. They were facing the same way, so it was easy for Kerian to slip around them unnoticed and into the room herself.

The scene inside looked like the aftermath of a sloppy Gardener's botched mission.

Cages had been hauled away from one wall, revealing a metal grate that was halfway peeled away from the brick. The tunnel beyond it was Maxwell's "secret" escape route, an underground road dating back to the Kings' War. Five Consultants waited in hiding at the other end, prepared to take Maxwell when he emerged.

But he hadn't made it that far. Maxwell lay facedown as though drowning in blood, five or six stab wounds in the back of his shirt. His killer had been shorter—they'd slashed him across the legs to bring him down so they could reach. One of his children, then, had turned on their master.

Perhaps this girl over here, the curly-haired one with the bullet in her chest. Tears had worn tracks down her cheeks and she still had a blue ribbon in her hair.

Not her, then. She'd died surprised and unarmed.

Kerian glanced around the room before she spotted the killer: a girl, probably less than ten years old, with her black hair spilling out of a cheap cap. She was curled up on a cage, a bloody knife still gripped in her hand.

Asleep.

The Gardener snapped her fingers twice and two Shepherds appeared, black-clad and black-masked, bowing their heads and awaiting her order.

"Finish collecting the rest of the children," she ordered. "Then bring them to the chapter house for the clients."

She nodded to the sleeping killer. "I'll bring this one myself."

CHAPTER TWO

'Intent' is what we call the power of focused will that all humans possess. If you use an object, you invest that object with your Intent. This, in turn, makes your tool more effective.

We have recognized these effects since ancient times, but only now are we learning to turn these principles to our own ends.

I believe the military applications are obvious.

– FROM AN ANCIENT RESEARCH JOURNAL IN THE MAGISTER'S GUILD
(EXCERPT STORED IN THE CONSULTANT'S GUILD ARCHIVES)

Fifteen years later, Shera was having trouble staying awake.

She sat in a padded chair behind a broad desk, forehead pressed against the paperwork she was supposed to be organizing. The room around her was well-appointed and comfortable; a chapter house of the Consultants had to be at least as inviting as this one. Paintings hung on the wall, plants on the windowsill, and the clients' chairs in front of the desk were even more comfortable than Shera's own.

If only they had a client.

This was the northern chapter house, one of three in the Imperial Capital. Even in a city the size of the Capital, not many people could afford the services of the Consultants, and they were usually rich enough to arrange a meeting beforehand. These days, the chapter house's flow of clients had effectively dried up.

Which meant paperwork. Lots and lots of paperwork.

The Shepherds' observations and Masons' reports would usually go straight to the Miners back in their catacombs, but some of the information was time-sensitive. It was up to the staff of the chapter house to sort through the piles of miscellaneous facts and decide exactly what they needed to keep and what needed to be sent back home.

The quicklamps on the wall glowed a steady orange—the alchemical fluid shone with the color of torchlight, or the blaze of sunset. It created an intimate, comfortable atmosphere for clients.

A little too comfortable for Shera. Her head rested on the paper, and her eyes slowly drifted shut. Maybe this time she'd be able to catch a few minutes of sleep before…

Her partner jabbed her in the ribs with what felt like a knife. Shera jerked awake, one of the sheets of paper sticking to her forehead and coming up with her.

Ayana's voice was a rough whisper, like paper over stone. "Control yourself. You should be able to lie motionless for a day and a night without losing focus."

Shera's partner was at least twenty years older than Shera herself, and she looked like an unquiet spirit from a five-bit horror novel. Her pale hair hung in strings like a torn burial shroud, her skin as pale as if it had never seen the sun. And that wasn't the worst of it.

She poked Shera's side again, with her six-inch iron fingernails. They were all-natural, gifts from parents who had not been entirely human.

And a plague on Shera's nap time.

Shera peeled the paper away from her forehead, slapping it back down on the stack in front of her. "Can we have this conversation after I wake up? It's too early for this."

Ayana looked pointedly at the gilded clock ticking away at the corner of the desk. "It's noon."

"Then we should at least wait until six."

Her partner jabbed her again, in the leg this time, but Shera didn't flinch away. That would only invite further punishment. Ayana sighed, drumming her metal nails on the surface of the desk.

"I beg you, take this more seriously. Yala will only relent if we prove ourselves indispensable. We have to be patient."

Shera propped her head in her hands. "*Yala* would execute me this second if she wasn't so afraid of the Regents. You've got a chance, though. Tell her you're sick of me, you'll listen to her commands from now on, and then kill somebody she doesn't like. She'll come around."

Ayana remained silent, still drumming her nails on the wood. Shera started to worry.

"…please don't actually do that."

"I didn't say I would."

"You looked like you were considering it, though."

"I consider many things."

Was she serious, or was she saying this to make Shera sweat? "Don't leave me alone here. I shudder to think who they'd send to replace you."

Ayana clenched her fist, which looked like she'd gripped a handful of knives. "Neither of us should be here. In a time like this, she's wasting not one, but *two* Gardeners? Inexcusable. I don't know why Kerian lets her live."

Kerian lets her live because Kerian doesn't see murder as the solution to every problem. It was an unexpected attitude in an assassin, but Shera had learned to accept it.

"Well, don't go too far," Shera said. "I don't mind being wasted. I've gotten more sleep in the last year than in the rest of my life combined."

"I've noticed."

"My problem is that I can't *enjoy* it. There's always something to do, and that's bad enough, but it's not even enjoyable. It's like raking leaves for a living."

Ayana scraped her iron fingernails together in a horrible cacophony that made Shera wince. "What I'm gathering from this discussion is that you'd like to live the rest of your life on a paid vacation."

Shera considered for a moment. "I've never heard it out loud before, but yes, that sums—"

The ring of a bell cut her off as an old man pushed open the door.

Shera's hands worked without conscious input, gathering up all the papers and shoving them under the desk. Ayana did the same, and in the blink of an eye the evidence of their morning's work was hidden from the client's view. Ayana kept her hands in her lap, smiling pleasantly. The expression made her look like a grinning skull.

Quickly swiping off the smudge of ink she was sure the papers had left on her forehead, Shera adopted the same expression.

"Welcome to the Consultant's Guild," Shera said pleasantly. By mutual agreement, they had decided that Shera was supposed to talk for both of them. Ayana's voice could be...off-putting. "How may we help you today?"

Their visitor was an older gentleman, perhaps in his early seventies, who had clearly seen better fortunes. His bowler hat was faded, his brown suit patched. He leaned on a chipped cane as he limped in—not as a pretense, but a prop to cope with a genuine injury.

He hobbled in with the mournful aspect of a man attending his own execution.

Straightening his back as much as he could, the man spoke. "My name is Ulrich Fletcher. Please, I need your help."

His voice trembled with desperation, as though he were asking for nothing less than his own personal salvation. That was unusual. Usually, the people who could afford Guild services were several thousand goldmarks distant from the poorhouse. For them, 'desperation' was just a word.

"Of course, Mister Fletcher," Shera said with a smile. "Please, have a seat." Beside her, Ayana covertly rifled through a drawer full of files marked 'F.'

With great effort, Fletcher levered himself into one of the padded chairs in front of the desk. "Ahem. Well, where to begin? I was once a man of great means and influence, you see. Eleven years ago, my business was destroyed by..."

He droned on, describing his personal history in unnecessary detail. Shera felt her smile slipping. She never had been suited for the false cheer that working in a chapter house required, but Ayana's smile sent small children running, and her voice could make a Champion shiver with fear. Next to her, Shera seemed as welcoming as a grandmother.

"...though I was compensated for this loss by the Emperor himself, may his soul fly free, it was still too late for my original fortunes. What was I to do? I could barely see a light in that deep darkness, and I'm afraid to say..."

Not only was Shera's smile gone, but her eyelids had begun to slide shut. She wondered if the old man would stop talking when she started snoring, or if he would keep going.

Ayana slipped her a file, careful to keep her sharp iron fingernails hidden from Fletcher.

On the outside of the file, in Ayana's wide handwriting, were the words *'Ulrich Fletcher.'*

Not even pretending to pay attention to Fletcher's story any longer, Shera studied the file. They kept information on any potential clients they were likely to encounter in each chapter house, which included essentially any citizen in the Capital with enough cash to hire them. These files had to be pruned, trimmed, and modified on a daily basis, which led to her waves of paperwork.

'Former warden of Candle Bay Imperial Prison,' the file said. *'Recent owner of an alchemical workshop at 1328 Regent Way. Kanatalia investigated him for the manufacture of illicit substances, but the investigation ended on uncertain terms.'*

The old man wiped a tear from his eye, his story not slowed in the slightest, and Shera scanned the file for any other relevant information. Her eyes locked onto *'Estimated total worth: five hundred silvermarks. The workshop is valued separately at approximately six thousand silvermarks.'*

Five hundred silvermarks? Shera had never settled on a contract for less than that. Ulrich Fletcher was becoming less interesting by the second.

"...so I invested everything in my workshop. If I can't get it back, I won't be able to feed my family."

Shera trawled through her mind for the bits of information that had trickled through. "So you say a gang of criminals has taken over your workshop? That seems like a job for the police. Or perhaps the Imperial Guard, since you have Alchemist's Guild contracts."

Fletcher's breathing grew a little rougher, and he looked anywhere except in Shera's eyes. "Ah, you see, that's the point. I've had some rough dealings in the past...anyway, you can't trust Capital police. What separates them from the street gangs? Uniforms and pistols, that's what I've always said. And I could never bother the Imperial Guard with this, their time is far too valuable—"

Shera cut him off before he could launch into another story. "I get it, Mister Fletcher. What are you making in there? Anthem? Drake dust? Undersong?"

Fletcher shifted in his chair as though he sat on a bed of hot coals, and Ayana elbowed her in the ribs. This wasn't the time to let him squirm.

"If you're cooking up something illegal, Fletcher, you can tell us. We don't care."

"It's very difficult to turn a profit with the classic solutions and formulas, you see, and even flashy potions have a surprisingly low profit margin..."

He trailed off, but Shera took it as an admission of guilt. "You're manufacturing recreational alchemy, and you need us to clear out the workshop before everything gets stolen. Great. We can certainly be of service to you, Mister Fletcher, but first there is the issue of remerration."

"Remuneration," Ayana whispered.

"Payment," Shera said.

Fletcher pulled a stuffed envelope out of his coat. When Shera took it, he let his fingers linger until the very last instant, as though he were a Soulbound and the paper contained his Vessel.

Shera pulled the gray banknotes out and flipped through them, counting in seconds.

Five hundred silvermarks. According to his file, that was the value of everything he owned outside of the workshop. He must be truly desperate.

"That's everything I could beg, borrow, or steal," he said weakly. "Without the workshop, I'll be living on the streets in a week. Please, I've given you all I have."

Shera handed the envelope to Ayana and gave the man a friendlier smile. "That was a good decision."

As long as the payment exceeded a certain minimum amount, it was up to the chapter house staff whether they accepted small-scale, limited-term contracts or not.

And in this case, Shera had nothing better to do.

Fletcher slumped in his chair, visibly deflating. "Thank you. What information do you need from me? I have blueprints, floor plans, inventories..."

He started to pull further papers out from his coat, but Shera stopped him with a raised hand. "That won't be necessary. We have all the information we need."

One of their Masons was employed in his workshop, so their file on Fletcher already contained everything he was likely to provide.

"Go home and rest," Ayana murmured. "We will contact you when your workshop is cleared. Rest assured: your problem is already solved."

Fletcher looked askance at Ayana, obviously disturbed by her hoarse whisper. But he didn't say anything about it, merely offering another word of thanks and departing to the ring of a bell.

As soon as he was out of sight, Shera hopped up and pulled her shears—a pair of bronze blades, still sheathed—out from under the desk. She would need to get her blacks from the back room, and she'd have to consult the file to see if she needed any climbing gear.

Ayana stopped her with a bladed hand on her arm. "We have four Shepherds on standby, and two Masons associated with this gang. I'll assemble a team."

Shera waved her off, walking toward the back room and calling out, "No need. Order a cleanup team for the workshop."

Iron fingernails drummed against the desk again, and Shera could hear it from the next room. "This won't impress Yala," Ayana said. "I think this is exactly what she wanted to avoid."

"Then she should give me more time off," Shera responded. "Or a more interesting job."

The alchemical workshop on Regent Way was unexpectedly boring. Shera had seen alchemist's lairs disguised as castles, made entirely of invested glass, and filling pyramids half-buried in the earth. This one was just...a warehouse. One identical building nestled among its brothers.

She'd climbed up on the roof of a neighboring building and slept until dark, which already made the mission worth her time. She would have taken the assignment for no more reward than these hours of sleep.

At the sound of a shout far below, she instantly woke and rolled onto her belly. Down by the workshop entrance, two men were pushing a third down onto the street.

She pulled a collapsible telescope out of her pouch for a closer look. The men certainly looked like they had dressed to intimidate rather than to impress: they wore rumpled suits with buttons undone, jackets that looked as though they'd been intentionally frayed, and far more jewelry than the situation deserved.

On closer inspection, one of the men had strangely colored eyes. She stared through the telescope until she'd confirmed her suspicion—the veins in the sclera of his eye had turned solid blue. A long-time Anthem user, then, and he wouldn't have long to live at this rate.

His partner scratched surreptitiously at the skin on his arm, and it looked like the skin rippled out of the way, as though trying to avoid his fingernails. Either he was an Imperial Guard who was kicked out for failing a graft, or else he'd taken one too many potions. His limbs twitched and jerked, and he rolled his shoulder as though the joint pained him.

Anthem user, potion abuser, she noted. *Must be the right place.*

The man on the ground tried to scramble away on his hands and knees, but Anthem User grabbed his heel and pulled him back. Potion Abuser walked up to the side, kicking him in the ribs.

Holding up an arm as though to ward off his attackers, the man on the ground said something in a pleading tone. Begging for his life, no doubt. There was a certain memorable cadence to people who were begging for mercy in times of certain death.

Potion Abuser hauled the victim to his feet as Anthem User pulled out a pair of knives. He tossed one to their prey, keeping one in his hand.

Victim missed the knife, which clattered to his feet, earning him a punch in the kidney from Potion Abuser. Thus encouraged, Victim bent over and scooped the knife up, holding it awkwardly in his right hand.

Anthem User tossed his own blade from hand to hand, spinning it around his wrist and walking it across the back of his fingers. Showing off, no doubt, but it made Shera roll her eyes. He had earned death for that display alone.

Anthem User stepped in closer, slashing Victim across the upper arm. Victim staggered and tried to retaliate, but he dropped his knife again. Potion Abuser took the opportunity to kick him in the forehead as he tried to recover it.

Growing bored, Shera considered her options. While they were playing around outside, they had left the workshop door open. She had planned to move from roof to roof and then lower herself down through one of the high windows, but if she tried that now, those three outside would likely get away. There was the possibility, in that case, that they would return to trouble her client after she'd left.

The client is Emperor.

She wouldn't allow that to happen. So she either had to wait until they returned to the workshop, or take care of them now.

Victim was bleeding from half a dozen cuts, and Anthem User was laughing hard enough that Shera heard him clearly. He had taken Victim's knife back, and was waving a blade in each hand, weaving a complex pattern of steel in the air before him.

That settled it. She couldn't risk the chance that Anthem User would escape, spreading his defective knife-fighting technique to an unsuspecting world.

Her rope waited for her, lying camouflaged against the wall, and she slid down to the street without a sound.

Tombstone had chosen his own name when he was fifteen, because he'd thought a tough denizen of the streets should have a name to match. Now, as he knelt in front of Wellin and bled from a dozen wounds, he wondered if he'd chosen his name *too* well.

Wellin widened his blue-stained eyes and grinned, flashing his knives so quick that they blurred into a mesh of steel. That was a technique of a master knife-fighter, Tombstone was sure. He could never hope to match that skill.

"What now, Tombstone? Hm? Never let go of your weapon, I told you that. I told you."

Behind Tombstone, Fisher laughed. "Hey! Hey. Where do you put a tombstone, huh? *In a graveyard!*"

Wellin flicked his eyes up to Fisher and back down, as though he didn't get it.

A few seconds ago, Tombstone had been filled with such terror that he thought the fear alone would stop his heart. He'd wet himself, for which the other two men had mocked him mercilessly, and he'd emptied his stomach onto the stones.

Now, he felt…hollow. Maybe it was the blood loss, he didn't know. But instead of being terrified, he simply wished they would stop toying with him and get on with it.

Wellin kept hurling insults about his lack of respect, his *betrayal,* but that didn't make much sense. Tombstone had simply sold a couple of the potions on the side. Where was the harm in that? Wellin and Fisher were using up the stock themselves, and nobody cared. But Tombstone decides to make a silvermark or two by moving the stock on the street, and suddenly it's a death sentence.

He steeled himself, trying to look death in the eye, as his father taught him. So he was looking straight at Wellin as the man's face tightened in confusion.

"Hey, what happened to…" Wellin trailed off, then threw his head back. "*Fisher!* Get back here you, you…Elder-spawned…trash. Thing." Wellin's insults trailed off into rambles.

Tombstone tried to turn and look behind him without taking his eyes off Wellin's knives. It was true: the presence at his back known as Fisher was gone. Probably off to water some alley somewhere.

A spark lit inside his heart. This could be his chance for *escape.*

He started scrambling away, pushing against the road with his feet, pulling himself along with the tips of his fingers. Wellin laughed.

Tombstone looked back in time to see the man throw a knife at his back. It struck him square between the shoulder blades with enough force to send him sprawling on the street.

The knife clattered down to land in front of Tombstone. *That's good news,* he thought dimly; it meant the blade hadn't pierced his flesh. It must have hit him hilt-first.

Unfortunately, Wellin had already caught up and retrieved his weapon.

His boots, scuffed and black, moved up into Tombstone's vision.

"Can't go anywhere my knives can't reach you, Tombstone," Wellin said from above.

It seemed that was true.

Then the boots turned away, in the opposite direction of the warehouse. "Private business, get gone." Confusion entered Wellin's voice. "Hey, what're you wearing? You...you're not Blackwatch, are you?"

Tombstone propped his head up with his chin against the cobblestones. There was someone in the shadows.

After a moment, the outline resolved itself into a slender figure, crouching in the darkness. Could be a woman, though Tombstone couldn't see enough detail to be sure. Black hair fell down around her face, and a black cloth covered her mouth. The rest of her body was sheathed in solid black, though irregular spots on her silhouette showed places where she'd strapped on weapons or equipment.

She said nothing, but she stepped forward into the dim starlight. With one hand, she reached behind her back, grasping a hilt.

Slowly, she withdrew a bronze knife.

The spark of hope in Tombstone's heart flared back to life. Rescue! Someone had come to rescue him!

He couldn't think who would have bothered to come save him, especially since he didn't know he was in trouble until a few minutes ago, but he wasn't picky. He scooted out of the way so he wouldn't get caught up in the fight.

And so he might be able to escape once the battle began.

Wellin grinned as soon as he saw the woman's knife, brandishing his own blades and waving them in a shining web. "Oooohhhh? You want a knife lesson, do you? Well, step up, I'm game."

Tombstone noticed a detail he hadn't considered before: there was a second sheath on her back, with a hilt sticking out from her left side. She had a second blade. Why not draw it?

She stepped forward, and Wellin advanced, and then *something* happened. Tombstone couldn't say what.

Wellin's knife flew out of his hand, ringing like a bell against the cobblestones. He didn't look like he had any better idea what had happened than Tombstone did.

The woman waited, still calm and half-bent, as though she meant to rush forward at any second. Her knife remained absolutely still.

Widening his blue-stained eyes, Wellin took a half-step back. "What… what did you…"

The woman in black straightened, walking casually closer to Wellin. He slashed desperately with his one remaining blade, trying to ward her off.

The second knife clattered against the street, coming to rest next to the first. Tombstone still couldn't tell how it had gotten there.

When the woman reached Wellin, she lifted her foot and stomped Wellin's knee in. From the side. Didn't look like she put any special force in it, or that she was in a particular hurry, but the joint sounded like crunching bone as it crumbled.

Wellin opened his mouth for a scream, but she jabbed him in the side of the neck with something in her hand. A syringe? A needle? He couldn't see. Was this an *alchemist* who had come to get revenge for the workshop?

Tombstone's spark of hope flickered, and he began to push himself farther away, closer to the shadows underneath the nearest building. His only chance was to stay out of sight.

The woman pushed Wellin roughly to the cobblestones as he choked and coughed, trying to get out a scream.

She leaned down beside him, whispering in his ear. Tombstone was close enough that he could hear each word clearly.

"This is *my* workshop. If I ever catch you within a city block, I will enter your home through the window. You know, the one that creaks? The one with a crack in the corner? *That* window. I'll slip in, and no one will hear me. While you sleep, I'll put a knife between your ribs. You'll never make a sound. No one will wake. They will find your body the next morning, soaked in your own blood."

Wellin whimpered, and Tombstone understood the impulse. He pressed himself against the far wall, his terror having returned in full force.

She walked over, picked up Wellin's knives, and then returned to crouching in front of him. She held the blades so he could see them.

"Also, if I ever see you pick these up again, I'll make you eat them."

She drove one of the knives down at the ground, and for a second Tombstone thought she had buried it to the hilt in Wellin's throat. But the man was still breathing, still staring wide-eyed at nothing, still struggling to scream.

The woman had wedged the knife in between two cobblestones, where the edge would be pressed against Wellin's neck.

She shoved the other knife down on the other side, pinning Wellin's throat between two blades. Then she stood up and walked away, closer to the workshop.

Tombstone couldn't believe his luck. His wounds burned as though his entire body had been dipped in fire, and his blood was leaking out more every second, but the woman had completely overlooked him. He was free!

Without turning around, she threw a hand back at him, and something stung him in the shoulder. Perhaps a wasp.

He moved his hand up to find the tip of a needle buried in his flesh, the outer edge sheathed in a small wooden handle. Rather than a needle, it might have been better to call it an oversized pin.

Tombstone pulled it out and let it fall to the ground. All things considered, it wasn't too bad. Didn't hurt much worse than a pinprick, and she was still leaving him alone.

He noticed the poison only seconds later, when he realized he couldn't move his arm.

It spread like ice through his veins, locking up all his muscles. He lay on the stones seconds later, rigid as a board, forced to watch the woman in black walk up to the glowing rectangle of the workshop entrance.

He didn't know who she was. He didn't know what she wanted. But in his heart, he fervently swore to the Unknown God of the Luminian Order:

If I live through tonight, I'm never coming back here again.

Someone called out from the inside of the workshop. "Hey, Fisher! Why is it so quiet?"

The woman walked through the workshop's open door. There were a few shouts.

A second later, the lights went out.

Even through his paralysis, Tombstone shuddered.

CHAPTER THREE

FIFTEEN YEARS AGO

GLADSTONE KIDNAPPER FOUND DEAD

During the early hours of yesterday morning, Rudeus Maxwell (previously known in this publication as the Gladstone Kidnapper) was found dead in his home, not two miles from the very same Gladstone Park in which he committed his fiendish crimes. Members of the public are no doubt fully acquainted with the infamous Kidnapper, who abducted some five dozen children from Gladstone Park and the surrounding areas over the course of his six-year career.

Professional investigators, Imperial troops, and the best Readers in the Empire failed to uncover any trace of the Kidnapper prior to yesterday's events, previously leading some to speculate that the "Gladstone Kidnapper" may have never existed at all. This theory has now been proven decidedly false, as Maxwell's corpse was discovered in the same house as many of the missing children.

The public should note that it was not an officer of the peace who discovered Maxwell's crimes, nor a judge who executed him. At an hour before dawn, members of the Consultant's Guild arrived at 75 Hanberry Street to investigate the suspicion of their clients. When they arrived on the premises, they found Maxwell's body still warm. It is presumed by Imperial investigators that the Kidnapper was dispatched by one of his own victims.

All the evidence needed to posthumously convict Rudeus Maxwell was found in his home, including the surviving handful of kidnapped children.

Forty-eight boys and girls were rescued by Capital police, and are currently residing in the local chapter house of the Consultant's Guild. If you believe your child may have been taken by the Kidnapper, please proceed to that location with all haste.

The name of the child who turned on his captor still has not been released.

Tapping her pen, Kerian regarded the child across the desk. The girl's feet didn't quite reach the floor.

"How old are you?" Kerian asked.

The girl leaned forward, eyeing the plate on Kerian's desk. Remnants of dinner still rested there—a half-eaten pork sandwich and a handful of fried almonds, bought from a street vendor. Kerian had the meal brought to her while she worked, but she'd been too busy to finish.

Kerian handed over the food, and the girl snatched it away, sinking her teeth into the sandwich before she'd settled the plate on her lap. She closed her eyes, savoring the flavor.

"Mmmm. This is *real* pork. I can tell."

"How long has it been since you've eaten?" Kerian asked. She wouldn't put it past the Gladstone Kidnapper to have starved his victims.

Still chewing, the girl twisted her face in thought. "Lunch? No, wait; I stole some dates from the cart outside. About two hours ago."

"Oh."

The girl tore into the sandwich like a ravenous wolf, and Kerian elected to stick with her professional questions. "How old are you?"

The girl shrugged. "Not ten yet, I don't think. The ten-year-olds got special treatment."

Kerian put a question mark in her ledger next to *'Age.'*

"How long have you been with Mr. Maxwell?"

The pork sandwich had vanished, so the girl held up a single salted almond to the light, examining it with one eye shut like a jeweler holding a diamond. "A long time," she said.

Kerian wrote another question mark next to *'Length of Confinement.'*

"Now, what's your name?"

The girl popped another almond into her mouth. "Maxwell called me Shera."

Kerian froze with her pen a half-inch from the ledger. That sounded suspiciously like an Am'haranai name.

Based on what the Shepherds observed and the Miners dug up, Rudeus Maxwell was a nobody. A malcontent who aspired to rebellion. He'd served in the Imperial army for almost ten years, but retired before the South Sea Revolution to inherit his family's remaining fortune.

Judging from a handful of Maxwell's letters the Consultants intercepted, some drunken talk with a Mason in a nearby bar, and the testimony of Maxwell's former squad members, it was good that he'd left the service when he had. He would have been more likely to join the Revolution than stay with the army.

That would not have ended well for him. The Emperor had signed the release—Baldezar Kern, Head of the Champion's Guild, was taking the field. The South Sea Revolutionary Army would be little more than splinters and twisted iron by the end of the month.

But it seems there's no escaping fate. Dead here, dead on a distant battlefield—Maxwell would never have made it into next week, no matter his choices.

Kerian made a note in the margins of her ledger: *Have someone Read his belongings.* She needed to know if he was imitating the Gardeners out of coincidence, obsession, or some secret knowledge.

If Rudeus Maxwell had been connected to the Consultants, then the Guild would have to answer some uncomfortable questions. As the Guild Representative for this chapter house, it would be up to Kerian to answer those questions.

"No family name?" Kerian asked, returning to her inquiries.

Shera shook her head.

Only Consultants, born on the Gray Island, had no family name. Kerian took a closer look at the girl. Black eyes, black hair down to the shoulders, pale skin…she was the typical breed of the Capital streets. Most of the Aurelian Capital's more dignified citizens had dark Heartlander skin, like Kerian herself, but the peasants came from a hundred mixed breeds.

Shera might have had an Izyrian ancestor, probably several from Erin, and maybe a dozen other mingled bloodlines. Without a full name, it would be hard to place her.

"Maxwell called you Shera," Kerian said. "What did your mother call you?"

Shera had finished her almonds, and was now staring intently at the sandwich crumbs on her plate. "Not much."

"Where is she now?" Kerian asked.

"Dead, probably," the girl said casually, placing a crumb of bread on her tongue.

Her voice sent a chill tickling down Kerian's spine. No one so young should be so cavalier about death. She even *spoke* like a Gardener. "Why do you say that?"

"Maxwell said that's what happens to Anthem addicts."

Whatever other lies the Gladstone Kidnapper may have told his victims, in this one case, he'd spoken the truth. If Shera's mother had been addicted to Anthem before the abduction, she would likely have died in two or three years. Shera could have been gone for as many as six.

"What about any other family? Do you remember anything?"

Shera reluctantly placed the empty plate back on the desk. "No brothers, no sisters. I may have had a father once, but I think he went away."

She didn't seem concerned about her fate. Instead, she craned her neck to see over the desk as if she expected to find another pork sandwich lurking in the shadows.

Next to *'Family Status,'* Kerian noted, *'likely deceased.'*

She hesitated before asking the next question. This was the important one, the reason why she had left Shera for last, after all the other children had been returned to their parents or to the care of the Empire.

"Do you know what happened to Mr. Maxwell?" Kerian asked.

All the other children had responded the same way to this question: they had shifted uneasily in their seat and pretended to know nothing. Some of them had glanced at Shera, but none had said a word.

Shera looked Kerian in the eyes as she answered. "I killed him," she said.

Kerian tapped her pen against the ledger, next to the words *'Relevant Testimony.'*

"Why?" she asked.

"He shot a friend of mine," Shera said. "We were only supposed to kill people who deserved it. I thought he deserved it."

In her mind's eye, Kerian saw the dead girl with the bullet-wound and the blue ribbon. "How did you feel, once you killed him?"

Shera's eyebrows furrowed. "Hungry. I hadn't had dinner yet."

Kerian rubbed the scar on her forehead, a nervous habit. She'd earned that scar when a client turned on her with his saber in lieu of payment, slicing her face straight down the middle from hairline to the tip of her jaw. She had overlooked his past as a professional duelist.

In other words, she'd earned the scar for being careless.

The Consultant placed her pen on the desk. "Shera. Do you have anywhere else you can go?"

"I'll find someplace. Do you have another sandwich?"

"No brothers or sisters? No relatives of any kind?"

The girl looked back at her, eyes flat and dead. "Why?"

Kerian tore the page out of her ledger, folding it in half, and then in half once more. The Council of Architects might not appreciate this, but Kerian herself would have a seat on the Council soon. And technically speaking, she already had the authority. Even if no one expected her to exercise it.

"Shera, I think you should come with me. I believe I can find you a place to stay."

The girl tilted her head in curiosity. "Am I going to live with you?"

"Something like that," Kerian said. She pulled a match from her desk, flicking it to life against the striker. She lifted the paper, letting the flame catch the folded corner and spread like spilled water. Kerian tossed the paper to the ground, watching as the only record of Shera's existence burned to ash.

"Tell me, have you ever been on a ship?"

Shera woke up lying on a nest of empty bags and coiled rope. A woman stood over her: brown skin, black hair in a hundred tiny braids, and a white scar passing down the center of her face.

Kerian, she remembered. The Consultant.

The slick wooden floor and the salty tang in the air reminded her that they were riding in the belly of a ship. On their way out of the Capital, the place she'd lived her entire life, and toward a place that Kerian called the Gray Island.

And none of that mattered quite so much as getting back to sleep.

She'd adapt to the Island in the same way that she'd adapted to the city.

"You can put that away," Kerian said. "Or you can try to use it, and I'll put it away myself."

Put what away? Shera wondered. Then she glanced down at herself.

She was holding a small knife, pointing it straight at Kerian. Maxwell had taught her never to sleep without a weapon, and punctuated that lesson by ambushing his trainees in their sleep. If you weren't alert, you never woke up at all. Shera had never gotten a satisfying nap with Maxwell around.

She didn't think she'd see any tests like that from Kerian, but it never hurt to be prepared. Now that Kerian was awake and aware of the knife, it wouldn't even work.

Shera slipped the weapon back into her belt, then tucked her shirt around the hilt to keep it hidden. The sailors up on deck shouted to one another, their boots pounding above Shera's head.

"Does that mean we're here?"

"We're docking now," Kerian answered. "We'll be prepared to disembark shortly."

Shera dropped back down and crawled into her nest. "Okay, then. Wake me when we're ready."

From a leather bag hanging at her side, the Consultant produced an egg. She began to peel bits of the shell away, revealing its white, hard-boiled flesh.

Shera's stomach rumbled, and she sat back up.

Kerian took a quick bite of her egg. The pale scar on her lips twisted as she chewed.

Before Maxwell took her in, Shera had survived for a while as a beggar on the streets. She found that people were prone to feed children that looked helpless, so she put on the most pitiable look she could muster.

The Consultant didn't look moved. She stared at Shera coldly for a full minute, slowly finishing her boiled egg.

That was why Mari had always played the Bait. Shera didn't look... vulnerable.

Then, without a word, Kerian conjured up another egg and tossed it underhand.

Shera snatched it out of the air, tearing the shell away and cramming the egg into her mouth. Experience had taught her that any food she had worth eating was food others found worth stealing. It was best to get rid of it as fast as possible, and then enjoy the memory.

When Shera finished the egg, Kerian pulled a set of folded black clothes out of her bag. "If you want to be a Consultant, you should look the part."

The pants and matching shirt were smaller versions of what Kerian was wearing: plain, unadorned black. But they were clean and smooth against her skin, so the outfit was better than anything else Shera had ever worn.

"Am I going to be a Consultant, then?" Shera asked, as she pulled on her new shirt.

"There are many different kinds of Consultants," Kerian replied.

When Shera had finished dressing, she started to slide her knife into her new waistband. Kerian stopped her by reaching into her leather bag and withdrawing a small sheath.

"From this point forward, the Consultants will provide maintenance for your equipment," Kerian said. "Especially your weapons."

Shera took the sheath and slipped her knife inside. It was a perfect fit. But she had only had the knife for two days; she'd stolen it from a sailor when they first set foot on the ship.

"How did you know?" Shera asked, impressed.

Kerian smiled, the scar on her lips shifting. "I take pride in my ability to anticipate a client's needs."

"Am I a client?" She had begun to think she was more like an apprentice than a customer.

"You're a little girl who costs me far too much money to feed," Kerian said promptly. "We'll have to see if you can provide a valuable return on my investment."

Struck by an impulse, Shera decided to test the limits of the Consultant's preparation. "Speaking of money, I'll need some."

"Check your pockets."

A little doubtful, Shera reached into her pockets. She had seen "magicians" on the streets of the Capital, claiming they could perform feats of entertaining magic for hire. From what she'd seen, they had used no powers greater than their own quick fingers. But there was no way Kerian could have slipped anything into Shera's pockets without alerting her, and she would feel the weight of any coins.

"There's…" *nothing,* Shera started to say, but she stopped when her left hand ran into a firm spot sewn into the inside. After a little maneuvering, she finally found the entrance to the hidden pocket.

She pulled out a small patch of neatly folded gray bills with the Emperor's face printed on one side. Shera had never used paper currency before, but she knew money when she saw it.

"Five silvermarks," Kerian said. "Not that you'll get much chance to spend it on the Island."

In addition to the money in the hidden pouch, there was a handkerchief in the back pocket, and she thought she felt hidden pockets in her sleeves. For storing knives, she guessed.

She was starting to like the Consultant's Guild already.

A gruff man's voice called from above, "We're…ah, that is, we've arrived, Consultant."

Shera still had vague ideas about returning to her nest and napping, but Kerian led her forward with a firm hand on her back. With regret, Shera gave up her ambitions of sleep and looked toward the future.

She had never traveled by ship, but she'd always heard of ships pulling up to the docks. She imagined a long, rickety wooden dock made of slatted boards, with the boat tied to a post at the end by a coarse rope.

The reality was far stranger.

Instead of wood, the dock was made of seamless gray stone, and it was wider than most major highways back home in the Capital. Three wagons, or a ship on wheels, could drive down the center of this dock with room to spare. Lampposts stood every few yards, made of what seemed to be the same stone and carrying blue quicklamps that lit the ocean like melon-sized moons.

The ship bobbed up and down with the waves, but it stayed locked about ten feet from the stone, as though it was moored with lines of steel. Shera saw nothing. Maybe Consultants tied their ships with invisible ropes.

But all of those details she noticed with only part of her mind. Most of her attention was taken up by the vast gray wall that swallowed the world.

Behind the ship, a blue sky stretched off into miles of ocean. In front of it, there was no sky. No land. Nothing but a towering wall of fog that stretched from the surface of the sea to the clouds above.

The fog swirled and billowed, like fog often did on a winter morning, but it never moved any closer to the ship. It stayed in line as though held back by a glass barrier.

"Welcome to the Gray Island," Kerian said, watching Shera for a reaction.

"There's land in there, right?" Shera asked.

"There is."

"Oh, good." Shera walked down a wooden ramp to the dock. The wall of fog was impressive and a little frightening, but she'd started to imagine that Consultants all lived in houses of mist and smoke. She wasn't sure she'd be able to walk on an island made entirely of gray clouds.

As long as it was nothing more than a foggy island, she knew she'd be fine.

A pair of sailors carried a polished chest down the ramp before them, hauling it onto the dock. They must have been here before, because they didn't pause at the sight of the fog wall. The pair pushed through it without hesitation.

As soon as they hit the fog, they vanished.

Shera couldn't even see the dock past the billowing gray. Only the quicklamps shone through, a string of blue pearls drifting off into smoky oblivion.

Before she stepped into the fog, Shera glanced up at the sunny sky. She gulped in the sight like a swimmer catching a huge breath of air. Who knew when she would be able to see the sun again?

Then, following Kerian, she stepped through the fog.

There came a flash of instant cold, like a cool, moist breeze, and her sight was swallowed up in endless gray.

Two steps later, she was through. Behind her, a featureless wall of gray fog blocked off any view of the ship.

"It's not very thick, is it?" she observed.

Kerian adjusted her leather satchel so that the strap sat more comfortably on her shoulder. "Most clients are not...professionally composed at their first sight of Bastion's Veil."

"Is that what you call it?" Shera glanced back again. "It's only fog."

The Consultant rubbed at the line of scar tissue running down her forehead. "You don't show your reactions. That's not as useful as you might think; it unnerves potential clients."

Shera had never given much thought to her expression one way or the other. What did it matter whether she smiled or frowned or gasped at the right time?

"An appropriate response is always more effective than no response at all. Laugh when you want to appear at ease, grimace when you want to appear reluctant, speak directly when you want them to trust you. When you want to seem mysterious, simply don't appear at all." Kerian glanced down at her. "You'll learn all this. But here's a current example: you pulled a knife on me earlier, and yet you've said nothing about it."

That caught Shera off-guard. What was she supposed to say?

Kerian saw her dilemma and rescued her. "Just so you know, most people will expect you to apologize for pulling a knife on them."

Shera frowned. "But I didn't even use it."

The Consultant took a careful look in Shera's eyes, then placed a hand on her shoulder. "With that attitude, you'll go far in this Guild. Now come along, we have an appointment to keep. And a Consultant never misses her appointments."

What attitude? Shera wondered, but she scurried to keep up with Kerian. The woman was walking up a set of white steps carved into a grassy hill.

At the top, the home of the Consultants waited.

CHAPTER FOUR

Kameira have lived on this planet for as long as humanity can remember, and perhaps longer than the Elders. They take the shape of animals—birds, fish, serpents, and furred beasts of all description.

But as different as they are, all Kameira share one common trait: a seemingly miraculous ability to control the world around them.

Kameira of the sea, like Waveriders or Deepstriders, possess the innate ability to command the motion of water in specific ways. Kameira of the sky, especially those in the shape of birds or winged serpents, manipulate air or gravity. Kameira of the forests can sometimes manipulate trees or lesser beasts.

If this is a function of Intent, such as we humans possess, then the implications are troubling. What separates men from Kameira if not our Intent? What does that imply about Soulbound and their Vessels?

– FROM THE MANIFESTO OF THE ORIGINAL GREENWARDENS
(EXCERPT STORED IN THE CONSULTANT'S GUILD ARCHIVES)

When the Emperor was alive, there had been no "street gangs" worth the name. Shera had been born in the underside of the Capital, and had spent years afterwards cleaning up the trash of the city under Maxwell. At the time, there had been nothing like criminals banding together, or organized crime, or anything that could be called a "gang" in more than the loosest sense.

Then came the riots that had almost torn the city apart.

Five years ago, when the Emperor had been murdered, much of the Empire had gone on just as before. The Emperor couldn't rule the whole world by himself, after all; he had to leave almost everything to the trusted delegates among his appointed governors and the ten Imperial Guilds. So for most places on the planet, the Emperor's death had changed very little.

But in the Capital, fires had followed news of the Emperor's death by less than an hour. It was the closest look into pure chaos that Shera had ever had: people hanging themselves in the streets, shopkeepers looting their own businesses, ordinary men and women banding together to set fire to anything in reach.

The Imperial Guard and the troops had worked together to restore order. They had even hired the Consultant's Guild to help, though Shera had been otherwise occupied for most of that operation. They had stitched the Capital together into working form.

But the wounds had only been bandaged. They weren't yet healed.

The crime rate had quadrupled overnight, even to the point of pitched battle against Imperial Guards. So-called "street gangs" had been the darlings of the newssheets for five years, haunting the poorer quarters like roving bands of Elderspawn. Burglary, extortion, and recreational alchemy bloomed on the streets like mushrooms after a rain.

Shera didn't mind. The increase in crime had meant an increase in her contracts, at least for the first few years. The city had mostly stabilized by now, which meant boredom had returned. But she liked to think she understood these gangs now: they were desperate and scared, banding together for the illusion of control in a world gone mad.

It was all she could do to stop herself from killing them all.

Inside the darkened workshop, Shera knelt beside yet another paralyzed thief. He lay sprawled between two aisles of meticulously labeled formulas, glowing softly in a rainbow of colors. His musket lay inches from his hand, loaded but not fired.

"...then I will enter your home through the window." Every home had at least one window. "You know the one that creaks? The one with a crack in the corner? *That* window." Every window in the poor quarters of the Capital creaked, and most of them had cracks.

As one of her teachers, Zhen of the Masons, had taught her, specific details were the cornerstone of any threat. Lack of accurate information was no excuse for a lack of specificity.

She kept up the threats, pressing the tip of her shear against the back of his neck until it drew blood. When he started crying, she knew her work here was done.

Only one left, hiding in the back behind a table, which he'd pushed up like a wall between him and Shera. She took him to be the boss, since he was fat, and he'd continued eating while the men around him fought. At first.

"I will *double* what they're paying you!" he shouted angrily, from behind his barricade. "Why won't you listen?"

I doubt you can afford it, she thought, but she said nothing. In cases like this, silence was more intimidating.

She walked up and kicked the table to the side. It was a cheap card table, and slid aside without resistance.

The fat man sat against the wall, holding his pistol in two trembling hands. Pointed straight at Shera.

The threat set her gut on fire, and she managed to drop before the muzzle barked and a bullet tore through the space where her head had been.

He screamed with laughter, cheeks turning red in the dim light from the glowing potions nearby, and hurled the pistol in Shera's direction. He spat threats, curses, and promises that he couldn't keep.

Shera had remained fairly distant from this whole mission. She was calm, cool, professional...but still concerned about keeping her targets alive. Still trying to treat them as if they mattered.

But now, under the threat of death, her thoughts were growing colder.

It would have been so much easier to simply kill everyone in the workshop and haul their bodies out for retrieval, but she had gone out of her way to paralyze and threaten them. This was her being *nice.*

And she'd come close to dying for it.

While the ice closed its grip around her heart, the fat man had pulled out a second pistol, cocking the hammer and swinging the muzzle in her direction.

This time, Shera had no interest in playing nice.

She seized the gun and his wrist in both hands, twisting in one sharp motion. The pistol came away in her grip, and something in his wrist snapped. He screamed, cradling his arm.

Shera reversed the gun, pressing the business end into his belly.

Briefly, a thought of her needles—each soaked in an alchemical solution designed to induce paralysis—flitted through her mind.

Then she pulled the trigger.

Blood spattered out behind him, and acrid smoke drifted into her face. She tossed the emptied weapon into the boss's lap, walking away without a word.

That was everyone she'd seen from above, present and accounted for. Her cleanup crew should be here soon, and the alchemist's workshop would be spotless and back in working order before dawn.

I almost made it without killing anyone. The thought came suddenly, unbidden, and it brought with it a surge of irritation.

She was *supposed* to kill people. For many years, that had been her only job. Now she had other options, but the Architects—the ruling council of the Consultant's Guild—wouldn't hold a body count against her. They only cared about results.

Shera didn't feel guilty, exactly. She felt as though she'd failed. Like she'd broken some unwritten rule, and she should be ashamed.

Lucan would have wanted her to let the man live.

He had killed his fair share of people himself, to be sure. But he liked to weigh the possibilities, to give the target every chance of redemption. To Shera, that had always sounded like an unnecessary amount of extra work.

"Their lives are worth just as much as ours," he'd say.

It was hard for her to believe that.

A noise echoed through the workshop, like a rabbit scuffling in underbrush, and Shera faded back into deeper shadows. She'd taken care of everyone she had observed from the roof of the warehouse next door, but there was always the chance that someone had escaped her notice.

She crept around a shelf of tanks, each containing some sort of water-dwelling creature. Some of them were ordinary animals, containing starfish or eels. Others carried juvenile Kameira—she saw a baby Deepstrider create a miniature waterspout in its tank, bearing its fangs at her in a silent hiss. Its blue scales rippled in the dim light as it undulated against the glass, trying to find a way through.

There were other creatures that she thought might have been Elderspawn. A tank full of black worms stood up in the sand, waving in time to a silent tune...music that, after a few seconds, Shera was sure she could *almost* hear, in the corner of her mind...

She shook her head and avoided looking at the tanks any longer.

Another sound broke the quiet: a soft whimper, followed by the scrape of cloth over stone.

Shera rounded the corner, bronze shear gripped in her right hand.

A round-faced man, a little older than she was, huddled in an apron, surrounded by food that looked as though it had fallen down around him. He clutched a bundle of fruit to his chest as if he meant to protect the produce with his life.

As soon as she appeared, he squeezed his eyes shut tight and whimpered again, waiting for death to come.

Shera reached to her side for a paralyzing needle, but she came up empty. Everything she had left in her arsenal was lethal.

Maybe he was right to be afraid.

Shera took a second to put the picture together. He was the cook, or the errand boy, or whatever this gang called the guy who carried food to the boss. Tonight, he was in charge of preparing food for his superior. He would spend most of his time in the kitchens at the back of the workshop, which was why she hadn't seen him from next door.

Her attack must have caught him in the middle of running for more ingredients.

Upon seeing him, Shera felt…indifferent. From one perspective, he was an innocent man who had been forced into serving a stronger master. He could be innocent. She hadn't seen him commit any crimes in particular, besides loitering in an alchemical workshop owned by another.

Then again, she had no reason to think this man was any less culpable than the others. As far as she knew, he had murdered someone for a bushel of apples. It was pointless to speculate, which was one problem she'd always had with Lucan's philosophy.

It was all well and good for *him* to investigate the guilt and innocence of his targets. He was a Reader. He could probably touch this guy's apron and tell what the man had eaten for breakfast three days ago. Shera had no such power.

And as a general rule, she felt no pity. It would make her night easier if she killed him and moved on.

But…

The Emperor himself had once given her a piece of advice. It was out of character for him, which was why she'd paid attention.

"I need you in a team because no one's judgment is correct all of the time. Not even mine. We all need other eyes to see in our blind spots."

So she made a conscious effort to consider what her old teammates would have told her in a situation like this.

Lucan wouldn't like it. It cost me nothing to leave this man alive. Meia would say I should kill him to be sure—the mission is more important than his life.

Then again, she'd never seen eye-to-eye with Meia either. She had a tendency to elevate the will of the Architects to the same level as an Imperial mandate.

An unwelcome memory bubbled to the surface, accompanied by a face she hadn't thought of in years: a little girl in a blue ribbon.

Mari would have wanted me to leave him alive. And Maxwell…

Maxwell would have told her she'd already wasted precious seconds by leaving him alive.

So, as always, it boiled down to this. She could listen to Lucan, or she could listen to Maxwell.

When she put it like that, it wasn't such a hard decision.

Shera leaned closer, making the man in the apron whimper again. After a moment of indecision, she plucked a single ripe-looking green apple from the bundle on his chest.

"I'm taking this," she said, tossing the apple up and idly catching it. "Now leave. Don't come back."

Fighting a battle didn't faze her, but enduring an internal debate made her feel like she'd run ten miles. She leaned back against the wall, pulling the cloth shroud down from her mouth to take a bite of apple.

As she chewed, she gestured to the black cloth now hanging from her neck. "You know, I've never understood why we wear the masks at all," she said to the shadows. "They only cover us from the nose down. It's not like they're not going to recognize me because they can't see my chin."

Ayana seemed to materialize next to her, watching the fleeing man with disapproval. "The shroud is a symbol of the Am'haranai dating back over two thousand years. It represents our anonymity, our denial of the individual self, our dedication to a life of service in the shadows…"

She trailed off, seeing that Shera had closed her eyes.

"No, no, keep talking. I'm still sleepy."

Ayana clashed her fingernails together in lieu of impaling Shera on them, for which Shera was grateful.

"What's the body count?" her mentor asked.

"One dead. Twelve immobile. One mobile and growing increasingly distant."

"Only one dead?" Ayana sounded surprised. "You were done so quickly, I assumed you'd killed them."

Shera cracked one eye. "Come to think of it, what are you doing here? I didn't expect you'd see to cleanup personally." She took another bite of the crisp green apple.

With the tips of two long, iron nails, Ayana reached down to her belt and withdrew an envelope. She tossed it to Shera, who snatched it from the air without thinking.

"This arrived at the chapter house a few hours ago," Ayana explained.

The front of the letter had Shera's name written in clear, simple handwriting. Nothing else. She flipped it over and saw that the envelope had been sealed in wax, pressed with the crest of the Consultant's Guild: a simple pair of gardening shears.

"Who seals a letter in wax anymore?" Shera wondered aloud, breaking the seal with her thumb.

"Gives Yala the excuse to use her signet ring."

As Shera continued munching on her apple, she scanned the letter. Its contents were mercifully brief:

Shera,

We have found a garden that requires your shears. Head northeast, where a bricklayer will give you a fish. Have no fear: a shepherd watches your flock.

Yala

"Since you can explain everything," Shera said, "perhaps you can tell me why Yala insists on writing a *secret* letter in code. Anyone who is capable of intercepting a Consultant's private communication has enough knowledge to break the code. If they can steal it, they can read it. And even if they *do* read it, it's not like there's any sensitive information here! She just wants me back on the Island."

Black shadows flitted around Shera and Ayana—Shepherds, with maybe a Mason or two, hauling paralyzed bodies away and generally cleaning up. Shera saw a Shepherd descend from the ceiling on a line, sweep a pile of broken glass into a dustpan, and then climb back up.

Ayana let out a sigh. With her rough voice, it sounded like the wind screeching through jagged rocks. "Yala has always been fascinated with the mystery of the Consultants. It would never occur to her that she could simply write what she meant to say. Besides, a little extra caution never hurt anyone."

"You know, when I was a girl, you would never have given me a straight answer. You would have told me to figure it out on my own. You've gotten soft."

Shera tossed her apple core in Ayana's direction. The other woman didn't catch it; she simply leaned to one side and let the garbage fly over her shoulder.

A Shepherd caught the core before it hit the ground.

"Soft," Ayana repeated, and poked her gently in the stomach with one of her sharpened iron nails. *'Gently'* here meaning that it didn't draw blood, but it still made Shera wince. "Who's gone soft, Madam 'One Dead Body'?"

Shera pulled the shroud over her mouth to conceal her smile, waving good-bye as she left the workshop. She preferred Ayana like this, as she was at the chapter house: relaxed, casual, even good-natured. As a child, Shera had seen Ayana as more of a monster mixed with a demanding stepmother.

Retirement had been good to her.

Briefly, Shera wondered if that applied to herself as well. But she wasn't retired—not at the moment. Yala had a mission for her.

And she was looking forward to it.

Ulrich Fletcher returned to his workshop the next day, shortly after dawn. Hope and disbelief warred in his heart; surely, one night hadn't been enough time for the Consultants to do their work. He couldn't help but believe that everything would be the same as it had been before.

So when he opened the door to the workshop, he was in for a surprise.

The door itself used to creak, its hinges crowded with rust. Now it swung open smoothly. His legal inventory, stocking the nearby shelves, shone with unprecedented clarity: every bottle, flask, case, and tank in the building had been dusted and polished.

He walked back to the office in a daze, lured by the scent of fresh pine. *Pine.* In *the Capital.*

His office, which he'd always kept in a state of cheery disarray, now looked as though it belonged to a particularly stuffy Imperial clerk. The files on his desk were organized and sorted into different piles—*arranged by urgency,* he realized, after a moment of inspection. The books on his bookshelves were rearranged and alphabetized, and his old chair had its stuffing replaced. Even the spare suit, which he kept hanging on a hook from the corner of his bookshelf, had been laundered and pressed.

He felt as though he'd stumbled into a dream. Where had they found the time to do any of this? He hadn't hired a cleaning service, he'd hired a private security team. Or so he'd thought.

In the very center of his newly cleaned desk rested a wooden case, secured by a pair of bronze clasps. With a little hesitation, he flipped open the lid of the case.

Inside, pressed into a velvet lining, rested a loop of thick chain, a padlock, and a key.

And sitting on top of the chain was a single card with a few lines scribbled on it.

'These contents have been invested by our private Readers,' the card said. *'Trash should no longer blow in your door so easily. Please enjoy, compliments of our Guild.'*

The back of the card was blank, except for a single picture: a simple pair of gardening shears.

Shera met with the "fisherman" on the docks only half an hour after she left the workshop. He was a Mason who worked for the Greenwardens training Kameira, and one of his charges was splashing around in the harbor: a dull brown creature as big as a horse that looked something like a flattened catfish. Its fins spread out atop the surface of the water, and its tail was flattened horizontally instead of vertically, slapping down on top of the water like a beaver's.

Waveriders, like this one, were one of the mounts the Am'haranai had used for centuries to reach their destinations in speed and stealth. Waveriders were bred for quick journeys, using their natural powers over water to skim the tips of the waves. They were not, however, bred for comfort.

Shera spent the remainder of the night clutching the Waverider's back as water tore at her skin, the fish gleefully hopping from one wave or another. Every time it plunged back down, Shera was soaked with bathtubs full of icy water.

This wasn't her first time riding out to the Gray Island on a Kameira, but this time she found herself longing for the relative comfort of a Navigator's ship. Even being dragged behind the hull on a rope would be more relaxing than this.

Worst of all, she couldn't go to sleep.

An hour or two after dawn, the Waverider slid to a stop on a tiny island. It was more of a sandbar than anything that qualified as an island in the Aion Sea, but a few scrubby plants and a single hardy tree sprouted from its surface. Shera collapsed against the base of the tree, shivering.

It wasn't wise to sleep in the middle of the Aion, even if by an experienced sailor's standards she was still close to shore. The deep Aion was where the true dangers lurked—ancient Elders, wild Kameira, hungry sharks, prowling pirates. If any one of those hazards happened to be taking a holiday close to shore, Shera could easily be dragged under and devoured as she slept.

She knew all that, but her body came up with an easy counterpoint: it was tired.

Shera woke after only an hour or two, ears filled with the true sound of terror: the rapid hiss of another Waverider approaching on the water's surface.

The second Mason dismounted, smiling, telling her that this Kameira would take her straight to the Gray Island. He would wait for a ship to pick him up here, but she was meant to meet with the High Council of Architects with all speed. He had offered his personal Waverider for her service.

Shera had to think of Lucan to avoid killing this man.

Once again, she set off on the Waverider. This time, the front of her body was frozen with ocean spray while her back cooked in the sunlight. The sun was fading into late afternoon before the Gray Island came into view, Bastion's Veil stretching from sea to sky like a vast pillar of cloud supporting the heavens.

By the time she staggered onto the dock, made it to her room, and changed into a fresh set of clothes, night had fallen again.

She made it to the Council room around midnight.

The home of the Council of Architects waited underground, as did most facilities on the Gray Island. The ceiling was nothing more than densely packed soil, with white tree roots sticking down like frozen lightning bolts. Shera suspected that they used Reading or alchemy to keep the ceiling in one piece—they couldn't have chunks of dirt raining down on a Council meeting.

Tiny quicklamps, each perhaps an inch around, hung like fruit from the branches; each of the lights was a subtly different color, ranging from white to orange. In total, they lit the chamber like a dim, pale flame, leaving the alcoves in shadow.

In fact, there were three tiers of such alcoves, each concealing an Architect's seat. Most Council Architects deliberated in shadow, voicing their opinions from a pretense of anonymity.

The three High Council members were the only ones who sat out in the open, around a waist-high white column that served them as a table. They were the voice of the Am'haranai, the leaders of the Consultant's Guild.

And tonight, two out of three were waiting for her.

Kerian sat to one side, a Heartlander woman with a faded scar down the center of her face. She wore her hair in a hundred tiny braids, as usual, but it always startled Shera to see that some of those braids had started to turn gray. The former Gardener sat with her leather satchel in her lap, shuffling through various items as though searching for a reason to keep her eyes off her counterpart.

Yala, meanwhile, leaned with both her hands on the white table. Where her palms met the table's surface, the stone glowed bright yellow.

"...this is *not* about your personal feelings," Yala said to Kerian. "Nor mine, for that matter. This is about minimizing risk. Sneak in, sabotage the Blackwatch, leave. If possible, reclaim the Heart ourselves. Once we've done that, we hold all the cards."

Shera hadn't made a sound, and in fact had barely set foot into the chamber at all, but Yala threw a hand up for silence. Whatever Shera thought of her now, the woman had once been a legend among the Masons, and she was keenly aware of her surroundings at all times.

Yala was tall and straight-backed, with long gray hair that still had a measure of blond. Her wrinkled skin was tanned and somewhat cracked, as though she'd spent years shriveling in the desert. Her whole aspect gave off a somewhat weathered appearance, like a traveler who wandered from battlefield to battlefield her whole life.

As Shera understood it, that was more or less the truth.

Kerian acknowledged Shera with a brief nod and the shadow of a smile, but she quickly moved her eyes back to Yala. "A single Gardener assignment could make that operation much safer. Harvest the target, remove any witnesses. They only have one suitable candidate. If he's dead, they're back to the beginning."

"Carry out both operations simultaneously, then."

"Sabotaging the Blackwatch will require at least a week of preparation, and cooperation from all the orders. It's a full-scale Guild action. Killing a Witness requires a team. We send Shera with a couple of Shepherds and a Reader or two, and we have them rendezvous with some Masons on the dock. They can leave tonight."

Yala tapped her finger on the table, leaving a shining yellow spot each time. After a moment, she beckoned Shera forward.

Shera walked around until she was equidistant from both Architects, and then she bowed at the waist. "Kerian, Yala. I heard you have an assignment for me."

Kerian spoke before Yala got a chance. "In fact, we've had a fairly important client make a specific request. It's directly relevant to your personal history, so we had you brought in."

Directly relevant to her personal history. That could only mean it was related to the Emperor in some way.

She'd hoped her connection to the Emperor had ended five years ago.

"Have you spoken with Lucan?" she asked. He was never allowed off the Island, so it should have been easier for them to consult him than to summon her from an active assignment.

"We have," Yala said, firmly taking the reins of the conversation back from Kerian. "He gave us what insight he could, and we are grateful. But he made it clear that you had more experience with the object in question than he did."

In its sheath, the bronze shear on her left—the blade she never drew—began to buzz. It was in her imagination, she was sure, but she still placed a hand on the hilt to keep it quiet.

"What object is that?" she asked.

"The Heart of Nakothi," Kerian said quietly.

An image swarmed Shera's mind: a gray heart with veins of green, still pumping sludge. An island made from the corpse of a Great Elder, ribs standing high like towers, guarded by the living dead.

In the distance, Shera thought she heard a woman's crazed laughter.

"That's not possible," Shera said firmly. "The Heart was destroyed when the Emperor died."

"*One* was," Yala corrected. "As I believe the Emperor taught you, the Dead Mother once had many hearts. You may remember that others have searched for them in the past."

Shera remembered cutting through members of a crazed cult. She remembered the Emperor putting their leader to sleep, so he couldn't defend himself as he was torn apart by creatures of living death.

She tried to think about that night as little as possible.

Kerian picked up the explanation. "The Blackwatch Guild has been searching Nakothi's corpse for another heart. We believe they've found one."

"We've been tasked to stop them," Yala said. "I don't have to tell *you* how important it is that we keep the Blackwatch from bonding with the Heart."

Shera's mind was spinning, but she managed to nod her head.

"In approximately ten days, we will be raiding the Blackwatch with all the force we can muster. Kill the Watchmen if we have to, and take the Heart if we can."

"To destroy it," Kerian added pointedly, looking at Yala.

Yala's mouth tightened, but she nodded. "Yes. To destroy it."

More than anything, Shera wanted this nightmare to end so she could get back to her dreamless sleep.

"I can kill the Heart," she said. Laughter seeped from her left-hand blade like escaping smoke. "But I can't do it myself. I need someone to contain it, or…"

"We're aware of all that," Kerian said smoothly. "And when the time comes, we will focus on bringing the Heart back here. There are many facilities on the Island where we can destroy it safely." She withdrew a pair of tiny scissors from her satchel and began trimming her nails. "We still have at least ten days before that point, however, and I feel that it would be foolish to waste that time."

Yala tapped her fingers on the table, leaving trails of yellow light. "The only *waste* is spending unnecessary resources on an action that will soon be made redundant."

Shera pried her thoughts away from Nakothi's Heart and started putting the pieces of their conversation together. Kerian wanted someone killed now, and Yala thought they should ignore the potential target until the Guild's main operation.

"Who do we need to kill?" Shera asked.

Yala turned an angry glare on her, but Kerian simply pulled a file from her satchel and placed it on the table. On the top was written the name *'Naberius Clayborn'*, above a stamped crest—the Quill and Candle, symbol of the Guild of Witnesses.

The table outlined the file in a soft yellow glow.

"Who is he?" Shera asked, flipping through the file.

"A Chronicler, working for the Witnesses," Kerian answered. "He was assigned to the Imperial Palace for many of the same years you were. I thought you might know him."

The memory surfaced, murky and dim. Naberius was a handsome man with long, dark curls who dressed as though he might have to star in a play at any given moment. He had something to do with finances, so Shera rarely interacted with him. She mostly recalled him thanks to his companion: a mute woman who walked around covered in bandages. She had quite the distinctive appearance, even for the Imperial Palace.

"I wasn't there to make friends," Shera said. "Is he the one who found out about the Heart?"

It made as much sense as anything else. Chroniclers were talented Readers by definition, so he had plenty of opportunity to uncover secrets of the Empire while working in the Imperial Palace. Including the existence of Nakothi's Heart.

"Not quite," Kerian said. "They want him to bond with it."

Shera looked more closely at the file.

If he managed to take the Heart as his Soulbound Vessel, then Naberius would become a Soulbound. Not only that, but he'd be able to call on Nakothi's power himself. There was only one reason why the Blackwatch would allow that.

"They want to name him the next Emperor," Shera muttered. Her head spun—this discussion was progressing *far* too quickly. She very much wanted a chair.

Except in certain special circumstances, the High Councilors stood, so there were no chairs around their table. The only seats in the room were the stone benches in the Architects' alcoves, and those were built into the wall.

Come to think of it, Kerian was seated on a folding chair. She'd always had a knack for packing the best gear.

Kerian swiped her nail file against the table, idly sketching in lines of yellow light. "We believe so. In that case, it would be prudent if he were *pruned.* As quickly and quietly as possible."

"You're presuming failure," Yala countered. "If we succeed in our attack on the Blackwatch, then we will have control of the Heart. Naberius Clayborn will cease to matter, and it's not worth the effort to send a team."

"Since when do we bet everything we have on a single play?"

"We have *no one to spare,* Kerian. Let's say we kill Naberius and lose those Shepherds and Masons you mentioned earlier. Now we've weakened our forces against the Blackwatch for the sake of killing *one man.* It's simply not worth it!"

Shera was getting sick of standing there, saying nothing, waiting for them to come to a conclusion. If they didn't want to hear her opinion, they shouldn't have called her.

Worse, they were wasting time. She could be sleeping.

"If we've got the chance to kill Clayborn, let's take it." Shera snapped the file closed. "I'll lead the team. If it gets dangerous, we'll withdraw. No losses."

Kerian gestured to Shera, palm-up, as though presenting her. "There, you see?"

Yala's hands trembled and she closed her eyes, like she had to restrain herself from attacking them physically.

Shera wished she'd try it. She had no chance against one Gardener, let alone two.

"We have. No one. To spare," Yala repeated. Then a smile crawled onto her lips as though she'd thought of something. "Actually, I believe we do have one extra person on hand."

She turned to Shera. "Would you like to attempt this assignment alone?"

Kerian started to interrupt, but Shera responded too quickly. "I'll do it."

What was the problem? She'd taken more dangerous assignments many times. Killing a Chronicler wouldn't take longer than a single night, even if she did have to fight a Silent One.

Kerian rose from her chair, and for a moment, Shera was reminded why she had risen to command the Guild's order of assassins. Her eyes hardened to chips of stone, and she straightened her back, delivering commands like the Emperor himself.

"I've grown tired of your attempts to downsize my staff, Councilor Yala," Kerian said coldly. "Shera is a valuable asset to us, and her loyalty to the Guild is beyond question."

Yala didn't back down; she sputtered in laughter. "*Loyalty?* She's a criminal. She turned her blade against her brothers and sisters. If circumstances were different, I'd send a Gardener after her myself."

Shera felt her heart freezing, and she forced the cold back. The last thing she needed was to kill a High Councilor.

Especially when she was right.

"We won't have this argument again," Kerian declared. "And we won't send Shera to her death."

Shera cleared her throat, hesitant to speak into the tense atmosphere. "They're Witnesses. What's so dangerous about them?"

Without looking, Kerian reached into her satchel.

"Not them. Clayborn has hired a Navigator to sail him and his partner out to Nakothi's island, where he will rendezvous with the Blackwatch and retrieve the Heart. If you want to kill Naberius Clayborn, you will likely do so on this man's ship."

Another file spun out onto the table, glowing yellow. This one read, *'Calder Marten.'*

"Twenty-six years old, former Blackwatch, once indicted for the destruction of an entire Imperial Prison. His father was executed for the theft of Imperial artifacts, and his mother is a commander in the Blackwatch Guild, nominally under the supervision of the Guild Head. He's another old friend of yours, though I doubt you'd remember."

She didn't, but she flipped idly through the file. The rough sketch of Calder didn't raise any memories, although one of the notes mentioned that he was of Izyrian heritage, with red hair. That tugged at something in her memory, but nothing she could drudge up.

Yala picked up the conversation. "Putting together information from the Shepherds and Masons in the area, we project that Clayborn will make contact with Marten in sixty to seventy-two hours from this point. If you *did* choose to go after him, this would be the best time. He'll be on the ship, which means immobile and isolated, and he won't have reached the deep Aion where we effectively can't touch him."

Kerian raised a hand to stop her. "Take a look at his crew, Shera."

Shera did, flipping to the appropriate point in the file, and she couldn't stop her eyebrows from climbing into her hair. "Light and *life.* He's got a Champion onboard?"

"You see now why this task requires a full team."

That she did. But at the same time...

Shera gathered up the two files. "It takes about a day to reach the harbor from this point. That leaves me with one day to spare. May I have twenty-four hours to think about it?"

Yala smiled, but Kerian's expression hardened even further. "Think about what?" she said. "There's no decision to make here."

The other High Councilor ignored her, looking directly to Shera. "It would be childish of us to invite you here and then ignore your opinion."

"We will *not*—"

Shera interrupted her by slapping the files against the table. "Kerian. Trust me. I'll see you tomorrow."

Without another word, Shera walked out of the Council chamber and all the way to her room.

Where, at last, she slept.

CHAPTER FIVE

FIFTEEN YEARS AGO

The beds on the Gray Island were spectacular, but on her first night there, Shera still couldn't get any sleep. It was a criminal waste, to her mind: she finally had a comfortable place to rest, but it wasn't doing her any good.

Thanks to Maxwell's attacks, she'd been conditioned to wake and respond at even the slightest sounds. The creaking of a board would send her rolling out of her sheets and reaching for a knife, and the sound of a door slamming was enough to make her scurry for cover. She could only catch up on her sleep when she was secure and alone, in a place no one could find her.

Here, the story was different. Far from hearing too many noises, she heard too few. The entire island seemed poised to strike, coiled like a snake. She never woke to a creaking board, or a footstep, or the sound of a fist on a door. Silence reigned over the nights of the Gray Island, and it kept her wide-eyed.

Somehow, the absolute quiet felt more threatening than Maxwell's thundering footsteps as he approached, sword in hand. Even the distant surf felt distant, muted, washed-out.

Shera had spent all her life in the greatest city in the world—the Capital of the Aurelian Empire. The Emperor himself lived there, in his palace that accounted for a fifth of the city's legendary size. Even in the small hours of the morning, the streets screamed. In the Capital, silence was a myth.

Her old home never slept, but it seemed that this new one never woke.

When Kerian slipped in through Shera's door at dawn, it was almost a relief. Finally, she would have an excuse to be awake.

As always, Kerian wore unrelieved black and carried her leather satchel. Shera had half-expected her to wear something more casual at home, but she was beginning to believe that Consultants never relaxed.

"Good morning," Kerian said, showing no surprise at finding Shera awake and alert. "I hope the accommodations lived up to your expectations."

"It was too quiet," Shera said.

The Consultant adjusted the strap of her leather satchel. "Silence is a gift," Kerian said. "You don't get to enjoy it as often as you might think.

Now, it's time for you to dress. I've made you an appointment."

"For what?"

Kerian pulled a mirror out of her satchel and began smoothing back the thousand tiny braids of her hair. "It's a job application, of sorts. We'll find a place for you on the Island, there's no need to worry about that. But some positions are more...rewarding than others." She ran a finger down the pale scar of her otherwise dark face.

For a few seconds, Shera wondered about the scar and Kerian's position among the Consultants, but then a more urgent issue pressed its way to the front of her mind.

"Where's the chamber pot?" she asked.

With one black-gloved hand, Kerian pointed to a small wooden door that Shera had assumed to be a closet. "We have indoor plumbing here."

"Indoor what?"

Kerian looked away from her mirror, pity evident in her expression. "You poor, poor child. Let me show you the true hallmark of civilization."

Glance out any window, and it seemed that the Gray Island was almost entirely untouched by mankind. Besides the towering white reception hall, where Consultants received guests and potential clients, there were only a few visible roofs and structures anywhere on the island. All the rest was rolling green hills and dense patches of trees.

As Kerian led her across the island, Shera saw a different perspective.

The unchallenged reign of nature was all an illusion. The home of the Consultants was every bit as packed with buildings as any street in the Capital.

Underneath the canopy of trees lashed together for camouflage, a team of workers patched screws and leather into a contraption that looked like a saddle the size of a house. From anywhere outside the woods, the scene would be completely invisible.

They passed by a hill that had been shorn in half, leaving the side closest to them little more than a wall of rough stone. As they walked by, an unremarkable square of rock spun out noiselessly on an oiled hinge, revealing a hidden door. Two men backed out of the door, carrying something green and tentacled that hissed when it spotted Shera.

Hidden in the shadow of that hill, Shera noticed something that seemed like a forest stripped of its bark and branches. Tall poles of solid wood stood thickly bunched together, and figures in black jumped from the top of one pole to another, occasionally spinning or sliding down the pole. After tapping the ground, they would shimmy back up to the top.

"Drills," Kerian explained, without looking twice at the Consultants. "When you're home, it's twice as important to keep the muscles sharp."

They walked through a few more drills behind the hill. In one, a line of black-clad Consultants threw tiny knives at targets painted onto archery butts. Not one that Shera could see missed the bulls-eye.

Kerian shook her head sadly, braids swinging. "Lenient. In my time, we had to hit the center of the target while under attack by Sandwolves. Let me tell you, *that* takes concentration."

One structure that Shera assumed was a giant boulder turned out to be another house, and a small copse of trees—from a different angle—became a watchtower.

When she asked Kerian about it, the Consultant took the opportunity to explain. "Perception is greater than reality. When the clients come here, we want them to see as little as possible of what we actually do."

"Who would care?" Shera asked honestly. "If they saw all this, wouldn't they be impressed by what you can do?"

"What *we* can do," Kerian corrected. "You'll have to start talking like one of us. And the point is not to show off how skillful we are. Our skill is in the minds of our potential clients. The less they know about us, the more mysterious we are. The greater the mystery, the greater our imagined powers. We are strongest when we are unknown."

At that moment, Shera spotted a man ladling white paint into a dozen hollow ceramic dolls. "Why is he doing that?"

"That's confidential. And because it is, you must speculate. It could be some personal training he set himself, or decoration, or perhaps he's preparing for a trap. As long as you don't know, it could be any or none of those."

That made sense, Shera supposed. But she still found the knife-throwing more impressive.

Kerian stopped in her tracks, shading her eyes with one hand and peering at the man filling dolls. "Actually, I'm not sure I do know what he's doing. Maybe it's for fun." She stood there for another second, then shrugged and kept walking.

They traveled on and on, into the gray horizon; the swirling wall of Bastion's Veil covered the island in mist. It was as though the island had been swallowed by a hurricane, with the eye clear and walls of fog on all sides.

By the time Kerian slowed to a stop, Shera was beginning to fall asleep on her feet.

"I feel it's my responsibility to warn you," Kerian said. "It can be difficult to find the doors."

Shera looked up blankly. They had reached the end of the island: a grassy outcropping that ended in an obvious cliff. All she could see beyond the grass was gray.

The Consultant stood nearby, appearing to expect something, so Shera started searching in the tall grass. "Is this one of those hidden doors?" she asked.

"Yes," Kerian said, and walked up to press her hand against the wall of mist.

Instantly the cloud swirled away, revealing a gray, three-story building that blended perfectly into the Veil. She could barely make out the edges of the wall against the background of mist. More, as she looked closely, she realized that every inch of the building was covered in doors. There was no room for a stretch of wall between them, so identical doorframes butted heads with identical doorframes. There looked to be a ladder that reached the second row of doors, though she couldn't see any way to reach the third story.

Kerian took a key out of her satchel—the key was, like everything else, dull gray. "Welcome to the House of the Masons, one of our most respected orders." She appeared to select a door at random, turning the key in the lock.

It swung open, revealing a fat man in an apron.

He had the pale skin of an Izyrian and a fringe of gray hair. By far his most distinguishing feature was his impressive mustache, hanging down like the tusks of a walrus. He clutched a carving knife in each hand, and he instantly pointed one at Shera.

"Young lady! Is that any way for an alchemist to dress? Did you finish rendering that compound I asked for? Stormwing ichor doesn't come cheap."

Shera shot a glance at Kerian, but the Consultant was rummaging around in her satchel again. Caught on the spot, all she could say was, "What?"

He eyed her for a moment and then heaved a disappointed sigh, pressing the heel of his hand into his forehead. "What? What, what, what? *What* am I to make of 'what,' Kerian?"

"You get common responses most commonly, Zhen."

Zhen tossed both knives in the air, where they disappeared behind the doorframe. "I don't need common! I need those who can be common on command. Young lady, for your information, a real alchemist would have told me that it didn't matter what she wore, as long as she's not in the lab. Of course you haven't finished rendering any compound, as we've never met. And you could have forced me to explain what I needed Stormwing ichor for in the first place. You could have said *anything*, and from all the words in the Imperial language you chose 'what.' Next time, I expect you to say something clever."

The knives didn't fall back down, so Shera assumed they had gotten stuck in the ceiling.

She thought for a moment, afraid to speak, and then cautiously said, "Something clever."

She continued watching his hands, wary of the knives.

It wasn't enough. He tugged a knife out of the ceiling and flung it in her direction. She staggered back, but the blade still sunk into the soil between her feet.

"No! None of that!" Zhen made a retching noise at the back of his throat. "False wit! I can think of nothing more disgusting."

Shera shivered—had he wanted to, he could have put the knife through her foot before she had a chance to react. She did pull the knife out of the soil and grip it into her fist. She never liked to pass up a free weapon.

Kerian pulled a silver pocketwatch from her satchel and popped it open. "We're spending a lot of time in your doorway, Zhen."

"I'm very careful about the sorts of people I allow into my house," Zhen said, stroking his moustache. He glared at Shera again. "And before I permit her to pass, I must have an honest answer to one question. *What is the average annual rainfall in the Dylian Basin?*"

This time, Shera was ready. "How am I supposed to know? Go find an almanac, but don't waste my time with pointless questions."

She looked up hopefully. As she understood it, the purpose of this game was to test her response to unanswerable questions. If she could deflect him, he might consider that enough to pass.

Zhen considered for a moment, idly juggling the other knife he'd pulled from the ceiling. He flipped it from hilt to blade, snatched the tip out of the air with two fingers, then spun it around and reversed his grip. "Six out of ten," he said at last. "The outrage was enough for a young lady, you redirected the burden of the conversation back onto me, and you were specific enough to direct me to an almanac. We can do better, though. Oh, yes we can."

He nodded and backed out of the doorway. Kerian walked in, seemingly absorbed in winding her pocket watch. Shera followed, and he held out a hand.

In a profound act of trust that made her shiver even as she did it, Shera gave him his knife back.

On the inside, the house looked like a textiles warehouse that had been struck by a tornado. Scraps of cloth hung from hooks and pegs, so thick that Shera couldn't see the wall's original color. A row of scarves hung down above the door in a rainbow of colors, and the wall opposite was papered in jackets. From the ceiling hung pairs of shoes, bound together by the laces: boots, slippers, dancing shoes, moccasins, sandals, even a pair of flippers that looked like a fish's fins.

Experimentally, Shera reached out and plucked a feathered purple hat from a stand in the corner. A paper tag had been pinned to the inside, with cramped handwriting spelling out, "Young woman aged between 16 and 25, dark complexion—high fashion in the Heartland."

She replaced the hat before Zhen could notice. *Costumes,* she realized. *This is where they keep the costumes.*

Maxwell had dressed them appropriately for their missions, but his outfits were hardly *disguises*. He insisted that he needed his trainees for what they were: poor, innocent children of the streets.

The two Consultants and Shera marched through a hall of capes, mantles, and cowls, pushing aside a curtain of aprons into a pristine kitchen. A side of meat rested on a stone slab, half-chopped. At least that explained why Zhen had been holding carving knives. Shera had pictured him carrying the weapons everywhere.

A layer of frost formed on the meat. Judging from that and the thin white smoke rising from the stone, Shera assumed that the slab was invested to keep meat cool. She couldn't imagine how expensive a device like that would be, but she supposed the Consultants could afford it. White quicklamps burned steadily at every corner of the kitchen, casting shadowless light brighter than noon.

Zhen reached up to pull a thin metal chain hanging from the ceiling, and water flowed out into a metal basin. He began scrubbing his knives in the stream.

Shera stared at the water. Surely they hadn't built this house under a stream—there was nothing above them. Her eyes followed the water, trying to trace the pipe.

"Plumbing again," Kerian said, answering her unspoken question. "Pipes carry the water up from underground."

Shera nodded, relieved. She still wasn't entirely clear about how water flowed *up* from underground, but she didn't want to waste questions on pipes. She hadn't had breakfast.

"What kind of meat is that?" she asked.

Zhen pointed a knife at her. "Any questions from you, young lady, had best pertain to dialect and character. If you can't pose as a Heartlander house servant or an apprentice of Kanatalia by the end of the week, then I'll have to retire."

With quick, smooth motions, he began slicing the meat into strips.

Kerian took off her satchel, hanging it from a peg next to a white apron. "I don't need her as a Mason. I need her briefed and ready for the Garden."

Zhen froze, looking from Kerian's dark eyes down to Shera and back. Shera felt a brief flash of irritation that they were leaving her out of the conversation, but she quickly reminded herself that she didn't care. As long as they kept feeding her, it didn't matter if they brought her to this 'Garden' or put her to work cleaning the kitchens. If it ended up being too much trouble, she could always run away. On an island with this many hidden homes and secret doors, there had to be somewhere she could hide.

"There must be more to you than I can see, young lady," Zhen grumbled. "Or less, perhaps." He resumed his butchery. "Tell me, what do you know about the Am'haranai?"

She responded instantly. "How am I supposed to know? Go find an almanac, but don't—"

Zhen slammed two hanging pots together, interrupting her. "Zero out of ten! Never repeat a story! And this is *not* a test, it is a genuine question."

"Oh. Well, then, nothing. I've never heard of it."

Zhen let out a deep breath, blowing out his moustache, and Kerian rubbed the scar on her forehead. He noticed.

"You should fix that habit," he said. "Draws attention to your scar. Dark skin like yours, you'd go unnoticed anywhere in the Heartland. People would believe it if you told them you were a child of the Emperor, but not if you insist on flaunting your one memorable feature."

Kerian scowled at him. "The idea is that I not be seen at all. Shera is the one in need of an education, not me."

"We are all in need of an education, my dear. Some more than others." He drew an onion and a handful of peppers from a cabinet, pushing the meat aside. "Girl. The word 'Am'haranai,' in a language that predates Imperial, means 'hidden counselors.' What's another word for a counselor? A word, perhaps, that relates to your present location?"

"Consultant?" Shera asked hesitantly.

Zhen shook his head. "Correct, but you should present your guesses as statements, not questions. You should sound most confident when you have no idea what you're talking about. Yes, we are the Am'haranai. The Consultants. And do you know what we do?"

"People come to you with questions," Shera said, sounding as confident as she could. "If they can afford to hire you, then you'll answer them."

"Eight out of ten," Zhen said with approval. He poured a capful of oil into a pan, followed by a handful of sliced peppers and onions. "Most children forget that we charge a fee. You're absolutely correct, but you have forgotten our slogan."

"The client is Emperor," Kerian said.

"The client is Emperor," Zhen repeated. "There are two meanings to this." He pulled a vial out of a cabinet, and carefully poured three drops into a small opening underneath the frying pan. Instantly, a wave of heat washed over the table, and the onions quickly started sizzling. "First, it means that we treat our clients..."

He trailed off as he saw that Shera wasn't listening. She was still staring at the food. How had he called the heat so quickly? He hadn't even started a fire. Maybe the pan was invested too, to stay hot. But he had added some kind of liquid, so that meant alchemy. She knew that you could start a fire in seconds with alchemical matches, but it didn't look like he'd struck a match.

"Alchemical stove," Kerian said, once again reading her mind. "Clean-burning, convenient, and with very little risk of burning your house down. It's mostly used by professional alchemists and old, rich families, because the fuel is worth far more than its weight in gold."

Zhen brandished a stirring spoon in one hand, stroking his moustache with the other. "Where else should I spend my vast fortune, if not on the preparation of delicious food? Now, back to the slogan of our Guild. Remind me, what are the words again?"

It took Shera a second to realize he meant for her to answer. "The client is Emperor," she said.

His spoon paused for a moment. "Correct. You were paying attention, then, that's good. Can you speculate as to the first meaning of this slogan?"

Shera was far more interested in breakfast than in Guild history, and she stared at the pan as she answered. "You treat the client as if they are the Emperor."

"Nine out of ten," he said, dumping the strips of meat into the pan. The room filled with the savory scents of onion, peppers, and something like pork. Shera wondered if all the clothes would start to smell like onion soon, or if they had some way to prevent the scent from clinging. Maybe they had some alchemy for laundry, or maybe you could tell a Consultant by the lingering smell of peppers and onions.

He nodded to her. "And the second meaning?"

She hesitated too long, so Kerian rescued her. "We treat our temporary clients as if their word is Imperial law, but we ultimately have one client whose interests supersede all others. The Emperor himself." The Consultant had seated herself at a nearby table, and she spoke without taking her eyes from her book. '*The Adventures of Lady Clearlove,*' the title announced.

"Essentially, these words speak to the heart of who we are," Zhen went on, folding his arms and leaning back against the counter as the meat cooked. "When a client hires us, they do not retain our services for a single task. Most of the time, they *think* they do, and they have a single purpose in mind. But as long as we are retained, we are the loyal servants of the individual who hired us. It is the main reason why our time is measured in hundreds of goldmarks. The only thing we do not do, that we will *never* do, is threaten the Empire."

Kerian spoke up from behind her book. "We are the architects who designed the Empire, and the masons who laid its foundation. We were born before the rule of man, and we will shepherd its people until the end. We are the counselors in the dark, the hand in the shadows, the gardeners among the weeds. It is through us that the Empire continues to prosper."

"A quote from *Foundation of Night*," Zhen explained to Shera. "Written by an ancient Architect regarding the foundation of our Guild. It's a piece of literature almost equal to that literary treasure in your hands, Kerian. Tell me, did it cost you a full five marks, or did you find it on sale?"

Judging by the look she was giving Zhen, Shera almost expected her to stick her tongue out.

"That's amazing," Shera said without enthusiasm. "You know, that meat looks like it's done. Do you want me to check?"

Zhen had already begun scooping the food into bowls. "I want you to eat quietly, while my former student and I have a nice talk."

That was an order she could follow. Before he had finished the sentence, Shera grabbed the bowl and started shoveling meat into her mouth.

"...after that, since Kerian seems to think you can handle it, I'd like you to help me with some business of my own," Zhen went on. "There's a little mess I was cleaning up before you decided to visit."

Shera hurriedly swallowed the last bite of her pork. "I'm not very good at cleaning." She nodded to the pan. "I can have more of that, right?"

Zhen turned to Kerian, who had pulled her own silverware out of her satchel. She was cutting each piece of meat into delicate pieces before placing them one by one into her mouth. The book lay open on the table in front of her, and her eyes never left its pages. "After Shera helps you clean up, I'll tell you where I found her."

The old man grumbled something into his moustache, but he did give Shera another helping. In Shera's estimation, he could complain all he wanted, so long as he kept cooking.

When Shera had first seen Zhen's gray building, the headquarters of the Masons, she had guessed that it was three stories. She'd been wrong.

It was much taller than that.

After breakfast, they descended down into the basement, which resembled nothing so much as a theater's closet. Maxwell had once ordered Shera to pick up a package from under the seats in a theater, but she had gotten lost. As she'd wandered the complex wondering if she had enough time to catch a nap, she'd come across their costumes: racks and racks of dresses, sailor's jackets, shapeless coats of brown sackcloth, and anything the actors needed to transform themselves into any given profession or station.

This basement put that collection to shame. It was a single room that seemed bigger than the house above it, and each rack seemed dedicated to a single article of clothing. Rather than one row of dresses, there was a whole roomful of them, and each rack held a single color in a dozen subtly different styles. Each item bore a tag with the same handwriting she'd seen on the hat: 'Older woman, age sixty or greater, pale skin, heavier than average—middle fashion, Izyria. Will seem outlandish.'

Shera stopped, assuming that they were going to pick out an outfit for her, but Zhen kept going.

"Keep walking, young lady," he said. "We've further to go yet."

At his signal, Kerian reached down and pressed a hand to the polished wooden floor. A trap door popped open, invisible a moment before.

She leaned over the opening, her braids dangling over the darkness. "Stairs? Are you getting soft?"

Zhen poked himself in the middle. "Feel for yourself. I had these installed five years ago, when I found that a ladder was beneath my lofty station."

"Broke on you, did it?"

"Like a matchstick."

The sub-basement was lined in blocks of rough stone instead of wood, and it was filled with crates. When Shera asked what was in them, Zhen replied, "The remains of little girls who asked that question."

She opened a crate herself when he wasn't looking, but it was filled with nothing more interesting than a bunch of papers. Nothing worth getting upset about, if you asked her.

The next basement down looked like the remains she'd seen of the Imperial Coliseum. Crumbling pillars holding up arches of stone. Four oversized coffins, intricately carved with the images of four different Kameira, lay arranged in a cross in the center of the room.

Zhen strode past them, stepping over yet another trap door in the floor and over to a rather ordinary door in the wall. He threw the bolt and stepped back, gesturing them through.

"As long as you're sure," he said.

Kerian shook her head, braids swinging. "It no longer matters if I'm sure, but if she is."

Inside the door, a man was strapped to a chair.

His hair hung in long, dirty strands down to his untrimmed beard. Sweat and grime clung to every bit of his skin, and his eyes were wrapped in a ragged blindfold. His hands had been twisted behind him and bound to the back of the chair.

Shera recognized the sight from Maxwell's house. He had used similar punishments on those he called 'insubordinate' or 'unruly.' Unlike the children in Maxwell's house, though, this man wasn't gagged.

"I said nothing," he croaked. "Nothing! Get a Reader! Test me!"

Stepping inside, Shera first checked his bonds. His wrists and ankles were secure, and the chair held firm at each joint. The Consultants had done a much better job than Maxwell had ever bothered with—Shera had escaped her first and only such punishment by disassembling her chair.

She looked back to Zhen. "Why is he being punished?"

The old instructor raised his shaggy eyebrows and nodded to Kerian, who gave a pleased smile without looking up from her novel.

"How did you know he was being punished?"

The prisoner gave out a choking sound halfway between a sob and the sputters of a drowning man. "I've done nothing! Committed no crime! Let me stand trial, I beg you, and I will prove my innocence!"

Zhen spoke over him. "This man has betrayed our order, leaking a client's secrets to his enemies. We cannot turn him over to the Imperial Courts, or we would be forced to disclose confidential details about assignments in progress. If we keep him here, he will waste away and die for want of attention. What, then, should we do with him?"

Shera had finished pacing a full circle around the prisoner's chair. She hadn't noticed any hidden weapons, or any weak spots in the rope. "You're sure he's an enemy?"

The prisoner had begun to cry behind his blindfold, making wordless sounds of pleading.

"One can never be completely sure," Zhen said. "But he *was* caught in the act."

That was good enough for Shera.

In one motion, she pulled her stolen knife from its sheath and plunged it into the prisoner's ragged shirt.

She'd meant to drive the blade up under his ribs and into the heart, as Maxwell had taught her, but she had barely touched skin before the prisoner slipped through his bonds as though they'd dissolved. He slapped the flat of the blade away, though he was working without leverage and from an awkward angle.

"Wait a moment," he said, his voice much clearer than before. "Shera. This was just—"

Shera seized his wrist, pushing it up against his body so he couldn't get any space. He would be three or four times stronger than she was, and more than twice as heavy, so she had to keep him from standing up. Using her whole body weight, she shoved against his ribs.

The chair pitched backwards, sending him sprawling.

He shouted as he fell, but she'd wrested control of her knife back, and she stabbed down into his chest. The knife scraped against bone, and he screamed as blood leaked onto his shirt, but her blow had been turned. It wouldn't be lethal.

Shera struck again, quick as a scorpion. If he had escaped his bonds, he could escape. If he escaped, then Kerian and Zhen would be in danger. She had to take care of him now.

Her second blow never landed.

A pair of arms grabbed her under the armpits and lifted her into the air. She kept struggling, trying to get back onto her feet, focused on nothing beyond putting her knife back into the enemy's heart.

Twin points of a mustache tickled the back of her neck as Zhen grumbled. "Settle...stop that! Settle down!"

Kerian knelt beside the prisoner, pulling a roll of bandages out of her leather satchel and wrapping them around his ribs with practiced skill.

The prisoner flailed around on the ground, teeth gritted against the pain. With one hand he clawed at his beard, finally pulling it away and tossing it across the room. A false beard, then. A costume.

"Oh, Dead Mother," he swore. "Dead Mother take me, it hurts."

"Never thought I'd hear a former Watchman call out for Nakothi," Kerian said drily. Her hands never stopped spinning bandages. "Especially not over something so small. When was the last time you got stabbed?"

The prisoner laughed weakly, showing a gap where one of his upper canine teeth was missing. "Winter of eleven ninety-two. Crawler sighting. It was dark, one of the others mistook me for Elderspawn. Said he thought my spear looked like a tentacle."

"That's enough out of you," Zhen said. "Save your biography for the Witnesses." Gently, he lowered Shera to the ground, but he kept a hand on her shoulder. As if he expected her to run off and try to stab the man again.

Which meant the man wasn't an enemy. She should have seen it coming. If he had been a real prisoner, they wouldn't have left him to a girl they didn't know.

Think like them, and they can never outwit you. That was what Maxwell had told her, and it had certainly proved true on the night she killed him.

Shera had forgotten to think like Kerian, and now Kerian had tricked her. Zhen had even fed her breakfast! But now they worked together to play her like a whistle.

Slowly, and with evident pain, Zhen lowered himself to his knees. He looked deep into her eyes, searching for something.

She glared back, embarrassed and betrayed. "He was your friend. Why did you make me stab him?"

Zhen reached out both hands, gently taking her knife from her. He rubbed the blade along his apron, leaving smears of red behind. "There is something broken in you, even more than in the rest of us. You have been shattered, melted down, and reforged into a lost and broken image of the one who made you."

He stared at her a little longer, then turned to Kerian. "Ten out of ten. You have my signature. Let us take her to the Garden."

CHAPTER SIX

Everyone uses their Intent subconsciously, but Readers are capable of consciously observing and manipulating the Intent stored in objects. This makes Readers better at crafting tools, investigating crimes, creating weapons, enacting subtle sabotage, and manipulating the information received by other Readers.

Yet, for some reason, none of our highest-trained operatives are Readers. We should remedy this lack immediately.

—CONFIDENTIAL CORRESPONDENCE,
PRESUMABLY RELATED TO THE FOUNDING OF THE GARDENERS.
(EXCERPT STORED IN THE CONSULTANT'S GUILD ARCHIVES)

The high-status prison, like almost everything else on the Gray Island, was hidden.

In the middle of the forest, Shera made her way to a familiar clearing. Amidst the grass, flowers, and scattered rocks, she found a trap door disguised as a flat, smooth stone. It lifted with surprising ease, revealing a staircase leading down.

She walked down the stairs and into the labyrinth at the heart of the Island. The foundations were laid by Jorin Maze-walker himself over a thousand years ago, and this tunnel was only the outer branch of a subterranean prison that stretched for miles. The cells here, bigger and closer to the entrance than the others, were used to house the most important of the Consultant Guild's guests.

As a rule, the Guild had very few prisoners; most cells had gone unused for decades. This wing had only one inmate, and he was perfectly happy where he was. So security was somewhat lacking, by Consultant standards.

Once inside the concealed trap door, Shera only had to pass a single guard—an old friend named Hansin, who had spent twenty years as an undercover Mason guarding the Imperial Palace. She'd come this way many times, and she gave Hansin a cheery wave as she walked up to his door.

The Mason stiffened visibly.

She held up a covered wooden bowl, opening it so that he could see the rice and vegetables within. "Here for lunch today, Hansin."

He shifted from foot to foot, uncomfortable. Hansin wore a Consultant's blacks—unusual for a Mason, who usually went undercover in whatever uniform their cover required. But his time as a guard was evident in his choice of equipment. He wore a black-dyed chain vest over his shirt, a dull helmet on his head, and carried a sword.

"We don't allow visitors without an appointment, Shera, you know that."

Shera frowned as though confused. "I didn't make an appointment last time."

"Last time you drugged me and stole my keys."

She brightened. "Should we do it that way, then?"

Hansin passed a hand over his eyes. "Dead Mother take you, Shera. Dead Mother take you." He unlocked the door.

Shera clapped him on the shoulder. "You shouldn't talk about Nakothi so much. She might hear you."

She was only half joking.

Lucan's cell was only a step or two from the door, embedded on the wall to her left. He had no privacy, concealed as he was only by a network of invested steel bars, but other than that minor inconvenience, his cell seemed rather comfortable.

He had a bookshelf and a blanket, a table and chair, and a second quicklamp to brighten up the gloom of his confinement. Several sets of clothes hung in a half-open wardrobe against the far wall, and he'd pasted an old, yellowed world map above it.

But Shera wasn't here for all that. After weeks apart, she was finally here to see Lucan.

He had the dusky skin of a half-blooded Heartlander, and he'd let his hair grow out a little longer since his confinement. He was still clean-shaven, though, which meant they allowed him a razor, and he still wore his old pair of invested black gloves. They were meant to keep him from Reading everything significant that he touched, to allow him a somewhat normal life not plagued by constant visions. Most Readers could get along without any such barriers.

But Lucan had received personal training from the Emperor. His skills came with certain drawbacks.

As she entered, he was lying back on his cot reading a book, but as soon as she stepped into view he sprang up, grinning.

"Shera! Light and life, that's a surprise. What brings you home so soon?"

Lucan stepped up to the bars and she followed suit, nerves blooming in her stomach. There was no reason for it, but she always felt that way after too long apart from him. Had he changed? Had she? For some reason, part of her always expected something terrible to happen every time they met.

And yet, it rarely did.

She moved close to the bars and hesitated, unsure if she should kiss him or not. Was that appropriate? Should they talk first? Maybe she should wait.

Lucan, apparently, had no such hesitation. He reached through the bars, pulled her close, and kissed her.

A moment later, Shera broke contact, stepping back and blushing thoroughly.

Which only made him laugh.

"It hasn't even been a month since I've seen you, and suddenly you're fourteen again."

She gave him a wry look. "I don't get much practice these days. Maybe if you were out here, with me..."

He sighed and rested his forehead against the bars. "I wish I could be."

"You *could* be. It wouldn't even be hard. We can break you out right now."

She put her hand on her left-hand shear. She hadn't used that blade in years, but if it meant breaking Lucan free, she'd do it in a heartbeat.

"I don't stay here because I can't leave, Shera. You know that. I stay here because I can't go anywhere else."

Shera's old frustration simmered up to the surface, woken again by the same argument. On one level, he was right. The Consultants would not let him go after the High Council had sentenced him to life imprisonment. Even if they got him off the Island—which, between the two of them, they could probably manage—the Guild would hunt him for the rest of his life. Yala would finally have an excuse to execute Shera.

The Am'haranai had eyes and ears in every corner of the Aurelian Empire. They'd never escape, not for long.

That was the truth, as Lucan saw it.

As Shera saw it, Kelarac could take the souls of everyone on the Council, and Othaghor could have their bodies. If Lucan would accept it, she would have started killing Architects one by one until they let him go. Starting with Yala. And if they sent people afterwards, well, her shears didn't run out of ammunition. She would kill anyone they sent until they couldn't afford to send any more.

But Lucan would never accept it. He couldn't live like that. And Meia... Meia could go either way. If she sided with Shera, then they had a good chance of escaping and opposing the entire Guild. If she sided against her—as she very well might, since the plan involved killing Meia's mother—then that was at least one assassin that Shera couldn't beat in a fair fight.

Sometimes, Shera was willing to risk it. Once, she had even watched Yala for a day and a night, tracking the woman's movements, preparing.

As usual, it was the thought of Lucan that stopped her. He might even fight against her, if it came to that.

But the alternative was him in a cage.

She sat down, slumping with her back against the bars, and began to eat her lunch. After a moment, Lucan slid down on the other side, resting the back of his head against hers.

"You have more stuff this time," Shera pointed out, deliberately changing the subject to something innocent. "I thought they took it away after three days, or something."

"They used to switch out all my possessions every three days." Lucan was a Reader, which meant he could sense and manipulate the Intent embedded in objects. A Reader of his strength and skill could have turned a folded paper into a hacksaw or bent the bars like rubber, given enough time. "I finally convinced the Reader that oversaw the inspections that I wasn't going anywhere."

Shera sensed a story. "Oh? How did you do that?"

"When he came to inspect the cell, I disarmed him, tied him up, left the cell, and locked it with his own keys. Then I walked back in, untied him, and gave him his keys back." He laughed a little. "Since then, he sticks his hand in every week or so, to make sure I'm not brewing a curse. Or a bomb, maybe."

"Relaxed supervision," Shera mused, chewing on a chunk of carrot. "Good thing you're not planning an escape."

"If I *did* plan to escape, which I don't, they'd be able to Read that in my Intent as soon as I made the decision. It's not as simple as you make it sound."

"Great! Let's improvise right now. I'll take out the bars."

He ignored that, as she'd known he would, but every move advanced her goal. The most persistent streams could wear down mountains.

They spoke for another hour before Lucan finally got to business.

"So what brought you here?" he asked at last.

She explained everything—about her life in the Capital chapter house, about the Blackwatch hunting for the Heart of Nakothi, about Naberius Clayborn and his hired Navigator crew.

"That explains why they were asking me about the Heart," he mused. "They implied that it was for the Miners' historical record, so I told them to talk to you. But it was a little too abrupt for a historical inquiry." He shook himself. "Sorry, focus on the situation at hand. Okay. You say Kerian wanted you to kill Clayborn, but Yala didn't. Why not?"

"She said it was too much of a risk. That she needed me to lead the expedition against the Blackwatch, and that we didn't have the time or the resources to try and pursue two goals at the same time."

"What resources?" Lucan asked. "It's killing one man. If you couldn't handle that, you'd have died ten years ago."

"Long before that," Shera said.

"But she eventually let you decide?"

"She finally realized that they had nothing to lose by me going. Meia can lead the expedition against the Blackwatch, even if I die attacking this Navigator's ship."

"And that worries you, I can tell," he said drily. "Here, leap into my arms and I will wipe away your tears."

Shera shrugged. "Maybe they'll get lucky and kill me. Nothing I can do by worrying about it."

She felt the bars vibrate as he shook his head. "There's no helping you. Well, setting aside you callously throwing away your own life—"

"I'm not *throwing* anything away!"

"—something still doesn't make sense to me. Yala is one of the most combat-experienced Masons in the history of the Guild. There's no way she suddenly realized that this was a one-person assignment. She thought it would take more resources than that, and she thought so for a reason."

Shera hesitated. Should she tell him that Kerian had considered it too dangerous? Or should she hope he didn't figure that out on his own?

"What do you know about his Silent One?"

"You don't remember her? They used to work in the Imperial Palace. She was completely covered in bandages."

He snapped his gloved fingers. "That's *right,* I checked up on her once. Something about Kameira burns."

Shera pulled the file out of her jacket pocket—she'd specifically worn a jacket today so that she could carry the files with her. She handed it to him, but spoke as he flipped through. "Tristania, no family name. She's roughly the same age as Naberius, but he adopted her nonetheless when he found her abandoned inside a building full of rampaging Kameira. She defended herself with a Stormwing's stinger, which he later made into her Soulbound Vessel."

Lucan clicked his tongue. "A Soulbound Silent One. That could explain why Yala wanted a team."

"I'm not going to fight Clayborn, I'm going to stab him in his sleep. If I can't do that, I'll wait until *she's* asleep, and kill him then. Not the first Witnesses I've killed."

"I can recall you killing witnesses many times," Lucan said drily. She pulled out her right-hand shear and, without looking, stabbed him in the back.

Gently.

"*Ow*, ow, ow. You *have* been spending too much time with Ayana." He handed the file back. "What about the Navigator and his crew?"

She took Clayborn's file and exchanged it for Calder Marten's. "There's a Soulbound on his crew. Former Izyrian gladiator. And I'll be murdering a passenger onboard a Navigator's ship."

Lucan sighed again. "You know, when I asked why Yala thought she'd need a full team, you could have told me. This is anything but a solo assignment." The sound of flipping pages froze. "His gunner is *the* Dalton Foster?"

"Allegedly."

"Then that's *three* Soulbound aboard this ship. At least. It's not common knowledge, but Foster is a Soulbound. The only craftsman I've ever heard of to bind himself to his tools. It's not directly applicable to combat, but I can't imagine the sorts of weapons he'd be able to create, given the right motivations."

"Not directly applicable to combat," Shera repeated. "You see? I'll be fine."

"Shera, if we were still working together, I'd want the whole team on this. Me, you, *and* Meia. And a team of Shepherds with full information, and preferably a Mason already onboard. That wouldn't even be my first choice—if I could, I'd strap the boat with alchemical munitions and sink it."

"Can't," Shera said. "Read the part about the ship."

Lucan flipped to the back and made a choking sound. "It's got a giant Elderspawn *tied to the hull?* I'm not kidding anymore, you *are* throwing your life away if you do this. This is insanity. If Yala allows you to do this, it's only because she hopes you'll die."

"You're right," she said. "I'll tell them. As much as I hate taking Yala's side, I'd rather not end up at the bottom of Candle Bay." Not unless she had to.

"Naberius Clayborn's life isn't worth risking your own," Lucan said.

No. So I'd better find something that is *worth it.*

Shera stood up and Lucan followed suit, handing the file back. She stood awkwardly for a few seconds before saying, "You've been in there too long."

"On that, we agree."

"...I miss you."

That was as close as she got to expressing her feelings. It felt like prying a diamond out of solid rock.

Lucan turned to her, a grin on his face. "Whoa, that was tender. Did you hurt yourself?"

"A little."

It would hurt a lot less if you were out here with me.

Shera met Yala and Kerian an hour later.

"If I succeed in killing Naberius Clayborn, let Lucan out."

Yala shook her head. "Can't do it. Same reason we have him in there in the first place: he knows far too much."

Shera was prepared for this. "That's a reason to keep him locked away from anyone who matters, not a reason to keep him in a cell. Move him to the Gray District. Put a Shepherd on him, if you need to. Then he'll be in the Capital, with me, and even farther from any sensitive secrets."

Yala folded her arms, thinking. Kerian didn't react at all, she simply pulled items from her satchel and moved them into a slick waterproof pouch.

"Tell me the truth," Yala said. "Why haven't you tried to break him out?"

"Because he refuses to leave."

After a moment, Yala nodded. "Done. Naberius Clayborn dies, and Lucan goes to the Gray District under provisional house arrest. You still have to lead the operation to retrieve Nakothi's Heart. Assuming you survive."

"To *destroy* Nakothi's Heart," Shera responded, for the sake of clarity. "And I like to assume that I'll survive. Hasn't let me down yet."

Kerian handed her the waterproof sack she'd finished stuffing. "A few essentials I'd prepared for you, in the event of this development."

Shera glanced through and saw climbing gear, a folded blanket, an invested breathing reed, a full set of poisoned needles—clearly marked lethal and non-lethal—and a new pouch of spades, among other things.

"Always prepared," Shera said, by way of thanks.

"I do my best," Kerian replied.

"You'll need to leave now if you hope to arrive in time," Yala said. "Reports indicate that Naberius is moving ahead of schedule. Your ride is waiting for you down by the dock."

When Shera saw the Waverider playing around in the surf, happily waiting for her, she had to choke back the urge to scream.

Back in the Capital, Shera spent the next day gathering information. Teams of Shepherds had been observing both Calder and Naberius, stalking them unseen from the shadows. According to their reports, Calder had recently sold gallons of Stormwing ichor to the local alchemists, and he was spending most of his time on the ship—*The Testament.*

That eliminated one possible plan: hiding herself aboard the ship. At least one crew member stayed aboard at all times, and if the Captain was also hanging around for repairs, there was no way she could stay there without being spotted.

The Shepherds following Naberius and Tristania were a frustrated bunch. Naberius had evidently taken steps to ensure that he was not observed, and those steps had been maddeningly effective. One team followed a decoy for two days before realizing their mistake, and another lone Shepherd was convinced that he was watching Naberius in a crowd. Then the man vanished into thin air.

It said a lot for Naberius that he was able to shake a team of Consultants with such apparent ease. Shepherds were highly trained in stealth and observation, and their information was usually flawless. For them to be so irritated at a target was rare.

It also meant that Shera had no choice but to wait for Naberius to approach the ship. If she acted on faulty information and ambushed a decoy, she would have both wasted time and alerted the target to her intentions.

The Masons had come up with slightly more useful information. Each Mason was trained as a professional in an actual field, and they simply relayed anything they learned to the Consultant's Guild. One of them was a worker on the docks helping deliver materials to Calder for *The Testament*'s repairs.

He delivered a new illustration of *The Testament*'s layout, more detailed than the one already in Calder Marten's file. According to him, the Captain and his wife would give up the main cabin to their passengers.

Since her options were rapidly disappearing, that would be Shera's best chance. She would attack as soon as the passengers slept.

But she couldn't take secondhand reports as evidence. To see for herself, she personally snuck aboard *The Testament.*

The Captain was obviously preparing for a long voyage, as he had so many strangers loading and unloading cargo. It took no effort for Shera to change out of her blacks, into the clothes of an ordinary worker, and slip aboard the ship carrying a box under one arm.

While no one was looking, she snuck a peek into the main cabin. Calder Marten was within, packing his clothes into a chest and wiping the floor down with a rag.

Judging by the state of the room, such a thorough cleaning was rare. So it looked like the report was true—he *was* cleaning the cabin for a guest.

That was all the confirmation she needed. When the Shepherds told her they expected Naberius that very night, she got ready for the mission.

As the sun passed its zenith, she slipped back into her blacks, strapping a sealed box of needles to her calf—non-lethal, in Lucan's honor. If she did succeed on this mission, and set him free, he would feel better knowing that she hadn't killed any more people than necessary. If everything went according to plan, she wouldn't have to use anything but her shears...but plans were always fragile.

To her left thigh, she tied a package of 'spades': tiny triangular throwing knives carried by Gardeners for generations. If she couldn't draw her left-handed shear, in the case of a fight, she could at least rely on her skill with the spades.

So far, these were typical preparations for combat. She carried these weapons into every battle.

Now it was time for the unconventional tools.

An hour later, Shera dangled from the bottom of *The Testament's* hull, fully underwater.

Her rope was affixed to the hull by means of a waterproof alchemical adhesive. She breathed through a clear reed that stretched from her mouth to the air—the tip treated with a Kameira-derived alchemist's formula that repelled water, so not a drop of liquid made it down the tube. Her eyes were covered by a set of tight-sealed glass goggles, invested to allow her to see flawlessly in the cloudy water.

At the moment, Shera wished her vision wasn't quite *so* flawless.

She stared directly at a titanic Elderspawn.

Its scaled head bore a mouthful of shark's teeth, and it had three jet-black eyes in a row on either side of its face. Gills flapped on its neck, and its arms—its huge, muscular, humanoid arms—were bound up in chains tied to the underside of the ship. Most of its body was concealed in the shadows at the bottom of the harbor, but Shera couldn't help the feeling that it was coiled and ready to strike.

The six eyes of the monster seemed fixed on her, its sharklike mouth opened slightly as though it meant to taste her. Whenever it shifted even slightly, Shera tensed, ready to pull herself up and climb up the side of *The Testament* at the closest hint of an attack. It could lean its head forward and snap her in half with no trouble.

There weren't many things that could get Shera to jeopardize a mission, but the threat of being eaten by a giant Elderspawn was one of them.

It didn't seem to move, simply keeping its eyes fixed on Shera, but she remained on high alert. She couldn't relax. If she missed a single movement of the monster's, it could have her in a second.

In that manner, she passed the next eleven hours.

When the moon emerged from the ship overhead, glowing down on the water, Shera judged that the time was finally right.

It took its time, she thought. If she had to stare at that monster for another hour, she would have turned around and headed straight back for the Gray Island. She could break Lucan out on her own, if it came to that; she hadn't signed up to fight Elders.

Silently, she edged her head out of the bay. Then she waited.

Water streamed down, out of her hair, over her head. She remained still, with absolute patience, waiting for the water to trickle back down in the bay. Then she lifted herself up a little more, baring her shoulders.

'Stealthy,' in this case, meant 'slow.' She would take all night to climb out, if she had to.

But that didn't stop her eyelids from growing heavy as she waited.

It took almost a full hour for her to pull her body fully out of the water, but as soon as she did so, she moved quickly. Shera clipped her goggles and breathing-reed to her belt, pulling a pair of hooks out and digging them into the wood of the hull. Once she was securely dangling from the hook, she unlatched her rope from the ship, wrapping it around her waist above the belt.

Out of habit, she moved her hand over all her equipment, reassuring herself that everything was in place and accounted for. The seal on the needles was still intact, so the poison hadn't washed off. That was a relief—as a girl, she'd almost gotten Meia killed when she hadn't protected her needles from the water.

Using her hooks, Shera hauled herself bodily up the side of the ship. It didn't take her long for her shoulders and elbows to start aching, but she didn't let herself slow. Now was when she was most vulnerable; a casual glance over the side would see her in full view. She had to be up, over the railing, and on deck as soon as possible.

When she finally reached the top, she hung on for a long moment, listening.

Most of the night was taken up by the gentle slap of water against the hull, or the creak of wood settling. The music of the city drifted out on the wind, sounding oddly like screams at this distance.

She remained still, focusing. At least one person should have remained awake, and if she simply paid attention...

There. Boots, thumping on the deck. A heavy stride. Likely the Soulbound cook, then: Urzaia Woodsman. He was the largest member of the crew. Naberius Clayborn was a tall man, so he could potentially match the sound of the boots, but leaving her target unguarded on the deck would be the height of foolishness. She would simply stab him in the heart and leave.

But she couldn't believe her luck was that good.

Having determined that her target was on the other side of the deck, Shera pulled herself up another few inches and peeked over the rail.

It was indeed Urzaia Woodsman, looking every inch the Izyrian gladiator. His skin was tanned and covered in a matrix of scars, his face bluff and handsome but battered, his nose having been broken and re-set a number of times. There was a single notch in his left ear, and as he muttered quietly to himself, Shera saw that he was missing at least one tooth. His blond hair was pulled back into a tail, and he wore a pair of black hatchets on his waist.

She lowered back down, processing what she'd seen. His torso was mostly covered by what looked like a breastplate of hardened leather, his left arm wrapped in a snake's hide—possibly Kameira skin—and his right arm in leather straps. It was an odd hodgepodge of armor, leaving several obvious gaps, but it was armor nonetheless. She would have to make sure her first strike took him down, or he would tear her apart.

She was an assassin, not a warrior. Certainly not a Soulbound. Though the Emperor had trained her to fight, while most Gardeners were trained to *avoid* armed conflict, she wasn't arrogant enough to believe she could fight a man who had survived the arenas of Izyria. If the rumors in his file were true, he was even a former member of the Champion's Guild, which meant she might as well slit her own wrists as fight him one-on-one.

In the Gardeners, Ayana had been clear: you avoided fighting Soulbound at all costs. If you found yourself facing a Champion, you abandoned your mission and ran.

Maxwell had his own piece of advice for such scenarios. *"If you're in a fight with a Soulbound, lie down and beg for mercy. It'll have the same result either way."*

The fight would be hopeless...so she had to avoid a fight in the first place.

When her target's footsteps carried him to the far side of the ship, Shera sprang into action. She vaulted the railing, rushing over the deck with more speed than silence in mind. Her luck was holding so far—Urzaia had his back to her. He turned slightly at the sound of her footsteps, but it was too late.

With one hand, she broke the seal on her pack of paralysis needles. She pulled out a pair, shifting one to her left hand.

A double dose of this poison would likely be lethal, even for a man of Urzaia's size. He would lose muscle control, and then even his heart and lungs would seize up. Most people would die in seconds.

But Champions were given resistance to poison as one of their many gifts. If he was indeed a member of that Guild, she couldn't afford to take any chances.

Before he'd turned all the way around, she embedded a poisoned needle in both sides of his neck.

He staggered, and Shera wrapped her whole body around him, clapping a hand over his mouth. The gladiator struggled weakly, fumbling at his belt for his hatchets, but she pinned his arm in place with an elbow.

As his weight settled down onto her, she noticed the flaw in her plan. Light and life, the man was *heavy*. It was all she could do to use her entire body to lower the man to the deck rather than dropping him.

His hatchets fell out as he hit the wooden planks, but she couldn't spare any attention for that. She did freeze for a few seconds, both to catch her breath and to see if anyone came in response to the sound.

No one did.

She plucked the needles from his neck and tossed them into the ocean—the ship had an alchemist onboard, and there was no need to leave any more clues than necessary.

Once again, she swept a hand over her equipment, taking stock of her remaining needles, making sure everything was still in place, loosening her shear in its sheath.

The major threat had been culled, and now all that remained was the target.

She felt her hopes swelling—she was *inches* from not only keeping the Heart of Nakothi buried, where it belonged, but also setting Lucan free.

When she noticed her own thoughts, she crushed the feeling with resolute force, letting the ice spread in her heart once again.

She couldn't think about anything needless until the mission was over. Hope had killed as many assassins as fear. Only cold, careful thought could keep her alive and successful now.

When her mind was cool and calm once more, she slipped up to the cabin door. She slid the latch open slowly with the tip of her knife, pulling at the door with her gloved hand. She took almost a full minute to open the door a crack, at which point she slipped through.

For a moment, she was surprised to see two people in the same bed. Did Naberius sleep with his Silent One? She'd heard the Guild discouraged relationships between Witnesses, which was one reason why they preferred sibling pairs, but Witnesses had to travel all over the world. There was little the Guild could do to stop Chroniclers and Silent Ones from doing whatever they pleased.

More importantly, the file on Naberius hadn't indicated any romantic connection between him and his partner, Tristania, but that could just mean they were discreet.

She padded closer, filling her left hand with a needle and her right hand with her shear. Since they were in the same bed, she would have to kill Tristania first; as a Soulbound, she was the bigger threat. So Shera would paralyze the Chronicler, then slit the Silent One's throat.

As she moved closer, she saw Tristania's black hair spilling over the pillow. The file had noted that Tristania preferred to cover her body in bandages at all times, presumably to hide some disfiguring injury, but it seemed she took them off to sleep.

Shera leaned over the bed, raising her needle and her blade...

Then she stopped as a shaft of moonlight fell through the porthole and landed on the man's head.

He had red hair. Naberius was supposed to have long, dark curls—the file mentioned them specifically, as well as the salons where he preferred to have his hair styled.

Calder Marten, she realized. The captain of the ship had stayed in his cabin after all. Which made the woman next to him his wife, not Tristania.

She cursed her own inattention, but it couldn't be helped. The file's description of Jyrine Tessella Marten was cursory and brief. She had never been a subject of interest for the Consultants, so the Guild knew very little about her. There wasn't even a physical description, and Tristania always covered her face, so there was no way she could have told them apart.

Shera leaned back, stepping away as quietly as possible. If she acted quickly, she could still salvage this. She just had to find where Naberius was sleeping.

At that instant, as if to curse all her meticulous preparations, the wood creaked under her.

And Jyrine Tessella Marten sat straight up in bed.

Shera whipped her left hand forward instantly, hurling the needle. Throwing a needle was an art, but mastery was almost impossible: unlike throwing knives, which could be weighted and launched predictably, needles tended to drift through the air. Getting the point in the target was as much luck as skill.

But this time, neither luck nor skill came into play.

An earring in Jyrine's left ear flashed green, and the needle burst into green flame in midair. It was made of metal, and should have at least melted, but not even ash drifted away.

Soulbound, Shera thought.

Of Jyrine, the file had only said, *"No combat training. No special powers."*

When the woman summoned a ball of acid-green flame into her palm, Shera began to suspect the file might be wrong.

CHAPTER SEVEN

THIRTEEN YEARS AGO

Of the two thousand Consultants living on the Gray Island, five hundred and twelve were students.

The Masons hosted the most, with two hundred and thirty-seven children of varying ages learning two hundred and thirty-seven different professions. They would be trained as librarians, alchemists, shipwrights, Witnesses, guardsmen, merchants, landowners, Kameira hunters, scholars, and even actual Masons. All so that when the Consultants needed an insider to deliver information, they would have already have an expert trained and perfectly positioned.

Next were the Shepherds, with their one hundred and twenty-three trainees. These young men and women learned skills of infiltration and observation, from memory training to scaling walls. For a young Consultant to be called a Shepherd, she needed to be able to swim from a river into a sewer grate, climb the walls of a clock-tower, then observe a target through a telescope for eight hours before returning and reciting all of the target's actions without error. This was how the Consultants built their legendary fortune of accurate information.

The Architects ruled the island, their students kept separate from the other orders. One hundred and seven children studied to lead their Guild, learning Reading and alchemy, history and strategy, linguistics and the secret machinations of the other nine Guilds. Where Masons and Shepherds would be sent out in the world to harvest knowledge for the Am'haranai, Architects knew that the Gray Island would forever be their home.

The Miners, a small and oft-forgotten order, housed only forty-two students. These were the archivists, those who kept and sorted the true wealth of the Consultants: their records. Not a single habit of a single Izyrian milkmaid was ever lost or misplaced; if the Consultants knew it once, they would know it forever. And the Miners trained to keep it so.

Miners, even more tightly than most Consultants, were sworn to secrecy. Because they also kept the personnel records for the Gray Island, and they knew that among the four orders of the Am'haranai, only five hundred and nine students were accounted for.

Three had gone missing.

Had this knowledge leaked to the wrong ears, it would lend credence to a nasty rumor, one that all Consultants publicly denied.

As everyone outside the Island had been told again and again: Gardeners did not exist.

All this Shera learned, as she and her two fellow students were taught how to kill people.

Nothing grew in the Garden.

The home of the Gardeners was a vast underground chamber that Kerian said had existed since the dawn of the Empire. Over the years, all that empty space—enough to swallow the Capital district where Shera had been born—had been filled with houses. Every conceivable type of shelter, from a simple lean-to to a sprawling Summerland estate, was represented here, recreated with impossible detail.

It was important that every inch of the dwellings was represented accurately, because you never knew where the assignment might take you. Targets could lurk in the back of a townhouse, or hide in the belly of a Navigator's cargo ship. No matter where they hid, a Gardener had to know a way in and a way out.

In her two years with the Consultants, Shera had learned more about architecture than knife-work. She still wondered who cleaned the hundreds of homes modeled here, or if they were somehow invested or alchemically treated to maintain themselves. The oldest houses in the back, made of fluted columns and towering arches of stone, seemed remarkably well preserved. Though they had to be at least eight hundred years old, they looked as if they'd been torn out of the streets yesterday.

Meia, the oldest of the three Gardeners-in-training, hissed and snapped her fingers to get Shera's attention. Shera jerked awake—she'd dozed off while thinking about the Garden.

"It's my turn," Meia declared, stepping up to the foot of a dusty stone tower. "Please pay attention."

Shera rolled out of the hammock she'd strung up between an eighth-century monolith and a Luminian chapter house. She sat on the edge of the hammock, adopting a look of intense concentration. "Your audience has arrived."

Meia tied her blond hair up and kicked some gravel in Shera's direction. For some reason Shera didn't understand, the entirety of the Garden floor was covered in fine gravel, as though it had been built to make stealth as difficult as possible.

"You should take this seriously," Meia said. "If you watch me, you'll have an easier time. You might not get punished today."

"Good point," Shera said.

She fully intended to be asleep before Meia made it down from the tower.

A whistle pierced the silence. Somewhere in the Garden, their mentor waited with a whistle, signaling the start and end of the training assignment. She would be observing everything they did.

And, as Shera had discovered, their mentor could be hiding anywhere. Sometimes she would be waiting in a far-off clock-tower watching through an invested spyglass, and other times she would have burrowed deep into the gravel beneath their feet. You never knew where she'd come from until she hit you with a blow dart or seized your ankle.

At the first sound of the whistle, Meia shot up the side of the tower.

For this assignment, the parameters were simple: scale the five-story stone tower, kill the straw dummy posing as the target, and return without being spotted. It was simple enough, and there was even a built-in time limit; Meia had applied tacky alchemical glue to her gloves and the toes of her shoes. It allowed her to climb up the stone walls as easily as a lizard, but it only lasted about five minutes before it dissolved. If it ran out while she was still in the room at the top of the tower, she would have to take the five-story trip down the hard way.

So she had to climb the wall, kill a straw man, and return within five minutes. Shera could do it in her sleep. She had proved that, once, when she had fallen asleep in the Garden and woken up at the top of a sixth-century bell tower. Sleepwalking was a terrible curse.

Meia would have no trouble with it either. Indeed, she was halfway up the tower before the echo of the starting whistle had faded. She scuttled up the stone like a black spider, reaching the shuttered window of the top room inside ten seconds.

It was an impressive feat of strength and agility, but Ayana—their mentor in the Gardeners—was not known to make tests easy.

Meia slid a thick knife from the sheath at her ankle, silently sliding the window latch up. She chewed on a loose blond hair as she worked, frowning in intense concentration.

She always took everything too seriously, in Shera's opinion.

The window slid open soundlessly, and Meia slipped inside.

Closing her eyes, Shera leaned back in the hammock. It was never this simple, with a test Ayana had set up. She didn't want to test their athletic ability, but their judgment. Which meant guards.

Through a yawn, Shera started counting. "Three...two...one."

As she finished counting, a door crashed open. Yellow light flooded the room at the top of the tower, and Shera could make out Meia's silhouette and the sounds of combat.

She let her eyes slip shut and drifted back into a state of relaxation. Maxwell had taught them to rest when they could, so that they would always be ready, and it was a lesson Shera had taken firmly to heart.

The whistle sounded again, and there came a 'crunch' as Meia landed back down on the gravel. Limping footsteps moved closer to Shera's hammock, and a panting voice said, "You should...have been...watching."

"I got the general idea," Shera said, without opening her eyes.

Metal scraped on metal, like a knife being sharpened an inch from her ear.

"Did you, now?" Ayana asked. Her voice drifted like a ghost's, but Shera snapped awake, rolling out of her hammock and onto her feet. Lazy she may have been, but Shera always responded to danger.

Ayana, the mentor assigned to train the three future Gardeners, looked like a phantom out of a play. Her hair was pale blond, her eyes light pink, and her skin looked as though she had never seen the sun. Worst were her fingernails, which grew six inches out from her fingertips and were made of solid black iron. They were sharp as knives, and she had the habit of scraping them together as she spoke.

One night, in a fit of courage, Shera had asked where the nails came from. To her surprise, Ayana had answered. Her parents were two members of the Imperial Guard, who integrated parts from Kameira into their bodies. Such people were usually infertile, but when they did conceive, their offspring often had...problems.

Ayana's father had dropped her off at the Gray Island when she was three days old.

"Meia was killed," Ayana said. "Why?"

"She tried to stay and fight," Shera said. It was a guess, but a good one. Meia didn't like retreating.

Ayana flexed her iron-tipped fingers, but gave no indication whether Shera had guessed correctly. "How many guards were there?"

"Two," Shera stated. As Zhen had once taught her, it was best to sound most confident when you had no idea what you were talking about.

The Consultant flicked one fingertip, drawing a red line on the back of Shera's hand. The pain made her close a fist, and a single drip of red crawled down the skin, but she was careful not to react any more than that. Excessive complaining indicated weakness, for which Ayana would punish her more.

"Shera," Ayana said, drawing out the word until it sounded like a specter's lament. "It's your turn. Try to stay awake."

Shera stepped up to the base of the tower, pulling on her gloves and wincing as the cloth slid over her fresh cut. For the first time, she looked straight up the tower's side. It seemed so much taller from this angle, stretching up like a highway into the sky. The stone bricks were cut rough and set wide, so they would provide handholds, but it wouldn't be as comfortable as she had imagined.

She should have borrowed some of that alchemical glue from Meia. Or better yet, thought to bring some herself.

When Ayana's whistle echoed through the Garden, Shera hesitated. It seemed like so much work, climbing this tower with nothing more than physical effort. Maybe she could fail intentionally, and share Meia's punishment.

But as always, she saw Maxwell holding a smoking gun over Mari's corpse. *Finish your work and rest,* he'd say. *Fail your work, and rest forever.*

Cold focus washed over Shera like an icy bath. Once again, the world was simple. The faster she finished her assignment, the sooner she could relax.

She hauled herself up hand-over-hand, reaching the top window in only ten more seconds than it had taken Meia.

The Masons posing as guards had closed and re-locked the window, so Shera had to slide the lock up again, slipping through the shutters.

This was where Meia had failed.

Shadows concealed most of the room, but there wasn't much to it. One large bed, with a straw man stuffed into the sheets. A bedside table holding a shuttered alchemical lantern and a single book. Against the opposite wall, a wardrobe.

Now, what would Meia have done?

Shera could see her now: creeping in the window, drawing a knife, and plunging it into the target's chest. Meia was skilled—having been born and raised among Consultants, she could do without thinking what took Shera two hours of planning—but she tended to think in straight lines. Shera had to do better.

Turning around, she closed the window and locked it.

Then she crept to the center of the room, taking a moment to think. The space under the bed was small and easy to check, and the wardrobe probably didn't have many clothes in it. This was a model, not a real home. More importantly, the Mason guards would almost certainly have instructions to check the obvious hiding places.

Shera took a second look at the wardrobe. Someone had carved it to satisfy a frail ego: it was built on a ridiculous scale, almost big enough to count as a closet.

And the top was spacious, wide, and shrouded in shadow.

Without any more hesitation, Shera slipped up the side of the wardrobe and curled into a ball on top. Her black hair should act as a hood, hiding her skin, and the rest of her outfit would blend perfectly into the shadows.

Now she only had to wait.

The two Masons may have been hired to act as guards, but they were still professionals. When they finally entered the room, they didn't fiddle with the doorknob to give her any warning. They pushed the door open soundlessly, leveling fake pistols.

When they didn't see anyone, they wasted no time. One of them ducked to check under the bed—leading with his pistol—and the other poked around inside the wardrobe. With one last glance up at the ceiling, in case Shera had suspended herself there with alchemist's glue, they left.

As soon as the door closed behind them, Shera palmed a spade. The triangular blade was weighted for throwing, and she could sink it into the mannequin's throat nine times out of ten at this distance.

But she stopped herself, reaching for a normal dagger instead.

This throw wouldn't be precise, and she could only make it sixty percent of the time. She tried anyway; holding it by the tips of her fingers and stretching her arm all the way back to get as much leverage as possible. It would have worked much better if she could stand up, as the dagger scraped the ceiling and she couldn't get her whole body behind the move, but she hurled the dagger.

Luck was with her, as the blade sank point-first into the dummy's straw chin.

Shera didn't know what signal the Masons were waiting for, but she expected that Ayana would alert them in seconds. Just in time, she curled back up.

The two guards kicked open the door, leveling their model pistols at the window. When they saw no one, they hesitated. One of them laughed, and the other made an appreciative noise.

Shera suspected that real guards wouldn't have reacted quite so pleasantly.

This time, they both moved to the window, throwing open the latch. Both of them leaned out, one looking down the wall, the other looking up. A sense of quiet relief crept through Shera: she had considered climbing up the wall and hiding on the roof to avoid the guards' search. Now she knew that wouldn't have worked.

Silently, she slipped down the opposite side of the wardrobe and through the door the guards had left cracked.

From her earlier studies, Shera was somewhat familiar with the layout of this tower. Outside the main bedroom there was a single landing, and then a staircase that crawled back and forth down all five stories. Now that she was past the guards, she simply had to make it down the stairs before they thought to check.

She was one floor down when she found out why Ayana had punished her earlier answer. There were not two guards.

There were four.

Another pair of guards stood on the landing below, clearly assigned to watch the stairs. One of them looked bored, as though he had expected to see her here. The other grinned and opened his mouth to say something.

Shera couldn't use real knives on these guards. Not only were they Consultants themselves, but a Gardener was expected to 'prune' only the necessary branches. If she made a habit of killing unrelated people, they would never let her off the Island.

But she did have an answer. Just because she had forgotten the alchemist's glue, that didn't mean she had forgotten alchemy entirely.

Shera withdrew a cloth pouch from her back pocket, tossing it at the laughing guard.

He slapped it out of the air with the butt of his pistol, never losing his smile. Any trained Consultant would be able to deflect that.

Which Shera had counted on.

The impact against the pouch shook loose a cloud of powder that blew into his face. He fell like a demolished building.

His bored friend hesitated for a moment, surprise flashing onto his expression. Shera took that instant to kick the back of the bored guard's knees, knocking him down to her level.

He recovered himself before his knees hit the floor, bringing up his fake pistol. This prop, used for training, would fire rubber balls. They wouldn't kill, but they would hurt. And more importantly, the discharge of a firearm would create enough noise to disqualify her from this exercise.

Shera leapt onto his back, wrapping an elbow around his throat and hooking her leg under his arm, forcing it out until the arm was fully extended. With the tip of her shoe, she pushed on his fingers, trying to keep him from pulling the trigger while she squeezed the air from his lungs.

He struggled silently for a moment. Silently, but not helplessly: he still outweighed her twice over, and her entire body was screaming with the effort of fighting against his physical strength.

At last, he tapped her arm twice with his free hand. She released him instantly, and he folded onto the ground. Somehow he managed not to cough, even with his bruised throat, which spoke volumes for the discipline of the Masons. By tapping out, he had agreed to stay silent and pretend to be dead for the duration of the exercise.

Shera half-expected another pair of guards on the ground floor, but she had no pouches of nightbloom powder left. She would have only improvisation to defend her from these.

But the ground floor was clear. Only a minute after leaving the bedroom at the top, she exited the ground floor.

Across the gravel lane, Meia stood with her arms crossed, wearing an expression of eternal stubbornness. Likely she was upset that Shera had cleared the assignment while she hadn't, but Shera would worry about that later. Ayana was the one who counted, and she stood with no expression, scraping her iron fingernails together.

Shera stood, waiting.

After a drawn-out moment of silence, Ayana blew her whistle again. The assignment was over.

Shera's whole body loosened, and she heaved a huge breath. Finally she let herself feel the exertion—the strain from climbing up the tower by her fingertips, wrestling a Mason who outweighed her by a hundred pounds, holding herself absolutely still as they checked the bedroom. Her body sang with aches and tight muscles.

She didn't know why Meia seemed to enjoy it. Work was too much *work*.

Meia looked over at Ayana. "Gardener? Did she pass?"

"...She did," Ayana admitted. Her nails struck sparks from one another.

After learning under Ayana for the better part of two years, Shera had the woman figured out. She wanted to give a compliment for the successful assignment, but she was reluctant to reward laziness with praise.

Fortunately, Shera didn't care. Laziness was its own reward.

She hopped back onto her hammock and closed her eyes.

Ayana drove an iron fingernail into Shera's side, deep enough to draw blood. "No sleep. It's Lucan's turn."

Shera squirmed away from the pain, but she didn't leave the hammock. She could watch well enough from there. "Is Lucan coming?" she asked. "I thought it was Reader training today."

Lucan hopped down from the roof of a nearby hut, sending up a burst of gravel as he landed. "Everything is Reader training, from the right perspective," he said. "And how will I ever accomplish anything with my life if I don't know how to murder Imperial citizens in their homes?"

"You think you will accomplish something?" Ayana asked softly. "Only the client matters. Now, up the tower. Harvest the target. Do not let yourself be restrained."

Lucan rubbed his gloved hands together as if excited. "So, who's the target?"

Ayana blew her whistle.

The boy didn't move.

Lucan was darker than either Meia or Shera; not the pure black skin of a full-blooded Heartlander, but dark enough that he could pass for Kerian's little brother, or a respectable citizen of the Capital. More importantly, he was a little older, and he had spent more of his life outside the Island.

He had learned to ask questions.

Meia never second-guessed her instructions; she had been raised on the Gray Island, and believed in the Consultants completely. Shera simply didn't care. But Lucan thought too much, and those thoughts bled out into questions.

Kerian said he would make the Council of Architects one day, if his mentor didn't kill him first.

Ayana flicked a hand in Lucan's direction. His smile never faltered, not even when a line of red appeared on his cheek.

"The whistle means you start," she whispered.

Lucan spread his hands helplessly. "I'd like to, but I know nothing about my target."

"He is at the top of this tower." She blew the whistle again.

"Who is the client? What has the target done to him? What defenses does he have around him? Why does he deserve death, and not some lesser punishment?"

Ayana flicked sparks at him. "Unnecessary answers. Begin climbing, or I will find a new Reader."

It was a bluff. If it were so easy to find Readers Lucan's age, she would have killed and replaced him years ago. But Shera still gripped her knife. She didn't intend to lose another friend.

The most likely result of Shera and Lucan attacking Ayana together was a pair of corpses lying on the gravel, and Ayana's not among them. But Shera wouldn't sit idly by and let Lucan get killed.

...If it came to that, which she doubted.

Lucan pulled one glove off and waggled his fingers in demonstration. "With my Reading, I'd be able to determine all those answers with a touch."

"The Emperor himself couldn't—" Ayana began, but Lucan hurriedly corrected himself.

"*Some* of those answers," he allowed. "But since I can't Read a fake target through a fake home, you'll have to tell me yourself."

Ayana's pale pink eyes stared out from her colorless face. Slowly she ran one iron nail over another.

"He is a smuggler," she said at last. "He transports illegal alchemy from the dump stations behind the Capital's Kanatalia chapter house, making a fortune on unregulated alchemist-grade materials. Over the past six months, his products have blown up a warehouse, poisoned an Imperial Guard, granted a burglar unnatural strength and the ability to breathe underwater, and intoxicated hundreds of street addicts seeking a cheaper alternative to Anthem. Our client is Nathanael Bareius, Guild Head of Kanatalia, who has offered us a fortune to eradicate the source of these leaks."

That was more words in a row than Shera usually heard from her mentor in an entire day. She didn't sound like she was making this up, either; usually their fictional training scenarios were much simpler.

"Is that…a real assignment, Gardener?" Meia asked hesitantly. "I only ask…I mean, it sounded as if…"

"The target is correct," Ayana went on, still addressing Lucan. "Wiser minds than yours have determined his guilt. With your questions, you suggest that you are better able to decide the course of this Guild than the entire Council of Architects. If you cannot trust the Council to make decisions for you, then you have come to the wrong place."

By the end of that speech, Ayana's dry voice sounded as if it had been scraped raw. Meia and Shera only watched, unable to say a word. Even Lucan seemed frozen.

Ayana blew the whistle a third time. This time, Lucan sprang into action.

By walking straight up the side of the tower.

This was flashy, even for Lucan, but he must have wanted to seem as competent as possible after questioning the assignment. Shera was no Reader, but she could guess what he had done, and it was as impressive as anything she'd ever seen. He would have to invest Intent into his boots, enhancing their ability to grip a surface until they could even support him on the side of a wall.

That would require boots with some sort of significance; maybe they had been worn by an ancient Consultant with some great skill at climbing, or assembled by a genius cobbler. Maybe the Emperor had kept them in his closet for a while. Then Lucan would need a personal connection to the boots—he had likely worn them for weeks, in preparation for a test like this.

Then he would need the focus and strength to Read the boots fully, to invest enough Intent to bring out their full potential. Shera had seen him convulse from the aftermath of a Reading before, and she didn't think he could handle making something like this.

His training as a Reader must have progressed faster than she'd thought.

Lucan strolled up the side of the tower, only stumbling once on a loose brick. When he reached the window, he pressed his hand against it, and the latch loosened itself.

He hopped inside, where Shera lost vision of him for a second. But only for a second, because an instant later, he was walking back down the wall. The window shut itself behind him.

"The target?" Ayana asked.

Lucan stepped onto the ground and shrugged, as if it were not worth mentioning. "I invested the blankets on his bed so that they clung to him and shut out all air. He would have suffocated in minutes."

For the first time, Shera felt a little in awe of Lucan. Walking up walls? Suffocating people with a touch? Opening windows that latched themselves back? That was the sort of Reading she expected from a Magister, not from a thirteen-year-old Gardener apprentice.

Meia looked as though someone had stolen her favorite toy. Shera could understand: the girl was used to thinking of Shera as her rival, and Lucan as the Reader who completed their team. If he could perform apparent miracles, then how could she ever compete?

After a few seconds with nothing to say, Ayana blew her whistle.

"Clean all of this up," the mentor said. "I expect everything spotless in two hours."

Without another word, she walked away.

Kerian waited by the subterranean gates to the Garden, expecting Ayana at any moment. Ever since her promotion to the Council, she had met with the Gardener mentor at least once a day. Those three would make up the entire next generation of Gardeners, and it was important to the Guild that they reach their full potential.

There was another reason, one that only the Council knew: the three Gardeners-in-training had already been requested by a client. And this one would not be kept waiting.

Ayana pushed her way out of the Garden, looking as usual like a black-clad ghost with razor-sharp fingernails. She didn't stop to greet Kerian, she kept walking and Kerian fell in beside her.

That wasn't exactly appropriate for Kerian's station, but it was acceptable enough between two old friends.

"How is our little flock?" Kerian asked, as always.

"If we could get them to follow orders, they could harvest the Emperor himself."

That was not a joke Ayana would have made to anyone. Some would have turned her in for treason, even though the statement was patently ridiculous. You couldn't kill the Emperor any more than you could kill the sun.

Ordinarily, Kerian would have laughed. This time, considering the news she was about to deliver, her friend's remark struck a little too close to home.

She cleared her throat. "I'm pleased that you would say that. In point of fact, we've received a visitor."

Ayana scratched herself absently. "Who?"

"The client."

"Which one?"

Kerian reached into her satchel, pulling out a copper half-mark coin. She flipped it to Ayana, who plucked it out of the air with the tips of two metallic fingernails. The coin landed with the Emperor facing Ayana.

"*The* client," Kerian said.

Ayana froze. "He's here?"

"The Council is assembling on the docks."

The mentor clashed her nails together, faster and faster. It was an old nervous habit, one that had the added benefit of frightening strangers. "Will he want to see them?"

"I have no doubt that he will," Kerian said. She could think of nothing else that would bring him here.

The Emperor had never needed to visit before.

"They're not ready," Ayana said. She turned back to the Garden, as if she thought she could prepare her students in the minutes before the Emperor's arrival.

Carefully, Kerian caught her friend's wrist. Seizing Ayana's arm was a risky proposition; as a trained Gardener and a born Imperial Guard, she reacted to danger without thinking. More than one person had startled her and ended up missing an eye or several cups of blood.

This time, Ayana simply took the hint and stopped walking.

"You assured me they *were* ready," Kerian reminded her. "Besides, who can know what the Emperor wants from them? Perhaps you've done an excellent job."

"Meia is stubborn and her ego is fragile. Shera is lazy and unpredictable. Lucan asks too many questions. They will insult the Emperor in person, and he will be displeased with us."

Kerian placed a hand on Ayana's back, guiding her down the hall. "I have no doubt that he can handle it, whatever the situation. Don't worry; I won't tell him what you said about having him assassinated. He'd probably understand, I'm sure he's faced assassins before."

She would have paid a thousand goldmarks to have an artist capture a picture of Ayana's expression in that moment. She actually laughed out loud.

Ayana slashed her in the arm, drawing blood, but the pain was more than worth it.

The Kameira winging its way toward the Gray Island was called a Windwatcher, and it was a work of living art. Its wings were at least forty yards from tip to tip, and each feather glistened in the sunlight as if they had trapped the shards of a shattered rainbow. Its beak was like spun glass, and its eyes glowed like stars in the distance.

Kerian watched it glide over the vast blue expanse of the Aion, fear and awe warring inside her, making her feel like a little girl again. It wasn't the Kameira that overwhelmed her, though it was an impressive sight. She'd heard that Windwatchers had gone extinct centuries ago.

It was the bird's passengers that had her in a sweat. The same passengers that had caused two hundred Consultants—including the entire Council of Architects—to gather on the dock outside Bastion's Veil, dressed in black silks, kneeling as though they never meant to move. The ancient wall of gray mist spun behind them, forming a backdrop for their panorama.

She expected the Windwatcher to alight on the end of the dock, but it simply dipped down, its golden talons clenching. It let out a single ringing note with all the subtle variance of a chorus.

And two figures leaped off the Kameira's back.

The first to land was a woman in full, heavy armor covered in red and black plates. She looked like a Luminian Knight in dyed armor, but this metal had never been dyed or painted. The Consultants had learned the truth years ago: the armor was forged from alchemical alloys and Awakened by Magisters that specialized in the working of steel. Legend said that this woman could take a cannonball to the gut without flinching a hair.

Then again, if her reputation was anything to go by, she could probably do that without the armor. This was Jarelys Teach, General and Head of the Imperial Guard, and she had risen to her current position on a tide of rebel blood. The hilt of a sword peeked over her shoulder—that would be Tyrfang, the executioner's blade that predated the Empire itself. Kerian was no Reader, but she could feel the weight of the sheathed sword from twenty yards away. If Teach wanted to kill everyone here on the dock, all she would have to do was draw her weapon.

General Teach hit the stone with a deafening crunch, both knees bent and one hand pressed against the dock for balance. She recovered instantly, sweeping the two lines of kneeling Consultants with pale blue eyes.

The Kameira's second passenger landed an instant later, as lightly as if he had stepped down from a curb. His clothes were cut in an ancient style: voluminous folds in many layers, as though he had wrapped himself in enough fabric to clothe a small village. Sunset colors, she noticed—layers of orange and red and gold. The only exception was a silver chain hanging around his neck, though it disappeared into the layers of his robes.

His skin was dark, almost black: the skin of a pureblooded Heartlander.

He is the original Heartlander, she reminded herself. *The father of every bloodline.* The idea was jarring. He might have been born before the island on which they stood.

She had to adjust her thinking, and quickly. It wasn't every day that she came face-to-face with the oldest man in the world.

He passed a hand over his bald head as if smoothing hair back, and then he turned and met Kerian's eyes. She hurriedly turned her gaze back to the stone beneath her, heart pounding, *pleading* with fate that the Emperor would not be offended with her.

"Rise, Kerian," the Emperor said, his voice rich and warm. "I understand that you have prepared the students I ordered."

Kerian rose to her feet, though she couldn't look any higher than his chin. Her eyes stuck there, staring at the silver chain around his neck. "I always try to anticipate the needs of my clients," she said.

The Emperor smiled broadly and clapped a hand on her shoulder, a father congratulating his daughter. "I know you do," he said. He placed a single finger on her forehead, tracing the scar down to her nose with a feather-light touch. "I see the proof of your preparation. You earned this in my service. Let me tell you something, Kerian: when people stare at you, they do not stare because they see a beautiful woman disfigured. They stare because they've never seen a hero before."

His words were so unexpected, they caught her entirely off-guard. Bands of steel closed on Kerian's chest, and she let out a single sob before she could stop it. Tears blurred her vision, and she blinked them back. He spoke as if he could hear her fears, her memories, her heart...and he probably could. There had never been a Reader as powerful as the Emperor of the Aurelian Empire.

None of the other Consultants made a sound.

He clasped her by the arms. "You have made me proud, Kerian. Do so again, and accompany us to the Garden. I'd like to meet these three in person."

He strode between the lines of kneeling Consultants, looking neither left nor right, his Imperial Guard clanking along behind him. Kerian followed, never questioning how he knew the way.

The Emperor knew everything.

CHAPTER EIGHT

Soulbound draw their power from a Vessel—an Awakened object, usually unobtrusive and small, that provides them with the abilities of an Elder or a Kameira. If you must engage a Soulbound in battle, first identify their Vessel. Destroy it if possible, and keep it from them if not.

If you cannot identify their Vessel, retreat.

– STRATEGIC ADVICE FROM THE ORIGINAL ORDER OF GARDENERS
(EXCERPT STORED IN THE CONSULTANT'S GUILD ARCHIVES)

Jyrine Tessella Marten stood on the stern deck of *The Testament,* only yards from Shera, with bright green flame in each hand. The hem of her white nightgown drifted in the night breeze, brown hair blowing behind her.

As she scrambled away from another lash of flame, skin seared by the heat of the nearby fireball, Shera couldn't help but notice the symbols tattooed on Jyrine's left ankle. They seemed to crawl all the way up the left side of the woman's body, ending on the left of her neck, under her chin.

There was something significant about those symbols that tugged at Shera's memory, some cultural detail that was supposedly important. Was it Vandenyas? As a child, Shera had met a man with similar markings. Where was it?

She couldn't remember. And Jyrine certainly wasn't giving her any time to think.

"I won't let you kill us," Jyrine hissed, whipping green flame at Shera's head. That was much better—it was easier to duck a strike aimed at the head. If Jyrine had been aiming at her center of gravity, Shera would have died by now. Fortunately for her, it seemed Jyrine was unused to her powers as a Soulbound.

And, for some reason, the other woman hadn't raised the alarm. As soon as Jyrine screamed, Shera would have no choice but to abandon the mission and retreat. But as long as Jyrine insisted on a fight, Shera had a chance.

"Who are you?" Jyrine asked, in a loud whisper. "A Consultant?"

Now, *that* was surprising. Very few people in the Empire knew for sure that the Consultants actually had an order of assassins. Most people knew the rumor, but there should be only a handful of people in the entire world capable of connecting 'an assassin in black' with the Consultant's Guild.

Shera flicked a spade in Jyrine's direction, sending steel spinning toward the Soulbound. Jyrine made a sweeping gesture with her hand, and green fire blasted the spade off-course.

The woman *still* hadn't called for help. So maybe Shera could talk her way out of this situation.

"Let's agree to go our separate ways," Shera said calmly. "You might not believe me, but you're in no danger from me." She didn't whisper, though she kept her voice low—people didn't realize that whispers actually caught *more* attention than simply speaking quietly. An ordinary voice was often best for stealth.

For some reason, the remark seemed to anger Jyrine further. Her earring shone like an emerald star, and she whipped both hands forward. Darts of flame licked at Shera's sides, and it took all her training to leap, duck, and sidestep each strike.

Of course, she returned some attacks of her own.

Every time she dodged, she pulled a spade or a needle from the pouch at her side—grabbing weapons based on instinct and reflex rather than conscious decision—pitching them in Jyrine's direction. None of them struck flesh, but they were able to keep the Soulbound's attention divided enough to allow Shera to escape unscathed.

"Your time's up," Jyrine said, still speaking in a harsh whisper. She had started to breathe heavily, and a sheen of sweat showed on her forehead. "Our family will lead this world forward into a new future."

Shera pulled her shear, slapping a slow-moving fireball aside. The invested bronze of her blade held, but the fire seared her arm even through the sleeve of her blacks. "Our family?" Shera asked, but Jyrine didn't hear her.

Fine.

If she wanted a fight, Shera could oblige her.

She rushed forward, dodging a whip of green flame and slashing at Jyrine's side. Her knife bit flesh, but too shallow—Jyrine counterattacked and Shera instantly flattened herself to the deck. Fire rushed over her head, and she hurled a spade from her prone position, trying to catch Jyrine in the neck.

The strike missed, and Shera was forced back, stepping to the side to avoid another lash of flame.

"I'm not here for you," Shera said again, mostly as a distraction. "I don't suppose I can convince you to go back to sleep."

"I won't let you get what you want," Jyrine whispered. "Time's almost up. That which sleeps will soon wake."

That which sleeps will soon wake.

The words slammed into Shera's gut, and she hesitated. The mission she thought she understood splintered and re-formed into a strange landscape. What was a member of the Sleepless doing here? Was she here to oversee the retrieval of the Heart of Nakothi? Maybe to steal it before Naberius could get it?

That didn't make sense. Jyrine had been married to Calder Marten for almost two years, according to the file, and had traveled with him for long before that.

What was going on?

Shera's shocked hesitation could have been fatal, but Jyrine hadn't moved. Her eyes were wide, staring at the lower deck as though she'd seen her own death.

Shera let out a deep breath and withdrew a non-lethal needle, closing the distance between her and Jyrine in one burst of speed.

The motion shocked Jyrine out of her paralysis, and she brought her burning hands up, but Shera had already moved. She pulled the needle out of Jyrine's neck.

Anticipating what would happen next, Shera grabbed Jyrine and hauled her to one side.

Jyrine had been staring at *someone* down there on the deck. If Urzaia had woken up, he would surely have attacked by now, and the sight of Naberius wouldn't have stunned the woman so much. There was only one person she could have seen: the captain of *The Testament,* Calder Marten.

And his first action, upon seeing his wife stabbed, would be to try and shoot the killer.

Sure enough, a pistol cracked an instant later, bullet buzzing by Shera's cheek.

Without pause, Shera shoved Jyrine overboard.

It would have been more merciful to stab her, most likely, but Shera had acted in the moment and seized the opportunity. With the paralyzing agent in her, Jyrine would remain fully conscious as she drowned. So long as she died.

At the edge of her hearing, a familiar whine grew in volume. A Waverider, on standby, mounted by a local Mason. He must have seen the fight on the ship and come to give her an early exit.

Now, how am I going to complete this mission?

The ship creaked and came to life, rope uncoiling and launching itself at her neck.

Shera had been prepared for this possibility—Navigators had the uncanny ability to control their ships. One of the Architects back on the Gray Island proposed that each Navigator was actually a Soulbound tied to their ship, but it was difficult to prove that theory. All Shera knew for sure was that Calder Marten was awake, and he could control the ship as part of his body.

So her only chance of escaping, let alone killing Naberius, was to neutralize Calder.

She ducked the rope and dropped from the stern deck, facing Calder.

He stood shirtless in front of her, his bright red hair practically glowing, a pistol in his left hand and a sheathed blade on his hip. He tossed his pistol aside and pulled his cutlass, flicking the blade at Shera with more speed than she'd anticipated. The file suggested his skill as a swordsman was *'Moderate,'* but she thought that information may have been out of date.

She turned his first strike, and his second, but soon he was pressing her back. It was to be expected. The shears of the Gardeners were not meant to hold their own against the superior reach of a sword.

Her back hit the door of the cabin, and the blade caught her forearm, slicing flesh.

Shera realized she was in lethal danger, and her thoughts turned cold.

She was letting herself be shackled by her reluctance to kill. Now was not the time for hesitation.

One more time, she slapped the sword aside with her knife, but this time she moved forward. It was risky; if he had anticipated her, he could run her through the heart with little trouble.

But his eyes widened in surprise, and she buried a needle in his arm.

One down.

As Calder collapsed, she walked past him. Now she wouldn't have to worry about the ship, or the Elderspawn chained beneath it. Along with the

Izyrian gladiator, that was the two greatest threats neutralized.

Now, where was Naberius?

A Heartlander, for some reason dressed in a full white suit and a broad white hat, leveled a pistol inches from her nose.

Not worth a thought. She ducked, swept a kick at the man's knees, and moved forward as his shot went wide.

A roar shattered the night, and Shera knew the truth without looking: Urzaia Woodsman had recovered. Out of the corner of her eye, she saw him scoop up a black hatchet in each hand and charge straight at Shera.

Her years of training as a Gardener, everything that Maxwell had ever taught her, and her own survival instinct all screamed that she should run. But at that moment, Naberius Clayborn stepped out onto the deck. He stood next to the mast, a blanket around his shoulders, and a cocky smile on his handsome face.

Lucan's freedom stood there, daring her to attack.

So she did.

She bolted across the deck, shear in her right hand. He held a pistol, but he only had one shot. She was confident that she could kill him before he killed her.

His eyes left her, crawling up the mast. His smile bloomed into a full-blown grin. "Too late," he said.

The warning cut through her focus, and she slid to a halt. Just in time.

The Silent One, Tristania, fell from the mast. As the file indicated, she was sheathed head-to-toe in bandages, with a brown coat settling around her like an eagle's wings. A dark whip fell with her, one end clutched in her fist.

Her Soulbound Vessel.

She snapped the whip, and Shera tossed herself to the side even more quickly than she'd run from the pistol. The file had been very clear about this Silent One's capabilities.

"Soulbound to the Awakened tail of a Stormwing. Extremely dangerous. Approach only with great caution."

Where the point of the whip struck, a white explosion blasted the air like a lightning strike.

Naberius stepped up beside his partner, smiling like the marble bust of a historical hero. "I can promise you safe conduct if you are willing to have a civilized discussion. Whatever your contract is, I can beat it."

Behind her, Urzaia was still clutching his hatchets. The man in white was reloading his pistol, off to her left. In front of her, Naberius stood with a gun in his hand, and his guardian had prepared her whip.

At last, Shera admitted that the mission had failed. It was time to escape.

Reluctantly, she closed her left hand around the grip of her second shear. She hated drawing it. The weapon seemed to laugh at her.

Naberius laughed. "If you choose to fight, I can at least promise you a good show. We even have a professional gladiator here, don't we, Urzaia?"

The big man said nothing, but she could feel his footsteps echoing over the deck.

No time to waste. Shera leaped straight at Tristania.

Without missing a beat, the woman flicked her whip. Crackling with light, the end flashed toward Shera's head. If it made contact with her skin, the force of this Soulbound Vessel would blast her entire head to pieces.

Shera struck the whip with her left-hand blade. In the distance, she thought she heard a shrill, cruel laugh.

Both of her shears were invested with years of Intent from generations of Gardeners, but the weapon at her left was special. Lucan said it bore heavier Intent than any other weapon on the Gray Island.

When a blade of such powerful Intent met a Soulbound Vessel in battle, the two powers clashed.

In this case, the flash of light from the Stormwing's tail flared like a newborn star. Heat seared Shera's entire left side, as though she'd stuck her arm in a pot of boiling water.

And she was the only one on her deck to squeeze her eyes shut in time.

Everyone else shouted out, blind, and Shera dashed for the side. Even through her eyelids, the light still left spots on her vision, and she could only see well enough to toss herself over the railing.

She struck the water only feet from the Mason and his Waverider.

When she surfaced, trying to keep a grip on both her shears while still treading water, the Mason reached out and hauled her onto the back of the Kameira.

But someone else had beaten her there.

Jyrine hung limp in front of her, between the two Consultants. As the Waverider sped off, Shera pressed two fingers to the woman's throat. Alive.

"You pulled her out of the water," she said to the Mason, raising her voice so that she could be heard over the churning whine of the Kameira's speed.

"Should I put her back?" he asked.

Shera almost shoved Jyrine into the ocean herself, but Lucan's voice stopped her. *"Death is too permanent,"* he would have said. *"We shouldn't kill, if we don't have to. It closes too many options."*

So Shera decided to leave Jyrine Tessella Marten alive. Maybe the woman would be useful for something.

But her second passenger didn't distract Shera from the unpleasant weight in her gut.

She wasn't used to failure.

Shera made it back to the Island almost unconscious and sheathed in pain from head to toe. She was taken to a room in the infirmary even before she had the chance to report.

The Council of Architects had seemed…perplexed, upon being confronted with Jyrine. They couldn't understand why Shera hadn't killed the woman, but they were unwilling to order her execution themselves. They didn't want to lose a potential source of information about the Sleepless cult and their cabal of leaders.

So they left Jyrine alone in prison, where she ended up in the cell next to Lucan. That was justice for you; now Jyrine would get to spend more time with Lucan than Shera did.

Yala, surprisingly, was perfectly happy upon hearing of Shera's failure. Perhaps seeing Shera exhausted and covered in burns did something for her mood, because she even smiled.

"I could have told you it wouldn't work," she said, "but at least you survived. We can't afford to lose anyone in a time like this, even you."

Shera wasn't sure the last part was strictly necessary, but she kept her mouth shut. Mostly because it hurt to move her lips, as though she'd suffered a bad sunburn. When had her *mouth* gotten burned?

Yala continued, still wearing that irritating smile. "I've sent word to Meia, in case you aren't recovered in time to leave for the next mission. Heal quickly."

Then she had the *nerve* to leave a basket of fruit on the nearby table!

Shera was almost insulted by the insincerity before she brought herself under control.

What was she thinking? Free food was free food.

A week later, Shera was stripped naked in her infirmary bed, with a cluster of alchemically trained Architects busying themselves over her blistered skin. The burns on her lips had healed, but there were a shocking number of more severe burns all over her body, especially the left side. Even she couldn't dodge fireballs and walk off unscathed.

One of the alchemists emptied a syringe into her upper arm, sending blessed relief flooding through her veins. At the same time, another woman spread a cream on her skin that made her burns blaze to life again.

Shera gasped as the pain outpaced the painkiller. "Couldn't you have waited?" she asked.

The Architects didn't even acknowledge that she had spoken, continuing their work without paying attention.

Someone else answered. Someone who wasn't supposed to be on the Island yet, let alone in the infirmary.

"Serves you right," Meia said. "Excuse me, Architects." She poked her face between two masked alchemists, blond hair falling almost down to her shoulders. "I heard you tried to fight a Soulbound by yourself."

"Trust me, I didn't know," Shera said, wincing at another shock of pain. "I wouldn't have fought her if I knew she could throw fire. That's way too much work."

"Not without me around," Meia said. She surveyed Shera's body and shook her head. "I can't remember the last time I've seen you hurt this badly. When I was a girl, I didn't even think you *could* get injured."

"That's because I avoid injury whenever possible. I don't know if you know this, but getting burned *hurts*. It's not worth the trouble."

"You should remember that next time, before you try and *fight* a Soulbound. Without me."

Shera closed her eyes and yawned ostentatiously. "You're interrupting my nap time."

"I came from the prison."

She snapped alert, pushing back the Architects who were wrapping new bandages around her burns. They protested, but she ignored them. "What does he know?"

Meia gave her a wry look. "That you were injured. His guard is free with the gossip."

Hansin. Next time, she would have to teach him to keep his mouth closed.

"Anything else?"

"You're asking me if he knows you did this for him? No, he hasn't figured it out."

Shera sighed and leaned back against her pillows, letting the Architects continue to do their jobs. "Did your mother tell you?"

"I knew as soon as they told me I could find you in the infirmary. When you fight with a clear head, you don't get injured."

"Your faith in me is inspiring." For the first time, Shera noticed what Meia was wearing: a close-fitting suit like the ordinary Consultant blacks, but white and padded with fur. There was even a fur-lined hood dangling behind her. "Is it snowing outside? In the middle of summer?"

As if she herself had realized what she was wearing, Meia started pulling off her heavy white gloves. "I rode in from the Fioran Reaches. Some of the tribes up there just found out that the Emperor was dead, and they had started causing trouble. Independence, rebellion, Elder worship, you know how it is. I'd finished pruning some of the low-hanging branches when I received my mother's message."

She shrugged. "As soon as I arrived, I headed straight to Lucan and then to you. I haven't had much of a chance to settle in yet."

Out of nowhere, Shera had a vision of Meia as a girl: haughty, fragile, and desperate to prove herself better than her friends.

That was a long time ago.

"Thank you," Shera said simply.

Meia adopted a stern look. "Lucan told me you were starting to express human emotion, and I can't approve of that in your condition. If you strain yourself, you could break something."

"In that case, I'll go back to sleep," Shera said. "Safer that way."

Meia's expression firmed, and she spoke more seriously. "I've begun preparations for the next mission. We leave in five days. My mother tells me that you might be in fighting condition at that time, and I do want you along. But if you haven't recovered, then leave it to me."

Shera gave another theatrical yawn. "I'll leave it to you. I've always wanted to try sleeping for a week straight."

But Meia wasn't having it. "I'm serious, Shera. If you're not ready, stay here."

"Fine," she said. "I hear you."

"I'm not kidding."

"I'm going to sleep now."

Meia shook her head and walked off, thanking the Architects before she left.

When the door closed behind her friend, Shera turned to the nearest alchemist. "You have five days to get me back into fighting shape."

"That's possible," she allowed, "but it depends on the efficacy of certain solutions. We can't predict—"

Shera cut her off by raising a hand. She had never trusted alchemists. Childhood trauma, perhaps.

"The correct response is, 'Yes, Gardener.'"

"...yes, Gardener."

As she left the infirmary room, Meia caught the end of Shera's threat.

How nostalgic, she thought. It had been more than ten years since she'd last heard Shera threatening a medical alchemist with death.

The muscles in Meia's hand rippled beneath her skin, stretching and pulling at her joints. Her fingers forced themselves painfully apart, her fingernails hardening into claws. An inhuman rage filled her heart, and from the prickling in her retinas, she knew her eyes had changed shape. Tiny movements in the corner of her eye made her jerk her head—the swish of a passing Shepherd's hand brushing against the wall made her snap to the side, looking for prey.

With a moment's concentration, Meia pushed the sensations back down. The anger subsided, her vision returned to normal, her claws retracted, and her arm settled back to its human shape again.

This happened four or five times a day since the Emperor had ordered her...'enhancements.'

When she was fourteen years old, the Emperor decided that her talent did not match her dedication. She was given a choice—leave his service and return to the Gray Island, or undergo a series of painful alchemical alterations to bring her up to the required level.

Meia had never given up on an assignment in her life. She would have rather died.

So she was left in the care of Kanatalia, the Alchemist's Guild.

Alchemists surrounded her, in their glass-eyed masks and long, stained aprons.

"The Emperor has given us permission to do everything we can," they'd said. "We have solutions that will give you the power of a Hydra, the constitution of a Nightwyrm, the fortitude of a Deepstrider...all the natural advantages that the Kameira have over man, they will be yours! You will be like a Champion, but unbound by their rules!"

They were so excited by their opportunity to serve the Emperor with their art, the alchemists had pulled out all the stops. She was poked, prodded, submerged, and injected day and night, forced to swallow potions, pills, and solutions with every meal.

And the pain...even twelve years later, Meia shuddered at the memory of the pain. She'd gone to bed every night shaking and crying, praying that this day's treatment would be her last. Worse, her body was out of her control. Before long, her room was covered in bloody scratches from the times she'd tried to claw her way through the wood and stone.

Two thoughts had sustained her through the whole process.

First, *I can't let my mother down.* Yala could forgive failure, but she could not forgive weakness. Even if she let her daughter continue to serve the Guild, she would never see Meia the same way again.

Second, *I can't lose to Shera.*

Meia had trained on the Gray Island her whole life. Not like Shera, who had come to the Island when she was almost ten. Yet somehow, Meia found that Shera outperformed her in every test. It had eaten her like a burrowing worm in her gut. If this process could help her surpass Shera, she would tolerate anything.

But her suffering did not go unnoticed.

One day, three months into the treatment, she lay strapped to an examination table screaming. Alchemists stood at each of her four limbs, simultaneously injecting her with a solution that was intended to prevent her muscles from twisting and snapping her bones.

The process felt like it was *doing* exactly what it was supposed to prevent. She shrieked until her voice was hoarse, begging for help, all the while thrashing about on the table trying to escape her own body.

She didn't expect help to actually come.

An apprentice had crashed into the room *through* the door, body tumbling to a stop against the far wall.

And a black-clad shadow had rushed into the room, bronze shears in hand.

Shera knocked a masked man over, paralyzing him with a needle, then leaped over to an alchemist who was trying to sound the bell that would call for help. Shera slashed across the woman's legs, rolling and landing next to Meia.

Meia remembered that day clearly, but one detail stood out from the rest: Shera's eyes, usually so cold and lifeless, burned with rage. She'd never seen such anger in the girl before or since.

Shera sliced through Meia's restraints, speaking through the black cloth covering her mouth. "Let's go. We'll tell the Emperor what they were doing to you. He'll burn this place to the ground."

She started to lift Meia up, pulling her off the table, but Meia raised one sweat-slicked hand to stop her.

"No!" Meia shouted, through clenched teeth. Her bones still felt like they had been replaced with broken glass, but she couldn't quit now. If she did, she'd never be able to face her mother.

Or Shera.

"I want this," Meia rasped. "Please. Don't stop them."

Shera quickly covered over the pain in her expression, returning to her usual stony mask. "I heard you," she said. "Last night, you were crying and screaming after you came back. They're not helping you. This is torture."

One of the alchemists tried to crawl up, but Shera kicked her back down without looking.

Meia had felt her consciousness fading, but she *had* to make Shera understand. She clutched at Shera's sleeve as she faded into sleep. "Please... keep going..."

Just before she lost consciousness, she saw Shera hauling a masked alchemist to his feet. "You heard her," Shera said. "Keep going. But if anything happens to her, I'm coming back. As long as she survives this process in one piece, so will you."

That was the first time Meia had ever thought of Shera as a friend.

Seeing Shera in the same position, helpless on an infirmary bed and surrounded by medical alchemists, made her feel…oddly protective. Part of her hoped that Shera would do the wise thing and stay home, recovering from her injuries instead of going on the mission.

But they were hunting Nakothi's Heart. Even the name brought up years of traumatic memories for Meia, and it had to be much worse for Shera. Meia's friend would do whatever it took to get rid of the Dead Mother's Heart for good.

She knew it was true, as she knew that Shera would follow her to Nakothi's island if she had to hobble there on a crutch.

Typical. The one time Shera could actually stay home and sleep all day, and she won't do it.

Five days later, when Meia woke up, she found Shera standing over her dressed in all black.

"You should be more alert, team leader," Shera said, taking a bite of an apple.

Meia sighed and rolled out of bed.

CHAPTER NINE

THIRTEEN YEARS AGO

Shera, Meia, and Lucan cleaned their training ground, as they always did. They sewed up the rips in their 'target,' stuffing it with fresh straw. They polished the armor of the Masons who had posed as guards, swept the tower floors, and hung suspended on ropes to clean the outside of the tower from alchemical residue.

And while they worked, they talked.

"You can't tell Meia," Lucan whispered. "She'll say I cheated."

Shera glanced over at Meia, who was busy hanging window-curtains. "Cheated? You either got the target or you didn't."

Lucan stopped pushing his soapy rag across the floor. "One might say I *didn't.*"

She bit back a laugh, hiding her expression while she scrubbed the floorboards.

"Nobody can Awaken blankets that fast," he went on, a grin in his voice. "But Ayana's not a Reader, so how is she going to know? I told her the blankets strangled him, and as far as she can tell, it's true."

"What about the window? How did you get it to close behind you?"

Lucan shot another glance at Meia. She was still grumbling into her curtains. He peeled his sleeve back, revealing a spool of white thread taped to the inside of his wrist.

Shera pressed a finger against the thread. It came away tacky.

"I've got a few friends in the Architects, you know that. Well, some of their alchemists are breeding spiders. Silk that's almost invisible when you spin it out, it sticks when you want it to, and you can pull it right off. One of the apprentices let me borrow it."

Now, *that* piqued Shera's interest. What else did the alchemists have that Ayana didn't know about? How much easier might they make Shera's job?

"And the boots?" she asked. "You walked right up the wall."

Lucan winced, putting a hand to his abdomen. "I don't advise it. It *kills* your stomach muscles, trying to stand straight out like that. I kept wanting to crawl, but then it would look like I was pulling my way up with my hands like Meia did."

"So was it a trick, or not?"

He sat back, tapping the side of one boot proudly. "Not this one. Took me three months to make a pair that worked, but now I've actually invested boots that let you walk up walls. I was trying to get them to hang me on the ceiling, like a bat, but it turns out alchemy's a lot better for that."

Shera only knew about Reading secondhand, from Lucan, but everyone knew about investing Intent. A new knife might be sharper, but an old knife held so much Intent that it would never fail. The pair of blades they would inherit, when they finally became full Gardeners, had been passed down from assassin to assassin for almost a thousand years. They were made of old bronze, but they would serve her far better than even new-forged steel.

"Still, that's got to be impressive," she said. "How many alchemists on the Island could do what you did?"

Lucan stretched out his legs so he could admire his boots in the light. "Not even five."

"Are you going to tell Ayana?"

He laughed bitterly, returning to his knees and starting to scrub the floor again. "Why should we share our secrets with them, when they don't tell us anything?"

It was the same old argument, and Shera was weary of it. "Why should they? They don't have to justify themselves to us."

"They don't justify themselves to *anyone*. The Architects get a contract, and so long as they're not killing a high-ranking Guild member or a famous philanthropist, they take it. Are human lives so cheap?"

"Three hundred silvermarks," Shera said automatically.

Lucan slapped his rag down on the floor. "Would you give me up for three hundred silvermarks?"

Shera closed her mouth. Of course she wouldn't, but that was completely different.

He nodded to the bed. "This target. He's somebody's husband. He tucks a little girl into her sheets at night, makes her feel safe. To someone, he's a best friend."

"He's a pillowcase stuffed with straw."

"Well, sure, *he* is, but that's not…my point isn't…" He grumbled in frustration, searching for the right words. "Maybe it's different for you, but I see things you can't. I pick up a woman's hairbrush, and I can see that she inherited it from her older sister when she was seven. It's all that she saved from her burning house. Once I know that, how am I supposed to kill her?"

"Brain, heart, lungs, arteries," Shera listed. "Same as everyone."

Lucan looked straight at her, his dark brown eyes piercing. "When you kill someone, you're ending a life that's *like yours.* Doesn't that make you feel anything?"

No, she thought. *It really doesn't.*

But she was beginning to wonder if maybe it should.

The end of a rolled-up rag snapped in the air like a whip between them. They both looked up, startled, Shera's hand moving to the dagger tied to her ankle.

Meia stood above them, her blond hair pulled back in a kerchief, twisting a rag in her hands. "I can hear you, you know. I'm still in the room."

Lucan held up a hand. "Listen, it's not like—"

She snapped the rag in front of his face. "There are Readers on the Council. They're older and stronger than you. You think they haven't heard these questions before?"

"Not from me."

"The Gardeners exist to maintain balance in an imperfect Empire," Meia went on, quoting from their lessons. "Through us, individuals settle their differences by relying on an Imperial Guild, instead of raising their own armies and dividing this Empire into a thousand petty nations."

Lucan scoffed. "That would never happen. Why would anyone want to be ruled by a thousand emperors instead of one?"

Meia smirked, as though he'd made her point for her. "It's never happened before because *we* do our jobs. Whichever side loses, the Consultants win, and the Empire is even stronger."

"Just because your mother told you that when you…"

Lucan's words faded away as Shera leaned her forehead against the straw man's stuffed mattress. He and Meia were so absorbed in arguing that they might not even notice if she slipped into the bed and under the covers. It would probably be half an hour before they wound down, and that was half an hour of sleep in a warmer, softer bed than her own.

Outside, something popped like a gunshot.

Instantly, all three Gardeners-in-training were pressed against the side of the window, weapons in hand.

"Where's the shooter?" Lucan asked.

"Didn't sound like a musket," Meia replied. She edged around, so that one eye could peek out of the window. "I don't see…wait a second."

Five more pops sounded from outside, and Shera slowly slid up until she could see out of the window. She caught a glimpse, prepared to duck back down instantly to avoid fire, but what she saw froze her in place.

A dark-skinned man had entered the garden, dressed in a tent's worth of flame-colored cloth. A woman in red-and-black armor strode along behind him, head swiveling for any sign of danger, the hilt of a sword poking up over her shoulder. Another woman followed *her,* and though it was hard to tell from this distance, Shera thought it might have been Kerian.

Wherever the man stepped, there was a deafening *pop*, and a floor tile appeared under his feet. He walked at a casual pace, headed straight for them, and behind him stretched a tiled path that hadn't existed a moment before.

"That's not possible," Lucan whispered. "He's Awakening the gravel."

Amid a shower of pops like an army's worth of gunfire, the brightly dressed man strode toward him. As he approached, the tower began to shiver.

Not just the tower.

Every single building in the Garden began to shiver.

The whole vast chamber quaked, as though a giant strode the Gray Island above. Something high-pitched burrowed into Shera's ears, as if every stone in the tower were shrieking at once.

Then he reached the bottom of the tower, five stories beneath their window, and he stopped moving.

At that exact instant, the island froze.

He turned his black eyes to the window, and Shera saw that his head was completely hairless.

"Jump," he commanded, and the sheer force of his voice told Shera that he was to be obeyed.

Meia leaped first, and as she fell, he whipped out one of his voluminous orange sleeves. It billowed forward like a ship's sail caught in the wind, spreading beneath her.

The sleeve caught the girl gently, as though she had fallen into a bundle of a thousand silk blankets. She rolled out onto her feet, but immediately lowered herself to her knees.

"Light and life," Lucan whispered. "That's the Emperor."

Shera had started to figure that out herself.

Lucan jumped next, and was caught in the same manner as Meia. But Shera hesitated. She was supposed to obey this man, she knew, but she didn't quite trust him.

He looked up at her, waiting. He didn't repeat his order.

Shera tightened her gloves, swung one leg over the windowsill, and began to climb down.

Kerian's voice came from below. "She has certain difficulties, as I expressed before. I can assure you, this won't—"

The tower shook once more, like a struck bell.

Shera's fingers slipped, and she found herself staring up at a flat gray ceiling as she tumbled down the last few stories.

And landed in a soft orange cloud. The Emperor released her, spilling her to the ground.

One corner of his mouth rose into a smile. "Lesson one: do what I tell you. You'll end up doing it, one way or another. You might as well take it easy on yourself."

Meia and Lucan both shot looks at her from their knees. Lucan looked ashamed and concerned, but Meia seemed like she was trying to suppress laughter.

Shera stood up. "How can we help you, sir?"

She looked over at Kerian proudly. *See that? I can treat a client with respect!* But for some reason, Kerian was covering her face with a trembling hand.

The armored woman behind the Emperor hadn't stopped looking around from empty window to empty window.

The Emperor chuckled, smoothing his sleeves, which had returned to their normal size. "I'll have an assignment for you in a few years. But before you can help me, you'll need to start training."

"So that we can better serve you, we receive training every day," Shera said.

The Emperor's smile widened. "No, you don't." He turned back to Kerian.

"They're exactly what I need. I will take them."

Kerian bowed, showing a look of pure relief. "I'll have them loaded onto a ship at once."

"No rush. I don't need them until next week. And get them their shears," he added, as if the idea had occurred to him. "I assure you, they'll earn it."

"As you wish."

"We won't be here anymore?" Shera asked. It didn't mean much to her, she just wanted to know.

The Emperor turned his smile on her, and the motion of his head set the silver chain around his neck to ringing. "From here on out, you'll be learning from me."

The other two were visibly overcome by awe, shocked at the idea that they would be taught by the Emperor himself.

Shera was less impressed. No matter what everyone said, the Emperor looked like a regular man. Like anybody else. Outside his fancy clothes, he wouldn't be out of place on the streets of the Capital.

And she couldn't help but wonder…

Why us?

CHAPTER TEN

At times, the Captain manipulates the yard or the planks of the deck as though they are extensions of his own body. He seems to communicate with the ship, and he claims that the ship communicates back.

Granted, the Captain's mind is Elder-touched, and he has lived a long life, scarred by grief. His stories could be lies brought on by sea madness.

But it is my belief that he is Soulbound to his ship, which is his Vessel. This could be the secret to the Navigator's mastery of the Aion Sea.

Further study needed.

–REPORT FROM A MASON UNDERCOVER IN THE NAVIGATOR'S GUILD
(EXCERPT STORED IN THE CONSULTANT'S GUILD ARCHIVES)

"The full team," Meia explained, "consists of thirty-three Shepherds, fourteen combat-trained Masons, a dozen sailor Masons to crew the ship, and us. Every one of us armed for battle. We're taking ten muskets, twenty pistols, and plenty of spare powder and ammunition, in addition to our normal weapons."

"That's very reassuring," Shera said. "But where are we going?"

Meia had led her around to the northeastern side of the island, down a narrow, twisting staircase that Shera never knew existed.

That wasn't a surprise, in itself—everything on the Island was disguised, secret, or hidden. There were probably so many hidden locations on the Gray Island that Shera would never have time to visit them all in her whole lifetime. The surprise was that this staircase went all the way down to the water. As far as Shera knew, the only way onto or off of the Island was the main dock to the west. Everything else was covered in high, jagged rocks.

But these stairs were leading down to the water. What's more, everyone else was already down there, prepared to leave. It was enough to pique Shera's curiosity.

Her imagination supplied her with a picture of a hidden bay filled with hundreds of happy, splashing Waveriders, prepared to take them on a long journey.

If that was what Meia had in mind, Shera might well stay here and recover. Even Nakothi's Heart wasn't worth enduring more days on those horrible creatures. She would be sincerely tempted to drown herself halfway to the destination.

"I'm sure you remember the last person to try and mine for a Heart of Nakothi," Meia said.

Shera did. The Emperor had killed the man personally, leaving him to be torn apart by Elderspawn.

"The Blackwatch found that island, " Meia went on. "Some of our Masons in their Guild got back to us and gave us the heading. We're going to meet up with them and determine the extent of their operation. If they've found a Heart, we'll take it. If they haven't, we'll slow them down a little. And if we have to, we're prepared to kill them all."

Shera couldn't conceal her surprise. "We're risking a Guild War?"

"War?" Meia asked, feigning shock. "A detachment of the Blackwatch were killed by an Elder attack. It's not so rare, in the Empire's history. We don't expect it to come to that, but we're prepared."

That brought up another question. "How are we going to get there?"

A third voice cut her off, and Yala appeared, standing on the stairs with her arms crossed as though she'd been waiting for them.

Meia stood straight. "High Councilor Yala," she said to her mother.

"Gardener Meia. Have you sworn Gardener Shera to secrecy?"

In an unusual display of uncertainty, Meia hesitated. "I'm sorry, Councilor, I...found that redundant."

"Hm." Yala turned her cold gaze to Shera. "Our means of transportation must remain secret. We have sworn every member of this operation to secrecy, including myself, and I don't mean to leave you out. You cannot reveal what we are about to show you to anyone, inside the Guild or out of it. This is a true Guild secret."

The High Councilor stood with the aspect of a judge, tossing out every word with the gravity of a collapsing tombstone.

Shera stared, wondering if this was Yala's version of a joke. "Do you realize how many Guild secrets I know? For years, my *existence* was a Guild secret. Lucan was arrested for telling me Guild secrets. Nine out of ten missions I performed in the field were off-record assignments for the Emperor himself. I know more Guild secrets than *you* do."

Meia's eyes had gone wider with every word, and Yala's face was flushed with anger, but Shera only felt puzzled. Surely she'd proven her ability to keep a secret by *now*.

"Gardener Shera, in the name of the Am'haranai, I call upon you to swear your secrecy on the mists and on your name as a member of this Guild!"

"I swear, I swear," Shera said, sighing.

"Next time, do that the first time I ask it of you."

Shera pinched the bridge of her nose. Next time someone wanted to execute her, maybe she should let them.

Only a few yards later, Shera saw the secret that Yala wanted to keep so badly.

She had to admit, it was probably worth the extra security.

In a secret bay, surrounded by rocks on three sides and Bastion's Veil on the fourth, floated a pitch-black ship. Shera was no judge of ships, but it looked three or four times larger than Calder Marten's *The Testament*.

On the hull, white letters declared the ship's name: *Bastion's Shadow*.

"Who named it?" Shera asked.

"I did," Yala said haughtily.

Shera actually liked the name, but Kelarac take her if she was going to say so *now*.

The fact that the Consultants owned a ship wasn't news—the Guild owned fleets of ships, spread out all over the Empire on various business. But keeping this one on the Island, in secrecy, and deploying it now...all the facts suggested one conclusion.

"I assume it's a Navigator ship," Shera said. That meant they weren't risking a war with one Guild, but with *two*. The Navigators protected their secrets more closely than the Champions.

"As close as we could make it," Meia responded. "It's been in development for years, with our Masons in the Navigator's Guild providing the secrets. As we suspected, each Navigator is indeed a Soulbound, bound to the ship, but it took us so long to figure out how they do that. Not only do you have to Awaken the entire ship, which is an impressive undertaking in itself, but parts of an Elder must be built *into* the ship itself. Without the powers of an Elder or a Kameira, it can't become a Vessel."

Shera didn't know much about Reading, but it sounded complicated. "Then why did you use an Elder? Why not a Kameira?" There were only a few thousand registered Soulbound in the whole world, and ninety percent of them used the powers of Kameira in their Vessels. Soulbound who used Elder powers tended to go insane in days.

"The captain doesn't guide the ship through the Aion," Yala put in. "The ship guides the captain. That was the breakthrough: if we used parts of Elderspawn in the ship's construction, it could guide us around the hazards of the deep Aion."

"Almost fifty people died before we figured that out," Meia said.

For a second, Shera almost asked what Elder parts they'd used in the ship's construction. Then she noticed the crow's nest at the top of the mast.

Instead of an open basket, it looked more like a solid, closed room. Was someone supposed to sit inside that? How would they see out?

The 'room' opened, and Shera saw that it wasn't a crow's nest at all.

It was a giant eye.

The eye was solid black, with a golden iris and a narrow pupil. It looked around as if searching for something, blinked a few times, and then settled back to sleep. Now that she looked closer, she could see dark veins standing out on the outside of the "crow's nest," blending organically with the mast.

The Testament had disturbed her at the time, and she couldn't understand how the crew sailed around knowing that there was an Elder giant chained beneath their feet. Now she found herself wishing for their problem. At least *their* ship couldn't watch them sleep. As far as she knew.

"We've spent everything we can spare on this operation," Yala said. "Bring us back a Heart."

Shera met her eyes, paying close attention to the Councilor's reaction. "Just be ready to contain it when we return," Shera said. "I don't want to destroy it on my own."

Because it would kill me, she thought.

Yala nodded expressionlessly and walked down the rest of the stairs. She moved in a stately and dignified manner, but she still outpaced Shera and Meia, putting distance between them quickly.

There was something strange going on there. Yala had been reluctant to even speak of the Heart's destruction, and she seemed more interested in getting it back to the Gray Island than about what they would do once it arrived.

If she didn't plan to destroy the Heart, what *did* she want to do with it?

Meia would grow suspicious if she stayed silent, so Shera continued with her questions. "How long will the journey take?"

"There's a Deepstrider migration across the coast," Meia said, jumping the last few stairs and leading the way to the ship. Shera followed, with less enthusiasm. "We've prepared countermeasures for that. And Lhirin Island has drifted west, but we don't have time to sail around it, so we'll have to fight our way through. All in all...five, six days."

Shera didn't like the sound of the Deepstrider migration. She'd seen Deepstriders before: huge, blue-scaled leviathans with mouths like dragons.

"When you say a Deepstrider migration, that makes me picture hundreds of hungry Deepstriders swimming under the ship."

"I've never seen it, but I've heard that's what it's like."

They had reached the base of *Bastion's Shadow,* and Shera found herself staring up at the closed eye on top of the mast. She'd never been too comfortable with Elders—not that anybody *was*—and her life's experience had done nothing but reinforce that fear.

"I see," Shera said.

Meia put a hand on her shoulder. "Think of it this way. One way or another, we'll be done with Nakothi's Heart by the end of this mission. Either we'll have taken it back here to be destroyed, or we'll be dead."

Strangely enough, that did make Shera feel better.

The Deepstrider migration was worse than Shera had imagined.

It was like they were sailing over an underwater river of a thousand sapphire-scaled, serpentine dragons, all of them thrashing and fighting and mating under the surface. The water swirled with whirlpools and clashing currents stirred up by the Kameira's conflicting water-controlling powers, and the surf chopped with white-capped waves.

The ship spun like a leaf in a storm, and Shera had her first experience with seasickness. Worse were Meia's "countermeasures": four Shepherds standing at the four corners of the ship, blowing whistles made of blue scales.

Whistles.

She'd seen one of them in use before, and those whistles were Awakened tools made to control Deepstriders. It was true that none of the Kameira had torn their ship apart. Yet. But it was no comfort to know that nothing more than a musical instrument stood between her and the mouths of a thousand hungry monsters.

What if one of them fell overboard? Would three be enough to protect the entire ship?

Shera spent the entire afternoon in a state of nausea and agitation before she finally gave up and fell asleep.

A day later, she caught sight of Lhirin Island.

"Ordinarily, Navigators would sail days out of their way to avoid Lhirin," explained the Mason acting as captain. "It's one of the 'floating islands' of the Aion, which means that it moves. Hunts, really."

The island looked more like a five-mile stretch of wet purple strings than a landmass, with black trees sticking up in the shape of jagged thorns. A flock of birds swirled around the island like a black halo.

"Hunts, you say?" Shera repeated. Then she noticed that the island was, slowly but surely, growing larger.

"Oho! Looks like it's caught our scent." The captain laughed, turning the wheel away from the pursuing island. "I don't know how it works, to tell you the truth, but Lhirin Island seems to hunt ships. Back in the early days of the Empire, it killed a lot of the first Navigators before they figured out how to deal with it."

"And how do you deal with it?" Shera asked. The island had sprouted several long, purple feelers that slapped at the surface of the water closer and closer to *Bastion's Shadow.*

"You avoid it, usually," he said. "But we didn't have time to do that this time, so we made some bait."

"Bait."

As she watched, three black-clad Shepherds pushed a crate off the ship's stern. It bobbed in their wake, drifting closer to the living island.

"Something the Architects cooked up, I understand. A mix of Reading and alchemy. Supposedly it draws the island in, pretending to be a ship, and then...poisons it? I'm sorry, Gardener, I'm just not sure."

"I see. Thank you."

Lhirin Island was closing on them, sprouting a wide, pinkish mouth. Its feelers snatched up the box, pulling it into the island's great maw.

Shera headed below, looking from room to room until she finally found what she was looking for: the place where the Architects kept their alchemy.

She plucked a syringe from an open box near the wall, holding it up to a young alchemist nearby.

"Take this," she said. "Fill it with something that will put me to sleep for the next twenty-four hours. Then hand it back."

He did as ordered, and she returned to the cabin she shared with Meia.

When next she woke, Nakothi's island was in sight.

The island looked much the same as she had last seen it: like a pale corpse, floating in the middle of the Aion Sea. For all she knew, that was exactly what it was: part of the Dead Mother's gargantuan body, stretching for miles in the ocean.

Ten curving, pale bone spires lorded over the center of the island in two rows of five. They curved inward toward each other, looking like nothing so much as a giant set of exposed ribs. The island itself was covered in pliant skin rather than sand or soil, broken only by patches of dark, waving seaweed that sprouted from naturally occurring wounds.

When Nakothi's nameless island first appeared as a speck on the horizon, the captain of *Bastion's Shadow* had swung in a wide arc around, hoping to avoid detection by the Blackwatch. According to their information, the Watchmen had clustered themselves on the western side of the island, around the makeshift mine they'd created to dig for a Heart.

Shera remembered her last trip here, and couldn't imagine anyone willingly spending more time in these surroundings than absolutely necessary. It was like crawling around inside a dead body—and one that was infested with monsters, no less. The horrific Children of the Dead Mother haunted this land, and she gripped her shears in preparation for a battle as the ship drew closer.

Nearby, Meia did the same, scanning the ocean's surface for any sign of Elderspawn. Her eyes had shifted, irises glittering orange and pupils transformed to vertical slits. Shera assumed that it helped her sight in some way, though she had a hard time keeping track of Meia's powers.

In the hours it took the ship to approach the island, neither Shera nor Meia saw a single speck of motion. The waters around Nakothi's corpse were entirely dead.

She hoped.

Ordinarily a ship of this size would have to anchor nearby and send smaller boats to shore, but *Bastion's Shadow* ran right up to the side.

"It doesn't slope," the captain explained. "And it's soft enough that it won't damage the hull. We can get as close as we want, so we'll lower a ramp and hop down."

It didn't slope...meaning that there was nothing supporting the island on the ocean's floor. It really was floating on the surface.

From the disgusted look on Meia's face, Shera knew she'd come to the same conclusion.

The island smelled like rotting vegetation and bloody meat, though not as strongly as Shera would have expected. The stench should have been overpowering, but it served as more of a backdrop to the ordinary scents of the sea.

Shera and Meia went ashore first, meeting the three Masons dressed in long Blackwatch coats. All three of them bowed at the same time.

"Masons. Have there been any developments since your last report?" Meia asked. Shera was too busy scanning the curving outline of the island for any signs of motion. Last time they'd been here, the place had crawled with the living dead. What had changed?

One of the undercover Blackwatch, a young woman, spoke up first. "We finally found what we believe to be a viable Heart, Gardener. Last night."

Shera could practically hear Meia's attention sharpen. "Do they have it yet?"

"Not yet. Attacks from the Children have made retrieval difficult."

"We saw no Elderspawn on the way in."

One of the other Masons, an older man, responded this time. "They seem to be concentrating their attacks on our camps at the western edge of the island. But it's true, they do seem to be tapering off these last few days."

"I don't trust it," said the last of the Masons, an old woman. "The Children don't back off without a good reason."

The male Mason coughed politely, as though he were embarrassed to have this discussion in front of the others. "None of them are capable of making plans. They don't have commanders."

"They did once," she responded.

No one had anything to say to that.

"What are our orders, Gardener?" the young woman asked.

"Standby," Meia said. "I need to consult with my partner."

She drew Shera off to one side, where they could discuss privately.

"We have to stop them from getting the Heart," Shera said. "Use everything we have and hit them hard."

Meia ran a hand over her blond hair, thinking. "Then we'll be leaving a Heart of Nakothi exposed. What if the Guild sends more people?"

"We mine it and destroy it ourselves."

"Without anyone from the Blackwatch? Do you know how to counter the powers of a Great Elder? Do you know anything about Elder biology?"

"What is there to know? Cut it out, take it back, destroy it. If we could destroy it here, I'd say we should."

But she knew they couldn't. They might be able to kill the Heart with the equipment they had on hand, but not destroy it completely.

"I'm still concerned about the Children," Meia said. "We're not equipped to fight both the Blackwatch *and* a horde of monsters."

That was a fair point. Whatever the Mason said about the Children not having a commander, Shera had found them more than capable of swarming last time. This silence had her concerned more than relieved.

If the Elderspawn attacked after their fight with the Watchmen, the Consultants might be the ones facing annihilation.

Shera thought for a moment, then proposed, "Let them do the work."

Meia remained silent, encouraging her to continue.

"They're going to mine it anyway. We get our people in position, hiding near the Heart. As soon as they get it free, we take it, hit hard, and fade out. Mission accomplished. If the Children attack then, so much the better. The Blackwatch will have to fight them instead of facing us."

Whatever Meia's faults, she certainly made quick decisions. She didn't so much as pause before turning back to the Masons, addressing the three of them as well as the small group of Shepherds from their own crew that had gathered to watch.

"Here are your orders," Meia said, and proceeded to hand out commands.

Shera liked her role. It involved hours of sitting around, doing nothing.

The Watchmen didn't know it, but they were surrounded by Consultants.

Masons moved among them, wearing the silver-buttoned black coats of the Blackwatch. Shepherds crouched behind patches of seaweed, in natural craters, or within the open, porous tunnels that riddled the island.

Meia remained close to the ship, a position she did not enjoy, but one she'd assigned to herself. Someone needed to coordinate all the Consultants, consolidating reports and dispatching new orders according to the situation, and Shera certainly wouldn't do it.

The mine was a huge crater a hundred yards from end to end, seemingly gouged out of the island's flesh. Its edges were an angry, oozing red edged with unhealthy patches of green. Holes dotted the crater walls where the Watchmen had dug through veins, each ranging from the size of a man's arm to bigger than a sewer tunnel.

Pink wires crossed from wall to wall, like a maze of thin tendons, though some of them had been severed to make it easier for the Watchmen to mine. Only one cluster of wires remained entirely intact, all terminating in a thick cluster at the bottom of the hole.

They were stuck to Nakothi's Heart.

The heart itself looked exactly as Shera remembered it: a pulsing, gray-green mass the size of a fist, throbbing and pushing sickly liquid into the island's flesh.

Its appearance brought back a hundred memories, none of them pleasant.

One last time, she thought. *We'll deal with this, and then I'll never have anything to do with a Great Elder as long as I live.*

Of all the Consultants in and around the crater-like mine, Shera had the best view. She was crouched inside one of the widest veins, deep in the shadows where the Blackwatch had no chance of spotting her in her blacks. Last time, the Children of the Dead Mother had haunted these tunnels, so she kept one shear drawn and her hand resting on the sheath at her left.

She was sitting with her back against the disgustingly flexible wall when everything went wrong.

Calder Marten climbed down into the crater.

He was fully dressed this time, thankfully, with a three-cornered hat over his red hair and a blue jacket over his shirt. He wore a cutlass on his left hip and a pistol strapped to his right.

They had no information on when Calder was supposed to arrive, but the captain had assured her that he would more than likely take the long way around Lhirin Island. That meant that they weren't expecting him for another three days, at least.

It seemed that he had indeed taken the longer route, or he would have arrived days before the Consultants, but the captain's estimate of his speed had proven optimistic.

Regardless, he was here now. And that meant his crew was here too.

Including the former Champion.

She had caught Urzaia Woodsman off his guard the last time, but she didn't expect that to work a second time. At least his fire-hurling wife was safely locked up on the Gray Island. Shera had gone to check on her once, back home, but she'd ended up leaving without saying a word. She had spoken to Lucan at length, though, mostly assuring him that her injuries were nothing and he shouldn't worry.

So Calder and his crew were here, but at least they hadn't all come down into the crater. At first glance, it seemed to be just the captain—he walked down with a brown-haired woman old enough to be his mother. Alsa Grayweather, if Shera remembered her briefing correctly. Calder's... mother? Stepmother?

They came down together, joining the six other Watchmen that dug at Nakothi's Heart.

Six Watchmen, and two Witnesses.

Naberius and Tristania had come down with the Navigator, the former in a dark blue suit, and the latter wearing her coat and bandages. Her black hair stuck up at all angles from gaps in her wrapping, and she turned constantly, keeping a hand on her whip. When the Silent One's eyes brushed past Shera's tunnel, she pressed herself back against the wall, hiding her shear lest the bronze glint in the dull light.

They had the worst *possible* timing.

Mentally, she urged them to leave. The Watchmen had been about to free the Heart. As long as they did it *without* a Soulbound down in the crater, Shera had a good chance of snatching her objective and leaving. But with Naberius, Calder, and Tristania in addition to the Watchmen, Shera didn't have much chance of getting through without a fight.

Then again, maybe this was better.

Shepherds with muskets had every angle of the crater surrounded. This could be their opportunity to leave Naberius dead, *The Testament* without a captain, and the Watchmen without a leader.

Personally, Shera had nothing against these people. But the Guild had a mysterious client, and the client was Emperor.

Besides, she would do whatever it took to prevent a Heart of Nakothi from escaping into the world once again. She'd witnessed the damage the last one had caused, and killing these people was a small price to pay for containing this Heart.

What would Lucan say? This time, she honestly wasn't sure.

Just when she thought the situation couldn't get any worse, one of the Watchmen started to wander over to her tunnel. It was a young man, a few years younger than Shera, carrying a shovel on one shoulder and kicking at the island's flesh as he walked. He peered carefully into the darkness as he walked by, and Shera froze.

He wasn't checking for her, she was sure. It was good sense to check any tunnels on this island before you walked inside. But she held her breath nonetheless.

After a moment, having ensured his own safety, the Watchman relaxed and leaned his shovel against the wall. Maybe he was trying to sneak a break, maybe he wanted to relieve himself. Shera never knew.

She took the opportunity.

Shera rushed forward before he knew what was happening, driving a needle into his chest and covering one of her gloved hands into his mouth.

He whimpered against her hand, eyes wide and terrified, before she pulled him into the darkness of the tunnel.

A second later, she came back for his shovel.

Shera hid him in the crevice to the side, where she had concealed herself. She hadn't made the smartest move—they would surely notice him missing. But they would have the Heart free in minutes, and there was every chance that he'd see her before that. She couldn't take the chance.

She watched the others in the crater closely, looking for any sign that they'd noticed her. Tristania still surveyed everything equally, giving no indication that she saw a missing member of her team. Naberius was on his knees with his arms raised, worshiping the Heart as though it were a primitive idol. Alsa watched Naberius with disapproval as an old man in a Blackwatch coat whispered in her ear. The other Watchman pried and hacked at the wires around the Heart, giving no thought to their surroundings.

Then she saw Calder Marten.

He looked from Watchman to Watchman, forehead furrowed as though something was bothering him.

Don't count them, Shera urged. *Don't count them. Don't count.*

When he spun to his mother, drawing his gun as he moved, Shera knew her cover was blown. She edged out of the tunnel, pulling a mirror from her pocket as she moved.

She angled the mirror into the light, sending a signal to the top of a nearby shack, where a Shepherd waited with musket ready.

Attack, she signaled.

Two flashes back.

Acknowledged.

"We're under attack!" Alsa Grayweather shouted, raising her sword.

Then the man next to her died in a musket-shot and a spray of blood, and Shera moved.

CHAPTER ELEVEN

When you must fight a Soulbound, do so with great care. Fight from a distance, or from the shadows, and be sure to gather as much information as you can.

If you must fight a member of the Champion's Guild, carry with you a small vial of poison. When the Champion defeats you, end your own life.

–GARDENER DOCTRINE

Bullets flew down into the crater from the ledge overhead. The Silent One, Tristania, did her order proud by standing over Naberius with her coat spread wide. It was apparently invested to stop bullets, which Shera recognized as a tricky bit of Reading, because bullets pounded against the fabric and failed to penetrate.

Naberius knelt under his partner's protection, saw in hand, and continued working to cut the Heart free.

Shera ran straight for him, but she found her way blocked by the back of a Watchman in a dark coat. He raised a musket, aiming for the exposed shoulder of a Shepherd locked in combat on the ledge above.

She straightened, plunged her shear into the back of his neck, and slipped away before his body fell.

Even Lucan would agree: there was a time for sparing your enemy's life, and the middle of battle was not it.

Shera ran around the action, sticking to the shadows at the edge of the pit. She dodged Tristania's attention more than the bullets; as long as she remained concealed, she had a single opportunity to secure the Heart.

Calder Marten, fortunately, had decided to make his way out of the crater. He had his mother by the arm and seemed to be moving away from the fight.

Good. That was another pair of eyes out of her way.

Then Calder shouted, in a voice that cut through the sounds of battle, *"Urzaia!"*

There was no way his Soulbound cook would hear him at this distance, over all the noise. No way.

But Shera froze when she heard an answering roar, and saw a black-clad

Consultant fly from one end of the crater to the other, screaming all the way. Urzaia Woodsman would be here in seconds, and if he caught Shera alone in this pit, she might as well attempt to surrender.

Calder changed direction, heading for a rope at the edge of the cauldron. She fought back a sense of relief—maybe he was going to meet Urzaia, and not the other way around. So long as she didn't have to fight the former Champion.

Almost absently, she cut down another Watchman who had started to notice her. Tristania's bandaged head flicked to the left, attention caught by something on the ledge. There, this was her chance: Naberius was still absorbed in sawing the Heart free from its bonds.

Shera rushed toward Tristania's exposed back. She could strike now, kill the two Witnesses, then finish cutting the Heart free herself while the Shepherds covered her from above.

She underestimated the Silent One.

Without turning around, Tristania snapped her whip behind her. The tip blurred toward Shera with invisible speed, already crackling with a Stormwing's concussive power.

Shera almost collapsed backwards, turning the motion into a sideways roll. There was a wide tunnel in the crater wall next to her, and she guided her body toward it.

The whip shone white and detonated. Heat and pressure blew Shera's hair back, but there were none of the scalding burns from last time. She continued her roll, sliding into the shadows inside the tunnel.

From there, she levered herself to her knees, keeping a sharp eye on Tristania. If the Witness had seen her, it was all over.

Tristania turned her head this way and that, scanning the entire cauldron. Her eyes moved to Shera's tunnel…and slid right past.

Shera exhaled in relief. Too close. That had been too close.

I've blown my best chance. She'd escaped by the edge of a nail, and now she would have to wait for another shot. Something else had to distract them, draw their eyes from her position.

With forced patience, she waited once more, watching as Naberius worked the saw with the intensity of a father saving his only child. His face was flushed, sweat soaking his hair, but he grinned like a hero accepting an award.

The battle above the crater began to quiet, and Shera found herself worrying for the Consultants. Had they been silenced? Were they forced to retreat? Would she have to escape with the Heart on her own?

She'd been forced into worse situations over the years, but none of them were circumstances she would care to repeat.

Two tendons left between Naberius and the Heart. Shera clenched the bronze shear in her right hand. Soon, now.

This was her last chance.

The first wire broke, leaving only one left. Naberius was panting now, working the saw feverishly, as Tristania circled him as though expecting an attack from any angle.

As soon as he gets it free, Shera thought. They would be distracted by their success, looking to protect the Heart instead of themselves. As long as she could kill one of them in that period of confusion, she could get away.

When the last tendon snapped, Tristania turned her attention to Naberius for an instant. Confirming for herself that the Heart of Nakothi was free.

With no intention of stopping, Shera ran.

Compared to the battle before, the cauldron was eerily quiet. No gunshots, no screams, only a few distant shouts. One man's voice broke the silence once again.

"Naberius!" Calder Marten yelled. *"They're after the Heart!"*

Shera should have killed him when she had the chance.

Commotion kicked up all around her, but one good thing had come from Calder's scream: Tristania looked up the ledge, toward his voice. Not back toward Shera.

She slammed into the Silent One knife-first, driving the blade with the full force of her body.

Tristania grunted as the air was forced out of her lungs, the invested blade slicing through her coat where the bullets had done nothing. The fabric held up better than Shera had hoped, blunting the strike, and preventing her shear from penetrating more than an inch.

Still, blood soaked the Witness's back, and she stumbled on her partner as Shera's charge bowled her over. The wound likely wouldn't be fatal, but Tristania wasn't the goal—Shera kicked her out of the way and bent down for Naberius.

He raised a pistol, which Shera knocked contemptuously from his hand. She turned her blade to the fist gripping the Heart, intending to cut it free.

It was at that point that she realized something she hadn't before.

She was *surrounded* by Children of Nakothi.

Something like a man-sized centipede made from scraps of skin and bone hissed, rearing up on its hind legs and striking at Shera, its rotting jaws wide open. She managed to slide away and slash at its exposed underbelly with her shear.

Milky white fluid spilled from its severed throat, and it curled up like a dead spider. A child-sized imp, its skin as blue as a drowned corpse, hauled itself up from an open wound in the flesh of the island. It hissed as it saw her, baring black fangs.

Behind that monster, a menagerie of bones and rotting parts shambled around, engaging Watchman and Consultant alike. Calder Marten slashed at a headless white gorilla on the edge of the crater, and a Shepherd fired a pistol blindly at a huge bat that looked like it was made of stretched human skin.

This was not the first time Shera had seen creatures such as these.

As the Emperor had once explained, the Dead Mother's Children were born when Nakothi's power bubbled up and embedded itself in human remains. In a way, their bones were invested with power like an object held Intent. In the days of the Elders, when Nakothi ruled a portion of the world, she would shape the Children for specialized purposes, designing perfect workers out of once-human parts.

Shera had known it was too good to be true when she heard that the attacks from the Children had slowed down. They were *waiting*. Waiting for the humans to free the Heart.

What she didn't understand was why. Surely they were here to protect Nakothi's Heart...but if that were true, why hadn't they attacked earlier?

Another piece of the picture clicked together.

A giant beetle, its face like a dried corpse and its shell formed of longbones lashed together into armor, clambered up on Tristania. She placed her hand against the shell and white light detonated *inside* the monster, blowing it into pieces. Shera herself had to leap over something that looked like a four-armed hairless monkey, driving her knife down through its spine to silence it.

But Naberius was completely unharmed.

He jogged away, Heart cradled in his arms, and the Children of Nakothi streamed around him. A few sniffed curiously at him, which made Shera wonder exactly how far his newfound immunity would take him, but none attacked.

They wanted the Heart to get out. If anything, they were here to cover Naberius' escape.

That made it even more imperative that Shera stop him.

Her left hand dropped to the pouch at her side, pulling a spade free and whipping it forward. The steel embedded itself into the Chronicler's calf, dropping him to his knees with a pathetic cry.

She stalked closer, intending to finish him and take the Heart herself.

Something slammed into the ground behind her, and she turned.

Urzaia Woodsman loomed over her, grinning his gap-toothed grin. He held a black hatchet in each hand, and the gold hide wrapped around his arm gleamed in the sunlight. He stalked toward her, muscles rippling between his patchwork leather armor.

Shera crouched on the balls of her feet, moving her knife forward into a guard.

I don't have to fight him. I have to get the Heart.

Urzaia spun the hatchet in his right hand. "I am Urzaia Woodsman. I am the cook for *The Testament,* under Captain Calder Marten."

He didn't attack, and Shera realized he was waiting for her to introduce herself. If that was what it took to distract him, she'd play that game. "Shera," she said.

His smile widened, and he reached out his hand, absently driving a hatchet-blade into the skull of an approaching monster. White fluid sprayed from every joint in its body at once, and it fell apart like he'd torn it to pieces.

Awakened blades, Shera noted. *Don't get cut.*

"Is this not better?" Urzaia said. "Let us fight. No tricks."

Not if she intended to live until sunset.

Shera drove forward, striking before his last word faded, driving the blade up into his gut.

With shocking speed, he knocked her wrist aside with the back of his fist, turning his body sideways and kicking her in the hip before she could react. His foot hit her like a hammer, sending her spinning away.

She landed on her feet more out of luck than skill, her hip straining as though her left leg had tried to tear itself free of her body. Her right wrist had gone numb, and she fully expected crippling pain soon. The shear was already shaking in her grip.

So this was what it meant to fight a Champion.

Urzaia roared so loud that it echoed from the crater walls. He leaped toward her with both hatchets raised. She rolled underneath him, side-stepping as though she meant to come up behind him.

Then she moved toward her real target: Naberius.

The man was still crawling across the moist ground in his blue suit, Heart clutched in his hand and living dead creatures swarming around him. Shera made it two steps closer to him before a demonic rabbit hopped in front of her, body held together by bones and tendons instead of skin. It hissed, revealing a mouth full of fangs.

She wasted a precious second driving her shear through its flesh and then shaking it free. By that time, she had to spin and catch Urzaia's hatchet on her invested blade.

It felt like trying to catch a collapsing tree. Her hip flared with pain and gave out, driving her down, and her wrist screamed at her.

He didn't seem focused on forcing the weapon down. In fact, he pulled the hatchet back, looking vaguely disappointed.

"I thought you had another weapon," he said, nodding toward the second of her shears. "You should release it."

Shera was beginning to come to the same conclusion. She never drew her second shear because the level of Intent bound in the blade distracted her. She could never get over the impression that the weapon was laughing at her. In a fight, that half-second of disruption could kill her, powerful blade or no.

And all the Intent invested in her second shear wouldn't mean anything if she couldn't cut him in the first place.

She moved her left hand as though she meant to reach for her shear, but flung a spade instead.

The gladiator didn't even blink as he slapped the dagger out of the air with the flat of his hatchet. "Not that one," he said. "The big one."

"I can't fight you," Shera said honestly. "If I had to kill you, I'd rather do it while you slept."

Urzaia's smile faded. "I am sorry for you." He stepped forward, an axe in each hand.

Then a figure in black landed between Shera and her opponent, knees bent, bronze blade in each hand.

"Urzaia Woodsman," Meia said. "My name is Meia. Pleased to meet you."

The Izyrian looked over her shoulder to Shera. "You see? These are manners."

Shera couldn't understand why Meia had landed in front of the man instead of behind him. She could have killed him already; what was she *thinking?*

Without looking away, Meia kicked a skinless dog with her heel. It flew back, over Shera's head, and slammed into the side of the crater. Urzaia's eyebrows raised.

"Shera is not a fighter. That's my job." She crouched, holding her shears ready.

Casually, Urzaia stepped forward and tested her by flicking his hatchet down. She caught his black blade on her bronze, and not only held him off—she actually forced him back.

The gladiator started to laugh. "Yes, *yes!* Come!"

They were insane. Both of them. Shera was surrounded by insanity. Resigned, she circled around the gladiator and palmed another spade.

Crazy Meia might be, but Shera still had to back her up.

Meia met a hatchet with each of her blades, forcing Urzaia's arms wide apart, then spun to plant a kick in his chest. The Kameira in her blood roared, reinforcing her body with strength and delivering enough force into the blow to knock a door off its hinges.

It didn't matter how strong he was: a kick like that would shatter his ribs and send his body tumbling over backwards. She had him.

It was like she'd kicked a mountain.

He grunted, his feet only shifting backwards a few inches. Nothing shattered or broke beneath her foot.

That wasn't *possible.* Her ankle flared with pain—the kick had almost broken her *own* bones, and she was enforced by all the power of the Alchemist's Guild. Soulbound or not, he should have at least taken a step backwards.

That's a Champion for you, she thought. Their physical enhancements were Guild secrets, but she had no idea they would hold up so well.

Urzaia brought his fist, still clutching the grip of his hatchet, down on her leg, but she was quick enough to pull back. She lunged forward as soon as her foot hit the ground, driving her right-hand shear at his ribs.

He countered with insulting ease, backing up and slapping her blade aside with his own. Urzaia raised his second hatchet, drawing it back too far for a simple blow.

He's throwing it, Meia realized, and raised her second knife to guard.

But Urzaia didn't complete the motion. He moved to the side, sweeping the hatchet in a circle instead of throwing it.

It knocked Shera's spade from the air. How had he even known it was coming?

Whatever his Soulbound power was, Meia wanted it.

She took advantage of his confusion to slash at his shoulder, though she succeeded only in slashing the strap of his leather breastplate before she had to retreat. He advanced on her, driving a black blade down at her forehead.

Meia raised both shears, catching his hatchet on her two crossed weapons.

That was when her own body betrayed her.

Power surged in her muscles, but it pulled in different directions. Anger urged her to throw her knives aside and use her claws to tear out his throat, savaging him with tooth and nail. Fear flooded strength to her feet, encouraging her to run. Animal cunning activated her eyesight, looking for easier prey. Shera could fight this one; she would take advantage of the opening to hunt elsewhere.

Shera noticed Meia's conflict and took the chance to throw another spade at Urzaia's back. He had to knock that dagger away as Shera engaged something like a blue-and-white mantis with bone claws.

Motion caught the corner of her vision, and Meia leaped. She landed on the shoulders of a heavily muscled, headless gorilla...but she didn't stay there. She launched off, using the monster as a platform to flip over Urzaia's head and drive both shears down at the base of his neck.

All of Meia snarled in triumph. *I have him.*

With some sixth sense, Urzaia had to have felt her coming. He opened his hands, letting his hatchets fall to the ground, then seized her by the wrists.

She fought with as much desperation as agility, wrapping her legs around his neck until she straddled the back of his head. She focused her strength on her legs, tightening calves against his throat, cutting off his air.

Just die, she urged.

But he didn't oblige her so easily. When Shera moved to stab him, he caught her, slamming her into the side of the crater. Then he allowed himself to fall backwards.

Meia had time to realize she was falling before she hit the ground hard enough to drive all the air from her lungs.

For the first time since her sparring matches with the Emperor, she was overwhelmed with a depressing realization: he was simply *better* than she was. Stronger, faster, more skilled at open combat. And his powers, whatever they were, worked in complete synergy. She constantly struggled to keep her body focused in the same direction as her mind.

Shera had the right idea. This wasn't the time for battle, it was a time to kill the target and leave. Meia *knew* that, but she'd let her own strength seduce her into a fight.

Fortunately, Shera had never taken her eyes off the goal.

As soon as Meia's eyes cleared, she saw Shera's black hair rushing through the crowd of Children. Calder Marten lifted the Heart of Nakothi from Naberius, holding it out of the Chronicler's reach.

Urzaia shouted and struggled to save his captain, but this was where Meia's strength could actually come in handy. She tightened her grip on him, arms and legs both, and refused to let him rise to his feet.

He didn't have his hatchets, so all he could do was pound blindly with his elbows and fists, trying to break her hold. It was like being pelted with bricks, but Meia's powers would heal this much in seconds.

She had to keep him away from Shera.

Calder spun at the very last instant, perhaps alerted by his Reader senses, and caught her shear on the edge of his cutlass.

Shera fought viciously, no words, launching spades and needles whenever she caught a gap, trying to keep him on his back foot. All she needed was one opening, then she could take the Heart and leave.

"Where's my wife?" he asked, voice burning, but she ignored him, sweeping a kick at his ankles. If she knocked him over, she could kill him and take the Heart.

Her injured hip gave out as she tried to recover from her kick, and she stumbled, still half-crouched.

Oh no. He wouldn't miss this opening.

And he didn't.

He cut her on the injured hip, blade sliding up to her side, and she ground her teeth to keep from screaming. She lunged at him, movements clumsy, and he kicked her in the ribs.

Calder shouted another question, but she didn't hear it. Her mind was filled with pain.

But a distant, cold, detached part of her recognized the opportunity. Her shear moved weakly, slashing at his leg. He was able to step back enough to avoid a more severe injury, but the blade still opened up a wide gash across his shin.

He screamed, flailing his sword, trying to keep her at bay.

And Shera knew: this was the time.

She reached her left hand behind her back, gripping her second blade. She could swear she heard laughter, and she couldn't tell if it came from the sheath on her back or the Children all around her.

The laughter rose to a crescendo, shrieking in her ears, and she froze.

She hated this blade. It remembered the Dead Mother too closely.

Shut up, Nakothi, Shera thought, and pulled her second weapon.

She advanced on Calder, both shears ready, ignoring the pain in her hip. As long as she stayed focused, she could kill him.

But his eyes were glued to her left hand, expression horrified. "What *is* that?" he asked.

He was a Reader—she'd almost forgotten. To him, the Intent in this blade had to be blinding.

She didn't answer him. Instead, she used that moment to attack.

He turned her right-handed strike with the edge of his sword, but that was more of a feint than anything. With his blade out of position, she swung her second shear.

In Shera's head, Nakothi laughed.

The knife cut through his sword in a shower of sparks and red-hot metal, sending the top half spinning to the ground next to a corner of his coat.

Shera stepped closer, closing the gap with him as he staggered away. A voice in her head whispered his earlier question: *Where's my wife?*

A memory of something that had never happened filled her mind—Shera plunging a knife into Jyrine Tessella Marten's throat, feeling the blood flow down her wrist. As though it were natural, she answered him.

"She's dead," she said.

Wait, that's not right.

But she didn't correct herself. She punched the Navigator's wrist, opening his grip. The Heart of Nakothi fell out.

She snatched it from the air and left, objective complete. Meia was still grappling with Urzaia, though the two of them were on their feet.

"Meia!" Shera called, running. "We're leaving!"

Instantly, Meia flowed out of the battle, pulling a cardboard tube from her belt and tearing it open with her teeth. She tossed the alchemical charge to the ground, and the two Consultants ran.

Behind them, the crater filled with smoke.

The closer they got to the ship, the fewer Children they saw. Shera and Meia supported one another, each injured, which surprised Shera more than anything else. She hadn't thought any wound could slow Meia for long.

One injury in particular seemed to bother her: a bite mark on her forearm, bleeding freely. The wound was now surrounded by dark blue scales, which Shera recognized as Meia's way of accelerating healing.

"It's not healing?" Shera asked, gesturing to the wound.

Meia shook her head, expression grim. "Not like it should. He bit me, and it's not healing. I *wish* I knew what his Vessel was."

Shera flashed back to the golden hide tied around the man's arm. "Isn't it a Sandborn Hydra? That would explain the strength, and the way he jumps."

Meia waved her wounded arm. "No Hydra does *this.*"

"Just sleep it off on the ship," Shera advised. "We won't see him again."

She hoped.

The Heart of Nakothi pulsed in her belt-pouch, laughing with the same distant malice as her left-hand shear.

"Quiet," Shera muttered, slapping the pocket.

Meia looked vaguely confused.

"Nakothi," Shera explained.

The other woman looked even more confused than before.

When they finally reached *Bastion's Shadow,* a cluster of Architects surrounded them as soon as they reached the beach. Two lifted Meia away from Shera, and three forced Shera to lie back onto a stretcher.

"How many did we lose?" Meia asked, turning to the captain. He shook his head.

"We only have twenty-four here, counting you. Still waiting for the others."

Meia gestured around her, issuing instructions to defend them as they waited, in case the Children attacked again. But Shera was distracted.

Twenty-four out of sixty-one. Heavy losses for the Consultants, even for a mission as important as this one.

She should probably be grieved at the loss of life—Lucan would have been, she was sure. Even Meia might feel that way. But all she felt was relief.

Now she could get rid of this Heart, and clear the Dead Mother out of her life once and for all. If she was allowed, she would stab straight through the Heart right now...but that would kill both her and Meia. She had no choice but to take it back to the Gray Island, where its deadly power could be restrained.

From her pocket, Nakothi laughed.

CHAPTER TWELVE

THIRTEEN YEARS AGO

For the first time, Shera stood before the full Council of Architects.

To her, the pale tree roots plunging through the ceiling looked like hands of bone, the tiny quicklamps dangling like suspended stars. The shadowed alcoves in which the bulk of the Councilors sat gave them black hoods, making her feel even more alone. Kerian would be in there, somewhere, but Shera couldn't pick her out from the overlapping folds of black.

Many of the Architects she had never met; some she had never even seen. Of the three Architects of the High Council, those who sat in the open around their short white column, she only recognized one: Yala the High Mason. Her long hair was equally blond and gray, and she had pulled it back into a single braid.

She greatly resembled her daughter, if Meia had spent twenty years drying in the sun. Yala was a legend among the Consultants for her exploits infiltrating the Izyrians and single-handedly stopping a rebellion. Rumor had her sneaking behind enemy lines, killing a Champion in his sleep, and then holding the rebel leaders hostage until they agreed to disband.

Shera only knew her as stern, disapproving, and entirely boring.

Her *table*, on the other hand, was fascinating.

This stubby column around which the three High Councilors sat looked like a big, round lump of chalk. But when one of the Councilors sketched something with their finger on the table, it lit up, like he was leaving a trail of glowing yellow paint behind.

An alchemist creation? It had to be. But was it an ancient relic of the early Empire, or a modern device from Kanatalia?

Yala leaned her elbows on the table, leaving spots of shining yellow. "Shera. We have brought you here, before the entire ruling body of this Guild, because the Emperor requires your service. But he needs a full Gardener, not a girl who can throw a knife."

Shera stared at the Councilor to Yala's left, who was doodling a knot on the table in front of him. Somehow, he was able to erase his old sketches and create new ones. How was he doing that?

Yala slapped the table, delivering a yellow handprint. "Shera! This is a grave matter. The Emperor finds you necessary, and we obey him in all things, but I will not permit anyone to call themselves a member of this Guild when they are *not.*"

It doesn't matter what I call myself, Shera thought. *The Emperor didn't ask for a Gardener, he asked for* me.

But it seemed to matter to Yala, so Shera simply nodded.

"Will you, under the sun and moon and in service to the eternal Empire, swear yourself to the Guild of Am'haranai? Or will you depart now, to live a life of exile and never to return to this island?"

That had the sound of ritual to it, but it made Shera crack a smile. At last, she was sure she had caught Yala in a joke.

"So if I don't swear, I can leave?"

Yala's face reddened in what Shera would swear was fury, but she jerked her head once. "The Guild has properties all over the Empire. You would not be allowed out of a supervised community, to ensure that you don't spread Consultant secrets, but you will not be harmed. We do not *coerce* anyone to join us, girl."

Shera managed not to laugh. She pointed to a door at the corner. "I'd walk out that door, then?"

One of the High Councilors nodded.

Lowering herself to one knee, Shera pulled a spade out of the pouch at her side. Instead of throwing it, she slid it flat across the floor. It slipped straight under the door, and through to the other side.

There came a *clink, clink, clink* as the blade struck the sides on its way down, and then—about six seconds later—a clatter as it struck the bottom of the pit on the other side of the door.

The High Councilors sat in frozen silence.

She was vaguely insulted that they had tried to lie to her. They should have told her to join or die. She never had any intention of leaving, and she hadn't expected they'd let her leave with the information she'd gathered.

Besides, she could feel the cool draft from the door all the way over here. It clearly didn't lead out, where the air was warm and wet.

"I'm not a Mason or a Miner," Shera said. "I'm a Gardener. I know how this Guild works."

From behind the High Councilors, among the ranks of the other Architects, Kerian laughed like a little girl.

Yala twitched and almost turned back, but she caught herself and kept her gaze fixed on Shera. "Yes. Well. We still expect you to swear."

Shera shrugged. "No problems here."

Kerian was still snorting out laughter.

Finally, Yala reached down and pulled out something that quieted Kerian's laughter and caused Shera to lean forward and pay attention. It was a glass box, perhaps two feet on one side and a single foot on the other, filled with rolling blue fog. It was as though Yala had managed to bottle a cloud.

"Place your hand on the box," Yala instructed, and this time, Shera obeyed without a word.

As she laid her palm flat on the cool glass of the box, the cloud surged up toward her flesh. The glass grew colder and colder, as though it were ice water instead of fog on the other side.

"Bastion was one of the founding members of our order," Yala said. "He was also a Soulbound of great renown, and the one who raised the Veil around this island. This was once his Vessel."

The cloud surged and rolled inside the box, as if hungry.

"On penalty of death or madness, repeat after me. Repeat only what I say, and know that the power of the Veil will hold you to this oath."

Shera waited in silence.

"I will protect the Am'haranai, its goals, and my brothers and sisters within it. I will never falter, nor betray my allegiance, nor work by action or inaction to undermine those I serve. I will work for the good of my clients to the best of my ability."

She repeated every word as Yala spoke them.

"Finally, I bind my will and my loyalty to the mists, never to be revoked."

For the first time, Shera hesitated. That sounded less like a Guild membership ritual and more like a binding magical contract. She didn't want some box controlling her mind for the rest of her life because she had mindlessly repeated a few words as a twelve-year-old.

But the glass grew colder and colder under her palm, until it felt like a layer of knife points. At last, she repeated the words.

The fog flowed out to fill the whole container once again, and her hand warmed. She pulled it away with a profound relief.

Yala's face was just as tight and pinched as ever, and she stowed the box of fog as though nothing had happened. "Now, though your training is incomplete, you may call yourself a Consultant and a Gardener. We can only trust that the Emperor, in his unending wisdom, will see to your education even better than we can."

She gestured to the High Councilor next to her, who pulled out a black cloth belt set with two heavy sheaths. He pushed the belt across the table toward Shera, leaving a trail of yellow light behind.

"If you are to serve us as a Gardener, you will need your shears."

Shera grabbed the thick bundle in both hands. It smelled heavily of leather and oil, covering a coppery metallic tang. It was heavy enough that she could barely carry it in one hand, and while it was clearly designed to hold the knives at the small of her back, she would have to tie the belt as tight as it would go to get it around her waist. Hopefully, she would grow into it.

She tugged on one leather-wrapped handle, revealing a blade of ancient bronze.

The hilt was a little too big for her hand, the blade almost as long as her forearm. She wouldn't doubt it if they told her the knife was a thousand years old: it bore enough nicks and scratches that she couldn't see a single spot of unmarred metal. Beyond that, it simply *felt* old.

Shera was no Reader; like all Consultants, she had been tested immediately upon her arrival, and the old crone who tested her had cackled after fifteen seconds of testing. *"I've seen squirrels with more aptitude,"* she'd said. *"This girl wouldn't know an Imperial relic from a shovel if the Emperor himself shoved it into her mouth."*

But you didn't have to be Lucan to feel the weight of Intent in this blade. It rested in her hand, quivering almost palpably with the hunger of ten thousand kills. When she slid it back into the sheath, it pulled itself inside as though guided by a magnet.

"Those blades have been handed down an unbroken line of assassins since before any Am'haranai first called herself a Gardener," Yala said. "Let them guide you in your service to the Emperor."

With a feeling of great ceremony, Shera tied the belt around her waist. The excess fabric fell down almost to her knees, and the blades felt likely to pull her over backwards.

But for the first time, she actually felt like a Gardener.

"Congratulations," Yala said, in a tone like the splat of cold porridge. "Now get out of here. We have two more of these today."

CHAPTER THIRTEEN

The captain of *Bastion's Shadow* had more skill than Shera would have expected. With a stiff tailwind and a few bold navigational choices, he had them back to the Gray Island in record time. Only two days after they left the corpse of Nakothi, the ship slid through Bastion's Veil and into the hidden bay.

Over the course of their two-day voyage, no less than three Consultants had tried to steal the Heart.

The first night, a young woman—a member of the crew, and a Mason-in-training—had slipped a few drops of sedative into Shera and Meia's stew, then snuck into the cabin where the Gardeners were supposed to be sleeping.

Unfortunately for her, Meia had tried the food first. The poison had no effect on her, and she was able to warn Shera. Together, the two Gardeners watched the young Mason head straight to the locked chest where they kept the Heart. She looked neither left nor right, as though she had been drawn straight to the power of the Dead Mother.

It wasn't the girl's fault, Shera knew. Nakothi's song, resonating between the Heart and her left-hand knife, woke Shera at all hours of the night. Even dead, the Great Elder possessed a will that few humans could resist.

Shera still beat the girl and left her dangling upside-down in the rigging for a few hours. Possessed or not, she'd tampered with Shera's dinner *and* forced her to stay awake watching for an intruder. For the sake of food and sleep, she deserved to be punished.

The second attempt came from a pair of Shepherds.

It was the middle of the next day, and *Bastion's Shadow* sped through a field of debris floating in the middle of the air. Chunks of bricks and masonry drifted against gravity, as though a giant had shredded a vast tower to pieces and then left floating in the wind. One corner of a wall spun slowly in place, revealing a strange clock-face almost as big as the deck on which they stood. Shera would have said it was the remnant of a clocktower, but each of the six hands pointed to a strange symbol instead of a number.

Though the clock was separated from any machinery that would keep it working, its hands ticked as they slowly advanced.

The spiral of debris stretched above them into the clouds, and beneath them until the depths of the Aion swallowed the sight. Shera leaned over the railing, looking down to watch something that looked like a finned tiger weaving its way between the submerged wreckage.

The captain took *Bastion's Shadow* around the obstacles at reckless speed, rushing by the severed half of a hovering cottage and squeezing between a spinning weathervane bigger than their mast. The black-and-gold eye on their crow's nest remained wide, gaze flicking between each new piece of gravity-defying masonry.

Come to think of it, the captain must be a Soulbound. If what Meia and Yala had explained to her was true, he could only pilot this well because of his connection to the ship, and the ship's connection to the Sea. The thought seemed strange for reasons Shera couldn't name. Somehow, the captain didn't seem *important* enough for a Soulbound Vessel—as though he was an actor cast to fill the role of a sailor, not a significant man in his own right.

Masons were trained their whole lives to fill a role. Maybe Mason training made one inconspicuous even when they performed great deeds.

At the thought, Shera turned to look at the captain.

And she saw a black glove before it clapped over her mouth, and the needle before it pressed into her neck.

The deck was packed with Consultants, but no one was looking. Every eye was locked on the spectacle of floating ruins around them. As far as assassinations in the middle of the day went, the Shepherd had chosen his moment well.

But his attempt had failed as soon as Shera saw him.

She had only a second or two before the poison started to interfere with her physical reactions, so she took advantage of that time. She stomped his foot at the base of the ankle, following it up with a quick punch into the solar plexus and the heel of her hand into his nose.

When her muscles locked up and she pitched over, the Shepherd was staggering and clutching a nose that bled through his black mask.

Meia had him facedown against the deck half a second later, her shear pressed against the base of his neck.

"What was your objective, sir?" Meia asked calmly. Two alchemy-trained Architects had rushed over to Shera, and one of them was calling for an antidote.

The Shepherd seemed to have trouble explaining. "I...just...it all must change. We all have to be different. It's not good...it has to change."

Meia sighed and pricked him with a non-lethal needle of her own. She raised her voice to address the entire crew. "Pay attention, everyone. If you hear a mysterious voice whispering to you in your head, giving you instructions, *don't listen to it.* I'm shocked that I have to tell you this."

The ship was filled with embarrassed silence, and Shera was sure that more than a few had already considered following Nakothi's whispered instructions.

That was more disturbing than her current paralysis. How close had they come to a full-scale revolt orchestrated by a Great Elder? Was there any way to transport the Heart without giving Nakothi a chance to infest the minds of good men and women?

She wanted to put one of her shears straight through the Heart...but she knew what would happen. The Emperor had warned her. Nakothi's powers would be released, all at once, and everyone in range would be killed and reborn as Children of the Dead Mother. The Heart, like any powerful remnant of a Great Elder, had to be contained and weakened before it could safely be destroyed. Though she was still tempted.

Out of the corner of her eye, she caught a figure in black sneaking into her cabin.

She couldn't move her head, but she finally understood the plan. One Shepherd attacks her, drawing attention, and his partner sneaks in and secures the Heart. It was a better idea than she expected from people following the whispered instructions of a dead Elder.

And it still had a chance of working. She couldn't move.

Shera whimpered impotently, trying to force out a warning. Her body wouldn't listen to her, her arms hung limp and useless, and her voice came out as the incoherent grunt of an animal. She choked back her frustration, trying again to attract someone, *anyone* who would look where she was looking...

It was no use. Even the alchemists administering antidote to her didn't pay her sounds any attention. She had to assume that the Shepherd in her cabin knew a drop point for the Heart; if all he had to do was take it to someone else onboard, or drop it into the Aion, then he had every chance of succeeding.

Without looking behind her, Meia pointed over her shoulder with the tip of her knife. "There should be someone sneaking into my cabin behind me. Someone catch him and tie him up. Thank you."

She turned to Shera and winked. "I can hear everything that happens on the ship."

A young Mason cleared his throat from behind her. "Uh...*everything*, Gardener?"

Meia looked at him with flat, disgusted eyes. "Everything."

He snuck off and hid behind a barrel.

A few hours later, they arrived at the Gray Island. On sight of the tall wall of mist, Shera felt no relief. Instead, her gut tightened.

Here we go, she thought. As though the real mission had just begun.

Yala waited in the hidden bay with an ornate chest in her arms, surrounded by three Architects.

It was easy to tell Architects apart from the other orders. Masons were usually dressed in the outfit of their chosen profession, Shepherds wore soft black clothing with strips of dark cloth masking their mouths, and Gardeners dressed like Shepherds but carried a pair of shears. Architects, in the same vein, wore black without the mask. But their blacks were different from those worn by Shepherds and Gardeners: fashionable, refined, expensive. One Architect's shirt had a row of gold buttons up the side, and another wore a black skirt instead of the usual tight cloth pants.

Each of them also carried the tools of their specialty, worn like badges of honor. Architects could be trained in alchemy, Reading, or leadership, and the three with Yala all carried miscellaneous junk strapped to them—tweezers dangling from a wrist strap, a coin hanging like amulet, a length of chain worn as a belt, a pair of scissors sheathed on the waist like a duelist's sword. They were all Readers, then, carrying invested items around with them as signs of their skill.

Shera carried the Heart down to Yala in a sack that was itself wrapped in a cloth and strapped with a leather belt. She had to ignore the song of the Heart even now: *Your old self can die, and your new soul will be reborn. Take me. Let me guide you.*

Yala's face was tight, as though she knew her time was short. She stepped forward, opening the chest. "Hurry, give me the Heart."

Shera hesitated.

"The longer we wait, Gardener, the more time Nakothi has to work on us all."

That was true, but...

Where were the other two High Councilors?

Standing in the bay, holding the Heart, Shera asked, "Where's Kerian?"

Yala's hands remained steady on the box, and her expression didn't change, but Shera knew she was preparing for trouble. "High Councilors Kerian and Tyril are waiting for us in the Council chambers."

"Great," Shera said, holding out an empty hand. "Hand me the box. We'll take it together."

Consultants stayed frozen all around Shera, but the tension was rising palpably, like a bowstring slowly drawing back.

"Why don't you trust me, Shera?" Yala asked softly.

Shera thought of Lucan, locked behind bars because he'd learned secrets of the original Am'haranai. Secrets that generations of Councilors had tried to keep buried. She thought of the Regents, who would have slept forever because Yala wanted the Empire to stay in anarchy after the Emperor's death.

Chaos was good for business.

But she didn't say any of that. She tilted her head to the side as though confused. "Don't you need me? I thought I was the only one on this Island capable of destroying a Great Elder." She hefted the packaged Heart. "Even a piece of one. The whole point of this was to destroy the Heart."

Yala stretched her fingers as if she itched to draw a knife. "We have developed some new techniques and resources that we think are very promising."

Shera's heart fell into her stomach. The woman was throwing up a smokescreen, and not even a good one. She had no intention of destroying the Heart.

"Light and life," Shera muttered. "I thought I was being paranoid. If you're not going to help me destroy the Heart, what are you going to do with it?"

"That's my concern, Gardener."

"The Emperor would have said it was *my* concern."

"And look what happened to him."

Shera lowered the Heart to her side. It would have been easier to hand it over, but the Emperor would have never forgiven her.

"The Great Elders will do anything to be free again," the Emperor had said. *"Don't give them that. Don't give them* anything. *You cannot let them win."*

Those were some of the last words he'd ever said to her. She'd seen what Nakothi could do to him, and she'd seen what the Heart had done to the Consultants on *Bastion's Shadow* with only two days of exposure.

Shera couldn't take any further chances.

The Readers shifted behind Yala, moving their hands to what Shera assumed were weapons.

The High Councilor raised her voice. "Please take the package from Gardener Shera and escort her to prison. She can share a cell with her lover."

No one moved. The moment creaked like a thin layer of ice.

"Just take me to Kerian," Shera said. "Don't do this again." Her emotions had already started to freeze over. There was no way she'd be able to get out of this without killing a fellow Guild member.

Which was exactly what had gotten her assigned to a chapter house in the first place. Yala had backed Shera into a corner, forced her to choose between the security of the Empire and fighting other Consultants.

Today, Shera would choose the same as she had then.

Before Yala could take the initiative, or the Readers could work something out to stop her, Shera attacked. She sidestepped the closest of Yala's pet Architects, ducked another, and had her bronze blade out and moving for Yala's throat before the High Councilor could defend herself. Shera had no intention of killing the woman, but if she could get a blade to Yala's throat, maybe the others would back off.

But as quick as Shera had been, Meia was faster.

In the split second it took Shera to act, Meia landed between her mother and Shera. She caught Shera's wrist in an alchemically strengthened hand, holding off the attack without effort.

Meia turned to Shera with eyes like a dragon's, snarling. Before she could say a word, her mother interrupted her by flicking a knife at Shera's chest.

No doubt Yala hoped to kill Shera while her daughter's attention was distracted, but Meia was far too fast.

With a snapping motion like a rattlesnake taking a mouse, Meia caught the knife in her *teeth*. She ground her jaws together, rending steel with the audible shriek of tearing metal. Shredded bits of the knife plinked to the ground.

Light and *life*, that was impressive. Shera would never have wanted to endure what the alchemists had put Meia through, but they *had* produced results.

"Everybody settle down," Meia growled, her voice overshadowed as though she were speaking in two voices at once. "We can still—"

One of Yala's Readers, taking advantage of the opening, whipped a length of spiked chain at Shera. She ducked her head out of the way, but her wrist was still held in Meia's iron grip. There was no way she could tear her way free, and the chain was still headed for her chest. She had no doubt that each was packed with lethal Intent. One hit, even from such a small weapon, could potentially splatter her like a ripe fruit.

Meia released Shera's wrist and stepped in between her and the descending chain.

The spike weapon struck with the sound of a war-drum, far deeper than it should have been able to produce, and Meia's back practically exploded. Blood and shreds of black cloth burst into the air.

Meia screamed, her eyes blazing orange. She spun around, revealing a back that had been laid open to the bone. Shera took one careful step back.

Blue scales had already started gathering around the wound, and the flesh was knitting itself together, as Shera had expected. She'd seen Meia recover from worse.

But that Reader was in trouble.

Meia tore the chain from the man's grip, ignoring the blood that flowed down her fist, and tossed it aside. Clumps of soil exploded away from the iron links as it landed.

The Architect's eyes widened, and he fumbled at his belt for another tool, but Meia's hand blurred. With a crunch, his nose broke.

"I asked you," she punched him again, "to please," she kicked him in the shin, snapping bone, "*settle down!*"

In the end, her voice rose to a shriek, and she was beating into the man with her fists as he lay helpless on the ground.

Nobody moved to help him. Even Yala looked away, disgusted. The other two Architects had bolted as soon as she punched their comrade the first time, which Shera thought displayed unusual wisdom. They hadn't stopped yet.

It was Shera who finally put an end to it, placing her hand on Meia's shoulder. "Personally, I don't care if you beat him to death," she said. "But Lucan would. And I think *you* would."

Meia stopped with her fist raised over the man's bloody face, eyes blazing orange. Her shirt still hung in dark tatters from her shoulders, but her body was already healed.

She stepped away shakily, legs unsteady. She didn't look at Shera or Yala as she spoke.

"This issue should be resolved between the High Council of Architects," she said quietly. "We will go find High Councilors Kerian and Tyril, and they will decide what is to be done with the Heart. Until that point, you will both remain in my care."

"You don't have the authority for that, Gardener," Yala reminded her, seemingly unimpressed.

Meia looked at her. Her eyes still hadn't reverted to their human blue.

All she said was, "Lead the way. Or will I have to carry you?"

As Shera had expected, Kerian and Tyril were *not* in the Council chamber, as Yala had claimed. When they arrived, there were a number of Architects gathered around, waiting for Yala.

When Yala marched in, she quickly announced that Meia and Shera should be detained for crimes against the Guild.

The two Gardeners drew shears. Those few Architects who didn't recognize them personally recognized their weapons, and no one attacked. None of the Architects looked at Yala; a few of them coughed nervously.

"I think I know where they are," Shera said at last. "Follow me."

Shera had taken a powerful piece of a Great Elder back to the Island before. On that occasion, they had brought the object to a single, ancient site, where its power could be safely dispersed.

The site itself was hidden, but the entrance was well-known to all Consultants: Zhen's House of the Masons.

Once Shera reached the edge of the island, she wandered around staring at Bastion's Veil before she finally spotted the camouflaged gray house. She hadn't brought the correct key this time—she had never expected to need it—so Meia kicked the door in.

Zhen wouldn't like that, but they were in a hurry.

Several floors down through a series of hidden trap doors, the three of them came to the room Shera remembered: it looked like the basement of a Luminian cathedral. The doors were all arches of interlocking stone, and the walls were carved with Kameira reliefs. Statues of knights lined the walls, and in the center waited a box of thick stone.

That box, as they had explained to her last time, was made to weaken objects of malicious origin. Jorin Maze-walker had designed it to break curses and draw the power from Elder artifacts so that they could be safely handled.

Sure enough, Zhen and Kerian stood waiting with the third and final High Councilor: Tyril. He lay sprawled against a nearby wall, snoring soundly, with a rolled-up blanket propped under his head. He had risen from the Shepherds, and he looked like he actually spent his time in the wild, caring for sheep: his gray beard was long and wild, spilling over his chest, and he wore dark rags instead of an actual set of blacks. He was almost painfully thin, but he looked as though he had walked a hundred miles to get here.

He always looked that way.

"It is about time," Zhen huffed, blowing out his moustache. "What took you so long, Yala?"

Yala looked back at the two Gardeners without saying a word.

"We have reason to believe that my mother was trying to take the Heart for her own purposes," Meia said, voice controlled.

"What reason?" Kerian asked coolly.

She was keeping herself under control, but Shera knew she would be pleased. Any chance to get rid of Yala would make Kerian's life easier.

Yala jerked her head in Shera's direction. "This one didn't want to let the

Heart out of her sight. She asked to accompany me back, and I refused her. Then she attempted to kill me."

Kerian turned to Shera, who nodded.

"That sounds about right," Shera said.

Zhen stroked his moustache thoughtfully. "Hmmm. The explanation is too practiced, and she even shifts the blame so that we will overlook the obvious holes in her argument. Two out of ten. I taught you to lie better than that, Yala. I am shocked and, frankly, disappointed that you couldn't do any better."

"I don't need to prepare a lie," Yala said, back straight. "I had not stepped outside my Guild-given authority. I need no explanation."

"Not until you never brought us the Heart," Kerian said. "What would you have told us then, I wonder?"

"It doesn't matter," she responded. "*She* was the only one who broke Guild law. Once again."

Shera had slept through most of her last trial, and she was fully prepared to sleep through another.

Kerian waved a hand. "Meia, take her away. Keep her confined somewhere until we can determine what she was planning. Until then, the Heart takes priority."

Meia bowed and left, pulling her mother along behind her.

Strangely, Yala didn't protest. She left without another word.

"Does it bother anybody else that she didn't argue more?" Shera asked.

"She seemed distracted," Zhen said. "The girl I knew could have spun a better lie than that on the day she came to me. Do you think she knows something we do not?"

Kerian heaved the heavy lid off the stone box, letting it crash to the ground with a thud. Tyril didn't even stop snoring. "Knowing Yala, she is looking forward to the next step of her plan. We can't do anything to her within the scope of our authority, and she knows that. As she said, she didn't defend herself because she doesn't need to."

"That's no excuse for letting herself get soft," Zhen said.

"You're one to talk," Kerian said, poking him in the gut. "And speaking of soft..."

She pulled a spade out from her own pouch, hefted the blade in her hand for a moment, and then hurled it at the sleeping Shepherd.

In the middle of a snore, Tyril rolled out of the way and snapped his hand up. He caught the spade between two fingers.

A second later, he blinked his eyes open. "Did you have to, Kerian?" he asked, voice mournful. "There are much gentler ways of waking me. A kiss, perhaps."

Kerian produced another gleaming silver knife, and he raised his hands in surrender.

Shera couldn't help regarding him with a little awe. She had somewhat ignored Tyril for most of her life: Kerian and Yala were much more impressive, in her opinion. Tyril had never had much of an impact on anything, as far as she could tell.

But a man who could sleep that soundly and still catch a knife in midair? That man was worthy of her respect.

He stared owlishly around, yawning. "Is Yala here yet?"

Everyone ignored him. Shera stepped up, raising the makeshift sack she'd fashioned to carry the Heart. She had focused on ignoring its song, but it was still there, like a steady whisper in the back of her mind.

"The road to perfection is through death. You can do nothing as you are: soft, weak, fragile. Only death is strong, only death is real, only death lasts forever—"

The song cut off as Shera dropped the whole sack into the box and Zhen slid the lid back on top.

A buzzing, grinding noise sounded from the box, so subtle that Shera wasn't certain she was hearing it with her ears. Perhaps it was something like Nakothi's song, and it played straight into her mind.

"How long did it take last time?" Zhen asked.

"Not long," Shera responded. "So I'm going to catch a nap. Wake me when I'm needed."

"Hear hear," Tyril echoed, returning to his pillow.

"I'd still like to hear what you have to say about Yala," Kerian said pointedly.

"We'll have plenty of time when I wake up," Shera responded. She was more than ready for this whole misadventure to end. Once the Heart was destroyed, she could go back to her quiet space behind a desk in the Capital's chapter house, and others could clean up.

She curled up on the dusty ground like a child, resting her head on her folded arms. There was still plenty to worry about—for one, her left-hand blade was always whispering to her in Nakothi's malicious voice, and that was after only *one* taste of the Great Elder's blood. How strong would it grow after a second helping? The Blackwatch would be calling for the death of the Consultants now, and Shera got the feeling that she hadn't seen the last of Calder Marten or his crew.

Naberius Clayborn certainly wouldn't give up on the Heart unless he knew it was destroyed, not after the covetous way he'd cradled it to his chest. He looked at Nakothi's Heart like a starving man facing the first morsel of food he'd seen in months.

There were still plenty of loose threads to snip.

But not for Shera. She'd be gone.

The rumbling in her mind grew louder, stealing her attention, as did the whispers echoing from her left-hand shear.

She rose to her feet, gripping the hilt of her blade to keep it from rattling in its sheath.

"Back away from the box," Kerian said calmly, pulling her own set of shears. Zhen also had a knife in each hand, though his were gleaming steel instead of battered bronze, and the blade Tyril produced looked more like a short sword.

The stone box started to shake, its buzz climbing to a rumble and the rumble to a deep throbbing. It grew in volume and deepened in pitch, until it sounded...

Exactly like a beating heart.

With a crack like thunder, the box snapped in half, slabs of stone falling away and leaving the Heart sitting there as if on a pedestal. The song of Nakothi rose to a crescendo, shrill and deafening.

Wake, wake, wake from your slumber! Come, come, come and taste fresh meat!

Wake, my Children, and rise!

To either side of the room, the stone walls—each carved with fanciful reliefs—shook under mighty blows, as though a construction crew had taken to them with sledgehammers. The room trembled, dust fell from the ceiling, and cracks appeared in the ancient stone.

"What's in the rooms around us?" Shera shouted.

Zhen turned to her, pale. "The Am'haranai crypts."

Shera didn't wait to hear anymore; she bolted for the Heart, wrapping it in the rags that she had once used to contain it. The Heart must have burst through its restraints at some point in the box.

Just as she lifted the Heart, the walls crumbled, and the dead forced their way inside.

CHAPTER FOURTEEN

TWELVE YEARS AGO

Lucan staggered back from the obsidian statue. Memories swirled in his mind—*the stoneworker chips away at the obsidian, terrified that he might fail; the soldier poses for a sculpture, eager to get back to the front; the stone itself remembers echoes of slow cold and unimaginable heat colliding.* In the rush, his own memories were all but lost.

"I can't," he choked out. "There's too much."

The Emperor stood over him, dressed today in all the colors of a glacier. "A Reader does not need the strength of a soldier, but the understanding of a poet."

This coming from the most powerful Reader ever born. "Then please, help me understand. There's too much identity here. Too *many* identities. How am I supposed to—"

"You hide behind questions like a coward. Try again."

With anyone else, Lucan would have debated, explained himself, thrown up more questions like a smokescreen to regain the upper hand. But this was the *Emperor.*

The gleaming black statue showed a soldier in ancient Imperial armor, his sword forgotten on the ground in front of him, clutching both hands together as if in prayer. Lucan put one hand on each of the statue's shoulders, staring into its stone eyes, and plunged back into the tide of remembrance.

As he did, he chanted silently to the obsidian soldier: *Move, move, move, move, move! Light and life,* please *move!*

The Emperor sighed and gestured for Lucan to take his hands from the statue. He did so, almost collapsing, grateful for the chance to catch his breath.

"When we first discovered Reading as a discipline, the ability to sense and manipulate human Intent, we didn't know what to call ourselves. Everyone had ideas, most of them grandiose: Soulweavers, Oracles, Enchanters, Fate's Chosen..."

In a train of blue and white robes, the Emperor paced around the obsidian statue. "Do you know why we settled on 'Readers' instead of 'Writers'?"

Lucan was still trying to wrap his mind around the story. Here, in front of him, was someone who had physically witnessed the birth of Reading itself.

"Because without understanding, without truly *reading* the depths of memory in an object, we cannot affect its power. Once we do understand, however, we can begin to make changes."

Gently, the Emperor placed one hand on the soldier's black stone head.

The room filled with a sharp, constant sound, like the crunch of snow or the crack of ice amplified and stretched to last minutes. The statue shivered…

And then abruptly shattered like black glass. Pieces of obsidian rained down, and Lucan took an instinctive step back.

"That's impossible!"

The Emperor didn't look back, merely brushed black dust from his hands. "And who taught you that?"

The older Architects had. The ones who could Read, anyway. They'd taught him from ancient books taken from Imperial Academies, written by some of the greatest Readers in humanity's history. Some of them written by the Emperor himself.

"It's an accepted fact," Lucan said. Sometimes, when you dug yourself a hole, you had to dig yourself out. "In your own work, *A Letter to the Young Reader*, you say that, 'An object cannot be made to gain a property that it does not naturally possess.' And also, 'An object's physical nature cannot be changed by Intent alone, save through the Awakening process.' This seems to violate both of those rules."

The Emperor raised one hairless eyebrow. "Yet I have done it. Surely you've heard the stories of the Magisters—burning homes to the ground, raising tornadoes of dust, growing forests overnight."

That had bothered Lucan as well, when he was a child, but he'd asked enough questions to kill the mystery. "Magisters carry staves possessed of potent natural forces. The powers of Kameira, Elders, or certain plants. With a staff, a Magister might produce such an effect."

Kneeling, the Emperor plucked a shard of obsidian from the floor. He stood and tossed it up, snagging it out of the air. "True, a Magister's staff can help. But it is a tool. And only in the hands of a master can any tool reach its true potential."

Lucan gave up. In the mind of the Emperor, the word 'impossible' had no meaning. Someone who had lived for a thousand years must regard the limitations of mortals as suggestions rather than rules.

"How?" he asked.

The Emperor caught the shard of obsidian again, then pinched it between two fingers and held it up for Lucan's inspection. "This process is known as 'active Reading.' It's a useful skill, but one that few possess. Perhaps twenty-four in the entire Empire, including several Magisters."

In his hands, the obsidian crumbled to black sand and blew away.

"It is similar in concept to Awakening, but it requires understanding the object at a fundamental, physical level. Once you do, you can alter the physical structure at will. Only in simple ways, and still taking into account the nature of the object."

He swept a hand toward the statue. "If you manage to crumble this statue to dust, you might be the twenty-fifth."

Lucan looked the statue in its black eyes. If he mastered this, he'd be assured a seat on the Council of Architects. From there, *he* would be the one to steer the Consultant's Guild.

In his opinion, that ship very much needed a pilot.

As Lucan's hands tightened on the statue's shoulders, the Emperor paused. "I'm told the process is painful at first, and there are some who end up insane. But you should be young enough. I believe you will adapt."

So much for encouragement.

Before his senses were swallowed up entirely by the Reading, he saw his Emperor nod toward the rows and rows of black stone soldiers kneeling behind this one.

"And when you're done with that," the Emperor said, "you only have three hundred and ninety-eight more to go."

Hardly daring to breathe, Meia clung to the thick branch like a squirrel. All around her, golden leaves drifted down from the canopy of the autumn forest.

She paused a moment to catalogue her injuries. The backs of her calves and thighs were spotted with acid burns—those wouldn't cause trouble yet, she simply needed to ignore the pain. Her left wrist was twisted, probably sprained. She could use it to hold a dagger or a needle, but she couldn't climb or throw a spade from the left. Her neck and shoulder still ached from where she'd been hurled into the trunk of the tree, but they hadn't seized up yet.

Worst of all was the long gash on her ribs. The cut had soaked through the bandages. Every minute or two, a tiny red drop squeezed out of the wrapping, crawled down the branch, and plopped onto the forest floor.

Her body was sending out too many complaints to ignore, and her head was fuzzing over. More importantly, the Duskwinder would smell her blood on the ground and find her in seconds.

Meia gritted her teeth in a forced grin. *The Emperor's supposed to know everything? Well, he doesn't know me.*

He'd been very open about his intentions. *"We will find your limits, Meia,"* he'd said. *"If I am to stretch you, I must know your breaking point."*

Shows how little he knew. Meia didn't *have* a breaking point.

A broad silhouette twisted through the air, snaking down and landing among the crunchy leaves. Bronze wings creaked as they folded back into the scaly body—a twenty-foot-long serpent with wings and a spiked tail. Its scales gleamed like bronze armor, its single eye jerking around the forest. It flicked three forked tongues out, tasting the air.

Tasting her blood.

The Kameira's eye shot upwards. Faster than thought, it had wound itself up the trunk of her tree, flaring its wings to intimidate its prey.

I'm not trapped, Meia reminded herself. *It's trapped up here with* me.

She attacked. She pulled the shears from their sheaths at her back, their blades gleaming like sunset, like the Duskwinder's scales. Her belly was still pressed against the bark of the branch, so she reared up onto her knees, striking with both blades like a snake's twin fangs.

The blades plunged toward the Kameira's single eye, but it swept them aside with one wing.

The impact shoved her arms aside, and the rest of her body followed. As she had been trained, she tossed her shears aside to avoid landing on a blade, but it wasn't a long fall. Her back slammed into the ground before she fully realized what was happening, driving the breath from her lungs. The back of her head thudded against the soil.

The Duskwinder was unwrapping itself from the tree. She had to reach it. She had to kill it. How was she supposed to kill it from her back? Her fingers scrambled at the pouch of spades tied to her thigh, but the blades had spilled out in the fall. Their edges sliced her fingertips, drawing more blood. It didn't hurt. Why didn't it hurt?

She finally palmed a single spade as the Kameira loomed over her, its huge serpent eye gleaming in the afternoon sun. It hissed, revealing a mouthful of fangs and tongues.

Meia hurled the spade. It pattered weakly against the snake's jaw, unable even to pierce the soft skin underneath its head.

The throwing blade landed lightly on Meia's chest, still wet with her own blood.

The leaves drifting through the autumn sky swallowed her vision, but Meia still did her best to glare at the Duskwinder. This big snake was lucky she couldn't get up, or she'd be peeling it down the middle and skinning it for steaks.

It was lucky that it got to eat her, before she could eat it.

Then a man with dark skin and bright clothes was standing between her and the serpent. He raised a hand and said something Meia couldn't hear.

The Duskwinder slithered backwards like a man scrambling away from a cliff, flapping its wings to push itself back faster. Half a second later, it was winging its way off into the afternoon sky.

The Emperor looked down at Meia, as though he'd simply happened to check his shoes. "Another failure," he said.

The words pierced Meia's chest like a spear, and she struggled to sit up. "Again, please," she managed to say. "Almost…I did…again."

She couldn't seem to sit up, so she flopped over onto her stomach. The pain nearly made her black out, but she seized her body in the grip of her will, crawling forward, trying to reach her shears on the leaf-strewn forest floor.

The Emperor laid a hand on her shoulder, and she froze.

"You have the heart of a Champion," he said warmly. She couldn't see his face, but he sounded like he was smiling. "Estyr Six herself would admire your spirit."

Tears burned in Meia's eyes, and she let her muscles relax, gulping down deep breaths.

"However, the spirit of a Champion will do you no good if you only have the strength of a Pilgrim. We have reached your limits, Meia. No matter how you push yourself, you will never fight among the best with this body."

Meia let her focus drop. All the pain of her injuries came flooding back, and she welcomed it, letting it burn her. She wasn't good enough. That was what he was telling her—irrefutable words from the Emperor himself. No matter how hard she tried, she would never be good enough.

Leaves crunched as nearby Luminian Pilgrims rushed forward, to heal her and carry her back for medical examination.

As golden light descended on her injuries, the Emperor spoke again. "This body won't do the job, so I'll have to give you a new one."

For the fifth time that morning, the hired thug put his boot on the back of Shera's neck, shoving her cheek down against the floor tiles.

The six men above her laughed and shouted coarse suggestions, clapping each other on the shoulders. An Imperial agent had hired them from a nearby prison, offering goldmarks and reduced sentences for a few days of beating up a little girl.

Their laughter cut off, and they each dropped to one knee. Shera knew what that meant: the Emperor had arrived. Even the scum of the Capital feared and honored him.

Shera lay panting against the tiles, not bothering to get up. Her Gardener blacks were soaked in sweat, her hair matted against her neck. The Emperor had roused her from her bed at dawn for combat training, and she'd spent the last five hours in an almost constant beating. Nothing was broken or bleeding, but her skin felt like a seamless tapestry of bruises.

The stone was cool against her cheek, and she let her eyes sink shut. Maybe she could snatch a few minutes of sleep without them bothering her…

The toe of the Emperor's slipper nudged painfully in her ribs, and she rolled over onto her back. "Some people would consider it an honor to be kicked by the Emperor himself."

He stood over her, draped in sheets of pink and purple and red. "Have you not had enough of kicking?"

Shera dragged herself to her feet, sweat pattering to the floor. "I told them to stop, but I think they only listen to you."

Two of the rough men laughed. The others glowered, rubbing or testing the injuries she'd given them in their previous bouts. She didn't take beatings lying down, after all. Well, not most of them.

The Emperor laced his fingers together, watching her. "You must be tired."

"Call off these dogs, and I'll be asleep in ten seconds flat. I don't even need a bed."

His hairless head looked as though it had been carved out of a boulder. "I am prepared to have them beat you twenty-four hours a day. The sun will never set on your training. You will never sleep until you die from exhaustion, or until you put six bodies on the floor."

The Emperor shrugged, layers of bright cloths shifting. "Or you can do it now, and take the rest of the day off.

Shera felt the old, familiar ice crawling over her heart...but the same ice waited in the Emperor's dark eyes.

"How am I supposed to fight six grown men?" she asked, finally.

He leaned closer, his expression as frozen and unyielding as the moon. "I'm not training a fighter. I'm training an assassin."

The Emperor walked out of the circle of kneeling men, to the edge of the courtyard. "Rise," he commanded.

The men rose to their feet, chuckling and cracking knuckles.

Shera took a deep breath, and ice bloomed inside her.

"Begin," the Emperor said.

Casually, Shera slid a poisoned needle into the nearest man's throat. He touched his fingers to the wound curiously, confused, but she had already turned to another of the prisoners.

Like all the others, he was wearing the bright red one-piece uniforms of an imperial inmate. A scraggly black beard spread across his chest, and his crooked smile flickered as he glanced up at his poisoned companion. A look of confusion passed over him like a cloud.

Too late. Shera's finger dipped into the pouch on her thigh, coming up with three spades, one between each pair of knuckles. She drove her bladed fist into his stomach, and then spun aside.

A whip-thin man carried an axe handle as a makeshift club. He had been forbidden from using it much until this point, but apparently all rules were suspended. He brought the club down.

Shera planted her shoulder in the bearded man's hip and shoved. The two men collided, the bearded man taking a crack in his skull. The thin man staggered backwards, and Shera spun a spade out of her fingertips and into his eye.

It caught him in the forehead, and then a dark-skinned Heartlander grabbed her about the throat with his one remaining hand. He shook her like a doll, while one of his remaining partners punched her in the back.

Her teeth rattled, and she felt her shoes pulling off the ground. Now that she'd killed someone, they wouldn't hesitate to kill her.

There's no such thing as mercy, Maxwell had told her. *There is only hesitation.*

She had left her shears outside the courtyard, still sheathed. No one had asked her for her other weapons, which was why she still had her needles and spades.

This fight would be easier with her shears, but Ayana had driven as many lessons into Shera's brain as Maxwell ever had. One of her favorites: *A Gardener is never unarmed.*

It was an echo of Maxwell and the useful lessons he'd taught her before violating them himself. *A warrior is never unarmed.*

Shera clutched the Heartlander's arm with both hands, pulling herself up. She twisted, driving a foot into his nose. He staggered backwards, but she kicked him in the head again and again, mashing his nose to pulp and spraying blood all over his neck and chest.

He roared and his hand loosened, dropping her.

Before she even hit the floor, she spun and threw the two spades left in her hand. The man behind her was young, and his eyes widened in surprise as twin blades sank into his neck.

Two dead, two injured, and two...

The other two men, a tattooed Izyrian redhead and a fat man that looked like a banker, stood with mouths open. They were *still* hesitating.

"Come on!" the Heartlander roared through a mouthful of blood. "Let's get this—"

She drove a pair of needles into his stomach, and he folded over.

The thin man didn't speak, just drove his club down at her. She raised her left hand, caught the club on her forearm, and felt her bone break. Didn't matter; he'd lost.

With her right hand, she threw a spade into his eye. He sank to his knees, screaming.

The other two *still* hadn't moved.

The Izyrian glanced at the Emperor as if for instruction. The father of the Empire stood with his hands folded together, patient as a stained-glass picture in a Luminian cathedral.

The fat man raised his hands, sweating. "Hey, I'm only in for tax evasion, you hear me? Taxes. I'll serve my years, no problem."

Shera was already behind the Izyrian, looping her silk belt around his throat. He struggled and gasped and clutched behind him, tearing out handfuls of Shera's hair.

She didn't let up.

There are men who stick it out until the job's done, and then there are dead men. Another of Maxwell's.

Shera waited for a full count of thirty after the Izyrian went quiet before she let his body slump to the floor.

The fat man knelt at the Emperor's feet, pleading. When he got no response, he heaved himself up and bolted for the courtyard door.

Shera pulled her last remaining spade and launched it smoothly overhand. It glittered like a shooting star as it flew through the air and landed in the fat man's calf. He shouted and pitched over.

The thin man was still screaming, clawing at his ruined eye.

The Emperor walked over to him, placing one finger directly on his forehead. The thin man quieted, then slumped down onto the floor. Dead or asleep, Shera didn't care; either way he was quiet.

For a moment, the Emperor was too.

Then he said, "I expected you to get three. Maybe four."

Shera shrugged. Her hands were sticky with blood, and she hoped he would give her a chance to wash off.

"I am not often impressed."

With the danger past, the ice inside Shera had started to thaw. Hesitantly, she asked, "So...does that mean I get the day off?"

The chain around the Emperor's neck tinkled like a bell as he shifted position, tucking his hands into brightly colored pockets. "How do you feel?"

"Tired," she said, but she knew what he meant. After a moment she added, "Lucan would not have liked this."

"Does he disapprove of executing criminals?"

Shera struggled to put Lucan's thoughts into words, because she didn't fully understand them herself. "He knows it's necessary, sometimes. But he doesn't believe one person is worth more than another."

The Emperor gestured toward the Imperial Guards who had been waiting against the wall. They hurried forward, scooping up bodies. Servants in livery of red, blue, and gold appeared as if out of nowhere, calmly mopping up blood.

"What do *you* believe?" the Emperor asked.

Shera glanced at the Heartlander's body, his body locked into early rigor mortis by the effects of her poison. An Imperial Guard who had traded in his arms for muscular reptilian replacements grabbed the body in one claw, stuffing the former prisoner into a bag.

"I didn't need them," Shera said at last.

The Emperor's smile gleamed. "Why don't you take the rest of the day off?"

CHAPTER FIFTEEN

The Great Elders might be strange, and hideous, and not at all polite, but they do follow certain rules. They use their powers through containers, not directly. They all act according to some kind of purpose, even if it's a horrible one. They are very focused.

Come to think of it, that sounds just like our Intent. How odd. I always thought only humans could use Intent.

Oh yes, and most Elders do want to see us dead. That's true.

– Bliss, head of the Blackwatch Guild
(excerpt stored in the Consultant's Guild archives)

The Gray Island looked like a stretch of untamed wilderness, but Meia and Yala knew where to find the hidden trails, tunnels, and clearings that made travel quicker than walking down a paved street in the Capital.

Meia walked a little behind and to the side of her mother, keeping her senses sharp. She could hear a mouse in the grass at fifty yards, but she'd learned not to underestimate Yala. The woman was a legend among the Masons for a reason.

Even though, for the last couple of years, she'd been acting more like a madwoman than a Consultant.

"You lost control today," Yala noted, not bothering to look around and meet her daughter's eyes.

She was looking for a fight, and parts of Meia wanted to take her up on that offer. The Shadeshifter urged her to prowl closer and finish off Yala while she was vulnerable. The Nightwyrm hissed at the perceived challenge, demanding that she meet the challenge head-on.

But Meia kept them both at bay and responded, "With due respect, Mother, you started it."

Yala made a noncommittal sound and walked a few more steps before she said, "You've started calling me 'mother' again."

Meia hadn't noticed. As a young girl, Meia had been taught to stop addressing Yala in such a familiar manner. *"Now that you have begun your Consultant training, I am no longer your only family,"* Yala had told her. *"The entire Guild is your family now. You should address me with respect, and I will treat you no differently than the other trainees."*

At the time, Meia had accepted the instruction without complaint. Yala was treating her strictly, but only because she had high expectations. Only because she wanted Meia to be the best.

For most of her life, Meia had been in the habit of calling her mother by title. So when had she stopped?

"I suppose I realized that I don't have to do what you tell me anymore," Meia said. "I apologize if that seems rude."

Yala took her eyes from the rocky path and shot her a reproachful look. "You *do* have to do what I tell you. I outrank you."

"Once, I heard a Mason addressing the Council of Architects. She made the case that authority, among the Consultants, was not a matter of enforcing rank but of earning respect. We are not an army, we are a family."

That Mason had, of course, been Yala.

"I was young then," Yala said.

"That's a coincidence. I'm young now."

Yala gave a single, dry laugh. "You sound like your friend."

That did sound more like something Shera would say. Which reminded Meia of a more important topic.

"Mother. I asked you this before, but you chose not to answer me. I'd like an answer now."

Yala let out a heavy breath. Likely she could predict the question.

"What problem do you have with Shera? She's done more service to this Guild than almost anyone." *Certainly more than I have,* she thought, but she wouldn't admit that aloud.

Meia's mother thought for a moment as she walked down a seemingly natural staircase made of an oak tree's roots. "Service to this Guild...I wonder if you mean that, Meia."

Yala turned, walking backwards down the steps. She ticked off points on her fingers as she spoke, spearing Meia with her eyes. "She has always been defiant. Lazy. More inclined to work by herself than with a team. She served the Emperor well, I'll grant you, but she started working against the Guild the *instant* she returned."

Meia had missed most of the ensuing conflict between Shera and the High Councilors; she had seen only the end, when Shera woke the four

Imperial heroes who had risen to become the Regents.

"As I understand it," Meia said, "she was working to keep the Empire together."

"Exactly," Yala said, turning around to walk straight again.

She didn't explain any further.

Stubbornness kept Meia's mouth shut. Yala obviously wanted her to ask further questions, and was stringing her along like a puppet. It was little moves like this, the tiny manipulations, that had finally woken Meia to her mother's true nature.

She just liked being in control.

After a moment, Yala continued as though she'd never paused. Silently, Meia celebrated a small victory. "The two years after the Emperor's death were the most profitable period for the Consultants in living memory. Perhaps the best ever."

Meia remembered. For most of her life, the Gardeners had worked in secret, and then the Emperor fell. Everyone in the world had wanted to hire assassins, and the Consultants had amassed a dizzying fortune in the first year alone. Eliminating rebels, silencing rivals, putting down would-be Emperors...it was the only time in Meia's life when she had a *backlog* of assignments.

The world had quieted since then, in no small thanks to the four Regents.

"She was trying to hold the Empire together," Meia said. "Surely we should reward her for that. We're taught to value the Empire above everything."

"We value the *client* above everything," Yala corrected. "And for over a thousand years, our client has been the Emperor. When he died, that contract was invalidated."

It made a cold, mercenary sort of sense. The Consultants could make far more money in a world without an Empire than with one. The only reason they had stayed in line so long was because of their ingrained commitment to their contract.

But they were getting away from the topic.

"We're speaking of Shera, not of the Empire."

"Shera turned her blade against us and worked against the best interests of the Guild. By rights, we should have executed her."

Except they couldn't. The Regents, having woken from a centuries-long sleep, had come to Shera's defense.

Forcefully.

"You can't, Mother. So you might as well learn to get along with her."

"I will not compromise with a traitor," Yala said firmly.

So be it. If that was how she wanted to play this game, Meia was holding a card up her sleeve.

"Speaking of treachery, what were you planning to do with the Heart?"

Yala snorted, but she replied quickly, proving that she had anticipated the question. "What do *they* plan on doing with it? I'll tell you: they plan to *waste* it. That power could be ours; we could even lend it to clients. The Emperor used the Heart of Nakothi for centuries with no ill effects, so why can't we?"

Meia stepped forward and seized her mother by the shoulder, turning her around roughly. She might have used a little too much force, but she didn't waste any thought on it. She pointed straight at Yala.

Meia's eyes tingled, telling her that they'd changed.

"Let me tell you one thing, High Councilor Yala. You speak of 'ill effects' lightly, as though the Emperor had managed to stave off the symptoms of some *disease*. I lived in the Imperial Palace for years. I stood as close to the Emperor as I stand to you now, and I saw the effects of Nakothi's Heart. He fought madness *every day*. That he lasted an *hour* without going insane was a testament to his incredible willpower, much less over a millennium."

Meia took a deep breath. "It's true, I knew the Emperor for several years before I noticed anything was wrong. But once he told us the truth, I watched him, and I realized he never went an *instant* without wrestling Nakothi for control. And I guarantee you that he would tell us to destroy it now. Tell me, Mother, do you know better than your Emperor?"

Yala leaned closer, ignoring her daughter's tight grip on her shoulder, paying no attention to Meia's predatory glare. She spoke quietly but firmly, with all the authority of the High Council of Architects. "The Emperor is dead," she said. "And so is the Empire."

They didn't speak until they reached Meia's room, where she locked her mother in the closet.

It wouldn't keep Yala forever, but it should at least slow her down—the door was reinforced with steel, the hinges invested to stay closed except in the presence of the key.

If Meia was lucky, it might hold Yala all night.

Perhaps because the Heart hadn't had long to work, none of the dead were twisted into the deformed shapes that the Children of Nakothi usually shared. The bodies were not skeletons, as they had been dried and alchemically preserved centuries before; rather, they were stretched, desiccated husks with skin the color of sand, lurching out of their graves and through the wall with weapons in hand.

At the founding of their Guild, Am'haranai had been buried with their blacks and weapons. It was supposed to be a sign of respect.

It now meant that Shera's dead opponents wore faded gray outfits and carried blades of rusty steel. If they were shambling and uncoordinated, as she thought centuries-old corpses *should* be, then they wouldn't have been a problem.

Unfortunately, Nakothi's power compensated them for what they'd lost. One ancient Consultant leaped, kicking off a nearby wall, and backflipped behind Kerian before sweeping his bony foot at her ankles. She managed to dodge, focusing on another opponent, but it was discouraging to watch. The enemy had three times their number, and twice their physical abilities.

The living had one advantage, though: they had the Heart.

Shera gripped Nakothi's Heart in her left hand, slashing dusty throats with the bronze blade in her right. The resurrected Consultants weren't interested in slaughter, not like the Children of Nakothi they'd encountered back on the dead island. They were consumed by the Heart, and only the Heart.

As a result, the living had clustered themselves around Shera.

Tyril drove the butt of his knife down on a brown, withered skull. The bone cracked and Nakothi's Child sank to the floor, still quivering with life not quite extinguished. Zhen drove his knives into two dead men at the same time, which did very little good. Shera could have told him not to bother; she had started off throwing spades, but had quickly given up. They did even less good than she expected, as the steel blades simply stuck out from dead flesh like splinters. The Children didn't even hesitate.

Her shear, on the other hand, actually did some damage.

Decapitation didn't work; the bodies would keep shambling forward, and sometimes the skull would hop forward on its own and try to bite nearby ankles. But breaking bones did. Destroying the skull could cause an entire body to lose its animation, and shattering a major bone in an arm or a leg would render that limb useless.

The invested shears that Shera and Kerian used were very effective, driving straight through bone with no effort. If only their opponents weren't so fast. Or so determined.

One bony arm thrust between Tyril and Zhen, clawing at Shera's arm, trying to knock the Heart out of her grip. She reacted by breaking its arm, but a second enemy leaped up and landed on her shoulders.

Why is he so light? she wondered. It was strange that his *weight*, of all things, caught her attention.

He leaned down, looking her in the face. Empty eye sockets stared at her above a faded black half-mask.

Then he drove a blade at her arm.

She brought her opposite hand up to stop the strike, but the knife still penetrated half an inch into her skin. She ground her teeth and pushed against the attack, pressing her strength against his, but the dead Consultant was even stronger than she'd expected. She pushed his arm to the side, away from the Heart, dragging the tip of the blade through the meat of her shoulder inch by excruciating inch. Finally, his knife left her flesh, and she tossed him off her shoulders.

He landed on Tyril, who shouted in surprise before stabbing wildly above him.

Shera took the second to assess her left arm. Blood flowed down in a steady stream, and she almost didn't have the strength to grip the Heart. She certainly wouldn't be able to use the arm in a fight, and if the knife had struck any deeper, the pain might have kept her from fighting at all.

Another dead Consultant leaped over Kerian while another crouched and drove its knife at her calves. In a single motion, she stepped over the strike while ducking under the one above, making it look effortless. Like the next step in the same dance, Kerian reached up with one hand and down with the other, slicing both skulls in half.

Dry skin and bones clattered to the ground around her, and her braids whipped at the air as she turned to Shera.

"We have to move the Heart to a safer location," Kerian said calmly.

Shera agreed. Kerian seemed perfectly at home, but Zhen and Tyril were having a worse time than either of the Gardeners. Slashes and cuts, most shallow, stood out all over their bodies, and Zhen was wheezing, gripping his one remaining knife. A dead Consultant struck at Tyril with powerful blows in quick succession, each of which he turned with his oversized blade. If the Children of Nakothi had possessed the intelligence they had in life, the live Consultants would have died in seconds, but these corpses moved with a singular purpose; as soon as Tyril stumbled back under the attack, the Child moved its empty eyes to Shera, refocusing on the Heart. It moved toward her, and Tyril and Zhen together severed its spine.

The room was empty of whole bodies, now: only pieces crawled toward the circle of living Consultants. They started to move toward the stairs.

Then two more corpses, even older and in worse state than the ones before, pushed through the remnants of the broken walls. If the Children kept coming, then the living had no chance.

"Run," Shera suggested. They did, shambling awkwardly in formation to keep Shera and the Heart defended from all sides. The group started to shuffle down the hall, between the statues of the knights that guarded the passageway in.

Sing, sing, sing with me and be reborn! the Heart declared.

And then the stone knights began to crack.

"I always...assumed...these were statues," Zhen panted, punching one stone face before the body inside managed to break free.

Shera looked to the exit, which seemed impossibly distant. They had no chance of making it while protecting her.

But she wasn't the only one who could carry the Heart.

She dashed the other way, back into the main room, leaving the others stranded in the hallway. There were two dead Consultants still there, and she engaged them, driving her shear at one Child's dry rib cage. It blocked with its own rusty knife, which must have been invested with years of Intent, as it did not crack under the Gardener's blade.

Its partner drove a kick at her ribs, knocking her off-balance, but she turned the stumble into a spin, lunging low and shattering one corpse's hip. It collapsed to the ground, using its hands to lope after her.

Shera met three attacks from the Child that was still whole and completely animated, then shoved him back and kicked the half-corpse away.

In that second of space, she dropped her bronze knife, and gripped the Heart in her still functional hand. Many of the Children that had been sealed in the statues had begun to run her way, so she threw the Heart over their heads.

She had assumed that they would simply watch as the Heart sailed over their skulls, but one of the first dead Am'haranai leaped into the air, catching Nakothi's Heart in both hands before landing. In an instant, the other Consultants fell into a defensive formation around the Heart, knives out and bristling like a porcupine's quills.

"*Why?*" Tyril shouted, tone sad and forlorn as though he were begging for an answer.

"I thought it would work!" Shera called back.

Now it was the living Consultants' turn to attack as the dried husks fought a retreat, trying to back through the broken walls. At first, it looked as if Nakothi was backing herself into a corner, but Shera knew better. The labyrinth originally constructed by Jorin Curse-breaker wove in and out of the entire Gray Island. If the Heart escaped this chamber, they would never be able to find it.

Shera threw herself into the fight with renewed energy, but it was difficult to make any headway. Even one of the ancient Consultants was quick and skilled enough to be a significant opponent, and they didn't necessarily die when you dealt a lethal blow. Sometimes disembodied hands gripped at her ankles, forcing her to waste precious seconds breaking it free, and distracting her in key moments.

The dead funneled through the remnants of the shattered wall, trickling toward the back, where Shera could glimpse a dark hole into the distance. The corpse carrying the Heart shoved its way through the crowd, kneeling to squeeze through the hole. Shera fought desperately, but she only had one arm.

I will give you a new purpose, Nakothi's voice hissed.

Then a hand on Shera's shoulder pushed her aside, and Meia stepped forward.

She flexed her hands, exposing short claws.

"Excuse me," the Gardener said. Then she went to work.

It was like someone had unleashed a sandstorm in the narrow corridor. In the first instant, Shera had wondered why Meia wasn't using her shears, as the Children of Nakothi were difficult to kill with any other weapon. She soon saw that Meia didn't need them—her own methods were brutally effective. She seized a dead Consultant and leaped, crushing its skull to powder against the *ceiling*. Before its body hit the ground, she had already put her fist through an empty set of ribs in another spray of dust, ripping that enemy in half from the inside out.

Two enemies came at her with knives, and she simply let them hit, accepting the shallow wounds for the opportunity to grab them each by the top of the skull and pitch them into the crowd. She waded in like a child into autumn leaves, stomping and crunching with each step, moving closer to the hole at the end of the room.

Shera had to back up, coughing. The air was filled with corpse-dust, and it was getting hard to see through the haze.

When she made it back into the other room, Kerian asked, "Did she get the Heart?"

"She will," Shera said, letting herself collapse against an intact section of wall.

The typical post-fight exhaustion crashed around her, submerging her in a wave of weakness, and usually she would do her best to fall asleep as soon as possible.

But the pain in her shoulder throbbed, and she held the wound tight with her opposite hand, slowing the flow of blood. More than that, she was too depressed to sleep.

She had thought this would be the end. She had wanted so badly for this to be over.

Now she had no idea what to do.

Her left-hand shear had been invested by Lucan and the Emperor on top of the hundreds of Gardeners who had used it before her, and it carried such a weight of Intent that it would be able to destroy Nakothi's Heart. That was still true.

But the same reason remained valid: if she destroyed the Heart without draining its power first, all of Nakothi's will would be released, and it would make what happened in this crypt look like a casual alley mugging. If the Heart was strong enough that it could do *this*, then destroying it might kill and resurrect everyone on the Island, not just Shera herself.

To Shera, trading the Heart for an island full of Nakothi's Children seemed like a bad exchange.

Meia emerged from the crypt a moment later, wiping dust from her eyes with one hand and holding the cloth-wrapped Heart in the other.

"Here," she said, tossing it to Shera. It landed in her lap with a wet splat. "I don't even want to touch it anymore."

"What now?" Zhen asked. Tyril was leaning with his forehead pressed against the wall, catching his breath, and Kerian rubbed at her scar with her eyes closed, thinking.

"I need to talk to Lucan," Shera said at last.

She couldn't think of any other way to destroy the Heart.

But maybe Lucan could *make* one.

When Shera brought the Heart down to Lucan's cell, he was writing furiously on a stack of papers. As she arrived, he tossed the top paper aside and continued, holding up his left hand to gesture for quiet.

She had assumed he would feel the Heart coming and would prepare for her, but he seemed absorbed in whatever he was doing. She cleared her throat. "Lucan, it's—"

He waved his hand furiously, urging her to be quiet, and his writing didn't slow down.

After another minute, she tried again. "This is important."

He waved her down and kept scribbling.

She gave him as much time as she could as her frustration overwhelmed her, which meant she waited another thirty seconds before lobbing the Heart into his room and onto his unmade bed.

He recoiled involuntarily against Nakothi's power, his pen falling out of his hand.

"We've got a time limit here," Shera said. "The longer the Heart goes uncontained, the more danger we're all in."

Lucan sighed in frustration, moved back to his papers as though he meant to continue writing, and then thought better of it. He rummaged around in his bookshelf for a while, eventually pulling a palm-sized chunk of masonry out from behind a book.

He walked over to the wall separating him from the cell next door and slid the stone into a crack in the wall. It fit perfectly, like he'd gouged it out of that exact spot.

The sound in the room deadened noticeably, as though someone had shoved a ball of cotton into Shera's right ear. It was an uncomfortable sensation, and she rubbed a hand against her ear, trying to dispel it.

"There," Lucan said contentedly, rubbing his gloved hands together. "Now we can speak freely."

"What did you do?"

He pointed to the wall. "I invested that chunk of stone to absorb sound, and I invested the rest of the wall to amplify its effects. It's called Sympathetic Investment, and it was one of the skills the Emperor didn't have time to teach me. But he always wanted me to learn, and I have nothing but time in here, so..."

"So...you decided to make me sound like I'm talking underwater?"

"Now Jyrine can't hear a word we say." He chuckled lightly. "The investment isn't perfect, she could break through it, so I told her she needed to be quiet or you would kill her."

"Jyrine?" Shera asked, blankly. There was something distantly familiar about the name, but she couldn't place it.

"The Sleepless girl," Lucan said impatiently. "You kidnapped her and brought her here." Gingerly, he picked up the wrapped Heart in his gloved hands. "Did you have to put this on my *bed?* They don't give me new linens until the end of the week."

Shera hadn't entirely forgotten about the Sleepless woman's existence, but she'd had more important concerns. The reminder raised an unpleasant realization, and she pulled her knife from behind her back.

"Thank you for reminding me," Shera said. She had left Jyrine alive as a mercy, but only because the woman didn't pose a threat. The last thing Shera needed was a Sleepless near the Heart of Nakothi. Who knew what problems she could cause?

Lucan jumped to his feet, leaving the Heart on the table. "Wait, wait, wait! Don't kill her *now!* I've made so much progress!"

Shera waited for him to explain, but she didn't sheathe her blade.

He gripped the bars, looking into her eyes, speaking intently. "Over the past week or so, I've been gradually getting her to open up about the Sleepless. She was eager to do it, actually; I think she's been waiting for someone to talk to. I've learned more about the Sleepless cult and their cabal of leaders than the whole *Guild* knows. I've been writing it down for you, so you can take it to the High Councilors." He gestured to the pile of notes on his desk.

So that was what he'd been scribbling when she walked in. At least he was working on something relevant.

"It's fascinating," he went on. "But here's the most important part: they've been communicating with her! In her cell! They contacted her again not ten minutes ago. Shera, they expect the power of the Heart to *increase*. And they've told her to...is that blood?"

Shera raised her collar and peeked inside, looking at her shoulder. She had worn the bandage under her blacks so that Lucan wouldn't notice, but it appeared that her wound had started to seep through at the edges.

"It's not mine," she said.

Lucan gave her a flat look and, without warning, tossed his pen through the bars.

Shera tried to catch it with her left hand, but a shot of pain through her shoulder made the limb freeze in motion. At the last second, she caught it with her right hand instead.

"I see your old war injury has been acting up," he said wryly.

"Only when it rains." She shook her head. "Never mind that, tell me about the Sleepless."

He didn't give up as easily as she'd hoped. "Who stabbed you in the shoulder? Come to think of it, why do you still have the Heart? I thought you were going to..."

His eyes widened, and before she could answer, he went on. "Jorin's curse box didn't work, did it?"

Once again, without waiting for a response, he turned back into his cell and peeled off his right glove. As soon as he did, he winced. Shera could understand why: Nakothi's song was a constant undercurrent even for her, and it must be much worse feeling that power directly with a Reader's senses.

He held his hand a foot back from the Heart, palm out, as though he pressed against an invisible wall. "Shera. It's getting stronger, even now. We have to keep it away from your shear, at all costs."

Keep it away? That didn't make sense. Nothing would happen unless she deliberately stabbed the Heart, and she knew better than to do that.

"I'm not going to destroy it," she said, but he shuddered back from the Heart, expression horrified.

"Light and life...Shera, this isn't Nakothi's stored Intent acting on its own. There is a *conscious mind* behind this. If you destroy the Heart now, and its power is released, it could wake the Dead Mother. We don't have room for any accidents."

Shera held a hand to the blade on her left, from which laughter trickled in a constant whisper.

"Wait! It makes sense now!" He dashed over to the desk, pulling the top paper off the stack. "The first time, I couldn't hear them very clearly, and we mostly spoke about the goals of the Sleepless afterwards. This time, I could hear more of it, though not everything."

"More of what?"

"The leaders of the Sleepless," he said. "Their cabal. They sent a messenger into her cell, probably an Elderspawn."

Shera seriously considered drawing her blade. If the Sleepless girl was capable of summoning Elders in captivity, then she needed to be killed, not contained.

He waved that way. "That's not important. I could hear some of what they said. They were quite loud, but their words weren't meant for me, so there was a little distortion. Okay, here we are: they're pleased that the Heart arrived on the Island, which means they can sense it somehow, and then they tell her, 'When you feel the Heart's power wax,' something. I'm not sure what comes after that. Either way, they're telling her that something is going to happen when the Heart's power *waxes*. They expect it to increase."

He jabbed his thumb over his shoulder, at the Heart. "I think they expect you to destroy it. And when you do, and you release the power stored within, that's a signal for something to happen."

Shera rubbed at her eyes. This was too much. She'd thought the Sleepless were all dead, only to find out now that not only were they here, but they'd been able to sense the position of Shera and the Heart all along. And they were prepared to act.

As though she didn't have enough to deal with.

"After that, they tell Jyrine to call for help after she feels the Heart's power increase, and they repeat it again. It's very important to them that you destroy the Heart." He gripped the bars again with his bare hand. "Which means that we have to find a *different* way to deal with it. Seal it away, or something."

Shera took a deep breath, refocusing. It was too easy to get lost thinking about how much she wanted to sleep, but she had a mission to complete.

"That's why I'm here, Lucan. The Heart overpowered the seal Jorin left us. And it turned a bunch of ancient bodies into Children of Nakothi, in the process."

Lucan's eyes flicked to her wound, and he nodded. "I can see how that might happen."

"So we need a different way to weaken it," she said. "We need you to come up with something else, because the rest of us are out of ideas."

He turned back to the Heart, and what she could see of his face clouded over. "I'm not sure how much I can do. It's dangerous working directly on an Elder artifact, much less a piece of their body. One slip, and I might turn on you."

"Don't slip," Shera suggested.

"You're a warm and encouraging beacon for these dark times." His tone was light, but he still didn't take his eyes off the Heart. "After an hour or two, I'll need you to take the Heart away from me. And...I might not want to give it up."

My power can become yours, Nakothi whispered.

"I'll take care of it," Shera said firmly. She sank down against the wall opposite his cell. "Two hours. That's a good nap."

He turned back to her, still looking grim. "And you can't always hold this yourself. I can't emphasize that enough. Assign a team of people to run it all over the island, spreading its influence around as much as possible. We can't let it pile up in one place."

"Don't pile it," Shera repeated, drowsy. The rock wall behind her back felt surprisingly comfortable.

He said something else, but she was already asleep.

The song of Nakothi was not quiet, so she dreamed of death.

And of horrible rebirth.

CHAPTER SIXTEEN

TEN YEARS AGO

The old alchemist strode along the ramparts of his castle, cackling. "I can feel your burrowing, little worms! Crawl, crawl, crawling along! Well, here I am!" He spread his arms wide, presenting himself to the darkness. "Take your shot, wormy-worm *worms!*"

The copper-plated staff in his left hand spat sparks. In his right, he clutched a bright green alchemical lantern.

He leaned out over his castle wall, raising the lantern to illuminate the ground far beneath him.

"Come along, now!" he called. "I've got all night, but do *you?*"

He continued to shout at the darkness as Shera watched from a cramped trunk three feet behind him.

Albadol Crane was one of the few men alive to have deceived not one but two Imperial Guilds. First, he trained under the Magisters, claiming an Academy education and a noble lineage, neither of which existed. Shortly before he was to earn his staff, the Magisters learned of his betrayal, and confronted him...only to find his room empty, scrubbed clean. He'd left days before.

But he hadn't gone far away, as it turned out.

Using the same document-forging skill that had gotten him so far in life, Crane lied his way in to Kanatalia, the Guild of Alchemists. Even after Crane spent five years among their number, they never spotted his deception. Fortunately, the alchemists proved themselves better at recognizing shattered minds than forged documents.

After the fourth release of Albadol Crane's "miracle elixir" coincided with the fourth disappearance of Guild acolytes, the alchemists called for his dismissal and arrest.

Only one of those actually happened.

Once again, Albadol Crane slipped the net, moving out to the Aurelian countryside, where he acquired an ancient castle through means unknown. Here he continued his experiments, crossing the Intent of a mad Reader with the cruel poisons of an unhinged alchemist.

Nearby farmers disappeared at an alarming rate, but no one noticed. Not until the local governor and the mayors of various regional villages scraped together enough coin to hire the Consultants.

When the Alchemists heard what was going on, they mobilized every Mason, Shepherd, and Gardener left on the island. Shera had heard, through Meia, that they planned to come down on this castle like the fist of an Elder.

Until the Emperor had decided that this presented a unique opportunity for his three personal Gardeners.

That was why Shera lay, cramped and shivering, in a trunk behind a mad alchemist. She had no idea where Lucan and Meia had ended up, but they were supposed to provide a distraction. And they were eight minutes late.

Worst of all, it was so cold and uncomfortable inside this trunk that she couldn't even *sleep*.

Gently, softly, it began to rain.

Shera cursed the Emperor to an eternity devoured by crabs in Kelarac's dungeon. She cursed Meia to be devoured by Urg'naut, and Kerian—who had allowed this to happen—to Nakothi's tender attentions.

And Lucan…

Well, she could forgive Lucan. Assuming he hadn't already gotten himself killed.

She felt a squirm of worry when she thought about Lucan, far greater than when she considered the others. Meia would survive, of that she had no doubt. Meia would survive anything out of sheer stubbornness. But Lucan? What would happen to Lucan without Shera around to protect him?

A metal grate burst open a few yards down the wall, and Crane leveled his copper staff.

Lucan pushed his head out, his dark skin smeared with some luminous orange fluid. He looked uncomfortable, but at least he was alive.

Blue-white sparks whirled from the tip of Crane's staff, crashing into Lucan. At the last second, he raised a wooden shield.

The sparks fizzed against the wood and vanished.

The shield was a device that Lucan had fashioned minutes before they entered the castle, out of spare wood and strips of leather. It would protect him from Albadol Crane's harmful Intent, he claimed.

Then Crane lowered his staff and raised a pistol.

Lucan dropped back down the grate as the pistol jerked back, sending up a crack and a puff of gun smoke. The bullet struck sparks from the stone next to the grate.

Crane tossed the empty pistol down—he would have no time to reload—and fumbled for a flask at his belt.

Meia vaulted over the far side of the wall like an acrobat, blond hair flipping in the dark. The heel of her descending foot caught Crane on the wrist, sending the vial crashing to the stone. It broke open and sizzled, raising a cloud of caustic-smelling smoke inches from Shera's hiding place.

She drove a punch at Crane's chest, but he cackled and spread his arms wide.

The whole castle shook. Shera rattled in her wooden cage like a coin in a bottle. The grate over Lucan's head crashed down, and Meia tumbled three steps backwards.

"This is my castle, worms!" Albadol Crane declared. "But while you're here, why don't I give you the *tour?*"

That was when Shera jumped out of the chest and cut his throat.

She used both her shears at the same time, just to be sure.

The alchemist choked and spewed blood over the stones at his feet, pitching forward. Meia gave him a little extra shove, and he flopped straight over the wall. Shera leaned forward.

He slammed limply into the ground, his alchemical lantern shattering in a pool of luminescent fluid.

"That wasn't so hard," Shera said. Then her leg muscles screamed at her, and she doubled over. "Ow, cramp...cramp..."

Meia glared at her, and that was when Shera noticed that her left arm was hanging at her side, mangled and useless.

"What happened to you?"

"Guard dogs," Meia snapped. "Kameira hybrids. They didn't die until I cut their hearts out of their chests."

"That explains why you're late." She turned to Lucan. "What about you?"

Lucan scraped some of the glowing orange goo off his face with a look of disgust, flinging it to the ground. "This was one of a pair of potions that were supposed to react together and cook me alive. If I hadn't Read the device first, they would both have gotten me."

Shera waved a hand over the wall. "I noticed you didn't stop to question him. How's your conscience?"

"Clean as a Pilgrim's hands," he said at once. "I did some Reading on the way up here. You have no idea what experiments he did in this castle. I can hear their screams from every brick in this place."

A weight Shera didn't know she'd been carrying eased.

Lucan approves...I'm glad.

Too often, when she killed people, she had to hear him wondering aloud if they had a brother, a lover, a wife, a mother. This time, they had simply rid the world of one more monster.

The three Gardeners stood on the wall, waiting.

Technically, this was the conclusion of their first official assignment as a team. They had done odd tasks for the Emperor individually and together, but they were usually mediocre jobs designed to hone one particular skill or another. This was the first official Guild mission they'd taken, and they walked away more or less unscathed.

"Did this seem a little easy to you?" Shera asked hesitantly.

Lucan scraped away more gel. "More risk than usual." Then he shrugged. "But not much. After all those lessons, I expected something more exciting."

Meia uncorked a bottle of dark blue fluid and drained it to the dregs, letting out a small sigh when she'd finished. "It looks like blueberries. It smells like blueberries. So why doesn't it *taste* like blueberries?"

Of its own accord, her shoulder shifted in its socket with a sickening *crunch.* Her wounds crawled together, sprouting dark blue scales where they joined.

"We got the job done," Meia said at last. "But yes, I did expect a little more of a challenge."

Shera looked away from Meia's writhing arm, vaguely nauseated. "Do you have to keep drinking those?"

"Until I stop growing. At least for the next two or three years, it's monthly checkups and lots and lots of potions." She grimaced and shattered the empty bottle on the castle wall. "So who's going to take care of the castle?"

Shera raised her eyebrows. "You didn't place the charges?"

"Yes she did," Lucan said, intervening before Meia could snap back. "But this place is defended against alchemical charges. He's invested every inch of the stone, and even some of the moisture in the air, to deaden explosions. I don't know how he got the pistol to work anywhere on the grounds."

Shera checked the shears in their sheaths, touched the pouch of spades, and adjusted the needles strapped to her belt. All secure.

"Your turn, then," she said. She gave him a smile. "See you down below."

He returned the smile, even as he stripped off his gloves and knelt to press his palms against the castle.

Meia and Shera hopped over the side of the wall.

Shera had to descend the old-fashioned way; digging for grooves in the stone with the tips of her gloved fingers and pressing flat-soled slippers against the wall. Like her shears, they were invested with generations of Gardener Intent, and they would never slip or slide on uneven terrain. But that didn't make climbing down any less painful.

By contrast, Meia jumped straight down. She threw one hand out for balance when she hit the grass, her knees slightly bent, but her whole body was alchemically reinforced. Sometimes Shera envied her that.

Sometimes.

By the time she reached Meia at the bottom, Shera's arms and legs were screaming at her. She rubbed at her wrist as she walked away from the castle and into the shadow of the surrounding woods. Meia walked at her side, keeping pace as blue scales flaked off her wounded arm.

Behind them, the castle started to shake.

"He could have taken this assignment alone," Shera commented. "Just brought the whole castle down from the very beginning."

Meia rolled her eyes. "Any of us could have. In, kill the alchemist, out. This was to test how we work as a team."

"We couldn't have brought down the castle. Not without alchemical charges."

"Yes, and I hear he walks on clouds, and sings with the voice of an angel!"

Shera's face grew hot.

"Hey, you see him special. Your heart's in your eyes. You're stitching your names together on a pillow." Meia clapped Shera on the back with her unwounded arm. "That's fine! I don't care. But don't let it affect your appraisal of the situation at hand."

A rumble grew like distant thunder as pieces of the castle fell to the ground.

Shera cleared her throat, cheeks still burning. "We *could* have done it without his help."

When Meia walked under the shadow of a tree, she was almost invisible except for her hair. "I do agree with what you said. For an assignment given to us by the Emperor himself, this did seem too simple. But he is the Emperor, and his reasons are not for us to know." Instinctively, they both stuck to the dark.

Behind them, a deafening roar shook the night as the castle collapsed.

Shera couldn't help herself. "You have to admit, that was impressive."

The Emperor sat in front of the three of them, for once wearing something simple: a plain white robe with a sash thrown around it. Evidently he had been sleeping when they arrived in the city, though he was awake and alert and holding a cup of tea when they finally reached him.

"How did you defeat the homunculi?" the Emperor asked curiously. "I wasn't expecting you back so soon."

Shera exchanged glances with the other two. "The what?"

He waved a hand. "Perhaps you have another word for them. In this case, Crane was building ten-foot monstrosities out of human parts he grew in his lab. They were infused with all the alchemy at his command, wearing invested armor. You saw nothing of them? There should have been a dozen or more."

"I cut his throat," Shera said. "Then Meia pushed him over a wall, and Lucan brought down the castle."

Delicately, the Emperor sipped his tea. "Well, that's a disappointment. I should have sent only one of you."

Shera looked triumphantly at Meia, who very carefully did not meet her eyes.

"Nonetheless, I am glad you've returned. Something significant has happened. It has left me quite disturbed, as I'm sure you've noticed."

He sipped some more tea.

"What's happened to you?" Shera asked in mock horror. "You're a wreck!"

The Emperor nodded to her as if to concede a point, unaware of the irony. "I do apologize for that. But there are certain issues that I can't address myself. And I can't trust the details to anyone else, not even to General Teach herself."

All three of their spines straightened, and Shera's gaze locked onto the

Emperor. Despite his casual tone, this meant matters were deadly serious. If she even thought about telling anyone outside this room, the Emperor could Read it and have her executed on the spot.

A bead of sweat rolled down her temple. Now that the idea had occurred to her, she couldn't *help* but think of it.

The Emperor swirled the tea in his cup, thinking. "What do you know about Nakothi, the Dead Mother?"

Shera's flesh seemed to crawl at the very mention of the name, and she thought she heard whispers coming from somewhere nearby.

"Only what everyone knows," Lucan said.

"Pardon me if I am somewhat unfamiliar with what *everyone* knows," the Emperor said drily. "I was the one who drove the spear into Nakothi's heart, before her death-throes leveled a continent and created the Aion Sea."

The impact of what he was saying struck Shera like a cannonball. Seeing the Emperor like this, in a night-robe and holding a cup of tea, made him look so human. She often forgot that he was *the Emperor.* There was only one man with actual living memories of the Great Elders, and he was sitting in this room.

Lucan bowed deeply, genuine regret in his voice. "I apologize, my Emperor. I spoke carelessly."

The Emperor waved a hand impatiently, but when Lucan went on, it was with a formal tone. "I know that Nakothi was one of the last of the Great Elders to rule before you united humanity. She ruled the domain of birth and death, and often tried to combine the two. The Luminians exterminated the last of the Dead Mother's cults almost two hundred years ago. Some say that it is Nakothi's touch that causes stillbirths, and when a corpse seems more healthy than it was in life, it is burned to prevent Nakothi from claiming it as a vessel."

Meia piped up. "Highness! I've heard that Nakothi waits at the bottom of the Aion, alongside Kelarac."

The Emperor looked up sharply. "One day we will have a longer conversation regarding where you heard that rumor. Nonetheless, there is much you don't know. And much to cover."

He glanced to the door, and presumably he did something with his Intent, because a pair of servants instantly pushed the door open. "Three chairs," he said.

They returned in seconds, and the three young Gardeners sat.

"I was born in Nakothi's territory," the Emperor said. "She ruled over what we now call the Heartlands, the birthplace of humanity. She had little use for living humans, so we scrabbled out our lives as best we could. What she did need were human corpses. By the thousands.

"She reforged them, you see. Stitched them together, brain and body, remade them into monsters. Her Handmaidens called it *rebirthing.*"

For a moment, the Emperor's face hardened with a hatred that predated the civilized world.

"When I learned I could sense the memories and potential in objects, the first thing I did was to leave Nakothi's lands, into the halls of Ach'magut. I wandered for years, seeking out others like me.

"When I next returned to Nakothi, I had an army behind me."

He stared into his cup, lost in memories. After almost two full minutes, he shook himself loose. Then he met each of their eyes in turn, staring at them with a gaze ancient and dark.

"Everything I have told you up to this point is historical fact. It's nothing you couldn't have pieced together with a visit to the Consultants' archives. What I will tell you now is a secret that I haven't told another living soul in centuries."

He held the teacup on his palm, and it began to shiver. After a moment, little white specks peeled away and drifted off on the wind. More and more specks joined them, until the teacup—and the tea inside it—dried up and crumbled away to ash.

Shera found the display unusually disturbing.

"This information is vital not only to the security of the Empire, but to my personal survival. I know you are all aware of this, so I have never emphasized it before, but I tell you now: if I even suspect you have leaked this story without my express authorization, I will kill you. I will have those who heard the story executed. I will print an official refutation in all Imperial news outlets, and I will put on a public display to shame and discredit your claims. Your names will be stricken from the record of Imperial citizens, and from the very stones I will strip all memory of your existence."

The sheer severity of the threat moved beyond intimidating and into the realm of absurdity, such that Shera was tempted to laugh. Why would they tell anyone?

But when the Emperor was so solemn, the very room exuded the air of an executioner's chamber. Shera found her muscles frozen, the mirth strangled in her chest.

Almost as one, all three of them nodded.

The aura of the room relaxed, and the Emperor dipped a hand into the front of his robes. He gripped a fistful of the silver chain he always wore around his neck and hauled it up.

On the end was a pewter shell, about the size of a big man's fist.

Gripping it gently in both hands, the Emperor pressed down on either side. It popped open like a locket.

Revealing a sickly, gray-green, still-beating heart.

"This," the Emperor said, "is a Heart of Nakothi. This is how I live forever."

CHAPTER SEVENTEEN

Investing Intent is a natural process, and one that we are learning to control. We believe Readers are the key to humanity's advancement. But in spite of everything we've learned, we still know next to nothing about the process we call Awakening. I will summarize our knowledge as best I can.

First, we know that Readers can Awaken objects, transforming their physical appearance and granting them increased powers.

Second, we know that Awakened items seemed to have a degree of awareness, the strength and nature of which are related to that object's original Intent.

Finally, we know that Awakened objects can no longer be invested further, or Awakened again.

However, we still do not have an answer to that most critical question: What effects do the Awakened have upon us?

– FROM AN ANCIENT RESEARCH JOURNAL IN THE MAGISTER'S GUILD (EXCERPT STORED IN THE CONSULTANT'S GUILD ARCHIVES)

"My mother believes that the Empire is already dead," Meia said, tossing Shera the Heart.

Shera sat down on a tree branch, idly passing Nakothi's Heart from hand to hand. She'd wrapped it in invested cloth and stuffed the whole bundle in a sack, but it did nothing to quiet Nakothi's song.

You are cold, the Heart crooned. *You are weak, you are sick. Let me make you strong, let me take away your pain...*

"I'm not even sure what that would mean," Shera said, ignoring the Dead Mother's voice. "The people of the Empire are still here. The Guilds are still holding together. Just because we don't have an Emperor doesn't mean that everything ended."

Shera tossed the Heart blindly to one side, and a Shepherd's black-clad arm reached out and snagged it out of the air. Now that her right hand was free, she swung from her branch to the next tree.

This forest was one part of the Shepherds' training course, and the trees were intentionally crammed close together, almost trunk-to-trunk. The idea was to get young Shepherds used to climbing over irregular surfaces, looking for the best vantage points. Meia had been the one to suggest it as an ideal place to take the Heart, to spread its influence around. As long as it didn't stay in one location for too long, the Heart of Nakothi wouldn't have a chance to corrupt its surroundings. In theory.

Meia didn't bother to swing; she leaped from one tree to another, landing with perfect balance. "We're not a single Empire anymore, though," she said. "We've already divided into regions, under the four Regents. And even the Guilds have started to work against each other."

"The Guilds were always unsteady allies at best," Shera said, stepping straight from one branch onto another. "But I take your point."

The Luminian Order and the Blackwatch had always stayed at each other's throats, and the Greenwardens sabotaged the Kameira hunting parties of the Champions and Imperial Guards whenever they could. But the Consultants attacking a Blackwatch operation, or acting directly against a Navigator on an officially sanctioned mission...that would never have happened even a year ago.

Only one thing bound the Guilds together: a mutual dedication to the Empire. And now those bonds were fraying.

Meia swung from a higher layer of branches over to another tree using nothing but her arms. When she reached Shera, she simply hung there, leaving her feet dangling.

Shera watched her with no small degree of jealousy. If she could climb trees like a monkey, she could nap *anywhere*. No one would ever find her.

"It doesn't have to be so bad," Meia said. "All of the regions can govern each other. The Izyrians rule the Izyrians, the Erinin rule over Erin, the Heartlanders rule the Heartland. It can be a noble goal."

Shera considered that for a moment, as a hidden Shepherd tossed the Heart to Meia. She caught it between her feet without looking.

"I'll grant you that the Regents didn't want to replace the Emperor," Shera said. "If they think the world can survive with a dozen little Empires, I believe them."

Meia released the branch with one hand, reaching down to grab the Heart, and then swung one-handed to the next tree. "It's not only that. If we don't have a single Emperor, we don't have a single weak point. The Emperor was so concerned about his own sanity because, if Nakothi corrupted him, she effectively controlled the whole world."

"Yes, but instead of one weak point, now we have four." Shera slid over and around a branch, following Meia. "If any one of the Regents are corrupted, that's a quarter of the Empire under the rule of one of the Elders."

"Not everyone," Meia said, grimacing and holding the Heart at arm's length. "Maybe the world can be like...like the Guilds. Everyone deals with their own problems unless something threatens everyone, and then we all come together."

It *sounded* good, but Shera couldn't help but think that a world without the Empire would be far too chaotic. What would keep the bigger regions from taking over the smaller ones? Who would force the different regions to help each other, in the event of a global emergency?

"Is that what your mother said?" Shera asked, taking the Heart from Meia.

Give your body to me, and I will grant you the gift of glorious purpose, Nakothi whispered.

Meia did a backflip from a lower branch to a higher one. *Now she's showing off.*

"My mother isn't concerned about the fate of the Empire. She's only thinking about our Guild. She wants the Empire to dissolve because that would be more profitable for *us.*"

"It would be," Shera allowed. If they threw away everything the Emperor stood for.

Shera pulled her arm back, ready to toss the Heart to one of the Shepherds, when a whistle cut through the forest. Instantly the black-clad Shepherds dropped from the canopy all around her, climbing down so quickly she almost thought they had fallen.

Meia actually did allow herself to fall, landing on her hands and springing up to her feet.

Shera clambered carefully down the tree, moving from limb to limb. "Are you trying to mock me, or do you want to make me feel slow?"

"I'm enjoying myself," Meia said. "I thought you would approve."

Shera joined her a moment later, following the Shepherds to the source of the alarm: Kerian, standing outside the forest, a silver whistle dangling from her lips.

Shera and Meia walked up to her, pushing through the crowd of Shepherds. It had been almost two full days since Lucan first proposed running the Heart around the Island. He had inspected Nakothi's Heart two more times in that period, and each time he invested its cloth wrappings. Its song had indeed grown weaker over the past two days.

Soon, he said, the wrappings would hold enough of Nakothi's power that they could safely place it in a box to have its Intent drained. The other Readers among the Architects were already working on such a box.

But now Kerian was here, stopping them on their rounds. It could only mean that something had gone wrong.

"What happened, Councilor?" Meia asked.

"Two Waveriders came back to the docks a moment ago," Kerian said.

Shera interrupted, "I can't leave the Island. I have to stay here. I can't go back to the Capital." The past few weeks had already exhausted her, and her left shoulder still throbbed despite the attentions of the alchemists. If she had to get back on a Waverider on top of everything else, she couldn't promise that she wouldn't stab the Kameira in the back when they were halfway across the ocean.

Meia, Kerian, and the surrounding Shepherds all gave her odd looks, but Kerian went on. "I'm not sure why you would need to go back to the Capital, but you can relax. We need you both here. Our scouts in the Aion have reported a Navigator's ship headed this direction. *The Testament.*"

Calder Marten's ship. Part of Shera had expected this, but she had hoped that she'd seen the last of that crew.

"Sink it," Shera said. "Bring the cannons on the docks. Send the scouts back out with alchemical charges. Whatever you do, don't let that ship make land."

She didn't look forward to facing Calder's captive Elderspawn in battle, but more than that, he had both a former Champion *and* Naberius Clayborn on his ship. The Consultants couldn't afford to let them make landfall, not with the Heart still exposed.

Kerian returned her whistle to the satchel hanging from her shoulder. "Our assignment has nothing to do with Calder Marten, or even Naberius Clayborn. We have to prevent the Heart from being used to raise another Emperor. How we accomplish that goal is irrelevant, so long as we do."

"The Champion will be coming for me," Meia said confidently. "He will want to finish our fight."

"That's good information," Shera responded. "We'll ambush him and shoot him to death at a hundred yards."

Meia rolled her eyes, a gesture that Shera remembered well from their childhood. Not fondly. "You think that will work? That wouldn't stop *me.* No, if I can isolate their best fighter and keep him from helping the rest of the crew, that can only be an advantage for us."

Kerian made a delicate noise in her throat. "I never mentioned fighting anyone. I'm taking a team to meet with him as soon as he gets here, which should be early tomorrow."

"You want to meet with him?"

"Despite everything, Shera, we are still Consultants. If he wants a consultation, I'm not going to turn him down. His money spends as well as everyone else's, and we might even be able to come to a peaceful agreement. We do have his wife."

That made sense to Shera. If Kerian could find a way to use Jyrine to get Calder under control, then that could only be an advantage.

"I came to warn you," Kerian continued. "I want you to be prepared when he gets here, in case we...fail to reach a mutually beneficial conclusion. And Lucan should be prepared as well. I don't like leaving the Heart unsecured if Naberius Clayborn will be coming here. There must be a reason the Blackwatch chose him to bond with the Heart of Nakothi."

Shera remembered Naberius from their fight on the dead island: hair ragged, suit torn, smiling insanely as he clutched the Heart to his chest. She wasn't as concerned about Naberius as she was about his Silent One. Tristania still had her bulletproof coat and her Stormwing tail Vessel, so that was another Soulbound that someone would have to fight, in addition to Urzaia Woodsman.

"Maybe we can throw the Heart into the sea," Shera said, only half-joking. "Then it's Kelarac's problem, not ours."

Kerian looked her straight in the eyes. "Do you want Kelarac to have control of Nakothi's Heart? Because I have no doubt that he'd take it gladly."

Shera winced. She'd mentioned Kelarac in the hypothetical sense—whenever you lost anything in the ocean, you said that 'Kelarac had it now.' She hadn't ever imagined the Soul Collector *literally* collecting objects of power.

It was a disturbing thought.

"We'll do our duty, Councilor," Meia responded, in Shera's silence.

"I'm sure you will. I'll be handling Calder Marten myself, so if anything goes wrong, I expect I'll have him and his crew killed. But as you know, I like to be prepared."

Shera and Meia bowed as Kerian walked away, taking a couple of Shepherds with her to prepare for the next morning's mission. After a moment of quiet, the two Gardeners and the remainder of the Shepherds returned to the trees, spreading Nakothi's influence as widely as possible.

When she took the Heart to Lucan that evening, she would tell him what was coming. Maybe he could speed up the process, and she was worried for nothing.

But if not, he might be able to give her another weapon.

"I need *at least* three days," Lucan said, grimacing at the Heart. "That's pushing it. For tomorrow morning...I can reinforce the investment that the wrappings already have, but the Intent degrades too quickly. I'm effectively starting over each time. And I guarantee you the Architects haven't finished their box yet."

They hadn't; Shera had checked before coming here.

He picked up a wooden box of his own—the same one Yala had used when she tried to take the Heart from Shera in the bay. "I tried making one myself, but again, it will take at least three or four more days. At its current level, the Heart will eat through this Intent in minutes."

"Do what you can," she said. Hesitantly, she placed her hand on her shear's hilt. She hadn't noticed before, but the voice of the knife in her mind was becoming stronger. And more distinct from Nakothi. The laughter, the whispers—they didn't sound feminine anymore. They sounded richer, deeper. Less like Nakothi, and more like the Emperor.

She wasn't sure why, and it was beginning to disturb her.

With one quick motion, she pulled the bronze blade out of its sheath and tossed it into Lucan's cell. "What can you do with that?"

He gave her an odd look. Lucan had invested her shears many times over the years, bringing out their power, preparing them to be Awakened.

But he had never taken the final step. Awakening was a permanent process. It would make the blade more powerful, but less predictable, and there was no going back.

"Are you...asking me to Awaken it?"

She remained silent, unsure. They had refrained from Awakening the blade up to this point for good reasons. She had enough problems with the corrupt Intent in the knife without making it stronger. For all she knew, Awakening it would bring out powers like the Heart's.

On the other hand, she was sick of being outmatched.

Her first night on *The Testament,* Jyrine Tessella Marten had taken her by surprise and almost gotten the better of her. Shera had fought the rest of the crew, but it was all she could do to escape with her life. On Nakothi's island, once again, she had almost been overwhelmed by the combination of Urzaia and the Children of the Dead Mother. And then two days past, the dead Consultants that had risen in the crypt might have easily killed her if they hadn't been so focused on the Heart.

And now everything was coming to a head. Even the Sleepless were planning something, and they expected the Heart to get stronger, not weaker.

"I don't know," she said finally. "But you don't have time to finish sealing the Heart, and I need an edge. Something else. If I keep fighting like this, eventually I'm going to...lose."

She had almost said "die," but she remembered to hold back at the last second.

Lucan picked up the shear reverently in both hands and placed it on his desk, next to Nakothi's Heart. Then he walked over to the bars, reaching out and holding her by the shoulders.

"Go back to the Capital, Shera," he said quietly. "It's getting so dangerous that you *can't* stay. Do it now. Jorin will know what to do with the Heart."

"Jorin's coming here?" That could change everything. The Regent of the South, Jorin Curse-breaker, was coming to deal with the problem personally. In that case, maybe Shera didn't need to be here after all.

"I suggested that they send word to him as soon as you told me his box was broken," Lucan responded. "It will take him at least a week to get here, no matter how fast he travels, but he should be on his way."

Shera considered it, but eventually she shook her head. "I can't. I might be needed today."

His grip on her shoulders tightened. "Shera, I know you *want* to stay, but I'm not sure you *should.*" He jerked his head toward the Heart. "It wants you here. That's more than enough reason for you to leave."

It would be easy to give in, to let someone else take care of the problem. She was sorely tempted.

"I'm afraid to do anything else," he went on. "Nakothi obviously has a plan. We should wait for Jorin."

As he spoke, she thought she could detect the mere fraction of a whisper, like a quiet breath blowing across dust.

...wait...

Shera moved her eyes between her shear, sitting on Lucan's desk, and the Heart. A moment later, the sound came again.

Wait...

Her blade and Nakothi's Heart were whispering in unison.

Shera backed up from Lucan, breaking his grip, scanning his eyes for any hint of madness. "*We* have to do something. The entire island is in danger." She started walking away, muttering more for her benefit than his. "We can't wait for Jorin to save us."

By the time the Regent got here, she had the suspicion he'd find them already dead. Dead, but not still.

Without knowing why, she found herself standing outside the cell next door, looking in on Jyrine Tessella Marten.

The woman looked worse than Shera had remembered. That should be typical for someone who had remained a captive for a month, but she didn't look weak or malnourished. She looked terrified, yet determined to fight to the bitter end.

She crouched against the back wall of her cell, with her knees drawn to her chest until most of what Shera could see was her red prison uniform. Jyrine's hair was tangled and frizzy, and she was clutching something tightly in her hands. A White Sun, perhaps? Shera had seen Luminians clinging that fiercely to symbols of their religion.

But this girl was a member of the Sleepless cult. An Elder worshiper. Maybe it was a symbol of Othaghor or Kthanikahr. In that case, Shera should probably take it from her, but she didn't have the energy.

Jyrine rose somewhat stiffly to her feet, slipping the Elder symbol around her arm like a bracelet and holding it behind her back as if to hide it. Her naturally tan skin was slightly pale, and the top symbols of her tattoos peeked out of her collar at the side of her neck.

With her right hand, Jyrine began to rake her fingers through her tangled hair. "Shera, isn't it?" she asked. "May I help you with something?"

She didn't *sound* like a woman who had been cowering in terror against the back of her cell five seconds before, but Shera attributed that to her acting skills.

Then again, Shera wasn't sure how to answer the woman's question.

What did she want to know? Why was Shera even talking to her?

Because I don't know what else to do. If the Sleepless were planning something, there was no way Jyrine would tell her, and she didn't have the energy for torture.

Then again, Lucan had said she was surprisingly open. Maybe they could have an honest discussion.

"Why do what you're doing?" she asked. "What is the point?"

Jyrine seemed surprised, but she covered it well. "I'm stuck in a cell, sleeping twelve hours a day. Just trying to while away idle hours, I suppose. Not much point to it."

Light and life, that sounds nice.

Shera sagged forward, resting her forehead against the bars. "I don't want to do this. Elders and the Emperor and living forever...any of it. I just..." She found herself talking, spewing her life out to this stranger, and she put a stop to it. "Well, that's the way it is. So I at least want to know why. What are you doing this *for?* What's the point?"

There had to be a reason that the Sleepless worshiped Elders, or even a goal the Elders worked toward. Maybe if Shera knew what it was, she could find the energy to oppose it.

"Humans are fundamentally selfish, aren't we?" Jyrine said. "No matter what else we do, when it comes down to a moment for action, we will *always* act for ourselves and those closest to us. We spend our whole lives worshiping one person."

She was growing more animated, more excited, as though she'd waited for weeks to deliver this speech.

Shera said nothing, letting the cultist go on.

"And where has that gotten us?" Jyrine continued. "Everyone agrees that it would be better if we were more charitable, more virtuous, simply nicer to our fellow man. But we don't change. We advance, we make discoveries, but the basic nature of humanity remains the same throughout the centuries."

She held up a single finger. "There is only one kind of truly selfless act. And that is anything done in the service of humanity as a *whole*. For all mankind. For anyone, present and future, whether or not we ever see a benefit for ourselves."

It all sounded good up to this point. Idyllic and a little naïve, sure, but good. The sort of utopian ideal that the Emperor had once held.

It sounded *too* good, actually, which meant that the bait was planted and Jyrine was about to set the hook. Sure enough, she stepped forward and gripped the bars, looking at Shera from inches away with a face filled with rapture.

"The Sleepless do not worship Elders. We're not a cult. Nor do we capture and examine them ourselves, like the Blackwatch do. Our goal is to *communicate* with the Great Elders, to establish a common understanding so that we can benefit from just the tiniest fraction of their wisdom. Not for ourselves, you understand. For all of mankind."

Jyrine finished the speech with a self-satisfied smile. "That's not so bad, is it?"

She's insane, Shera thought.

Something inside Shera must have wondered if she was doing the right thing, if keeping the Heart safe was worth all her time and energy. But now, hearing Jyrine's story, she knew she had to keep the Heart out of Sleepless hands at all costs. Out of everyone's hands.

They wanted to *learn* from the Great Elders. From the Dead Mother, whose voice whispered eternally, trying to talk humans into dying so that it could remake them into a horrifying monstrosity. From Kelarac, who kept the souls of those who fell afoul of his deals. From Kthanikahr, who wanted humanity replaced by worms. From Tharlos, who simply wanted to burn it all to the ground.

Shera had wondered why she was fighting, and this was why. Because the alternative was to leave the world to people like this.

She leaned back from the bars, loosening her arms, rolling her neck, and rubbing the ache in her wounded shoulder. She felt as though she'd been taking a long nap, and she was finally waking up.

"So you're idiots," Shera said aloud. "Thanks. That tells me what I wanted to know."

With her right hand, she reached back and pulled out her remaining shear.

Jyrine stiffened and stepped back at the sight, her hand going to the Elder symbol on her bracelet. It wouldn't help her. Shera's knife had enough Intent that it would break straight through the lock, with a little force.

She couldn't afford to let Jyrine live. The woman's own story had made it clear. She was crazy, and she would work as hard as she could to steer the world toward anarchy and destruction.

Then she looked at Jyrine's terrified expression, and she stopped herself.

Lucan would say her life was worth as much as Shera's.

Shera heartily disagreed.

But at the same time...insane and misguided as she was, Jyrine at least seemed to be sincere. *For the good of all mankind.*

Shera turned away, walking toward Lucan's cell. The woman was a danger to herself and others, but she wasn't malicious, and she *was* locked away. If the Sleepless did do something today, Shera wanted to have a prisoner around to question. And Jyrine wasn't going anywhere.

Then the door burst open and Calder Marten walked in.

Shera went into a fighting crouch instinctively, holding her shear steady in one hand. He was flanked by his second-in-command—*Andel*, she thought—a Heartlander man wearing all white. Shortly behind him walked Dalton Foster, the grizzled old man with two pairs of spectacles hanging around his chest. He looked skinny and weak, but he was supposedly one of the greatest gunsmiths in the Empire's history, so Shera didn't discount him.

Behind them, the hall was filled with Consultants. Including Hansin, Lucan's regular guard.

And Kerian, wearing purple. Her eyes were filled with fury and she had her shears in her hands, but she didn't attack.

What was going on? Was this the settlement they'd reached with Calder? Allowing him to visit his wife made sense, but why the show of force?

Is Lucan in danger?

At that instant, Shera noticed a thin golden crown nestled in Calder's red hair. The surprise she'd felt from seeing Kerian was *nothing* compared to the shock that struck her when she recognized that circlet.

He was wearing the Emperor's crown.

"On your knees," Calder commanded, and the order resonated through the hall. It echoed between the stone walls, driving into Shera's skull, pressing on her back like a heavy weight. The order carried with it all the authority of the Emperor himself, all the charisma and influence he'd built up over a dozen centuries.

Shera understood why the other Consultants were following Calder. They were under his control. For a loyal Imperial citizen, someone who had sworn their allegiance to the Emperor and the Empire, such a command would be impossible to resist.

But the Emperor had already set her free.

"Protect the Empire," he had commanded her once. *"Even, if necessary, from me."*

Shera stayed on her feet.

Calder's expression grew frustrated, and he put out a hand as if he thought it added to his power. "Shera, I order you to put down the knife."

She gripped the blade tighter. It was still difficult to move—her body was convinced that any attack against him would be a betrayal of the Emperor—but she didn't drop the weapon.

Dalton Foster seemed satisfied, smirking as he stroked his beard. "There, you see? That's what I expected it to do. This absolute command thing is unnatural. It shouldn't work so well."

Beside him, Kerian glared helplessly, but she didn't say a word.

Ice crawled over Shera's heart once again.

They were keeping her fellow Guild members hostage, using the Emperor's own crown to force Consultants to betray their cause. If she had considered letting Calder live before, now she was determined to see him dead.

"Where did you get that?" she asked coldly, still staring at the crown.

Instead of answering, Calder looked to Lucan. Shera's body tensed, and she held the knife so tightly it shook. She may have problems attacking Calder, but if he threatened Lucan, she would put her knife through his heart no matter what it took.

Lucan seemed calm enough. He lifted a closed chest the size of a jewelry box, from which Nakothi's Heart still spewed whispers. "What do you intend to do with this?" he asked Calder.

With his other hand, he gestured to Shera. *Move over.*

She edged to one side, where he had a clear line to her between the bars. As soon as Calder's attention fully focused on Lucan, and he opened his mouth to speak, Lucan hurled the box at Shera.

She was ready, snatching the box out of the air with her left hand despite a scream of pain from her shoulder. Without looking back, she bolted past Jyrine's cell and farther down the tunnels.

Calder shouted an order, and the hallway filled with the padding of soft Consultant shoes rushing afterwards. She started to dodge from side to side as she ran, expecting a spade in her back at any second.

Nothing struck her.

She didn't dare look back, but she stopped dodging and focused on speed. *He can order them to follow me,* she thought, *but he can't order them to do it well.*

The idea encouraged her as she rushed down the tunnel, and she remained encouraged for exactly ten more seconds. Then she realized that she was lost.

"Does anyone know how to get out of here?" she called.

"Right," Kerian grunted, as though it were difficult for her to speak.

Shera turned right.

CHAPTER EIGHTEEN

TEN YEARS AGO

The Emperor lounged in his chair while the three Gardeners sat stiffly in theirs. He closed the Heart of Nakothi back into its pewter cage, tucking it back down the front of his robe.

That's how he's lived for more than a thousand years. The information stuck in Shera's throat like a chunk of meat. She had never wanted to know *that.* Someone could kill or torture her for knowledge like this, not even counting what the Emperor would do if he thought she had let something slip.

And it was...disappointing, somehow. Shera had never worshiped the Emperor in the same way that others did; she knew that, behind his immense power and centuries of experience, he was just a Reader with more skill than any other. There was nothing divine about him.

But he was still *the Emperor.* The symbol of everything good about humanity, of Imperial stability, of civilization itself. He was beyond change, beyond corruption. Knowing that his long life came from a Great Elder was like learning that he feasted on baby hearts.

Meia kept her expression stoic and her back straight, but her hands were trembling in her lap. Lucan had gone slack in his chair, eyes wide and staring at nothing. It was hard to tell with his dark skin, but it looked as though he'd gone a shade paler than normal.

Compared to those two, Shera figured she was handling the news rather well.

"Forty-eight hours ago, the Blackwatch reported that a member of their number had stolen certain sensitive documents regarding Nakothi and her spawn. Thirty-six hours ago, he hired a Navigator and set out into the Aion. An informant aboard suggested that he means to travel into that sea, to the location of Nakothi's corpse, and remove another of her hearts."

Shera was the only one of the three Consultants still capable of speech, so she asked the question. "She has more than one?"

The Emperor stood from his chair and began to pace. "Twelve. Most of them are no longer viable, but if he can revive one...I am the only one alive who can bind myself to the heart of a Great Elder without going entirely mad. In the worst-case scenario, we'll have an insane immortal wandering the earth, doing the bidding of the Dead Mother."

Meia finally found her voice. "I'm sorry, Highness, but...surely you must have placed *some* security around the island."

"Enough to repel a fleet of ships like this one," the Emperor said. He turned his back to them, staring out a dark window. "Even if I hadn't, there are certain dangers associated with plumbing a Great Elder's corpse. Realistically, this voyage has no chance of success."

"Then why are we here?" Shera asked bluntly.

He turned back to them, clutching the amulet through his robes like a man suffering a heart attack. "I'm not used to basing my decisions on intuition. I prefer plans and data. But I have a feeling that we're not dealing with realistic odds tonight."

As he clenched his fist around the Heart, Shera could have sworn she heard distant whispers.

The Emperor nodded slowly, as if to himself. "Yes...Nakothi's hand is in this game. But it's not the final gambit. If we can stop her here, we may buy ourselves twenty or thirty years. No more."

Shera remained silent, having no idea how to respond.

Suddenly decisive, the Emperor marched over to a blank wall and placed his hand against it. The painted wood shifted and flowed away from his touch, bunching at the corners.

Behind the wall stood a set of ancient armor on the stand, lacquered white, painted with the sun-and-moon crest of the Aurelian Empire. Beside it rested a pair of matched swords, each with a bronze blade.

Shera could feel the pressure from the weapons all the way across the room, like a wind pressing against her mind. Lucan staggered backwards, knocking over his chair and throwing up a hand to protect himself.

"Make your preparations," the Emperor said, without turning around. "We leave in one hour."

Meia had gone to see the alchemists about potions, solutions, and general upkeep she might need for the mission ahead, leaving Shera and Lucan behind.

Shera tied her belt, tested her shears in their sheaths, replenished her stock of spades, refreshed the poison on her needles, and checked the silk sash she wore wrapped above the belt. The sash had a thousand uses, from a garrote to an emergency climbing rope, and she had been reluctant to replace it with her new knife-belt. After a second's thought, she added a few more trinkets she might need: her breathing-reed, a waterproof case of matches, and an emergency flare.

She kept checking her equipment to keep her mind occupied, but she knew she was ready. They had returned from an assignment only hours before. Her gear hadn't gone anywhere.

Lucan's preparations were more complex. He had his own set of shears buckled onto the small of his back, but the rest of his belt was hidden behind pouches, loops, and pockets filled with invested bric-a-brac. As she watched, he stuffed a thumb-sized hammer into one loop, poured some glittering sand into a pouch, and filled a pocket with what looked like acorns. Finally, he tucked a copper spoon into his boot.

"Preparing for breakfast?" Shera asked.

Normally he would have returned a joke of his own, but this time he rubbed his hands together, glancing around the room as if looking for something else to add to his collection. "It was forged by a young smith who wanted to escape his apprenticeship, and stolen by a petty thief. He used it to burrow out of a makeshift prison. With all the Intent invested in this spoon, it will be better for digging our way free than any shovel."

"It's still a *spoon*, though," Shera said, striving for levity.

"Not if we need it. I'm prepared to Awaken it, if I have to." Then he stared at her, so hard and so long that she shifted back.

"You don't feel any different, do you?" he asked.

Quickly, Shera catalogued her emotions, trying to discover if she did, in fact, feel any different than usual. Her heart was beating a little faster, and she might have been a tad more self-conscious. Both normal, considering that Lucan was asking her personal questions out of a clear sky.

"I'm getting ready to go to work," she said, hoping that would pass for an answer.

"We could *die* tonight."

"Technically, we could die any night."

But nothing would shake Lucan out of his dire mood. His hands flexed, as though he meant to knead each word as it passed through the air. "We're not strangling a wine merchant in his sleep. If anything goes wrong tonight, we could be facing Elders and Navigators and disgraced Blackwatch. We're so far past our depth we can't even see the shore. And you're not nervous?"

Shera placed a hand on his arm to steady him; alone, this close, the simple contact felt unusually bold. "There's more at stake in this game, but it's still the same old game we've been playing our whole lives. There's nothing new here, so long as we keep winning."

In truth, she didn't feel much about the upcoming mission. If there were targets, she would kill them. If not, she'd have a night relaxing with Lucan and Meia. Even in the worst case, she could still catch a nap on the ride out to the island.

Sure, they might die. But a storm might capsize their boat, or the Emperor could choose to have them executed on a whim. No amount of worrying would change it, and there would be nothing to complain about afterwards.

Death did what she wanted, when she wanted, and nothing could stop her.

Compared to the outcome of the mission, Shera was far more nervous about the results of this conversation.

Then Lucan threw his arms around her, and her heart tried to drill its way out of her chest.

"I'm not going to let you go," he whispered into her ear. "This time, I can stop it."

She would have wondered what he was talking about if she hadn't been too busy wondering what she was supposed to *do.* No one had taught her this. Should she return the embrace? That seemed logical, right? Maybe she should kiss him; that's what the girls in Kerian's romance novels would have done. But maybe that was too much, too fast. What would a normal girl her age do?

For the first time, she realized that the only people she knew were spies and assassins. And that maybe a Consultant's training didn't prepare her for everything.

Ultimately, she stayed frozen for far too long. Until Lucan lowered his hands, seized the hilts of her shears, and pulled the knives from their sheaths.

For that situation, she *had* been trained.

She drove a knee up between his legs, doubling him over. Then she slipped under one of his arms and slid around behind him, pulling his own set of shears from his back. She faced Lucan with one of his bronze knives in each of her hands, knees bent, balancing on the balls of her feet in a knife-fighting stance.

Shera came back to herself when she realized Lucan was still kneeling on the ground, groaning, her shears forgotten on the floor next to him.

Lucan would never hurt me, she realized. She *knew* that, and had never really doubted it, but at the same time…

Trusting too easily is asking for a knife in the back. That was one of Ayana's sayings, not Maxwell's, and she'd meant it to apply to non-Guild members. But it seemed Shera had taken it too much to heart.

She dropped the blades and stepped hesitantly over to him. "I'm sorry, I just…reacted."

Lucan flopped over onto his back, looking up at her with a strange expression. It looked like a mix between amusement and pain and sadness and resignation, and she wished she had his powers so that she could know what he was thinking.

"It was my fault," he said from the floor. "I should have seen that coming. But, I—"

He interrupted himself, levering up to a sitting position. "We've been together for so long, I feel like we're on the same page of the same book. We spend every waking minute together, and there's no one else who's done what we've done. It's you and me, and maybe Meia, and then the rest of the world."

He picked up one of her shears, staring into it as if to find his reflection in the dull blade. Maybe he was looking into the weapon's past, Reading it, or maybe he found it easier to face the knife than her.

"You're like a sister to me, and a friend, and maybe something…else. I don't know. My point is, I look at you one second, and it's like you're perfect. And then…"

He didn't take his eyes away from the knife. "…and then you scare me. You might be the most frightening person I've ever met. You go dark, and cold, and the person I know goes away."

Shera was starting to long for the Emperor and his horror stories about the Great Elders. They hadn't disturbed her nearly this much.

Because he was right.

Something was broken inside her, a part was missing, a cog had been stripped away. Maybe Maxwell had taken it away from her, or maybe she'd been born without all the pieces that normal people got. But she *was* different, and she wasn't sure how to change.

Or even if she wanted to.

Lucan smiled, an expression without any humor whatsoever. It was the smile of a Gardener. "But I can tell you one thing, Shera. If I had to put money on one of us making it through this mission alive, I'd bet on you. So that's what I'm going to do."

He crossed his legs, arranging her shears in front of him. "I'm investing everything I can into your shears. I thought about Awakening them, but I'm not sure we have the time."

"What will that do?"

"Give you a better chance. I do need to be alone for this next part. I wanted you to know..." he waved the words away. "It doesn't matter. But I'm doing everything I can to make sure that if Nakothi herself rises tonight, you'll be able to handle it."

She thanked him, and tried to say something, though she wasn't quite sure what.

In the end, she just left.

CHAPTER NINETEEN

Let's say you want to become a Soulbound.

First, you should get yourself something with power. And I mean real power, not a gardening can that your grandmother invested to grow daisies. I'm talking about a spear you used to kill a Duskwinder, or the eye of an Elder.

Second, you need to know this thing inside and out. Don't take somebody else's spear—use it to kill the Duskwinder yourself. Blind that Elder with your bare hands. If you can't do that, at least carry it around for a few years. The more the object means to you, the better your chances of bonding with it.

Third, get a Reader to Awaken your object. This might take a while.

If you did it correctly, the object will become your Vessel. You'll be a Soulbound. Congratulations.

If you didn't, you'll probably be dead. Awakening powerful artifacts isn't a game.

—UNKNOWN SPEAKER

(FROM THE THIRD JOURNAL OF ESTYR SIX, QUOTING AN OLDER SOURCE)

Calder Marten stayed outside Lucan's cell for a long time, arguing with his wife. Lucan tried to write down most of it, but the stone wall did a surprisingly good job of muting sounds. Remnants of his own Intent, perhaps.

When Calder finally left, leaving Jyrine silent in her own cage, Lucan counted slowly to one hundred. Then, once he was certain that someone hadn't lingered in the hallway, he pulled out Shera's knife.

He had taken the glove from his right hand, so his senses were exposed to the raw nature of the world. Nakothi's influence drifted in this cell like a stench, tingling his skin, drawing his thoughts to dark places.

I can rebuild you, it promised him. *I can make you strong.*

He placed his fingers to the surface of Shera's blade, and instantly recognized that the malevolent, whispering voice wasn't *only* coming from the Heart.

The knife is hungry. It has tasted the blood of Elders and of great men, and it thirsts for more. It needs not only their blood but their Intent, the power of significant death, for this weapon feeds on more than simple meat. It is a greedy thief, a covetous glutton, stealing the power of its victims for its own.

While the Dead Mother destroys bodies and builds them anew, this blade breaks down defenses, building them back up into its own weapons. The stronger the target, the greater the damage.

The blade is aware of Lucan, in its own rudimentary way, and it wants *him. It can feel his strength, his willpower, his focused Intent. If only it were capable, it would lunge from the table and bury itself in his throat.*

Lucan managed to tear his hand away from the knife, jerking it back while breathing as though he had run five miles. In addition to the weapon's own long and significant history, the Emperor himself had laid a hand on it, he was sure. As had Lucan, multiple times, trying to give Shera a better weapon for her own protection.

Well, it seemed he and the Emperor had done their jobs too well. The Dead Mother's power had soaked into the blade, corrupting its original purpose and its deep store of Intent.

It was easily significant enough to Awaken, now. The weapon was on the verge of Awakening *itself.*

But Lucan had to decide if he wanted to.

He jerked his glove on with more than necessary force, pacing the length of his cell. *Five steps, turn. Five steps, turn.* He had been in here so long that the process was subconscious.

Lucan rubbed his hands together, building up friction, staring at the battered bronze as he thought. Shera's safety came first, of course. Now he regretted that he hadn't taken her up on her offer to break him free; if he was out, he could help defend her on his own.

Defend her. In some ways, it was a ludicrous idea. In battle, having him standing in front of her would only slow her down. He had all the training of the Gardeners perfected by years studying under the strongest Reader in history, but Shera and Meia were deadly in a way he could never match. He thought too much, and it interfered with his instincts.

There was only one thing he could do for her: support her from behind. As he'd always tried to do, with his powers.

And now she needed him more than ever...but *what* did she need?

Did she need a more powerful weapon? This shear had always been powerful enough, but she couldn't keep it under control. So she never drew it anymore. He could Awaken the blade, but that could easily make her control problems worse. More importantly, it could give Nakothi more influence. If Nakothi's power had infested the knife to the core, corrupting its Intent entirely, then the Dead Mother would also corrupt any Awakening. Then, in addition to the Heart, they'd have *another* artifact of a Great Elder to deal with.

He glared at the knife as though blaming it for his problems.

So he could Awaken the knife and give Shera a more powerful weapon, but put her at greater risk. Or he could do nothing, and hope she didn't need to fight anyone truly formidable.

Like a Champion. Or a Great Elder.

...both of which would be present, in one form or another, on the Gray Island today.

He had to resist the urge to kick the knife.

Okay, start over. He was thinking about this in the wrong way, turning over the problem in his mind again and again instead of searching for a solution.

What did she actually need?

She would need a second blade. One that could kill Elderspawn and alchemically enhanced Soulbound, preferably.

But she needed it to work *with* her, instead of distracting her. To do what she told it to do.

Struck by inspiration, Lucan seized the knife by the hilt, ignoring its delighted cries. He folded his legs and sat, placing the shear on his lap, peeling both his gloves off.

For a full minute he sat there, focusing his Intent, picturing clearly what he wanted.

I don't want to change its purpose. I want to channel *it. I will learn this blade, I will know its very nature, and when I finally understand it...that is when I will bring it to life.*

Mind firm, vision clear, Lucan placed both hands on the knife and Read.

The weapon's lifetime stretches back through the entire history of the Empire. There is no life it can't take, no power it can't steal, no defense it can't break. And even among others of its kind, this blade is unique. It has harvested lives of unimaginable significance, unfathomable depth...and Lucan needs it to do so again. He begs for every shred of power the blade can offer him.

To protect Shera, he needs this knife to Awaken.

Guided by Kerian, Shera eventually made it out of the maze. She emerged into the blinding sun, but she threw herself out of the trap door and over a nearby boulder before she could get adjusted to the light.

The other Consultants had caught up.

She wasn't sure how the crown's orders affected them, exactly, but when one of the Shepherds reached her, he slashed at her legs with a knife. Clearly, it didn't prevent them from giving her advice, but it must pressure them to use force when necessary.

She jumped over the knife, kicking the Shepherd's face into the dirt. "Sorry," he muttered into the ground, pushing himself up and renewing his attack.

Another Shepherd reached her, and she slammed the Heart's box over his head. It broke his scalp, leaving a stain of blood on the corner of the box, but it was still better than using her shear. She didn't want to kill anyone.

Then Kerian reached her, still wearing a purple dress instead of her blacks, and the situation got much more dangerous.

Kerian was probably twenty years older than Shera, so she should have been at least a little slower and weaker. But Shera was exhausted. She still hadn't recovered from the fight on Nakothi's island, her left shoulder was beginning to leak through its bandages, and she was fighting with one blade. Worse, she had to fight with the Heart's box in one hand.

Her mentor had no such restrictions.

Kerian slashed with both shears, following up with a kick that almost took Shera in the gut. Meanwhile, the Shepherds that Calder had snared tried to sneak around, coming at her from all sides. They attacked with hands and feet whenever possible, trying not to use blades, but Shera could do nothing but evade and withdraw.

The field with the exit to the labyrinth was wide and scattered with boulders, like many of the spaces on the island, and Shera tried to use the elevation to her advantage. She leapt from one boulder to another, staying ahead of the crowd, forcing them to react to her. There was a ring of trees around the clearing, and she even trudged through the undergrowth, hoping that the bushes would slow her attackers.

But eventually, they would catch her.

She had no choice but to find help. Any Consultant who wasn't commanded by the Emperor's crown should help her, once she had a chance to explain the situation. Kerian might even be able to back up her story.

Of course, that was only if she managed to get away for that long.

Kerian dropped down beside her, driving a shear at her neck. Shera almost didn't notice, but Kerian managed to choke out a whispered, *"Dodge,"* before she struck.

Shera raised the hand with the box and used it to stop Kerian's wrist, but the Councilor's other knife came around at Shera's ribs.

She managed to knock the second strike aside with the box, but that freed the first shear to nick her shoulder. If she hadn't lunged forward at the last second, it would have been worse than that.

The pain freed her anger. This wasn't fair. She hadn't asked for this. All she wanted was to go back to her room and sleep.

But she couldn't leave the Heart of Nakothi free. It was her responsibility: the Emperor had seen to that. She *could not* let it go, no matter what she had to do.

With her pain and anger came the cold.

Shera dropped the box, letting a Shepherd dive for it. Even Kerian was distracted by it, the Heart drawing her attention for one instant.

Stay, stay, stay and be reborn, the Heart whispered. For a brief second Shera wondered what that meant. Did Nakothi want them to "stay" in one place? Stay close to the Heart? Stay on the island?

And then a second later it didn't matter.

She kicked in the side of Kerian's knee. There came the snap and tear of cartilage, but no other sound—the older Gardener remained absolutely silent. She slashed out with both shears, more instinct than skill, and Shera dodged one while seizing her left wrist. Then she twisted, releasing another painful sound, and Kerian's left-hand knife dropped to the ground.

Her face was pale, set in an agonizing grimace, but she said nothing. She tried to attack with her second shear, but this time Shera could be merciful: she withdrew a non-lethal needle, sticking it into the base of Kerian's neck.

With that, the Shepherds were on her.

She fought ruthlessly this time, standing over the box like a bear defending her cub. With her right hand, she slashed at limbs and joints, trying to remove her enemies without killing them. They were still fellow Consultants.

But she wasn't too careful anymore. If they got themselves killed, they could blame Calder Marten.

One man lunged at her, and she cracked the hilt of her shear against his temple. His body fell limp on the ground, forcing her to kick the box out from under him like a ball lest he collapse on top of it. Head injuries were tricky; he might wake up in a few hours, and he might not wake up at all.

She knew what Lucan would have thought, but only one thing came to her mind: *Good. He won't be getting back up.*

A dagger flashed in the air, and she struck it down with her bronze blade, meeting a lunging Shepherd a second later with a fist to his throat. But a third was behind him, and this one caught her in a tackle around the waist, knocking her off-balance.

As they rolled, her foot caught the tip of the box and sent it rolling into the clearing. The Heart didn't tumble out, but the lid cracked.

Fear shocked Shera's limbs into action, and she moved on instinct.

She stabbed the Shepherd in the chest.

It was a young woman behind the mask—younger, even, than Shera herself. Her brown hair spilled out over the ground, and her eyes widened in shock.

Shera didn't hesitate, pulling her blade from the woman's chest and wiping off the blood. *A casualty. Oh, well. I tried.*

She should have had some other reaction, she was sure, but she couldn't quite bring herself to care.

The remaining Shepherds seemed to slow down. Either what she had done to their companion had shocked them into immobility, or the crown's command was beginning to wear off, or both. No matter what the reason, she was grateful for it.

Because it allowed her to reach the box quickly.

...at least, it should have.

When she got to the gap between boulders where the Heart should have been, where she *knew* it had flown after she'd kicked it, she found nothing but disturbed grass.

"Who took it?" Shera asked flatly, looking around at the Shepherds. She raised her voice, *"Who took the box?"*

No one answered.

Finally, she raised her bronze shear, the symbol of a Gardener, over her head. "Find the box!" she ordered.

Slowly, they dispersed, the injured limping off and the healthy blending smoothly with the surrounding trees. She had hoped that would work: by playing off what remained of Calder Marten's order, she was able to get them to listen to her own.

The Shepherds bled away, leaving only Shera and the crippled Kerian.

Shera regarded the woman who had adopted her into the Consultants and had no idea what to say. She didn't feel quite as cold anymore, and when the ice retreated, it left only shame.

"I'll find an Architect," she said eventually.

Kerian's face screwed up in confusion. "What? Go after the Heart!"

She was right, but Shera still felt like she needed to say something. "I'm sorry."

Kerian shook her head, braids waving. "You did what you had to. I'll take it out on Calder Marten, not you. But now you need to *go.*"

With nothing else to say, Shera ran away from the clearing, thinking as she moved. She had virtually no chance of tracking the Heart at this point, so she had to anticipate where it would end up.

Had one of the Shepherds taken it while she was distracted? In that case, they would likely hide it somewhere on the Island and listen to Nakothi's song. If Calder's crew had managed to take it, on the other hand, they would likely bring it back to their captain. He would give the Heart to Naberius Clayborn, who would bond with it for immortality.

The best bet, then, would be to find a member of Calder's crew. Either Naberius would be with them, or they would know where to find him.

To do that, she could simply return to the docks and wait for them to board *The Testament...*

But there was another way. She knew where one of his crewmen had gone.

And it was a lot closer.

In an underground arena, unused for centuries, Meia fought an Izyrian gladiator.

Urzaia Woodsman's scarred face was transported by focus and sheer enjoyment, his hair tied back, his mismatched armor creaking as he ran. His black hatchets remained dull in the light of distant quicklamps, as though they ate the light.

He ran at her like a charging stallion, feet kicking up sand, and brought one of his weapons down at her head.

She slipped aside with inhuman speed, and that black blade hit a chest-high wooden crate. The arena was surrounded by rows of stone benches big enough to hold thousands of people, the floor wide enough to show off dozens of gladiators or fighting Kameira at once. But the men and women who once filled these seats were not interested in a plain spectacle. They wanted a game. So the floor was littered with not only sand, but devices and obstacles of every description.

Stone pillars, pits filled with nets, wooden blocks of various heights and sizes. One portion of the sand was even covered in inch-long spikes beneath the sand, as she learned when Urzaia walked over them without care, crushing them beneath his feet.

Most of those obstacles were now destroyed.

Meia returned the strike, swinging her shear with enough force to drive a nail through stone. He stepped back, grinning his gap-toothed grin, and then actually *flipped* all the way back, landing on his hands and kicking up.

The toe of his boot caught her wrist, sending up a flare of pain and knocking her blade wide. That much agony in the joint meant that her grip *should* loosen. Instead, she tightened it, forcing the power in her veins to bend to her will.

The Kameira inside her screamed. They demanded rage, fury, cowardice, stealth, hunger, deceit, and a thousand other childish, mewling desires.

She gave them only the iron bars of self-control.

Heal me, she demanded, and forced the Deepstrider blood to the surface.

The Deepstrider couldn't understand why she wouldn't attack with overwhelming force, sweeping him aside and devouring him in one bite. Protracted battles were foreign to it, and it was growing impatient.

But it wasn't the Deepstrider's body. It was Meia's, and the Deepstrider's power served her.

Her wrist sprouted a ring of blue scales as it began to heal.

She felt her eyes blaze as she launched forward, tracking every tiny motion of Urzaia's muscles. She didn't need to win in this arena today, but she needed to delay her opponent.

And there was only one way to delay a Champion: to give him a good fight.

So she attacked, because if she only dodged and defended, he would get bored. His fist flashed, too fast for even her to catch, and she almost fell for it. But she had anticipated the attack and ducked, driving her left-hand shear at his stomach.

He jerked out of the way, catching her shoulder with his elbow and slamming her aside.

"Good!" he shouted. His voice was sized for the arena, and he held both hatchets up as though calling for applause from his invisible audience. "Very good! There are not only cowards and thieves in your guild, I see."

The Nightwyrm raged and rampaged, and for a moment she had to endure a spasm under her skin as her flesh tried to attack Urzaia without her.

She was playing a strategic game, but the alchemists had given her a body meant for open combat. Like any weapon, it could be used against her as well as by her.

"What are you doing here?" Meia asked, taking advantage of the lull in the combat. "What do you want out of this?"

He pointed his hatchet at her head, though he didn't stop moving, even for an instant. He was constantly taking slow, smooth steps as if he meant to circle around her. Even as she listened for his answer, she forced herself to match him.

"To fight you," he declared. "On the ship, that first night, your friend ran away. Then, on the cursed island, *you* ran away. You will not run this time."

And he leaped at her. No matter how strong he was, he shouldn't have been able to leap that distance, over the stalagmite obstacle in his way...but he did, sailing over it as though he meant to fly.

So his Vessel does come from the Sandborn Hydra, she thought. *It has to.* Most Kameira had at least one miraculous ability, which Greenwardens claimed derived from their inhuman Intent. The Sandborn Hydra was one of the Kameira that the alchemists had used in enhancing her, but only as far as improving her strength and durability. She had no extra power.

But in the wild, Sandborn Hydras were said to have developed the ability to control their weight. They could creep over dunes of sand without leaving a footprint or disturbing a single grain, or they could strike from the air with the force of a collapsing temple.

That was the rumor. She wasn't sure how much was based in fact.

However, as Urzaia Woodsman fell toward her, she thought it would be prudent to get out of the way.

Your power is mine, the blade whispered.

"I will give it to you," Lucan muttered back. "You will need as much power as you can get, to protect Shera."

To take lives, the knife countered.

"You must take lives to protect Shera."

To feed.

"In Shera's service."

From the knife's history, he pulled out images of Shera, brightening each picture as though refreshing a coat of paint. Shera receiving the blade as a girl, determined to become a Consultant. Shera focusing herself before a kill. Shera encountering invested armor, pushing the blade deeper, begging it to break through the defenses.

...to break down barriers.

"Any that stand in her way."

To turn power against the powerful.

"Against any that threaten her."

His head began to throb painfully, as though he had taken a big bite of snow. Reader burn, he could feel it. It happened when he overused his powers, and he'd been pushing himself to the limit today. The pain could overwhelm him, knock him flat on its back, if he kept Reading.

But he only had a little farther to go.

As long as he wasn't distracted.

"Lucan?" Jyrine called, from the cell next door. "Is there someone else there?"

Lucan remained silent, trying to stay in his trance, trying not to lose the thread of the Reading. If he ended an Awakening halfway through, it would be worse than simply having to start over; the blade might Awaken on its own, without his guidance, and no one could predict what it would become then.

"Lucan, can you hear me?"

She slapped her palm against the stone separating them, trying to get his attention.

"No!" he shouted back. "No one's here! Please, I'm trying to concentrate!"

His vision of the knife's history wavered, cut with an image of his actual cell, and he focused all his attention on the Reading. His head felt as though it would split in half, but the vision stabilized.

"But I heard voices," Jyrine shouted.

"It's me! I'm talking to myself! Now will you please be *quiet!*"

The image shook again, and he almost lost it, the knife's memories flashing by one by one as though he had been hurled through a vast gallery of paintings. He froze at the sight of one in particular, a memory that should have been significant beyond all others, but that he had failed to find until now.

The bronze blade, piercing a gray-green heart. Sludge pumped out of the organ's exposed flesh, and somewhere an Elder let out a harsh scream.

Just next to this image was another, as though they were two halves of the same event. The blade piercing another heart, this one red, and human, and inside layers of skin and muscle.

Two kills, two different times, inextricably linked.

Lucan seized on those images, pouring all his Intent into them, focusing their significance and giving them purpose.

In his lap, the bronze weapon floated into the air. After a few seconds, it hung in front of his eyes, slowly revolving.

This is you, he said, shining a beacon of light onto those two related images. *This is what you are.*

Two powerful kills, both at Shera's hand, greatly increasing the blade's power.

I am... the knife whispered.

To Lucan's senses, the whole room shuddered with power, and the bronze blade flickered green.

Sweat rolled down his temples, and he felt like a Watchman had pounded seven iron nails into the back of his skull. But he persevered.

He couldn't stop now. He'd prepared for this moment for years.

Everything I've done for Shera, everything she's done for me, everything we've shared...that's the only way I could do this. He shared a connection to this weapon as deep as to his own shears, maybe deeper.

Through his connection to Shera, he was bound to this blade.

Everything was prepared. His Intent was gathered, the blade's history waiting at the surface. He'd stacked the wood, soaking it in alchemist's fire-oil.

Now he only needed to provide a spark.

He drew on his desire, his need, his *Intent* to make Shera as powerful as possible. He forced it all into the blade—even the pain of Reader burn simply forged his will, making him shout with effort. Wisps of pale green light sprung into being, floating around the knife like disembodied spirits.

He felt the spark take, the fire begin to kindle.

And the blade began to whisper to him once again.

"You are the taker of lives, the thief of secrets," Lucan declared. His words bound the blade once spoken, fusing with its significance, defining its purpose. "You are that which turns power against power. You are the death of the powerful."

As the Awakening came to its end, the cell filling with green light, the ancient weapon said one more word to him.

Its name.

He reached up, seizing the floating blade by its hilt, reversing it point-down. "You will be called Syphren, the Whispering Death!"

And with one final surge of Intent, he slammed the weapon down into the ground.

It sunk easily into the stone, filling the cracks with green light.

The room shook, and he could swear he heard Jyrine shouting next door. He even thought he felt the power of the Awakened weapon echo over there, but his Reader's senses were so burned out, it could have been nothing more than his imagination.

He collapsed, falling onto his cot, panting. He barely had the strength to pull on his gloves, but once he did, he felt much better. The gloves were invested to keep his Reading under control, to prevent him from sensing anything he didn't want to, and pulling them on felt like shutting his eyes after staring directly into the sun.

Now, he understood why most Readers took days to Awaken an object, even after they spent months or years getting to know the subject. Doing it this quickly risked more than a mistake; he could have killed himself.

For the first time, he rolled over to look at the weapon he had helped create.

Syphren had changed shape slightly—it looked longer and sleeker, for one thing, though it was hard to tell when all he could see was the hilt and the inch or so of bare blade sticking out of the floor.

And the blade was what *really* caught his attention.

What had once been ancient, battered bronze now looked like a glass window. A window looking into some strange netherworld.

At first glance, the blade seemed to be filled with solid green light, but closer inspection revealed that they weren't lights, but hands. Dozens and dozens of shining green hands, pressing against the weapon as though trying to push their way through into the world.

It was a busy crowd, as some hands got shoved away and others shoved forward to press their palms against what looked like glass. But every inch of the hands, where they touched the blade, glowed bright green.

Well, that's disturbing.

His Reader's senses were so closed that he couldn't hear the blade whispering, though he was sure it wasn't quiet. He glanced around the cell for a moment before he spotted them: the rags he had used to bind Nakothi's Heart before he had finished that box. They were invested to restrain power, especially that of the Elders, and they would do nicely to keep this knife from killing anyone until Shera wanted it too.

Gingerly, careful not to let any of his bare skin touch the weapon, Lucan wound the strips of cloth around the knife from hilt to tip. When it was fully covered, he tossed it onto his blanket, and then wrapped that around it too. He didn't want it to cause any accidents when he took it to Shera.

Then he turned and regarded the bars on his cell. If he used the knife himself, he wouldn't be able to hold himself back from Reading it, and then the pain of the Reader burn would likely have him screaming on the ground. Besides, he had Awakened the blade specifically for Shera to use, and it might turn on him.

So how am I supposed to get out of here?

CHAPTER TWENTY

TEN YEARS AGO

The knife's first memories had faded over the years, like rumors of a dream.

The totem-man is the only one in the refugee tunnels trusted to make bronze. Once he worked the forges of Kthanikahr, blending the alloys that became the chains, cages, and muzzles keeping human slaves in check. He has little knowledge of his own—something less than an alchemist, in an age before alchemy.

When he pours this batch of bronze into its mold, he adds a splash of his own special concoction. A potion, he believes, that will allow the metal to steal souls.

The bronze cools into ingots, making their way to a smith. He knows the totem-man is a little crazy, but crazy or not, he still delivers good material. Maybe the metal will steal souls, and maybe not, but the smith knows what matters: the skill of the craftsman.

It's up to him to make blades that will kill anything. He's heard all the tales of the liberator, going around murdering the Great Elders and their servants, so the smith is determined to do his part. His *blades will free mankind.* His *blades will cut through even the immortality of the Elders.*

Every beat of his hammer carries that Intent.

In Lucan's mind, the scene shifts.

The Reader kneels inside a trench, pouring her Intent into these fresh-forged weapons. Now that she's about to die, her mind is even sharper and more focused than ever.

The forces of Kthanikahr surround the trench, squirming over the ground like mobile nests of tentacles. She can hear them on the approach, a sound like a thousand slurping tongues. No one captured by the Worm Lord returns with their sanity intact, so she has no intention of being taken alive.

But before she dies, she invests all of her hopes, her dreams, and her wishes into these newborn blades. She urges them to leech power from their targets, to destroy the enemy with its own defenses.

She believes that's the only way to defeat an Elder creature: to turn its power in on itself.

The knives survived that battle. The Reader did not.

Some time later, on a land Lucan will know as the Gray Island, an assassin kneels. For years, she has served the Mistress of the Mists as one of the Am'haranai: an order of killers for hire in this long war. Now, the whole order has been hired by the man they call the Liberator. The one who, it is whispered, will one day lead mankind.

As a symbol of their new contract, the Mistress' twelve most capable servants each receive a pair of bronze knives.

The assassin's focus bleeds into the shiny, new weapons. With these blades, she will cut down the Liberator's enemies. She will deliver death with one strike, and she will never need a second.

Then the blade draws blood.

Again and again and again and again.

Conflicting purposes, powerful Intent, crossed and compounded and reinforced one another for a thousand years, building a matrix of significance so complex and powerful that the single pound of bronze feels like a living thing. Layers of hopes and dreams and beliefs and emotions were stacked one upon the other, forming strata that stretch down to the core of what this weapon *was.*

And in that core was a common thread, a seed of inspiration.

If only he could seize it.

With enough time, Lucan could Awaken the knife, but that process would lock the object in a single form. It would never absorb Intent again. And he got the feeling that Shera would add to the story of this blade, such that when it finally was Awakened, it would rival any weapon the Empire had ever produced.

One day, Elders will tremble before this blade. But not today.

This is just one step forward.

With all the force of his will, with everything the Emperor had ever taught him, Lucan dragged out a piece of the knife's potential. Then he added his own power to it, feeding it, like slipping twigs one by one into a fire.

When he'd finished, the blade seemed to hum in his grip. Curls of the carpet pushed away slightly, as though pressed down by a phantom wind.

One down. One to go.

Shera found that she liked sleeping aboard a ship. Once she got used to the motion, it was actually quite soothing, and the lapping of the waves against the hull could form a lullaby to the right ears. Most important of all, she was surrounded by water. No one would show up and bother her, at least until they reached their destination.

Which, in a ship propelled by the Emperor, did not take long. Scarcely had they boarded this abandoned ship when a shadow seized it from beneath and carried it off into the Aion with the speed of a musket-ball.

The vessel itself was fully stocked and ready to sail, but the sailors had abandoned it only minutes before the three Gardeners and their Emperor had arrived.

Even at those unnatural speeds, it would still take several hours to reach the island. The Emperor stood motionless at the bow, navigating. Even the other two Consultants slept; Meia to recover from whatever the alchemists had done to her body, Lucan to restore himself after his efforts investing Shera's shears.

Now the twin blades hung from a tack on the opposite wall of her cabin. They all but quivered with eagerness to be used.

Shera, meanwhile, had taken this opportunity to sleep. She'd curled up on a bunk and let the spray of the waves and the occasional hiss of the sea monster sing her to sleep.

When the ship crashed, she awoke in midair.

There was no time to react. Her left shoulder slammed into one of the beams on the overhead, narrowly missing the quicklamp that shook at the end of its chain like a bull trying to break free.

She tried to get her feet underneath her before she landed, but she only succeeded in landing—hard and painfully—on her knees.

The ship continued to buck as she scrambled to her feet, the Kameira and the ocean both roaring around her. She grabbed her knife-belt, but the ship pitched forward, bruising her knuckles. Her pouch was full of spades, but when the ship rocked back, she cracked the back of her head and almost spilled the throwing-knives all over the cabin.

Whatever's happening on deck, it's got to be better than this.

She finished scooping up her gear and scrambled up the ladder, running headfirst into a spray of water so thick that she saw nothing else.

The ship jerked to port so hard that she pulled one of her shears, driving the blade deep into nearby railing. By the time the ship finally steadied, her eyes burned from the salt water, and her knuckles ached from keeping a grip on the blade.

Then the spray subsided, and she could see again.

The Emperor stood on the railing at the very prow of the ship, as rock-solid on the slippery wood as if he'd been nailed there. He had his arms raised as though to embrace the oncoming waves, a bronze-bladed sword in his right hand and pale armor gleaming in the moonlight.

Meia stood behind him, seeming just as comfortable on the pitching deck as the Emperor. Lucan, Shera was pleased to see, had tied himself into the rigging.

Ahead of them, the ocean writhed with the dead.

At first, she could only see a pale mound of bones, like an island made entirely of human skulls. Then something pushed its way through the cave at the front: the long, pale, neck of a giant slug, with a human head as big across as any ship's sail. The disturbing face turned to the ship, its expression full of mourning, and let out a howl.

Shera staggered her way over to the outer railing for a closer look. All around the skull-tortoise, the surf frothed with a thousand other monstrosities. Human corpses, still wearing tattered clothing, with the snapping claws of crabs. Sharks clad in exoskeletons of yellowed bone. Colorless worms with rows of gnashing teeth. Hundreds upon hundreds of horrors.

All locked in battle with a great leviathan.

The same Kameira, she now realized, that had been pulling their ship.

Its serpentine head rose from the water like a lighthouse, towering over their mast. Its maw filled with hundreds of needle-fine teeth, its eyes orbs of solid blue. It reached out with long, webbed claws, slashing through legions of the dead until the water clouded with milk-pale blood.

The skull-tortoise howled again, and the leviathan's jaws snapped it up, lifting it high into the air. Drops of seawater fell from the bruise-purple underside of the tortoise, pattering the ship's deck like rain.

The leviathan closed its jaws, and the giant tortoise was sheared in half. A legion of skulls dropped from the sky, most plopping into the water. A few struck the deck with the sound of cannons, rolling back and forth across the planks.

"What *is* this?" Meia shouted, her voice full of horror.

For once, Shera knew how she felt. Killing men had never bothered her, but this…this was the stuff of nightmares.

The Emperor pointed his sword up at the sea serpent, which still chewed on the tortoise's rubbery flesh. "That is called a Deepstrider. Once, they made long-distance sea travel impossible."

A group of the corpse crabs had swarmed onto the Deepstrider's tail, slicing off long bits of flesh and sending purplish blood dribbling back into the water. The Kameira howled in pain, tossing the remains of the skull-tortoise aside, and set about raking the enemies with its claws once more.

"Are these *your* defenses?" Shera yelled. "Is this how you protect the island?"

The Emperor gripped the hilt of his blade in both hands. "I have steered us through my own defenses. These are the children of the Dead Mother."

He raised a small whistle to his lips and blew. It glinted blue in the pre-dawn light; Shera found herself wondering if it was made from the same stuff as the Deepstrider's scales.

The Kameira turned at the shrill sound of the whistle, clawing its way through waves of the dead. It circled their vessel once, shaking off unsavory passengers, and then drew to a stop parallel to the ship.

"This ship will no longer serve us," the Emperor said. Calmly, he walked around the curve of the railing, and then hopped on to the undulating back of the sea serpent.

Meia followed without hesitation, though she didn't bother to jump on to the rail first. She leaped clear over it, landing lightly on the Kameira's scales. The benefits of an alchemically enhanced body.

Shera was somewhat less enthusiastic.

Lucan steeled himself, holding on to a fistful of the rigging while he waited for the right moment. When he finally jumped, he shouted, wheeling his arms in the air as he flew from ship to living creature.

He landed unsteadily, but Meia caught him and hauled him to a steadier perch.

For the first time in her life, Shera hesitated during a job.

It was one thing if she died in a fight, or because a target had more skill than she expected. When you played a game, you had to be prepared to lose.

But she knew ships. She was no sailor, but she understood how they worked, and that this ship had been assembled by a crew of men. It was solid, reliable. Now she was meant to leap onto the back of a sea serpent, fleeing a swimming army of the animate dead.

Not what she had ever expected.

Then the hosts of Nakothi boiled up the sides, hauling themselves up and over the railing using fleshy tails and claws of bone. When the first fanged skull showed itself, Shera's hesitation shriveled and died.

She retreated, as she often did, into the cold.

Ice grew around her heart, and she took off toward the side in a running start.

At the last instant, when she pushed off into a jump, her foot slipped on the damp wood.

Shera fell.

The dark water rushed up to meet her, blue Deepstrider scales sliding past her nose. She scrabbled at the serpent with her hands, but she succeeded only in shredding the tips of her gloves.

Then she hit the water.

She spun around in a chaos of bubbles, foam, and wisps of cloudy blood. The rushing water choked her ears, leaving her deaf.

When she gathered enough of herself to wonder which way was up, she saw only an endless black sky. And, out of the distance, a dozen pale hands stretching out to meet her.

Then the rest of her brain reported for duty, and the picture clicked into place.

Not a black sky; the depths of the ocean. The hands weren't reaching down, they were reaching up. For her.

Something's down there.

Shera spun the opposite direction, kicking for the glimmer of the sky and the smear of blue that must be the Deepstrider. Now that she was facing the right direction, she could make out the Kameira's webbed claws, paddling the water as its serpent body bobbed up and down in waves.

She pulled herself through the water, away from the hands.

They followed her, rushing through the water with the speed of launched harpoons. As they got closer, she saw that the all-too-human hands sprouted from the ends of long, worm-like tentacles stretching up from the deep. Twelve hands, all reaching for her, snatching blindly, flailing for an ankle or the heel of her shoe.

She looked back up, trying to gauge distance, and she found herself face-to-face with a wall of fangs.

And above that teeth, solid blue eyes.

The Deepstrider growled, so deep that it shook the water. It opened its mouth, giving Shera a dizzying view of its titanic gullet.

Then it snapped its teeth down on the corpse-white tentacles, severing them.

Something beneath Shera let out a sound like a screaming whale, and the disconnected hands still grabbed at nothing as they floated under the waves.

Finally, Shera's head breached the surface, and she gasped for her life.

The Emperor sat on the Deepstrider's neck, not three feet away. He extended one dark hand, wearing an amused smile.

"Next time, jump sooner."

Shera took his hand and let him haul her up.

Minutes after they abandoned the ship, the Deepstrider reached the island.

Shera couldn't believe she hadn't noticed it before.

The ground was a vast expanse of clammy skin, stretching upward like a distended belly into a huge hill. Towering over them were ten curved and pointed bone spires, as though the island had grown in the middle of a colossal rib cage. The sun rose red between the ribs, like a bleeding heart.

At the base of the bone spires grew small clusters of sickly green fungus, like bunches of seaweed bursting through the skin of the ground. Over all the island hung the pervasive stench of coppery blood and rotting fish.

And the strewn parts of a dozen dismembered monsters.

Lucan winced. "I can feel the battle from here. They must have fought their way up from the beach."

"It seems I was right to worry," the Emperor said. He clutched the Heart of Nakothi in one hand and a sword in the other, and Shera couldn't tell which he held tighter.

The Deepstrider finally slowed, drawing near the vessel bobbing on the waves a few dozen yards from shore: a ship almost as strange and impressive as the island itself.

On the hull, in shining red alchemical paint, glowed the words, *The Eternal.*

Every inch of the ship was red. *The Eternal's* sails were furled, but she could clearly tell that they were the color of bright, fresh blood. The hull was made of naturally red planks, and the quicklamps hanging from the bow and stern glowed like the rising sun. Most noticeably, *The Eternal* seemed to drift on a tide of flame rather than water.

Orange flames licked at the bottom of the ship, illuminating the surrounding water in sunset hues. The wooden belly had been charred black, but the flames neither died nor grew. They lapped patiently at the ship's sides as though they would never run out of fuel.

At full speed, dragging a line of fire on the water behind it, *The Eternal* must be a truly spectacular sight.

Sailors hurried around the ship's deck, one of them raising a spyglass.

"Do we leave witnesses, Highness?" Meia asked, flexing her right hand. Bones shifted beneath her skin.

The Emperor's gaze was locked on the shore. "The Navigator and owner of that ship is Cheska Bennett, a very promising young woman. I will not deprive the Empire of her service. It is not illegal for a Navigator to accept a contract. Besides, she's the one who alerted me to this voyage in the first place."

The Deepstrider slithered past the ship, pressing its chin against the soft skin of the beach so that they could depart. All four of them scrambled ashore before the Emperor blew his scaly whistle again.

With a hiss like escaping steam, the Kameira turned around and dove into the ocean. In a flick of its tail, it was gone.

"Will you call it again when we leave?" Shera asked.

The Emperor marched up the hill, looking neither left nor right, resting a hand on each of his sword hilts. "If we are successful, we will be departing with Captain Bennett. If we aren't, then we will not be departing at all."

The three Gardeners fanned out around their Emperor. As the one with the sharpest senses, Lucan took the lead, with Meia flanking to his left and Shera to his right. The Emperor was more likely to protect them than the other way around, but he did not protest.

In fact, he hardly seemed to notice them at all. Only when he spoke did he acknowledge them at all, and only to expand their education.

"There are wider implications to this than my individual survival. The Watchman in question, the one who betrayed his Guild, knows far more than the secret to my youth. He had to know exactly where Nakothi died, how to get here, and that the Dead Mother once had eleven other hearts. I've only shared that knowledge with one other soul."

"Could he have given you up?" Lucan asked from higher up the hill.

"*She* is not capable of betrayal. I don't know where this Watchman found his information, but before this day is out, I will."

With all the secrets the Emperor had revealed to them, Shera almost didn't notice the one crucial detail he hadn't shared.

"This man who betrayed the Blackwatch. What's his name?"

The Emperor stopped, holding up a circle of glass to one eye like a monocle. "He has none. I've had his name stricken from Imperial records. From this day forward, when he is spoken of, it will be as a traitor and nothing more."

Through the glass, he peered over the crest of the hill, at the base of the towering ribs. Then he tucked the glass back into his pocket and drew one sword.

"I will engage the target first," the Emperor said. "Once I have him secured, everything else dies."

They made no sound of acknowledgement, but they didn't need to. Shera's Consultant training told her that she would obey the Emperor's orders without question and to the death.

But her instincts whispered that something was wrong.

First he shares ancient Imperial secrets with us, and then he takes us on a secret mission to remove a target we know virtually nothing about. No one knows we're here. There's no record of this assignment. He's rushing us forward, keeping us from asking questions.

Why?

And then another question bubbled to the surface, one she hadn't considered in years. *Why us? What did he need three Gardeners for in the first place?*

The wind gusted over the ocean, parting another copse of fungus, and Shera saw what the Emperor had seen through his glass: an intricate mausoleum of red muscle and yellowed bone. A circle of men had gathered in front, clustering around a wide gray-green hole, a wound that burrowed into the living flesh of this island.

There was no cover between them and the gathering below, so they all reacted the same way: they sprinted forward, weapons drawn, relying on speed instead of stealth.

Weapons drawn, Shera dashed headlong into the Emperor's mysterious plans.

CHAPTER TWENTY-ONE

When space warped around her as though she were standing in a heat haze, and dust began drifting up from the ground in streams, Shera started to wonder if something had gone wrong.

When she heard a malicious, inhuman voice shrieking with laughter from everywhere at once, and when she saw what looked like a newborn star hovering over the center of the Island, she wondered if she was about to die.

The light split at the bottom, cracking and releasing a mass of writhing blue-white tentacles, as though a pale squid had crammed its way into a chicken egg and was now oozing out. From this distance, it was hard to be sure, but what looked like little feelers on the tentacles might actually be *human hands,* covering the waving limbs like patches of fur.

When the tentacles were all the way through, instead of a squid's head, the bony upper torso of a long-dead woman squeezed out of the light. It looked like the dead Consultants she had fought in the crypt: as if someone had taken a human corpse and sucked all the moisture out, leaving only tight skin, shriveled muscle, and bone.

But this body was ten times bigger than any human. The creature would stand over the trees of the Gray Island.

Its arms were long and bony, like a skeleton wrapped in pale skin, and it seemed to have *two* elbows. Its long, pointed fingers curled into claws. The monster's neck was long and flexible, bending almost like a tentacle itself, but when its head finally emerged from the white light, Shera was forced to look away.

The face looked *wrong*, as though someone had crammed a bulb of mismatched organs onto the creatures neck with no order or reason. The rest of its body looked somewhat like a woman, albeit a titanic, hideous woman—with tentacles instead of legs—that had drowned a week before. But the head didn't belong on anything natural. Most Children of Nakothi were made out of human parts, but the head was a shifting, seething mass of pulp and madness.

Unfortunately, this was not a Child of Nakothi. It was what every Child aspired to be.

The Emperor had prepared her for it, as he'd prepared her to deal with all of Nakothi's tricks, if necessary.

This was not one of the Great Elder's "children," but one of her attendants. A Handmaiden of the Dead Mother.

The Emperor rarely told stories of the days before the Empire, when Elders ruled the world, but once he had spoken of the Handmaidens.

"To look in their faces was to court madness, and I knew many who had been driven insane by exposure to a Handmaiden's gaze, day after day. Unlike Nakothi's children, a Handmaiden has a cruel intelligence, and they often worked as overseers or managers, supervising the Dead Mother's 'harvests.' When the Dead Mother needed to build something out of specific human pieces, the Handmaidens were the ones who picked out the parts."

Shera had never expected to see one, so long as Nakothi herself remained dead. Or asleep. With the Great Elders, those two seemed to be somehow interchangeable.

This Handmaiden stood head and shoulders over the trees around her, and upon first landing on the Gray Island, she took a look around as though gauging her surroundings.

After a moment, she let out a gurgling whistle that sounded like a teapot caught in the grip of hysterical laughter. The white light above her swelled from a star to a moon, and then it cracked like glass.

After a single frozen instant, it shattered, flinging specks of dust all over the island. The pieces were dark and tiny, as though it had scattered a handful of sand over the land, but after a moment the specks grew larger, and Shera understood.

The Handmaiden brought an entourage.

Shera went down into a crouch as, with a series of crashes, Children of Nakothi landed all around her.

She waited an instant to make sure that no monsters were going to land on her head, but she didn't wait long enough for the Children to get their bearings. She launched herself forward, leading with her shear.

The first she encountered looked something like an anemone with waving limbs instead of tendrils. Something like a hand, but not quite the shape of a human hand, clasped down on her upper arm, and she sheared its limb off with a sweep of bronze.

A moment later she slashed the Child in half, and she was through and into the woods.

Many of the trees around here had been toppled by impacts, with dead monstrosities unfolding all around her. A spider of bone and sinew clambered down a nearby trunk, bones clattering like a rattlesnake, but Shera simply kept running. They might chase her, but she couldn't afford to fight each one. If she did, she would soon be overwhelmed.

A hideous bear, wrapped tightly in greasy hair, roared and charged her, lashing a spiked tail behind it. She couldn't avoid this one, so she matched the bear's charge, ducking under at the last second and slicing across its belly as she slid on her knees over the forest floor.

From the stench and the splatter of liquid, she knew she'd struck a blow, but she didn't stop and see if it was vital. She kept running, putting as much distance as she could between her and the rotten, stinking bear-creature. Not to mention the other hungry monstrosities ready to kill her.

How much running have I done today? she wondered. The stitch in her side was beginning to pain her as much as her wounds.

She kept running, headed for Meia. Or at least, where she *hoped* Meia would be. She had planned to fight Urzaia in the underground arena, so that's where Shera was headed. If she got there and found the tunnel packed with Children of Nakothi instead...well, she would likely die.

Hopefully it wouldn't come to that.

Two or three times, she caught glimpses of Consultants doing battle with monsters in and around the trees. Steel flashed, monsters screamed, and men and women called to one another, stealth forgotten.

Shera longed to go and help, which surprised her. She had spent most of her time as a Consultant away from the Gray Island, so she had few friends here. She likely didn't know those people personally. So why did she want to help them so badly? Why did it pain her to leave them behind?

Lucan would probably call it progress, but she wished it would go away. It was distracting her.

The entrance to the arena was concealed within a giant boulder, but when she finally found the right clearing, she couldn't figure out *which* giant boulder. There were several to choose from. She ran from rock to rock, checking the symbols that generations of Consultants had hidden, to give those who knew where to look directions to the hidden entrances.

The sounds of slavering beasts drew closer, and Shera made a mistake:

she turned to look.

The bone-spider had indeed continued to follow her, as had the bear—dragging a loop of blue intestines behind it—and a pale slug bigger than a man which she hadn't even *seen*. Other things loped behind, white and blue and fused together from mismatched parts, but she didn't stop to look.

Inches ahead of the Children of Nakothi, she slid into the boulder and jerked open the hidden door, crawling inside and tugging the door shut.

Nerve-scraping shrieks cut at her from outside, and sturdy limbs pounded at the door in impotent fury. Shera stopped in the tunnel to catch her breath, watching dust stream upward in the dim light. Anything more than four or five feet ahead still looked distorted, as though space had turned in on itself.

The Dead Mother's laughter echoed throughout the Island, and Shera shuddered.

Had someone destroyed the Heart? Or had something else gone wrong?

Either way, her best chance of fixing it was to find the Heart, if possible. And Urzaia could lead her straight to it.

Hopefully.

The air warped in Lucan's cell, and dust drifted from the floor to the ceiling. Worse, Nakothi's laughter drowned out even the whisper's from Shera's new shear.

His head still pounded, and he was afraid to open his Reader's senses, but he hated feeling so blind. What had happened? Had Shera destroyed the Heart? He doubted her remaining knife would be powerful enough to do it, but he'd been wrong before.

Whether this was Shera's mistake, or a Sleepless attack, or simply a natural consequence of his Awakening Syphren on an island with the Heart of Nakothi, he didn't know. No matter what, his first step remained the same: he needed to get out of here.

Once again, he stopped and looked at the bars on the front of his cell.

The Emperor had taught him the trick to active Reading: making physical changes to objects using nothing more than his Intent. That alone made him one of the most accomplished Readers in the Empire, with the ability to escape this cell whenever he wanted. In theory.

There were a few problems.

First, active Reading required a serious mental effort. One that he wasn't prepared to make, suffering as he was from Reader burn. Second, *destroying* an object was much easier than *changing* it. And that tended to get...out of hand.

Even if he succeeded, he had a very real chance of bringing the whole roof down on his head. Active Reading was a lot like planting an explosive charge, and it had many of the same applications.

A wet shriek cut through the air, and the whole island shook, sending plumes of debris falling from the ceiling to match those rising from the floor. Now he certainly couldn't risk it. If the cell was already unstable, anything he did to remove the bars might kill him.

Speaking of killing himself, he did have an equally insane option that was just as likely to result in his death.

He walked over to the bundle of blankets and folded the corner back, regarding Syphren.

The knife looked the same: like a clear slice of glass with a thousand bright green hands pressing against it like they were trying to escape.

Take, the blade whispered. *Take, steal, drink, break...*

It went on, dropping below audibility several times, and Lucan was doubly glad that he had his gloves on. If he could Read the Intent behind those words, he would never have the courage to do what he needed to do.

Gathering up his courage and taking a deep breath, Lucan picked up the whole bundle, gripping Syphren's hilt through layers of blankets and his gloves.

The knife hissed. *Take you! Take you, steal you, drink you, break you!*

His hands trembled and weakened, cold stealing into his bones. He lifted the whole bundle, moving the blade forward awkwardly, pressing the edge of the blade against the lock between the door and the bars. The edge hissed as it met the steel, and the hands on Syphen's blade moved more furiously.

But it didn't cut through the steel, as he'd hoped.

He pushed down with all the strength he could gather, despite his awkward position. The more force he used, the louder the knife's words became.

Take me to the strong one, it demanded.

Lucan ignored it, pressing against the lock.

TAKE ME!

"I'll take you wherever you want," Lucan muttered, icy hands shaking against the metal. "Just let me out of here."

The blade sank half an inch into the metal.

He couldn't believe that worked.

Hurriedly he wrapped the knife back up in its restrictive bindings, folding the blankets back over it. When it was entirely covered, its voice returned to a muted, annoying buzz in the distance.

Lucan shook out his hands, which trembled uncontrollably. The cold hadn't gone away, but it didn't feel like he'd carried a block of ice; rather, it felt like blood loss, as though the dagger had sliced his palms open and let him bleed.

Then he drew his foot back and stomped in the door.

At least, he tried.

Almost two years of captivity hadn't done much for his athletic ability. He exercised as much as he could, in his cell and on the few occasions where they let him out into the hallway, but that was no substitute for active duty.

The door shook and rattled loudly, but the latch didn't break.

The island rumbled around him again, and he gathered himself, kicking once more.

Was it his imagination, or had that kick done *even less?*

Lucan backed up all the way to the wardrobe at the back of the room, until his shoulder blades were pressed against its doors. He ran with all the force he could muster, striking the bars of the door with his shoulder.

Blinding, *stunning* pain. It felt almost as though he'd crashed straight into a metal wall. His shoulder throbbed, and he'd managed to clip the side of his skull, which had done nothing for his headache.

A moment later, another shriek came through the air, and the island shook once more. But instead of fading away into echoes, this one grew stronger. And stronger.

He was thrown off his feet and the world seemed to dissolve around him in a fury of howling sound and random color. He tumbled about like a bird in a hurricane, though he managed to grab Syphren's bundle in all the chaos. If the knife escaped from its bindings and slid out into the hallway while Lucan was still trapped in here, he couldn't imagine the sort of trouble it would cause.

Chunks of stone the size of his two fists together fell from the ceiling, narrowly missing him. In the far back corner of his cell, high up on the wall, another stone block fell away from the wall separating him and Jyrine.

If I went through all this trouble only to be crushed to death in my own cell...

He didn't complete the thought. With a squeal of metal, the bars warped, the latch broke with a sharp *ping*, and the door swung open.

For a moment, he stared at it.

His room was covered in dust, gravel, and chunks of masonry, which distressed him more than he would have thought. He'd spent a long time keeping this room organized.

Now his door was open, and he couldn't believe it.

He could have waited. He didn't have to do anything with the knife, he could have just *sat there* and waited.

It was enough to make a grown man want to cry.

Scooping up Syphren's bundle, Lucan started to walk out of the room. He pushed the door out of his way, and what remained of the hinges squealed loudly.

A woman shouted behind him. "Lucan! Light and life, *Lucan!* Can you hear me?"

Jyrine.

He stopped in place for a second, considering. She was in danger here; if another of those earthquakes hit, she could be crushed to death with no one to save her. He could at least check her bars for weakness, perhaps see if he could weaken them with Syphren.

Then again...she was one of the Sleepless. He couldn't release her onto the island in the middle of an Elder-related disaster. She would likely try to make things worse.

It pained him to leave her there: he could imagine being helplessly trapped as the ceiling caved in little by little, eventually crushing the air from your lungs...

"I learned a lot from you, Jyrine," he called, hardening his heart. "I'll be back." Once he delivered the knife to Shera, he would come back and do what he could for Jyrine.

She slapped her palm against the wall again. "No, let me out! Lucan!

Come and get me! I'm a Soulbound! If you get me to my Vessel..."

She kept shouting, but Lucan had already left.

On the way out, he found Hansin's ring of keys sitting on a small table, next to a weighted lead chest. His breath caught.

He hadn't dared to hope...

Fumbling with the keys, as the ground shook beneath him, he finally managed to find the right one and open the chest.

Inside, in a bundle of black, his gear sat waiting for him.

The guards occasionally let him out for exercise—it wasn't as though he'd spent the *entire* last two years in the cell—but he still emerged blinking into the unexpected brightness of the sunlight. It took him a second to get his bearings.

So he had to find Shera. How, exactly, would he go about doing that?

Not for the first time, he wondered how people got anything done without a Reader's senses. He might as well fumble around the island blindly.

Lucan considered the pain in his head. Maybe he could Read the ground a little, risking the pain.

He shook the thought away. He might need to use his powers when he reached Shera. He couldn't waste it now. He had to do what Shera or Meia would do, and actually think the situation through.

Shera had run deeper into the labyrinth. Either she had died in a corner there, or she'd found an exit. If so, it would be...this direction.

He turned around and started to walk, coming face-to-face with a monstrosity like a six-handed man with a thousand eyes.

The jaws split in half vertically, like the mandibles of an insect, and the Child of Nakothi let out a wet, threatening whistle.

Lucan's instincts may have rusted after two years alone, but he wasn't *that* far out of shape. He drew a shear in half a second, driving it straight through the eye on the creature's forehead and withdrawing, stepping back to avoid its death throes.

Use me... Syphren whispered. *I want them. Give me their lives.*

He ignored the blade, though he did pick up the speed.

He was back in his blacks again. How long had it been? Even the shroud over his mouth felt right, as though these were the clothes he was meant to wear. The weight of his shears at the back was a comfort.

Lucan felt dangerous again, competent, which was a comfort when monstrous things moved in the shadows of the woods.

He ran faster.

Finally, he came to one of the many boulder-strewn clearings on this part of the Island. Even this place looked beautiful after so long.

Nakothi's Children, of a dozen wildly different descriptions, crawled, oozed, and lurched all over the clearing. Nearby, the body of a black-clad young woman was being dragged off into the woods by something that looked sort of like a white mantis.

At least, he hoped it was a body.

Something like a dead horse with a ridiculously elongated neck waved its head around, hissing in frustration. It dipped once again, opening its mouth to feed on something behind one of the biggest boulders in sight.

A woman shouted, and when the tall horse's head withdrew, its lips were split open and spilling pale blood.

Lucan adjusted course. He might be looking for Shera, but he couldn't abandon someone fighting off the Children.

The tall horse burbled through its long neck as Lucan leapt off the top of the boulder, slashing at its throat with his shear as he sailed past. He landed in a crouch as the woman stumbled forward and plunged her own bronze knife into its chest.

The woman was a Heartlander wearing a purple dress. A Mason?

Then he realized that she had used a Gardener's shear, and he noticed the white line down the middle of her face. Not a Mason. *Kerian.*

She gripped her shear in obvious pain, her left arm hanging limp and useless at her side. She limped forward, dragging one leg behind her.

"Lucan," she said, her voice tight and full of obvious pain.

Before he said a word, he shoved Syphren's bundle into his belt, then stepped up to support Kerian's shoulder.

"Where can I take you?" Lucan asked.

"I need to get to the Council chamber. There's something there that might help." She nodded toward the center of the island. "As long as you can find a way to take care of *that*."

Lucan looked where she indicated and almost dropped her.

There was a monstrosity looming over the trees at the center of the Gray Island, shoulders set against a backdrop of slate-gray mist. Its chest and arms were the pale, sunless gray of a dead worm, and through the gaps in the trees, he saw that it was slithering forward on a nest of tentacles.

But its head drew him with a horrible fascination even as it repelled his gaze. It looked like a rib cage full of fish guts, or a maybe a mass of bodies all churned together...

He stopped thinking about it. The face was everything horrible he could imagine stuck on a long, flexible neck, and the more he imagined it the sicker he would get.

Kerian noticed his horror. "Did you not see it before?"

"I was looking for Shera."

"It was my understanding that you could sense her anywhere on the Island."

They both froze for a moment as a Child, like a small elephant, ambled past.

"I overdid it today," he whispered. "Have to find her like an ordinary—"

He was cut off by his own realization. Syphren, which had kept up its constant whispering ever since its birth, had gone completely silent at the sight of the Handmaiden.

Lucan had been the one to Awaken the blade. He was its father, in a way, and he understood the weapon's nature at a fundamental level.

It wasn't silent out of fear, or respect.

This was the silence of a child presented with a present so unexpected, so huge, and so massively generous that the only appropriate response was a stunned silence.

And like that child, Syphren would eventually...

GIVE IT TO ME! TAKE ME THERE! LET ME TASTE ITS SPIRIT!

...start shouting.

Lucan had to release Kerian, stumbling into the underbrush, and pull the knife's bundle from his waistband. Keeping it at arm's length helped, but it only kept the volume down. Syphren was still screaming, lashing out with its own power, and *writhing* in its container. It wanted that Handmaiden with a pure, overwhelming desire that Lucan could only envy.

Kerian came to a stop and eyed the blanket-wrapped package. "What's in there?" she asked.

"Shera's knife," he responded.

She pressed the heel of her hand against her forehead and nodded.

"I don't know where Shera is," Kerian said. "She ran off, chasing the Heart, and I don't know where that took her. The monsters showed up after she vanished, so she might be dead."

His mind refused to take in that idea. He didn't even consider it.

"But Meia should be in the arena. She was supposed to lure the Champion, Urzaia Woodsman, there and keep him occupied." Kerian looked around her, at the destruction of the forest and the Children lunging around in the trees. "I don't know how well that would have worked, given how things turned out, but that was the plan."

It wasn't as good as having his Reading back, but at least it was something. He gathered up her shoulder again, ignoring Syphren's hysterical shouts.

"Let's get you to the Council chamber," he said, but she pushed him away.

"No," she said. "Get going. I'll make it if I have to crawl."

Nearby, a snake that looked like it was made entirely of a stretched-out spine raised its "head" and hissed at them, then continued on its way.

"...are you sure?"

"Don't worry about me," she said. "Worry about Ayana. She's still doing paperwork."

Meia leaped at Urzaia, so that when he dodged, her shears were planted straight into the stone. Rock fragments burst up, slicing open her cheek, but she didn't bother to pay attention.

The Kameira had taken control.

She'd given herself almost entirely to her body's instincts. There was too much effort involved in the strategic approach—she had to borrow *more* and *more* from her Kameira to keep up with Urzaia.

Finally, she had given in.

Now she fought like a beast, slashing at his flanks and leaping out of harm before rushing in to snap at his throat. He seemed to enjoy this even more, judging by his frozen grin.

She was getting stronger now...but so, it seemed, was he.

The arena was shot through with cracks, from their wild blows as much as the earthquake. When one of his hatchets struck the ground it was like the wrath of a thunderstorm unleashed, blasting away a circle of debris as though a star had landed on earth.

When the Children of Nakothi arrived, she almost didn't notice.

Something on four legs with a pair of crocodile heads came lumbering down the steps, but she was locked in Urzaia's grip, trying to push her shears into his eyes. He held her wrists back, muscles straining, as she snarled into his face.

He laughed and looked as though he was about to say something, but then he noticed the creature she'd seen out of the corner of her eye. His expression grew somber, and he pushed her aside, waiting.

When the Child reached him, it howled with one head and struck with the other.

His hatchet blurred in a rush of black, and both heads were blasted to dry pieces.

The stench was awful to Meia's enhanced senses, but the Kameira within her roared their approval. The weak should not interrupt a battle between the strong.

She threw herself back into the fight, redoubling her efforts. Whenever the Children approached, they were crushed, decapitated, or simply slammed out of the way.

After a few minutes, the two humans both began to laugh.

As Urzaia grabbed her by the ankle and hurled her into a still-standing stone pillar, he laughed. As she lunged from the rubble, seized a rock the size of a cannonball, and launched it at Urzaia's head, she laughed.

When the Izyrian broke the missile in midair, but the debris still slammed into his face and chest, knocking him backwards a step, they *both* laughed.

They soon refocused, attacking each other with renewed ferocity, but Meia knew he thought the same as she.

At last, she had a chance to cut loose, to push it forward and find out what this body she'd earned could *do.*

It was the most fun she'd allowed herself to have in ages.

CHAPTER TWENTY-TWO

TEN YEARS AGO

As Gardener training and common sense dictated, Shera targeted the gunmen first.

One, a woman with her head pulled up in a cap, spotted them as they rushed down the hill. She pulled her musket to her shoulder, took aim, and squeezed the trigger.

Shera ducked to one side, but the shot was wide. It struck the skin-covered ground ten feet from Lucan, sending up a spray of gray-green blood. The woman in the cap was the only one with a musket; two others had pistols, but they kept their weapons raised, waiting for the Emperor and his assassins to get closer.

They waited too long.

The woman with the musket was driving a ramrod down the barrel when Shera reached her. She raised her gun to block a descending strike, but Shera ducked low, driving one of her shears up under the woman's ribs.

The blade slipped in and out of flesh as if through water. Had Lucan's one hour of attention done that much?

Shera shot behind a nearby patch of fungus, instinctively seeking cover, but she stopped halfway there.

Everyone else was already dead.

The Emperor flicked his two long blades, ridding them of excess blood. His white armor had been spattered with a red spray, and three bodies were still crumpling behind him. Two of the corpses clutched pistols.

Meia stood over another body with a spade in his throat, and Lucan stood in the center of a cloud of glittering sand, a corpse at his feet. But none of them had moved as quickly as their Emperor.

None of them paused, walking straight over to the burrowed wound in the island's flesh.

Kneeling down, Meia peered into the hole. Shera thought she saw the other girl's pupils flicker, as if they had changed shape for an instant.

"Highness, there's someone down there," she reported. "I can see movement."

The Emperor stepped out over empty air. "It's *him.*"

He dropped straight down the hole.

The rest of them had to descend less dramatically. Shera slipped climbing-hooks onto her gloves and the tips of her shoes. They were made to gouge handholds in wood, but they had no trouble driving wounds into the strange flesh of this island.

Lucan's gloves and boots seemed to stick to the wall like the legs of a fly, and he descended as quickly as if he were walking down a staircase. Meia merely flexed her hands, and her fingernails hardened into claws. She climbed down in the same way as Shera, though with far more grace.

Not for the first time, Shera wondered what the alchemists were doing to her.

As they moved farther down, Shera got a better look at the anatomy of the island. The sides of the wound were dotted with holes the size of her head, so deep they vanished into darkness. It looked as though they were burrowing through dry veins. Once, Shera rested on the lip of a hole big enough to drive a wagon through. Something moved at the far end, but she didn't have time to investigate. The Emperor was already down there, somewhere, and Lucan and Meia were about to catch up.

Past that point, the hole was crisscrossed with sticky red wires no wider than her thumb. They looked like thin tendons, or perhaps threads of a spider's pink web. The wires were sparse at first, and many had been cut to get them out of the way. But the closer they got to the bottom, the thicker the wires clustered.

At the end of the vertical tunnel, the room opened up into a cavern. Nothing as gargantuan as the Garden, which could safely hold a city, but it was at least the size of a rich man's basement.

The air between them was thick with those reddish wires, which bunched closer and closer together as they terminated at a single point. The flickering, unsteady light of a flame lantern illuminated the room, casting shadows into the corners.

Meia simply jumped down, and Lucan unspooled a quick climber's rope for a few feet before he followed. The floor they landed on was gray and squishy, like the giant tongue of a man long dead.

Shera wanted more information before she followed, but she could neither see nor hear the Emperor. This was not the time for hesitation.

Stretching out, she seized one of the reddish wires and gave it a tug.

Seemed solid enough. She disengaged her climbing-hooks, swinging from one wire to another like an ape through the Izyrian jungle.

When she landed with a *squish* on the gray surface, she dropped into a crouch, both shears drawn and ready.

Nothing. The lantern rested on its side a few feet to her left, feebly casting its unsteady light. Somewhere in the distance, liquid dripped into a pool with the regularity of a bleeding wound.

Shera looked away from the lantern, letting her eyes adjust to the darkness. There, in the corner, the Emperor's white armor showed up as a slightly brighter patch of shadow. Lucan and Meia stood nearby, weapons in hand, still hesitating.

Seeing Shera, the Emperor walked out of the shadows, dragging a ragged-looking man by a fistful of his hair.

The Blackwatch traitor was older than Shera had expected, maybe fifty years old, with the naturally tan skin of Vandenyas heritage. An intricate, squirming tattoo masked half his face, and the design made her nauseous for reasons she couldn't quite name.

The Emperor knelt, pushing the side of his captive's head down into the moist floor. "Tell *them* what you told *me*."

Whimpering, the captive still managed to summon an insane smile. "You lose!" he gasped. "The long game is over! Make this easy for all of us—"

The voice of the Aurelian Emperor rang out in the confined space, so packed with Intent that Shera flinched back. "Say it!"

When the words finally came from the disgraced Watchman's throat, they crawled out. "That which sleeps...will soon...wake..."

The Emperor's answering smile was as mad as his captive's. "Soon for me, yes. But not today. And not for you."

Before Shera could fully register what was happening, the Emperor had seized another handful of black hair and dragged the traitor over to her, closer to the lantern. The Watchman struggled weakly, but his captor gave no notice.

The Emperor pulled something out that Shera hadn't noticed before: a white sash, which he had tucked between plates of his armor. He placed one boot on the tattooed man's chest to prevent him from squirming, and then he stretched the sash out between both hands.

"What a comforting pillow this will make you," he said, and folded the sash in half. "You'll get a good night's sleep." He folded the sash again. "Nothing will wake you. Not a sound. Not an itch. Not a scratch."

The Watchman sputtered something out, slamming his fist into the Emperor's armored leg, but the Emperor simply knelt again, tucking the sash under his captive's head.

"Pleasant dreams," he said, then he removed his boot from the man's chest and stepped back.

For a second, the traitor tried to rise, but he couldn't seem to pull his head from the makeshift pillow. His eyes drifted closed as he tried to speak, but Shera heard only mumbling. His right hand lifted, then fell back down without strength. His legs kicked like a dreaming dog's.

Then even that motion stopped, and his only sign of life was the slow rise and fall of his chest.

"Would you like us to kill him?" Meia asked. Her voice was flat and businesslike, which meant she was uncomfortable and trying not to show it.

The Emperor didn't answer. He staggered away, gripping a handful of red wires as if to steady himself. "It's not enough. It's never enough. Century after century, and it's *never enough.*"

Shera followed the red wires as they ran from the Emperor's fist down to the floor in a corner of the room, one still bathed in shadows. Most of the wires in the room ended at that point; the Watchman had severed several near the base, as though trying to dig through them.

Struck by curiosity, Shera moved toward that spot.

"Back where I started," the Emperor murmured. "It begins again. They're not ready. They need to be ready. They need to be better!"

A soft wind picked up from somewhere, hissing through the chambers like a thousand distant voices.

Then Shera saw what waited at the end of those sticky red tendons. They terminated in a gray-green heart, but not as sickly as the one the Emperor wore around his chest. This one was healthy as a ripe apple, pumping in a steady rhythm. The wires stuck to it, fused with it, carrying blood or nutrients or whatever the Elder needed back to the rest of Nakothi's vast, not-quite-dead body.

Now Shera could hear it, echoing through the whole island: a faint heartbeat.

The Emperor's hand had slid from the wires down to the hilt of his sword. "I can *make* them better. I can *remake* them, reforge them. I can give them *rebirth.*"

And the voice of Nakothi howled through the chamber, echoing the Emperor's final word.

"REBIRTH."

Then the Emperor slammed his booted heel down on the glass lantern, and the light went out.

CHAPTER TWENTY-THREE

Awakened objects may be powerful and somewhat self-aware, but they are no substitute for a living human being.

From this day forward, non-human entities are no longer allowed a seat on the Council of Architects.

– Secret Laws of the Am'haranai, Number Seventeen

Kerian lunged on her one good leg, almost collapsing on a fused monstrosity that looked something like two drowned men trying to escape a shapeless blob of flesh. The Child of Nakothi spurted up foul-smelling milky blood, curling in on itself as it died.

Some of the rotten fluid got on Kerian's clothes, but she was past caring. If the stench could distract her from her pain, so much the better, and she was already going to tear the purple dress off her body and burn it as soon as she had half an opportunity. That was what she'd earned, dressing for negotiation instead of battle. She'd been thinking like an Architect and a Councilor, not like a Gardener.

Sitting back and kicking at the Child's corpse with her good leg, she managed to push it away from one of the secret entrances to the Council chamber: a brown metal hatch fused to the back of a fake tree, hidden behind a thornbush.

For a second she sat on the ground, regarding the entrance. Having everything concealed and difficult to reach was a long tradition of the Gray Island, stretching back to the origins of the Am'haranai. It spoke to their philosophy: humble in appearance, complex within.

But she was only beginning to realize how impractical it all was. It was all well and good to have secret entrances and tunnels everywhere as long as all of your Guild members were able-bodied, but what about during a battle? What if they were injured? Even a Consultant who knew the Island like her own home couldn't get around any more quickly than an ignorant enemy, if she couldn't rely on both legs and both arms.

She felt a newfound sympathy for those Guild brothers and sisters who lost a limb during a mission. They had all retired to the Gray District in the

Capital—the block of expensive homes where long-serving Consultants lived out the rest of their lives. She had once wondered why so few of them chose to stay on the Island.

Now she knew.

She gripped the hatch in both hands, shivering and sweating through the pain in her injured wrist. Kerian didn't blame Shera for doing what needed to be done—it was Calder Marten's fault for abusing the power of the Emperor's crown, not anyone else's—but she couldn't help but feel that the girl could have taken it easy. Kerian wasn't as young as she used to be, after all.

Finally, with a shot of pain like an alchemist's needle pressed straight against the bone, Kerian managed to wrench the hatch open.

Inside, cloaked in shadow, waited her greatest opponent yet: *stairs*.

She pulled herself through awkwardly, grateful that there were no witnesses around, and pulled the hatch shut behind her. The last thing she needed was another Child of Nakothi crawling through, forcing her to fight in the dark, on the cramped stairs.

She slid down on her backside, scooting down one stair at a time, ignoring the foul stink coming from her clothes. She was tempted to tear the dress off now, but she didn't enjoy the thought of pushing her way down the stone steps in nothing but her underthings. That could result in some scrapes in awkward places.

Finally, after what seemed like an eternity of pain and discomfort and wire-taut fear, Kerian reached the Council chamber at the bottom.

The pale lights hanging from the roots on the ceiling had never felt so bright, as she'd never come down the stairs in complete darkness before. With all the agility of a ninety-year-old invalid, she pushed herself to her feet and staggered closer to the white table of the High Council of Alchemists.

It looked like nothing so much as a waist-high column of chalk, and the Councilors mostly used it to doodle in yellow light during meetings, but it was an ancient artifact created by the greatest Readers and alchemists of the early Empire. The table had been used to plan attacks on Great Elders, and given to the Am'haranai to train their strategists.

And for one other purpose.

Kerian pressed her palm against the surface of the table, activating her handprint in yellow light. She tried to focus her Intent, though she was never sure how well she'd done; she wasn't a Reader, so she couldn't see the results of her own Intent.

When she thought she was properly focused, she spoke out clearly and firmly. "I am Kerian, Architect of the High Council. I seek the wisdom of Bastion, and the safety of the Veil."

It took long enough that Kerian had begun to wonder if she had done everything correctly. She had tested this process out once, upon being elected to the High Council, to see if it would work. Since then, there had been no need: Yala took the swearing-in of new Consultants as a religious duty, and guarded that right covetously. Kerian had never minded, since she normally had more important things to do, but now she wished she'd had a little more practice.

Just when she'd resolved to try again, a rectangular slice of the table's center withdrew, sliding down into itself with the scrape of stone on stone. Kerian withdrew her hand, slumping against the edge of the table, breathing deeply in relief.

It had worked. Maybe they would have a chance.

After a moment, the stone slid back up. A glass box sat on top, packed with clouds of silver mist. At a certain angle, the mist almost looked blue, whirling and twisting as though it were buffeted by invisible winds.

She placed a hand on the device—the Vessel that had once raised Bastion's Veil—and focused her Intent once more, speaking loudly and clearly. The instructions she'd received upon being raised to the High Council clearly stated that she didn't need to speak the words out loud, so long as she held them clearly enough in her mind, but she felt more comfortable speaking. It seemed easier to control.

"Our home is threatened," she said. "The Veil is breached. Lend us your power and cleanse this island of that which is unclean."

Once again, nothing happened for a moment, but this time she was prepared. Prepared for anything, in fact: this was one of a dozen emergency procedures she'd had to memorize upon her election to the High Council. She'd never expected to need it.

A moment later she gasped as her vision was stolen away, and she was given a view of Nakothi's Handmaiden, rampaging across the Island, directing the Children of the Dead Mother like a shepherdess with her flock.

It's a Reader's vision, she thought. This must be what it was like for Readers, though as she understood it, they mostly viewed the past instead of the present. But this certainly felt like a trance, as though an outside force had taken over her imagination and plugged an image into it.

Kerian's view wasn't steady; it whirled and spun, as though battered by the wind. After a second she realized she was seeing out from within Bastion's Veil itself.

The sound of the wind tore around her, and she had listened for almost a minute before she realized that the furious wind was trying to *speak* to her.

"...break us..."

She screwed up her ears and her mind, focusing on picking out the words.

"...she will break us," Bastion's Veil whispered.

The Intent bound within the ancient Vessel flowed directly to her, and she understood the full story from those few words. As Kerian had been warned years ago, releasing the Veil was an action of dire emergency. Using all of the mists at once would cleanse the Gray Island of Elderspawn, but the island would go without cover for weeks afterwards as the Veil recovered.

Now Bastion's Veil was telling her something else, something that Yala and Tyril hadn't known when they inducted her. The Handmaiden could *break through* the Veil. If Kerian collapsed the mist and attempted to drive the Elders away from the island, she'd be pitting Bastion's power against the power of the Handmaiden.

And the creature of Nakothi would win. Easily.

The Veil would be just as broken, requiring weeks to recover, but the Elders wouldn't even be inconvenienced. They would have free reign of the Gray Island, and by the time the mists returned, there would be no one left to save.

Kerian broke the trance, stepping back from the table and dropping to the floor in defeat. Until someone killed the Handmaiden, she couldn't take care of the other Children.

So she had only to sit here, holding the Vessel and waiting for someone else to solve her problems for her.

She hated even the thought of doing nothing while her fellow Guild members died above her, but she stayed where she was.

Because she was a Consultant, and Consultants did their duty.

Shera made it to the base of the arena, but between the earthquake and the two combatants, the ancient stone wouldn't last another five minutes.

Rocks fell all around her as she rushed through a tunnel at the arena's ground level, so that she had to blink grit from her eyes and stare through the dust as she ran, leaping over the jagged maze of debris on the ground. For the first time, she was actually glad for the mask over her nose and mouth, because it kept her from taking in a lungful of dirt with every breath.

But the clouds of dust in the air still worked against her, because she was dodging more than rocks.

A fat Child of Nakothi, little more than a blob of blubber, waddled toward her, raising a pair of bone clubs and howling. She stabbed it at the base of the neck, dodged its strike, and slashed it in the side before moving on.

Something like a swarm of hermit crabs had taken up residence in human skulls, and they scuttled up to her as she ran, trying to grab her feet with sharp claws. She leaped over them, kicking off one skull and landing on a stacked pile of rocks, before continuing to run.

She had one goal, and one goal alone: she had to find the Heart. Maybe then, somehow, she could put an end to this.

Even if she had to destroy the Heart herself, Nakothi's unleashed powers couldn't make the island any worse than it already was.

Finally she emerged onto the sand of the arena floor in time to see the Gardener's shears meeting the gladiator's hatchets. They struck one another, ringing like a bell struck by a cannon, but then Meia managed to land a kick in his armored gut. When he doubled over, she struck at his throat with her shear.

Too shallow, Shera thought. If Meia had leaned forward a little more, the fight would have been over. Instead, Urzaia was able to dodge backwards, though he lost his balance and rolled down a flight of arena stairs. He tumbled down every stone bench, landing on a chunk of rock.

Meia advanced on him, blade raised, and Shera rushed forward to stop her.

She had to talk to him, to find out if he knew where the Heart was.

She'd be willing to offer a truce, a ceasefire with Calder Marten, whatever it took if they could stop this madness on the Gray Island.

Out of the corner of her eye, she saw that someone had pulled a pistol on her.

Fueled by instinct and training, she threw herself into a roll, and the bullet struck the sand next to her shoulder. She came up in a crouch, shear leading and spade in her off hand.

Calder Marten stood in the arena, his blue jacket covered in stains and grit. The Emperor's crown sat in the middle of his red hair like gold in a fire, and when he tossed his pistol aside, he readied a sword.

This one was new.

The cutlass blade was long and black, mottled with spots of orange that... well, they didn't quite glow, but they *shifted*, like the patterns on a hot coal. It was as though the blobs of color on the blade weren't really there, but were made by some alchemical paint.

Either he had invested in a clever forgery, or Captain Calder Marten had found himself an Awakened weapon.

They regarded each other without moving, sand rising up from the arena in streams even as pebbles clattered down from the ceiling far above.

I should have killed him weeks ago, Shera thought. It would have saved her a lot of headache, though not as much as if she'd simply thrown Nakothi's Heart into the ocean. Even if Kelarac got his hands on it, it couldn't be worse than what was happening now.

Her left shoulder still throbbed, the cut on the back of her neck blazed like a hot poker, and every muscle in her body felt as though it had been tenderized like a fresh-cut steak. But she ignored all that, focusing on Calder.

She shouldn't have let him live before. Now she had a chance to correct her mistake.

So tight was her focus, that she almost didn't notice one distinctive fact—the man had an *Elderspawn* on his shoulder.

It was a stubby little thing, more humanoid than most, with dark green skin and little wings that she thought surely couldn't carry it into the air. Its black eyes glared at her with tiny fury that would have been adorable under other circumstances, and its mouth was covered by a nest of writhing, twisting tentacles.

The tentacles parted, and a noise resounded from the creature that Shera would never have imagined: a deep, resonant, masculine laugh.

It laughed hard enough to hurt her ears and then got louder, laughing like a Great Elder waking to consume the world, like a phantom from a nightmare. Its laughter grew in volume until the stones around her shook.

"KILL," the Elderspawn declared, and then flapped its way off of Calder Marten's shoulder.

That was a signal if she'd ever heard one.

Shera hurled her spade at Calder's eye, more to distract him than anything else. He jerked his head out of the way and brought that orange-mottled blade down on her as she closed the gap between them. She knocked his cutlass out of the way, unfolding to stand inches from his body, driving a poisoned needle at his neck. This one would be lethal.

He stepped *closer* to her, slamming his elbow into her nose.

The world flared white and pain flashed through her head as blood, warm and wet, flowed over her mouth.

He was better than she'd expected. Swordsmen kept their distance against knives, using their reach to their advantage. Few of them had the presence of mind to adjust on the fly, to step even closer and fight her without their weapon. Even those that did try usually ended up dead on the end of her knife.

But he'd caught her off guard, and she staggered back, losing her grip on the needle.

I need to see.

She was still blinded by tears, but she anticipated his next move: he would try and finish her with a thrust to her midsection. She dropped into a low crouch, reversing her grip on her shear as she did.

The rush of air over her head meant she had chosen wisely.

Shera slammed the knife into a black blur that she thought was his boot, but he slid it across the sand and away from her in time. As soon as he did, she rolled away, expecting the counterattack.

On the way, she reached out and slashed his leg. The same leg she'd injured in their last encounter.

The edge of her blade tugged through a bandage beneath his pants and then bit flesh, telling her that she'd remembered correctly. She'd torn open his old wound.

She felt a surge of satisfaction that matched her pain. He deserved to hurt at least as much as she did.

And then he deserved to die.

Her emotions cooled to the familiar block of ice as she reached down for a spade. The triangular blade felt light in her hand.

She could see it now: she'd throw the spade, and he would react. Whether he swung his sword to try and knock it out of the way, or jerked back to avoid it, or even if it hit its mark, either way he would lean backwards half a step. She was close enough to take that opening. She'd bury her shear in his belly.

Her left hand had already started to come up when he met her eyes and issued an order.

"Stop where you are!" he shouted.

The crown seemed to pull her attention, and for a moment, she was a little girl standing in front of the most powerful man in the world.

When she finally broke free and threw the spade, he had already dodged, moving behind a half-shattered wooden rectangle standing on its end. It looked like the remnants of a woodshed that had been struck by lightning—or, more likely, caught in the battle between Meia and Urzaia.

Shera almost ran around the "shed" to pursue Calder, but she caught herself. He would be waiting for her, sword ready.

With that in mind, she pulled herself up onto the broken wood. It started to collapse, so she leaped from it to a nearby pile of stone that had once formed part of the arena. She hurled a spade from above him, and as she'd expected, he leaned back as he tried to knock it aside with his sword.

The spade kicked up sparks as it hit his cutlass, deflecting off the flat of his blade and embedding itself into his shoulder.

She started to lunge forward, but something in his eyes stopped her. Even as he pulled the spade out of his flesh and let it fall to the ground, dripping blood, his expression said he had a plan. He looked firm, determined, as though he had one final card up his sleeve that he was simply looking for the opportunity to use.

He could have been baiting her, but she doubted he had the presence of mind to do so at this point. He knew something she didn't.

And she'd already underestimated him once, earning a broken nose for her trouble.

So when he started limping to the side like he meant to find a better position from which to attack, she matched him from the other side, prowling opposite as though they each stood on the other side of an invisible circle. She pulled a poisoned needle into her left hand, waiting for the opportunity to use it. It was easier to jab with a needle, but she could throw it if she had to. As long as he was distracted.

When a shadow loomed up behind her, she realized her mistake.

He's a Reader. He could feel the Children of Nakothi coming.

All he'd wanted to do was keep her eyes on him.

She spun with her shear in one hand and the poisoned needle in the other, facing the pale-skinned bulk of a headless gorilla from only an inch away. The needle pierced its skin and the knife drew a line of pale blood down its chest, but neither had any visible effect.

She tried to dodge as its fist descended, but it still caught her on the right shoulder with the force of a hammer. The blow flung her from the rock on which she stood, sending her tumbling to the arena sand.

At last, the pain was too much. She couldn't see anything—there was dirt in her eyes, blood in her mouth, and pain in her whole body. She tried to roll to the side, to avoid the attack she knew was coming, but her body only arched and writhed.

She couldn't see. She couldn't move.

He was going to kill her.

Meia saw Shera run into the arena, saw her stopped by Calder Marten, and heard the echoing declaration of Calder's horrible Elderspawn pet.

But she didn't have the luxury of watching their fight, because she was in danger of losing her own.

By all rights, Urzaia should have been exhausted by now. His hair had been cut loose by one of her strikes that had come close to stabbing him in the back of the neck, and his face was covered in cuts—as much from debris and shattered rock as from her knife.

Instead of backing off, he came at her even stronger before, as though he *fed* on the battle.

Even the Kameira inside her were growing weary, snapping and growling in her mind but seldom pressuring her into action. The Deepstrider's healing was growing slower and slower, leaving the minor injuries alone, and her stomach seemed to gnaw on her backbone. If she could think of hunger at a time like this, she must be starving indeed.

Her shears trembled in her grip, but she bit her lip, savoring the pain and blood that flooded her mouth. It focused her, kept her eyes on Urzaia, reminding her what she needed to do.

She needed to *tear him to pieces.*

Meia had rushed at him when, to the side, she saw a Child of Nakothi slam its fist down on Shera's shoulder. She tumbled off of a rock, landing on the ground, and Calder killed the Elderspawn. For some reason, the heavily muscled gorilla dissolved into a pile of foul black waste. She wondered if that was the effect of his sword.

After killing Nakothi's Child, Calder walked up to Shera. He reversed his strange orange-stained cutlass, ready to drive it through her and into the ground.

Meia's vision filmed with rage.

She was already rushing at Urzaia, so instead of turning away, she *doubled* her ferocity, kicking off with speed that even he couldn't match. She didn't have to kill him; that would take too much effort. She had to tear him up, keep him out of her way.

Meia slammed into him with her left shoulder, jabbing her shear into his side.

At *last*, she got in a clear hit, slicing through what remained of his leather breastplate and carving a piece out of his ribs.

Even Urzaia screamed, sweeping at her with his hatchets, but she'd already pushed him away, turning around and rushing for Calder Marten.

He had gathered the hilt of his cutlass in his fists, prepared to drive it down into Shera's chest.

She ran faster than she'd ever run before, the muscles in her legs bunching and changing shape.

It was all she could do to stop, kicking up a spray of sand as she arrived, one foot on the ground and one resting flat on Calder Marten's gut.

He looked up, eyes wide beneath his bright red hair.

She's not yours, Meia thought fiercely, but all that came out was a Kameira's snarl.

Strength flooded her legs again, and she *pushed* him as much as kicked him.

It was enough to launch him into the air, sending him skimming over the ground as he tumbled backwards. His sword skittered free from his hand, sliding over the sand until it came to rest against a rock.

Much like Calder's body.

His back crashed against a boulder that had once formed part of the roof, knocking the crown from his head. The Emperor's crown rolled away like a coin on the street.

A roaring voice filled the whole underground chamber, as loud as Calder's laughing Elderspawn from earlier. "*Captain!*" Urzaia shouted.

A second later, he was on her, driving his hatchets down at her head.

Her shears came up to hold him off, but she couldn't understand where he found such *strength*. Even the Nightwyrm inside her was urging her to retreat and tend to her wounds, and she felt as though she would collapse from sheer exhaustion, but Urzaia hit her with more power than he'd ever used before.

He pounded at her blades relentlessly, and it was all she could do to hold on.

First she lost her grip on her left-hand knife, then his eyes lit up. He shouted, grinning like a maniac, and slammed one hatchet down on the flesh between her shoulder and neck.

The sheer pain...it was like nothing she'd experienced since the alchemist's table. It didn't feel like a shoulder wound, it felt like every one of her bones had turned to flame, and her muscles were being pulled apart until they tore.

Blood sprayed into the air, but she couldn't even get the breath to scream.

As she fell backwards, she saw someone that she hadn't expected to see—free and walking around—ever again.

Lucan.

She allowed the dark to take the edges of her vision. The three of them were all together again. They couldn't fail a mission when they were together, no matter the odds.

Everything would be okay now.

Lucan saw the instant Meia took the black hatchet to the shoulder, and it was all he could do not to pull his own shears and leap into battle himself. If it was an opponent that could overpower Meia blade-to-blade, he had no chance. Certainly not without his Reading.

But there was one more thing he could do to ensure the big Izyrian's death.

The blanket fell away, and for the first time since he'd created the weapon, he gripped Syphren's hilt.

He has power... the knife whispered. *Let me taste it.*

You will, Lucan promised.

Shera was climbing to her knees, hidden behind Calder Marten, her mask soaked in blood. Lucan raised his voice.

"Shera!"

At the same time, Calder seemed to sense something. His eyes fell on Syphren, and they widened. He turned to his Champion.

"Urzaia!" he shouted.

With all his strength, Lucan hurled the blade. Syphren cackled as it flew, delighted at the chance to draw blood.

At the same time, Urzaia Woodsman kicked Meia away, his face the very picture of bloody fury. He readied a black hatchet, turning to Lucan and glaring like death. His muscles bunched, and he prepared himself to lunge.

Shera's hand caught her Awakened shear out of the air, and Lucan smiled.

The blade filled her mind with whispers. Not one, but a thousand voices, all speaking in unison.

They all wanted the same thing.

Power.

Power in his blood.

Power in the gold on his arm.

Let me taste it.

Let me take it.

Let me tear it apart, and use it for us.

The voices were all one voice, and it sounded like Nakothi, like the Emperor, like Shera herself. Even like Lucan, like some dark part of him that she didn't know. Something inside Shera told her to cast the knife away, that the whispers were disgusting and shouldn't be heeded.

But Shera was a Gardener, and each Gardener had a *pair* of shears. She couldn't throw one of hers away now.

Not when she had a weed right in front of her.

"Behind you!" Calder screamed, pointing with desperate urgency at Shera. Or at her weapon.

It didn't matter; he was already too late.

Urzaia spun, his hatchet blade swinging at Shera's midsection, but she simply ducked the attack.

The moment seemed to freeze. He was wide open, committed to his attack, his chest exposed. In her left hand, she gripped her shear, stabilized and Awakened. The weapon with as rich a history as the Empire's own: passed through generations of Consultants, of assassins, until it passed into her own hands. The blade that had taken significant lives, again and again, for over a thousand years.

The blade she'd used to kill the Emperor.

A memory, one that she avoided above all others, floated to the surface of her mind. The Emperor's personal chambers were torn to pieces as if in a great battle, blood both inhuman and human spattering the walls. Shera crept out, bloody knife hidden in her sheath, listening to the Imperial Guard running here and there, shouting that they had to protect the Emperor.

Taking the opening, she plunged the blade into Urzaia Woodsman's chest.

The knife let out a contented sigh, flaring green, the hands pressed against the inside of the blade freezing in place. Emerald lights sparked to life and floated like ball lightning around his chest, running all over his body, spinning around the gold hide wrapped around his upper arm.

Urzaia's mouth hung open in surprise. He started to say something but coughed instead, toppling over backwards.

Shera kept her grip on her shear, letting the gladiator's falling body pull the knife free. For an instant, the blade was covered in thin smears of blood, but then those evaporated.

Such strength... the knife whispered.

And somehow, perhaps because of her connection to the weapon, Shera felt stronger. As though Urzaia's death was a breath of new life, rejuvenating her and bringing her new focus.

It steals strength, she realized. The voice of the knife was familiar to her; it was the blade she'd carried for years, strengthened by the significance of her own actions, invested by Lucan and by the Emperor...and by Shera herself.

She'd always wanted a blade that couldn't be turned. Now she had a weapon that would tear through any defense, turning the target's own power against them.

Now she needed to ask Lucan its name. She was sure he'd have named it; it was something he'd do.

Lucan walked up beside her, standing next to her without saying a word. Meia rose to her knees, blue scales gathering around the torn flesh at her shoulder. Her face was pale and pained, but she focused her gaze on Calder Marten.

The Navigator was nearby, scrambling in the sand and rocks. After a moment, he pulled the Emperor's crown free, cramming it on his head. He lifted his orange-and-black sword a second later, pointing it at the three Consultants.

Shera readied both of her shears—bronze in her right, green in her left.

The Awakened blade whispered drowsily, beneath hearing, as though it were simply murmuring in its sleep.

Calder drew himself up on shaky legs, feigning a strength he obviously didn't feel. "Let's get to it, then," he said.

Beside Shera, Meia let out a snort that might have been a laugh.

And then the Handmaiden of Nakothi tore off the roof.

CHAPTER TWENTY-FOUR

TEN YEARS AGO

As soon as he'd set foot on the moist gray floor of the cavern, Lucan felt something wrong. It was more than the persistent aura of death that surrounded the whole land—he had caught flickers of death and wisps of deadly Intent ever since they'd landed on the beach, as though the entire island wanted them to die.

Down here in the bowels of the beast, he sensed something even worse. Birth and death twisted in on one another, a perversion that filled his mind with visions of dying as an infant and being reborn as a withered corpse. Ordinarily he had to touch an object to Read anything, but here it was taking all of his concentration to avoid being carried away on tides of madness. He wouldn't remove his gloves for all the goldmarks in the Gray Island vaults.

And that aura, that madness, was pouring from the Emperor of the Aurelian Empire like waves of heat from a fire.

Lucan stood, mute and frozen, as the Emperor dragged the treacherous Watchman to the center of the room and put him to sleep with an invested pillow. Only when the Emperor began muttering to himself, and the visions of murder and mutilated corpses whirled around his head like leaves in a high wind, did Lucan finally force his paralyzed hands into action.

From a pouch at his belt, he pulled a black cloth mask.

For once, he had brought the right tool for the job.

The mask had been created to his exact specifications, months earlier: woven out of wool sheared from sleeping sheep, by a seamstress who thought she was weaving a sleep-mask for an insomniac Magister. Then he had invested it in his free time, rubbing it through his hands and meditating on a very simple Intent: *bring me peace. Calm. Stability.*

Many Readers had been driven mad by their powers, and he didn't intend to be one of them.

He pulled the mask down, over his face.

The wool was soft, though it still felt strange against his skin, and some of the seams tugged at his hair. But none of that mattered in the rush of cool, dry relief.

The visions vanished, the gibbering whispers of insanity silenced. His fear died away, leaving only peaceful focus. He wouldn't be able to Read a thing through this mask: Reading required a degree of openness and emotional empathy that this deadening of sensation would not allow.

But he needed his senses closed now, not open. Reading would do nothing but make him vulnerable to Nakothi. And to the Emperor.

Lucan had the feeling that the Emperor was no longer on their side.

When a white-armored boot crashed down on the lantern and doused the room in darkness, Lucan was ready.

He drew his shears and confronted his Emperor not as a Reader, but as a Gardener.

Lucan may have been prepared, but Meia was not.

When the Emperor spoke the words of Nakothi and the island echoed them, senses she didn't understand screamed at her to run away.

When the alchemists had taken her away on the Emperor's orders, they had primarily focused on enhancing her natural abilities. Potions administered intravenously increased her reaction time, solutions injected into her major muscle groups increased strength.

But they hadn't stopped there. When the Guild of Alchemists received an assignment from the Emperor himself, they set about making a masterpiece.

A formula derived from the Shadeshifters of the Heartland swamps gave her the ability to temporarily restructure her nails and bones. A potion of Deepstrider blood healed her wounds. Regular doses of Nightwyrm venom kept her immune to the vast majority of poisons.

And a dozen other treatments strengthened her in ways she didn't understand.

She understood the pain. Pain like fire flowing along her bones, like her bones shifting and cracking all at once, like her body was trying to eat itself from the inside out. And the needles. All those needles.

Every night, she woke in sweat from dreams about the needles.

The worst of the treatments had ended, and Meia had been thankful more than once for their effects. She was faster, stronger, more capable than any other Consultant in the Guild. Best of all, she was finally better than Shera.

But now, those very advantages worked against her.

All the Kameira whose power rested inside her—the Nightwyrm, the Deepstrider, the Shadeshifter, the Duskwinder, the Sandborn Hydra, countless others—all of them begged her to run.

Meia didn't want to run. She wanted to stand, and fight beside her Emperor.

The Kameira didn't see an Emperor. They saw a predator.

So when the light went out, Meia and her heightened reflexes stayed frozen, locked in an internal battle.

When her eyes adjusted to the darkness, and she saw a blur moving toward her, she moved on instinct. She leaped backwards, pulling her shears into a defensive stance.

Bronze met bronze as the Emperor's swords crashed into Meia's knives. But his weapons had more than one man's strength driving them. They had been born in ancient war-forges, invested with a thousand years of rock-solid Intent. Those blades could carve the heart out of a mountain.

Meia's knives were just as old, and almost as heavy with Intent, but they had been carried by assassins. Not warriors. If a Gardener needed to block an opponent's blade, she had already failed.

When swords struck shears, Meia's blades were knocked aside with enough force to drive her to her knees. If not for her alchemy-reinforced body, the bones in her wrists would have shattered.

The Emperor's eyes were fevered, his scalp slick with sweat, but he did not slow. He pulled a blade back, and then a white sun exploded in the room, driving a spear through each of Meia's dark-adjusted eyes.

She shrieked and scrambled back, throwing up a hand. Even more than the Emperor's ancient blades, at that point, she feared the light.

But the back of her mind realized what had happened: Shera threw a flare.

Meia's eyes adjusted quickly, if painfully. The tube of alchemy blazed in the corner, lighting the chamber up like noonday. Creatures of bone and pale flesh, which had been invisible in the shadows, hissed and slithered back into the tunnels from which they had come.

She expected to see a bronze sword plunging into her chest, but Lucan was there, a black cloth mask over his head. A spade flashed in the light, aiming for the Emperor's neck, but the sweep of one sword knocked it aside.

Lucan held a shear in one hand and kept the other open, throwing spades and needles and what seemed to be junk from his pouches at the Emperor to maintain distance as he backed away. Leading the enemy away from Meia.

Once again, Meia hesitated.

We never abandon our brothers and sisters, her mother Yala said.

And then, *We obey the Emperor without question.*

If the Emperor wanted them dead, who was she to argue?

Lucan launched a low kick, hitting only air, and a white-armored boot crashed down and shattered his shin. Lucan managed not to scream, hopping back on one foot and tossing a handful of glittering powder at the Emperor's face.

It landed in the Emperor's eyes, but did nothing. He didn't even blink. He drew one sword back for a fatal blow.

And Meia hesitated no longer.

She bunched strength in her legs and leaped across the chamber, her shears in each hand, driving them down toward the Emperor's shoulders.

He slipped aside and her knives bit only air. His foot met her forehead and she tumbled back, head and heels in a jumble, landing in a pile against the wall.

The Emperor stomped on Lucan's other leg, smashing it, and the young Gardener finally screamed. The sound broke Meia's will.

He's the Emperor. Who are we to resist him?

Then Shera joined the fight.

Her black hair fell around her face like a hood, shrouding her expression as she knocked the Emperor's legs out from under him.

He caught himself with one hand against the ground, impossibly agile, and still managed to counterattack with a kick. Shera didn't block it; she ducked her head aside and brought up her knife, scoring a cut along the back of his knee.

For the thousandth time in the past five years, Meia watched from her back while Shera did what she could not.

A steady stream of silver flowed from Shera, spades and needles and hidden daggers flashing through the air. The Emperor batted most of them aside, but each time he did, Shera was there to deliver a strike with her bronze blade.

If he met that attack, she would simply move out of the way, flowing through a shadow like a shark through the depths. From every angle, with every weapon at her disposal, Shera kept up a furious attack.

Most of them failed to land, but some did. A nick appeared high on the Emperor's cheek, and on the backs of both knees, and at each joint in his armor.

Meia couldn't understand it. Shera was slower, and weaker, and less experienced than her opponent. But somehow she stayed unharmed, while the Emperor picked up a collection of injuries that would slowly cripple even him.

Without looking, Shera hopped backwards, over the still-sleeping form of the Watchman. As she turned her head, eyes tracking her opponent, Meia finally got a clear look at her expression.

It was absolutely blank. Like an anatomical sketch of a human girl, instead of an actual person. Her eyes were as dead as a snake's, and she scarcely seemed to breathe. Even the Emperor, in the grip of madness, looked more human than she did at that moment.

A sense of despair settled into Meia's belly like a chip of ice. *How am I supposed to compete with that?*

I'm only human.

But she wasn't. Not anymore.

She gathered her strength, the power that a team of skilled alchemists had given her as a gift, and prepared to show Shera how a *real* killer took its prey.

Shera stopped, like a dog reaching the end of its rope. For a second, her eyes flicked over the Emperor's expression. Then her shoulders relaxed, and she wiped her shears clean on her black pants.

"Don't play games," Shera said at last, her voice flat. "Either kill me, or tell me the truth."

The Emperor's back was turned to Meia, so she couldn't see his expression. He spun one sword through the air, idly, like a bored duelist.

"Which truth would you like?" he asked, at last.

Somehow, he didn't sound nearly as insane as Meia had expected.

Shera slammed her shears into place behind her back. "I like finishing my jobs quickly. I can't do that if I don't know what the job is."

He laughed, warm and rich, as though they were all enjoying a leisurely ride through the countryside. Then he plunged both his swords into the ground, sheathing them in the squishy gray floor.

"Do you mind if I tend to him first?" the Emperor asked, with a nod toward Lucan.

Shera said nothing.

All Meia could think was, *What happened?*

As the ice shrank back from Shera's heart, anger took its place.

She didn't get angry often. Most things, she could shrug off. But if the Emperor was going to string her along like a puppet, she at least wanted to know her part in the show.

Besides, he broke Lucan's legs.

The Emperor held out his hand to Meia, who looked as though she wasn't sure whether to run, fight, or throw up. "Lord Bareius gave you a canister with a pink cap. Give it to me."

Meia fumbled at her belt before she found the canister he was looking for. She tossed it to him underhand, and he snatched it out of the air.

Lucan drifted in and out of consciousness, the cloth of his mask moving up and down as he tried to speak.

"When did you realize?" the Emperor asked, dumping a pill from the canister into his open palm. After a moment's thought, he added a second.

"You fought like anyone else would have," Shera responded. "Not like you." She'd seen the Emperor jump from a hundred feet up in the air and land safely, catch a falling girl in his sleeve, Awaken a sea of gravel, and dissolve a teacup with nothing but his will. Any one of those feats, a normal Reader would call fundamentally impossible.

Yet, when he fought her, he relied entirely on the power of his invested blades.

The Emperor nodded, absorbing the information. He rolled up the bottom of Lucan's mask, giving him enough room to force the pills into the boy's mouth.

The room rumbled again, wind hissing between the wires.

"REBIRTH!" Nakothi shouted. Cold fingers brushed Shera's skin, and she shivered.

Facing into the shadows, the Emperor stood. He laughed loudly, defiantly, into the dark. "This is *my* world! Take your whispers back to the dead!"

The wind howled away, like breath leaving a dying throat.

But Shera noticed that his hands were shaking.

"Were you...faking, then?" Meia asked hesitantly. "We thought..."

He turned a smile on her. "Nakothi has no hold on me yet."

It was a lie. *Something* had laid its hand on him at the beginning. Maybe he had allowed it, for whatever reason, and had shaken the spell away later. But for a moment there, he had changed into a different person.

"Yet?" Shera asked.

He leaned forward on the hilts of his swords, which stood up like twin flagpoles from the gray floor. "That was the bargain I made, a thousand years ago. While the Dead Mother sleeps, I can use her power freely. But death will not hold her forever. When she begins to rise, her authority over me will be greater than mine over her. She will control me. And I will need to be stopped."

With an audible crackle, Lucan's legs pulled themselves together. He gasped, like a scream in reverse, and Shera felt a sympathetic pain shoot through her own body. The Emperor placed a hand on his knee, and Lucan's cries eased.

"Why do you think they allowed Lucan into the Gardeners?" he asked.

Meia and Shera looked at each other, uncertain.

"His disposition is *clearly* unsuitable," the Emperor continued. "He's empathetic, clear-headed, has a strong moral compass, and he questions everything. He's far from the template of an ideal Gardener, and under normal circumstances they would have inducted him straight in the Architects. So why did they raise him with you?"

"Because you told them to," Shera realized aloud.

"I needed a Reader that fit several criteria, including age. His disposition as a killer was not one of those criteria. I don't need him to be ruthless, I need *you* to be ruthless." He pointed at Shera. Then he turned his finger to Meia. "I need *you* to be strong. And I need *him* to be skilled."

The Emperor swept a hand to encompass all of them. "Today was meant to be a practice game. We have years more before the main event, and before that time, I hope to come up with an alternate solution. But in case I fail, I *will not* let the Elders win.

"You three have one task, and one alone.

"When Nakothi rises, you will kill me."

CHAPTER TWENTY-FIVE

Do Soulbound Vessels have their own consciousness? My sword says yes, but it's a liar.

– Jorin Curse-breaker

The Handmaiden pulled the dome of earth away from the arena like a child lifting the roof off her dollhouse. Pieces of earth and stone rained down, shaking the ground.

Shera leaned on Lucan's shoulder, limping to shelter. Meia crawled behind them as the three of them limped to the broken wooden shed. It wouldn't offer much cover, not from the rocks falling from the ceiling, but it was overshadowed by a stone chunk of the arena that loomed overhead. Hopefully, that would break up the bigger rocks and pieces of earth, while the shed's crumbling roof kept the dirt and smaller stones away.

Calder, she noticed, didn't seek shelter. Instead he knelt by Urzaia, heedless of his own safety.

Good. Maybe he'll get crushed.

She sunk down, sitting with her back against the shed, and listened to the patter of stones like rain. A thunderous impact shook the arena as the Handmaiden dropped the roof to the side.

Shera put a hand on her shear to quiet its laughter.

"What did you name it," she asked, without looking up at Lucan.

"Syphren," he replied, grinning down. "It means 'The Whispering Death.' The knife helped me choose the name, so it wasn't all my fault."

Meia looked at him suspiciously. "That sounds like an Elder name."

"It killed a Heart of Nakothi. There's a little Elder in it."

The Handmaiden loomed over the exposed arena, her face shifting and horrible. "Speaking of Elders," Shera said, "what are we going to do about that?"

Lucan squinted up. "You should be able to kill it. Syphren can feed on anything it does to protect itself."

"I'll walk up and stab it, then." The Handmaiden's tentacles writhed, each big enough to tear a shark to pieces. The Children of Nakothi swarmed around her, vague and shapeless at this distance, but surely enough to keep

Shera from approaching.

Meia looked at her blue-scaled shoulder wound, which was taking longer than usual to heal. "Come to think of it, Lucan, how did you get out?"

"The cell fell apart in the earthquake," he said. "I just sort of...walked out."

So it had been that easy, had it? "If I had known all it would take was an earthquake, I would have made one years ago," Shera said.

He looked skeptical. "How do you *make* an earthquake?"

She gestured around her. "Maybe I made this one."

"Did you?" Meia asked, suddenly serious. "What happened? Why is there a Handmaiden here at all? Where did the Children come from?"

Shera leaned back against the wall of the shed, resting her injuries, but still keeping a wary eye on Calder. "I don't know. I'm sure it has something to do with the Heart, so I was coming here to find out if Calder Marten had done something with it. Not much chance of that now."

Meia looked to Lucan, who sighed and pulled off his glove. "I assumed Shera had destroyed the Heart and this was the result," he said. "But I'll see what I can."

He held out his bare hand, wincing in pain. He must have overdone it, working on the Heart's seal and then Awakening her blade. But he stayed in that position for thirty seconds before his eyes snapped open.

"I think the Heart is *gone,*" he said. "It's hard to tell, since the power of Nakothi is everywhere, but I don't hear anything like the Heart. Someone must have destroyed it."

"It wasn't me," Shera said. She had assumed that she was the only one on the Gray Island with an invested weapon significant enough to kill Nakothi's Heart, but that was nothing more than an arrogant assumption.

She thought of Calder Marten's orange-and-black sword, and the effect it had on Elderspawn. He had stabbed that headless gorilla once, and it dissolved into a rotten black mess. Would it have the same effect on a Heart of the Dead Mother? Maybe he *had* destroyed the Heart, and somehow survived the ensuing release of Nakothi's power.

If it had that effect on the Heart, then what would it do to a Handmaiden?

Urzaia Woodsman had given up even his tentative hold on life, and Calder rose. The falling dirt and rocks had stopped, now that the broken roof was gone, but the distortion in space was still there. Sand and smaller pebbles drifted up in streams, clouding the air.

Through the cloud of dust, the Navigator walked toward them, Awakened sword in his right hand and the Emperor's crown on his head. He stopped only a few yards from their shelter.

Meia tensed, and Lucan slid his glove back on, his hands drifting toward his shears.

Shera rose to her feet, unconcerned. Calder wouldn't attack them head-on like this unless they'd backed him into a corner; it was more his style to run. Unless the rage over Urzaia's death had gotten the better of him, in which case she would kill him.

"It seems we have a common obstacle," he said. The Handmaiden, she assumed. His voice was bitter, as though he resented even having to speak to her.

He pointed his orange Awakened blade at her green one. "Can you kill it?" he asked.

Why was he asking her? If he could destroy the Heart, surely he had the power to deal with a lesser Elder.

But she had received her knife only minutes ago, and she was already learning the nature of its power. If he had carried his sword for longer than that, then he should know its limitations. And he was a Reader as well; maybe he knew he couldn't fight the Handmaiden.

She turned to Lucan, silently asking for his opinion. He was the one who had Awakened the weapon.

"If we can get you close enough," he said. She could tell that he didn't think they *could* get close, but he was willing to try.

Calder rubbed his right arm with his left. Now that she looked closely, there was a red mark visible through the tears in his sleeve. It looked like some sort of brand, or an angry bruise left from a monster gripping his arm too hard. Even with a sword that dissolved Elderspawn, it seemed he couldn't fight through an army of Nakothi's Children without taking an injury or two.

"It's planning on attacking soon," he said, which Shera accepted as a product of his Reader's senses. "When it does, I'll hit it as hard as I can. You'll have to find your own opening."

So she would have to go up and stab the giant Elder after all. Great.

Her wounds pulled at her body and spirit like weights, dragging her down into exhaustion, but there was some core of her that had plenty of energy. Her mind and her flesh cried out for sleep, but somehow she felt that, right now, she could push herself beyond those limitations.

It was the energy she had stolen from Urzaia, she realized. That, or the Awakened weapon itself did something to increase her stamina. Either way, she'd take it.

If it would even help.

"What are the odds that it will stay dead?" she asked wearily. Maybe as a Reader, he knew something she didn't.

"Based on my experience with Elders? Abandon that hope right now."

She'd been afraid of that. She rubbed a hand over her closed eyes, wishing for sleep. "Maybe if I get wounded killing an Elder they'll give me some time off. Meia, here's your chance to stab me in the back."

Meia opened her mouth to try and respond, but muscles shifted unnaturally under her skin, and the blue-scaled flesh around her wound crawled. She shut her mouth, giving up.

Every time Shera grew jealous of Meia's enhanced power, she only had to remind herself of the drawbacks.

Lucan patted Shera on the shoulder. "Don't worry. I'm sure she would stab you if she could."

Something about that statement seemed to make Calder angry. His fist tightened on his sword as though he meant to use it, and his face turned red. "Just do your part," he said roughly, and marched away.

Lucan and Shera looked at each other. After a moment, Lucan shrugged.

Meia pulled herself to her feet as her skin settled down. The blue scales faded from her shoulder, the wound having closed to an angry red scar. She gulped down air like she had emerged from a river.

"Sorry," she panted. "Had to...take care of that."

"It's not like we were doing anything important," Lucan said.

Shera held Syphren's hilt and looked up, staring at the Handmaiden in the...chest. It was too painful to look directly at its head.

The Handmaiden stood there at the ledge, bubbling like a teakettle gone mad, Children running around its "feet."

"What is it waiting for?" she asked.

"It's afraid," Lucan began, but whatever else he was going to say was drowned out in a bellowing, threatening voice that bounced around in the hollowed-out arena as though an army of men were all shouting at once.

"TESTAMENT," the voice shouted. The three Consultants all grabbed their weapons and turned, looking for the threat.

Calder stood only a few yards away, speaking to his pet Elderspawn. The creature flared its wings, tentacles writhing over its mouth, and its cruel, dark eyes seemed to sparkle with laughter.

"Foster," Calder said, and a second later the creature boomed out an echo: "FOSTER!"

The Consultants ran, both to distance themselves from the voice and to prepare. Calder was obviously doing something, and they needed to be in position.

As soon as they left the shelter, they saw that they were surrounded.

"READY CANNONS!"

The Children of Nakothi weren't just waiting above; they had snuck down into the freshly opened crater around the arena, gathering around the sandy arena floor, waiting to attack. Now monstrosities of dead flesh filled the seats built for the living, gnashing teeth and snapping claws like dogs held on the end of a thousand leashes.

Just as Shera saw them, pulling her shears, the Handmaiden slithered to the edge of the hole. She shrieked, pointing down into the arena.

And every one of the Elderspawn exploded into action.

"AIM," Calder's pet declared, and then Consultants met Children blade-to-bone.

Shera was sure they'd be overrun in seconds, given Meia's condition, but she underestimated her new weapon. The bronze blade in her right would cut through children perfectly well, but Syphren...

The Whispering Death *reveled* in its role. A nick of the green transparent blade stole all of Nakothi's power away from the Child struck, reverting it to nothing more than an inanimate pile of body parts. Green wisps of light floated around each of her victims, spinning around her and around the Children like an army of ghosts.

And with each enemy struck down, she got a little stronger, a little faster. She vaulted over something like a wingless, crawling wasp made of petrified muscle, slashing it as she flew. It died, and another green ghost was born. A blue-skinned imp rushed at her, screaming, and she did something on pure instinct that she'd never imagined.

She reached out with her mind and *tore* its power away.

An emerald wisp of light was ripped from its body, and Shera hadn't even come near it with her blade.

As an experiment, she stopped, listening to Syphren's whispers for a moment. They didn't cohere into words—the blade was having too much fun to converse—but she drew some meaning from it nonetheless.

And a second later, she drew in her Intent as though taking a deep breath.

A *wave* of green light, like an ocean's tide, surged out of the surrounding Elderspawn and into her. For a moment she was blinded by a verdant flash, as though she'd stared directly into an emerald sun.

For fifty yards around her, all the Children collapsed.

The surge of strength was like nothing she'd ever experienced. Every grain of sand stood out in distinct contrast to its fellows, every hiss of the wind was like a symphony. The world was bright and clear, and power *shone* through her body. She felt like she was glowing.

She glanced down at herself for a moment to make sure she wasn't actually shining.

"FIRE!" the hideous voice shouted, and the Handmaiden staggered back as though she'd been struck by a cannon. A second later, the sound of a cannon firing caught up, and Shera realized what Calder was doing.

His ship was in the water, off the edge of the island. He was ordering his gunner from *here.*

Shera started to run toward the edge of the hole, where a ladder went up to yet another hidden entrance. It should come out right under the Handmaiden's tentacles.

She slowed when she realized that Lucan and Meia weren't following.

Blades at the ready, Shera spun, ready to kill whatever threat her two teammates were facing. Only to realize that she already had.

Body parts in the shapes of animals and monsters lay in piles before Lucan and Meia, messy and rotten. They both had their shears in their hands, staring at her as though they couldn't believe their own eyes.

"Shera," Lucan asked unsteadily, "what did you do?"

"FIRE!" the Elderspawn announced again, and the island shook again.

"What do you mean?" Shera held up the dagger, showing him its shining green hands. "I'm using Syphren."

"Awakening can give a weapon powers it didn't already have," he said. "It can't give them to *you*. Shera, I think you may be Soulbound."

Meia's left eye twitched, and she looked like she was holding herself back from screaming in frustration.

She glanced at the dagger and then up to him, skeptical. "I don't think so." She didn't feel any different. "I'm not any stronger than I was. That Izyrian gladiator could punch through stone. You *know* what the Emperor could do."

"FIRE!"

Above them, the Handmaiden collapsed.

"What a Soulbound can do depends on their Vessel," Lucan explained. "Most of them aren't any stronger than anyone else. Urzaia was a Champion—his body was enhanced, like Meia's. That's likely where his strength came from."

Shera waved that away, heading for the ladder. "That doesn't matter now. We have our mission." And she had so much energy now that was begging to be used.

Lucan hurried after her, still speaking out of concern. "This is important, Shera. There are risks in the bonding process, and there are certain dangers facing Soulbound...you're not listening."

She wasn't.

She leaped up the ladder, landing with her feet on the fifth rung, and kept climbing.

Behind her, Meia grumbled.

They emerged from the hatch at the top of the ladder amid a forest of undulating white tentacles and flailing, grasping hands. The hands were made out of the same pale flesh as the rest of the Handmaiden, seeming to grow out of the flesh of the tentacles, but otherwise they looked human.

The whole mess of tentacles smelled like an open sewer filled with fish, and Shera had to breathe lightly through her mouth as she staggered away from the hatch.

Optimistically, she pulled Syphren, slashing at one of the nearby tentacles. Maybe it would affect the Handmaiden as easily as it had the Children, and they could all go home.

The limb slithered out of the way, and her strike bit only air. A second later, the Handmaiden pulled back from them entirely, gathering her tentacles underneath her body. It was difficult to appreciate from down in the arena, but the Elder was *huge,* towering sixty or seventy feet in the air at least. Her arms, bony and double-jointed, looked as though they could smash buildings and uproot forests. Her head...

Shera tried not to think about the creature's head.

The Handmaiden let out a long, wet scream, like a singer drowning in the middle of a solo.

At that signal, all the Children in the forest charged toward the three Consultants.

It was like facing down a hideous army, but fueled by her newfound strength, Shera ran straight toward the onrushing wave. The first rank died, collapsing in a whirling storm of green wisps.

But the second rank was right behind them, hitting Meia with slashing claws, whipping tails, and gnashing mandibles.

Shera couldn't react in time, stunned as she was by the incoming energy from the dead Elderspawn. The Children of Nakothi met Meia instead.

Eyes shining orange, Meia hit the monsters with a shout. Her shears cleaved through the first creature, something like a hollowed-out bull with swollen, jet-black horns. She leaped over it and landed with both feet on a skinless dog, planting both knives in its back.

Lucan followed up, impaling two Children at once on his shears. He stayed behind Meia, careful not to get in her way, catching only the ones that first made it through her.

It took Shera a few seconds to blink the light from her eyes and catch her breath after the influx of strength.

This will take some getting used to.

Syphren didn't seem to agree. *I want it,* it whispered. *Bring it to me.*

Shera's eyes moved to the Handmaiden, and she ran forward once again. She passed Meia, slashing Elderspawn with her green blade, leaving a trail of emerald ghosts spinning in her wake. The Children were trying to get in her way; up *there* was her real target.

The trees were packed with Children of Nakothi, so thick that it looked like the underbrush had sprouted rotten flesh. Shera scrambled over them, walking from crawling beast to crawling beast. She killed them when they got in her way, but her eyes were still fixed on the Handmaiden.

Behind her, Lucan called out, but she ignored him. He wasn't important.

"It's mine," she and the knife whispered at once.

A moment later, a figure in black hurled a bone-white insect out of her way. Meia came to a halt, kicking up the dirt of the forest as she skidded to a stop. Her blacks were torn, stained, and even *burned* in a few places, though her mask was still in place. Her blond hair fell around her eyes, in worse state than her clothes, and her gaze burned orange. Black sleeves flexed and moved as muscles squirmed under her skin.

Meia was clearing the way for her. Good. That would help her reach her real target even faster.

Shera started to walk past Meia, but a hand caught her on the collar and shoved with superhuman strength. Shera staggered backwards, managing to stay on her feet, flailing for purchase with hands that held her shears.

Meia was trying to get in her way. What was she *thinking?*

Didn't she know that was dangerous?

One of the Elderspawn leaped at her from the side and she stole its power without looking, green wisps spinning around her body. Shera fell into a fighting crouch, Syphren on her left and bronze shear on her right.

If Meia wanted to stand in her way, so be it. Shera could go *through* her.

Someone placed a hand on Shera's shoulder, and it was a presence even her knife recognized. Lucan.

"Put your blades up, Shera," he said desperately. His hand vanished from her shoulder and there came the sounds of combat: grunts from him, and a weird whistling growl from one of the Children.

She killed his opponent without looking around, setting another pale spirit of a fireball spinning around her. Put her blades up? Why? If she did that, she wouldn't be able to kill Elders anymore.

She looked up at the Handmaiden with the longing of a starving woman staring at a feast. It was *hers.* It was all hers. And the giant was wounded! Bleeding! The more time she wasted, the more strength it would lose. She had to act *now* if she wanted to take it.

And she did want to.

She started forward, but he begged her again. "Just sheathe it, please. I'll teach you how to kill it."

How? It was simple. All she had to do was kill Meia, kill any Children that got in her way, and then kill the Handmaiden. A three-step process.

But she and Syphren both recognized Lucan, even as they resented the delay. She slammed both shears into the sheaths at her back.

And a second later, when Syphren's voice retreated to a dull whisper, the world looked much clearer.

Meia relaxed, her eyes lingering on Shera for a moment before she went about the work of clearing out Elderspawn again. Had Shera almost attacked Meia? Really? Meia could tear her limb from limb.

She shuddered, both in fear of herself and of what she had almost done.

"I..." she said, but she wasn't sure what to say. "I don't..."

Lucan's eyes raised past her, and without a word he tackled her out of the way.

A tree fell where they'd been standing a second before. The Handmaiden had another in her hand, roots and all, and this time she howled before she threw it like a javelin.

Shera and Lucan rolled in different directions, but this time the tree struck at such an angle that it drove itself straight into the ground like a spear. The ground rumbled like a struck drum.

The Elder reached down and tore up another couple of trees, readying them to throw. Children skittered closer to Shera.

The two of them ran next to Meia.

"We need a plan," Shera yelled, as they got close to the Elder's tentacles.

Meia gestured to the Handmaiden with one hand as she punched a skeletal horse out of the way with the other. "Kill it! Do what you've been doing to the others!"

"Won't work," Shera said briefly. That would be like trying to inhale a tornado. "I have to stab it." If the blade penetrated the Handmaiden's flesh, it would turn the Nakothi's power against her servant, and the Handmaiden would effectively destroy itself.

But she didn't explain any of that out loud, nor did Meia ask for an explanation. As they closed on the tentacles through the trees, and as the Handmaiden prepared to throw another tree, Meia threw out a hand for Shera to stop.

When she did, confused, Meia scooped her up in both arms.

It was both shocking and a little embarrassing, and she couldn't help but fight it. "What are you doing? Let me go!"

"I'm going to throw you!"

"...what?"

"I'm throwing you!"

Shera looked up the sixty feet to the top of the Handmaiden's neck. "I'll die. I will definitely die."

Meia threw her.

The wind tore around her as though she'd been launched into a hurricane, and her scream was sucked into her lungs by the speed of her flight. She had expected to tumble head over heels, but she flew surprisingly straight. She supposed that was thanks to Meia's aim.

But her flight path had at least one drawback: she could clearly see that she wasn't going to make it to the top of the Handmaiden's torso.

Instead, she was falling toward the creature's bed of tentacles.

Shera managed to pull her shears as she fell, hoping that she could at least deal the Elder a blow when she hit.

Instead, one of the tentacles whipped up and grabbed her out of the air.

She hit hard, blowing all the air out of her lungs, but not as hard as she expected. She survived the impact, at least. Hands, sprouting out of the Elder's flesh, grasped fistfuls of her clothes and every inch of her body.

And Syphren, cackling with glee, stuck into the meat of the Handmaiden's limb.

Green light crawled out like moss spreading over a boulder, and the Elder shrieked loud enough that the sound tore at Shera's ear.

Then Shera was falling. Again.

The giant limb had lost its strength, releasing Shera and falling limp. That allowed her to plummet on her own.

But the strength lost by the Elder had gone somewhere else.

Into Shera.

The world blazed with light and motion, and for a second Shera felt like she could see everything perfectly, as though she was focused on each individual detail all at once.

She was falling toward the Handmaiden's other tentacles, and most of them were easily the size of thick tree branches. With enhanced reflexes, Shera landed on her feet, dashing down a tentacle as though running on a narrow bridge.

The Handmaiden lashed the limb, flailing it about and trying to knock her off, but Shera kept her balance. Green lights swarmed around her like a parade of fireflies.

A moment later, she reached the creature's torso, a vast wall of pale and desiccated skin.

Shera raised Syphren, prepared to plunge it into the exposed flesh. The Awakened blade hissed in anticipation.

Then the Handmaiden doubled over, sticking her face in Shera's own.

She was staring directly into the heart of everything disgusting and vile that had ever existed. A nest of writhing worms, a disemboweled corpse, a mass grave, a plague-infested heart, it all watched her from inches away. The smell alone was enough to make her retch, but she couldn't look away, couldn't tear her eyes from the horror.

The Handmaiden spoke into her heart, but it was nothing that she could translate into words. She spoke hatred, death, bile, a thousand twisted torments and a million exploitations of human flesh.

Distract us? Syphren whispered, sounding amused. *We are your death.*

Once more, Shera's thoughts grew cold.

The Handmaiden's shock tactic only worked if she thought of those pieces as people. She didn't. The people were dead, and what was left was nothing more than garbage.

Shera was here to kill this thing. That was it. That was all she needed to know.

There was nothing left to think about.

Shera plunged her Awakened blade straight into the center of the Handmaiden's head.

A shriek obliterated thought, Syphren laughed like a madman, and the Dead Mother screamed from somewhere out on the Aion. An emerald light swallowed Shera's vision.

The next thing she knew, she was falling. Meia caught her.

Lucan jogged up next to them a second later. "I'll catch you next time," he said. "Just don't fall from quite so high up."

Meia snorted, carrying Shera away. "Don't hurt yourself. Leave it to me." Her eyes were back to normal, and she carried Shera with no trouble, but her steps were weak. She had to be exhausted, maybe even more so than Shera herself.

Tired? Who's tired? Shera wasn't tired, she realized. She felt *great.* She wanted to jog around the Island once or twice to burn off some of this excess energy. Why was she letting someone else carry her?

She started to say so, but then Lucan peeled Syphren out of her hand and shoved the blade into her sheath.

"Get some sleep," he said gently.

That was all she remembered.

CHAPTER TWENTY-SIX

When a world dies, it starts to decay. It breaks into fragments, and these fragments float on an empty sea: splitting, changing, and merging with one another. They will fade forever, until they latch onto a healthy, inhabited world…or until there's nothing left.

Living inhabitants can sometimes survive the death of their world. They're often twisted, grotesque, and powerful beings, forever altered by their exile to the void.

Something very much like your Elders, in fact.

–The Unknown Wanderer, from *Observations of the Unknown Wanderer* (held in the Architect Council's secret archives)

A group of Shepherds, Masons, and Architects hurried over as soon as the Handmaiden toppled, fighting their way through the maddened Children of Nakothi to provide aid. Lucan started to explain the situation to them, but Meia simply handed Shera over with a polite request for medical attention.

Then she left. There was one more thing she'd left undone.

She limped and staggered her way back toward Lucan's prison, so exhausted that she didn't remember half the trip. Her body raged at her, muscles screaming in pain and writhing for control, but she didn't give them an inch.

Everyone seemed to have forgotten, but Calder Marten had escaped.

Calder Marten, the Navigator who had brought the Heart here in the first place. The one who had been working against them all along. The one whose wife was a member of the Sleepless.

If Shera hadn't caused all this, it was a good bet that one of the Martens *had.* And they would stand trial for it if she had to drag them before the Council of Architects herself.

If Calder's wife was in her cage, Meia would stand guard and make sure she could be brought to trial. If she wasn't, Meia would hunt her down.

She may have felt like she was going to collapse at any second, but Meia never left a task undone. Besides, she still had more than enough strength to overpower a merely human opponent.

Meia found the trap door leading down to the prison standing open, the stairs lit. She followed them down, and even the second door—the one within the tunnel, the one that should have been guarded—was standing open.

She didn't visit this underground prison often, certainly not as often as Shera did, but she was surprised to see the far end choked with debris. It must have collapsed under the Handmaiden's weight.

Lucan's cell seemed intact, if dirty, but the one next door had hundreds of pounds of earth and stone spilling out of it. If Mrs. Marten had been in there, she was dead.

And Calder looked like he knew it.

He stood with eyes closed and hand stretched out, obviously Reading for a glimpse of his wife.

This was too good of an opportunity to miss.

Meia pulled her shear quietly, sneaking down the hall toward him. Her knees felt as though they would buckle, so she had to move even slower than usual or risk breaking him out of his trance, but he was gone. There was no way he'd hear her.

She was weaker than she'd thought; she couldn't drag him to trial if he resisted. She hadn't brought any non-lethal needles with her, and he would be too heavy for her to carry in her condition.

Well, that was fine. She was a Gardener, after all.

She slashed at the base of his jaw with her shear, intending to spill his blood on the stones. He must have felt her coming, because he jerked back, bending all the way backwards at the waist.

Meia leaped after him, drawing her second shear in the same motion...

Or she tried to.

Her legs locked up, the Kameira within her resisting her control. Her body screamed at her to rest. She staggered to the side instead, propping herself up with one hand.

Just because she couldn't control her limbs was no reason to give up. She had a mission to complete.

"You...will not...escape," she said between breaths.

Maybe he would give up.

Calder looked at her for a moment, horror and pity mixed on his face. He looked as though he was about to rush her to a surgeon, not attack.

I must look three days dead, she thought. Maybe this hadn't been such a good idea.

Then his expression firmed, and he pulled his orange-and-black sword. "You should have checked behind you," he said.

The words took a moment to register, but when they did, she glared at him. He thought he could beat her with *tricks?* On the verge of collapse she might be, but she wasn't going to put on a farce for his amusement.

A sound behind her caught her attention, like a snapping flag or flapping wings. And a voice like Othaghor himself bellowed out, "BEHIND YOU!"

There was something behind her.

She spun, bringing both shears to bear, slashing out in front of her. A pain and a white light flared in her skull.

Meia struggled weakly, but the blow and exhaustion took their toll. Her consciousness faded to black.

Her last thought: *I can't tell Shera about this.*

When Shera woke, she found herself alone in the infirmary.

Over the last two weeks, she'd spent more time in the Gray Island infirmary than in the ten years prior. She'd have to be more careful. Well, considering that she was heading straight back to a desk job in the Capital, she effectively had no *choice* but to be careful.

The thought of working at a desk actually seemed appealing at the moment, which Shera took to mean that she needed more sleep.

But she needed answers, and she needed to relieve her bladder, and most importantly she was starving. She spent most of the next ten minutes easing herself out of bed.

It was like her body was having a contest to decide which could hurt the worst: her joints, her muscles, or her impressive collection of flesh wounds. When she pressed her feet against the floor, even the soles of her feet hurt, as though she'd bruised them.

Straightening her back was another exercise in agony, primarily because her chest, both shoulders, and her neck were all stuck in the same network of bandages. She couldn't turn her head without causing the stiff cloth around her stomach to tighten.

Shera found her knife belt sitting on a table nearby, and she realized that someone had done to Syphren what the healers had done to her. The blade was wrapped, sheath and all, in a full case of bandages. A few bare spots of the sheath peeked out, but not a speck of the knife showed through.

After a moment's concentration, Shera determined that she couldn't hear a single whisper coming from the weapon. That could only be a good thing. Whatever Syphren had done to her—whether she was a Soulbound or not—she didn't like it. It seemed complicated.

And she wanted to avoid further complications for the moment, not embrace them.

A few pointed questions led her to Lucan. From combining the stories of several passing Masons and Architects, she was able to piece together what Lucan had done during the day she'd been asleep. First, he'd invested and woven bandages around her blade to stop it from whispering. Second, he'd reported to the High Council of Architects, telling them his version of the battle against the Elderspawn.

Finally, he'd found a new prison and reported back to his cell.

It took her longer to find his new cell, as everything on the Island was hidden, and all the Consultants were still in chaos. Most of them were still panicking over the single, most obvious change: Bastion's Veil had vanished.

The island was still surrounded by low wisps of fog, like smoke that hadn't quite blown away yet, but the sun shone brightly on the Gray Island. Shera didn't know what had caused it, but every single Elderspawn on the island—dead or alive—had vanished.

The Veil was supposed to protect them; well, maybe it had finally done its job. Somehow.

Shera finally tracked Lucan to an open cell at the base of a cliff. His walls were mountain rock, and the door—instead of being made entirely of bars—was a single piece of solid wood set with a small barred window at the top.

And a familiar face stood outside the door: Hansin, the same Mason guard that had watched over Lucan before. His shoulders slumped when he saw her, and his hand moved to the hilt of his sword.

An unconscious gesture, she was sure.

"Why do you always come during my shift?"

Shera held up another covered wooden bowl. She smiled as cheerily as she could, though even smiling seemed to stretch the bandages around her throat. "Because you work lunchtime!"

He sighed and backed away, giving them some semblance of privacy.

Shera chatted with Lucan for a while as she ate, though it took her far too long to get through all his questions about her recovery. "Should you be out of bed?" "Do the Architects know where you are?" "Do you need to be resting?" "Should you be throwing knives right now?"

But after she assured him that she was fine and recovering comfortably, he spoke about his new situation. "At least I get some fresh air," he said, peering out the window. "And I'll get to see the sunlight. They managed to recover most of my belongings from the old cell, so I'm right at home."

"You went *back* into prison," Shera said. She couldn't keep the bitterness from her voice.

He gave her what he likely intended to be a comforting smile, but it came across more sad than comforting. "I was never here because I couldn't escape, Shera."

Shera let that go, for the moment. She had plenty of time left to get him out. Kerian was on the High Council, and she would eventually see reason.

After that, Lucan explained the wrapping on her knife.

"I used the wrappings on Jorin Curse-breaker's sword as a guide," he explained. Jorin, the Regent of the South, carried around a full-sized sword wrapped in cloth everywhere he went. It looked incredibly inconvenient, and she said so.

"You won't be able to draw it quickly," he admitted. "And you'll need to change wrappings every few days. Jorin should be here soon, and he might be able to come up with something that lasts longer, but this was the best I could do. At least you'll be...yourself."

Shera remembered the unnatural focus that had come over her at the sight of the Handmaiden. The focus, the greed, the rush of *energy* as she fed on the power of her enemies.

She had almost attacked Meia.

"Thank you," she said eventually.

Nearby, Hansin cleared his throat.

She pointedly looked away from him, taking another bite of her lunch.

"Gardener," he said, a little louder.

Shera eventually gave up and looked at him. "Is visiting hour over?"

He gestured to the side, where an Architect in a flowing black dress bowed before her. "There's a messenger here for you."

"I come from the High Council," the woman said, without rising from her bow. "They would like to see Gardener Shera."

Shera wolfed down the rest of her food and slid the bowl through the bars to Lucan.

"Hold that for me until I come back," she said.

Hansin stepped toward her. "I have to inspect every delivery to the prisoner."

"Come back tonight," Lucan said. "I want to know what the Council said."

She nodded.

"The prisoner can only receive one visit per day!"

Lucan frowned at the tiny, barred window in the door. "I can't kiss you through these."

"It's okay," Shera said. "I'll pick the lock later."

Hansin groaned.

Lucan did stick one hand through the bars, and she gripped it. "I love you," he said firmly.

Shera cleared her throat and looked around. "There are…other people… here."

He raised his voice. "I love you!" he shouted. He turned to Hansin, pointing back to Shera. "I love her."

"I heard you," the guard said wearily.

Shera stiffened, afraid to turn around, but she quickly murmured back. "…I love you too."

She hurried away, keeping her head ducked so the Council's messenger couldn't see her bright red face. When they were far enough away, the other woman laughed. "Ah, young romance."

Shera blushed further.

"What are you, thirteen? Fourteen? I've got a little sister who blushes when she holds hands with a boy. She turns twelve this winter."

"I *will* kill you."

The High Council, for once, was not meeting in the underground Council chamber. Instead, they brought Shera to one of the largest conference rooms in the Island chapter house, reserved for meeting with the wealthiest clients.

The room was situated on the third floor of the chapter house, and surrounded on all sides by windows. Normally this would only allow the dubious view of Bastion's Veil and the rough, natural charm of the island's landscape. But now that the Veil had vanished, the conference table was bathed in the light of the setting sun.

Five thick-padded chairs sat around the table in the center of the massive room, but only two of the seats were filled. Kerian—swathed in even more bandages than Shera herself—and Yala sat at the table, directly across from one another.

Without waiting for permission, Shera took the chair next to Kerian.

Yala glared at her. "My daughter left me locked in a *closet* for a full day. Where is she?"

Shera fought back the smile brought on by that wonderful mental image and answered the question honestly. "I don't know. I only woke up three hours ago."

She turned to Kerian, who was rubbing at her bandaged wrist. "Bastion's Veil?" Shera asked.

"Emergency protocol," Kerian responded. "Sweeps all lesser Elderspawn off the Island. I had to wait until the Handmaiden was gone, so thank you for that."

Shera gestured to Kerian's injuries. "Sorry about your...body."

"We have some talented healers among the Architects," Kerian said. "Most of my injuries are minor."

She shifted her leg as she spoke, which was bound in a splint.

Most of her injuries.

Shera winced. "Your leg?"

Kerian looked at Yala and forcibly changed the subject. "I think this is the appropriate time to clarify some misunderstandings, don't you, Yala?"

The blond Councilor nodded, but she didn't look happy about it.

"Very good. Shera, what is the purpose of this Guild?"

Shera looked from one High Councilor to another, caught off-guard by the apparent change of subject. "To serve our clients as we serve the

Empire." It was an easy question to answer; any Consultant would have answered the same.

Yala leaned closer, eyes hard. "What Empire?"

Shera recalled her conversation with Meia a few days before. If she remembered correctly, Yala thought the Consultants would be better off without an Empire.

She sagged back into her chair, tired. She wanted to go back to *sleep,* not debate political philosophy with her superiors.

"I worked with the Emperor," Shera said wearily. "I knew him as well as anybody did. He would tell us that the Empire is made up of people, first and foremost. As long as those people still exist, we should serve them as best we can."

"Well said," Kerian responded. "And we agree. We simply doubt that raising another Emperor is the best way to serve the Imperial citizens."

Shera narrowed her eyes, looking from Kerian to Yala. Both of them were fixed on her, judging her reaction.

We agree. We doubt.

"You agree with her," Shera said to Kerian. "You think the Empire is dead."

That explained why, despite their obvious dislike of one another, Kerian and Yala were always working together. For all their friction, they were on the same side.

It took her a moment to wrap her brain around the idea.

Kerian raised a hand to the scar on her forehead, speaking softly. "Think about it, Shera. You knew the Emperor. Do you think we could ever raise anyone like him?"

Absolutely not.

"Maybe Estyr Six, or one of the other Regents," she suggested. They weren't immortal, not in the same way that the Emperor was, but they had helped found the Empire. Surely they wouldn't want to see it break into pieces.

"We offered," Kerian said.

"You should remember," Yala added drily. "You were there."

"And as you know better than most," Kerian continued, "the Elders seek to corrupt leaders first. They *want* one point of vulnerability for the human race, one person that they can control, and thereby control all the rest. We're not leaving people undefended. We're *trusting* the world to govern itself."

Shera had only met with the Regents once, and spoken face-to-face with Estyr Six herself. The current Regent of the North was the Emperor's first companion, and the woman the Emperor had spoken of most fondly. She was a legend.

"You have grown beyond an Empire," she'd said. *"Let us see how the world handles its first taste of freedom."*

After that, the Regents had split the world into four. They'd made it clear that the arrangement was temporary, but Shera had always assumed that meant a return to one Empire.

Now she heard the words for what they truly meant.

Slowly, she nodded. "What about the other Guilds?"

Yala barked a laugh, and Kerian looked to the conference room doors. "That's why we've invited you here," she began, when the doors burst open.

The third and final High Councilor, Tyril, strode into the room. He looked nothing like a farmer this time, having traded in his raggedy, faded blacks for a crisp suit of fine black fabric. His hair and beard were trimmed, and he moved with a vigor that he had always lacked in their previous meetings.

He looked like a different man—like a successful banker instead of a vagabond.

And he was not alone.

His companion was at least twenty years younger than Tyril, perhaps slightly younger than Kerian. His hair was solid black, like the thick rims of his spectacles, and he wore a gray suit and coat that looked as though they had been polished. A man in the exact same suit entered behind him, so subtly that Shera almost didn't notice him. He stood unobtrusively in the corner, a writing-board under his arm.

The newcomer spread his arms and smiled. "Ladies! Pleased to meet you at last. My name is Nathanael Bareius."

Yala rose smoothly to her feet, and Kerian struggled to follow. Shera remained seated. She hurt too much to bother.

Not even for the Head of the Alchemist's Guild, and the richest man in the world.

"Sit, sit!" he declared, sliding into his own seat. "It seems like the situation here got a little *dicey,* if you don't mind me saying it, so I thought I'd personally check on my investment. No disrespect intended."

"None taken," Kerian said. "You have every right to be concerned. Before we get started, is there anything we can do to make you more comfortable? Refreshment, perhaps?"

He rubbed his palms together quickly, as if in anticipation. "Not necessary at all! My only refreshment is the meat of *commerce,* the cooling draught of a new deal. Isn't that right, Furman?"

The man in the corner spoke without looking up from his writing-board. "That's right, sir."

"You see? If I could get a fruit tea, though, that would be *splendid.*"

Yala gestured to one of the Mason servants hiding nearby.

"So, first things first. What happened to the Heart? And Naberius Clayborn as well, I suppose."

Kerian opened a file on the table, though she didn't glance at it. "Our Readers confirmed that the Heart disappeared on the Island. It did not leave, and so we conclude that it must have been destroyed. We—"

Bareius threw up his hands. "Excellent! That's all I needed to know. If it's gone, it's gone. Do keep your Readers looking for it just in case, though, hmm?"

"Of course," Yala said sourly.

A Mason clad in an apron slid a porcelain cup of reddish tea onto the table.

Shera's mind finally caught up to the reality. This was the *client*, the one who had hired them to seek the Heart in the first place. She had known the Guild wouldn't do anything so expensive without a client backing it, but she had never considered the client's identity. She simply hadn't thought of it.

"Naberius Clayborn was recovered by the Navigator Captain Calder Marten," Kerian went on. She turned a page in her file, though Shera was fairly certain that the file was completely unrelated. "We assume that the Captain will take him back to his sponsors as soon as possible."

Bareius raised his tea. "Not a problem! He was irrelevant anyway, I only wanted to know. We've made progress here, certainly progress. Not as much as I'd *like,* sure, but we've gained valuable information. You'll be paid immediately."

Shera spoke up. "I'm sorry to interrupt, uh...Mister Bareius, but I was wondering—"

He slammed his teacup down onto its saucer. "Speak up, then! *Wonder-*

ing doesn't do anybody any good. Only questions do! Speak your mind, and don't hold back!"

So much for her attempt to respect the client. She went on bluntly. "I was wondering how much we're making. We've practically gone to *war* with two Guilds. How could that possibly be worth it?"

Yala glared at her, and Kerian rubbed her forehead as though she had a headache.

Bareius sputtered in laughter. "*Two?* Furman, the bag."

A second later, his servant—Furman—placed a velvet bag into the alchemist's open palm. Bareius upended the bag, spilling four silver coins onto the table.

He snagged one before it rolled off the edge. "My alchemists are accepted absolutely *everywhere,*" he said. "As a result, I am able to get a fairly accurate sense of the workings in most Guilds. Based on my own information, and what you all have brought me, this is what I've been able to piece together."

Bareius held out the first silver coin to Shera. It was stamped with a symbol: a ship's wheel with a single eye in the center. The crest of the Navigator's Guild.

He slapped the Navigator coin down onto the table in front of him. "Cheska Bennett isn't unreasonable, but for now, she's firmly against us. She has invested too much in a second Emperor to back out now." Next to that coin he placed another, this one marked with the Elder Eyes—the crest of the Blackwatch. "The Watchmen, we believe, are set on producing a series of disposable Emperors. When one is corrupted by the Elders, they will simply replace him."

He lined the other two coins up with the first two, forming a line. This pair bore the Open Book of the Magister's Guild and the Aurelian Shield of the Imperial Guard, respectively.

"The Imperial Guard, you see, has no reason to exist without the Emperor. Will they join us? Absolutely not. They're a relic of the past, I'm afraid. The Magisters...to be quite frank with you, I don't know why the Magisters want an Emperor at all. Maxeus has always been an enigma to me."

Bareius gestured to the line of four coins. "These represent the Guilds most committed to returning an Emperor to the empty throne. Those who hold on to the archaic notion of one global Empire."

His eyeglasses gleamed in the setting sun as he leaned toward Shera. "I would call them *the enemy.*"

He held out his hand, and Furman placed a second bag onto his palm. These coins were gold, and he lined them up quickly, with no explanation. The White Sun of the Luminian Order, the Emerald of the Greenwardens, the Bottled Flame of Kanatalia...and the Gardening Shears of the Consultants.

"These," he said proudly, "stand for those of us who seek to progress *beyond* the Empire of the past, free of Imperial restrictions. Three days past, I received confirmation that the Greenwardens will no longer allow enemy Guild members into their territories. And the Luminian Order has begun reinforcing their own borders."

He indicated the coins, lined up opposite one another like game pieces, four gold and four silver. "My friends, we have gone beyond threatening *two Guilds.* Our course is well and truly set. This will be a full-scale Guild War, the likes of which the Empire has never seen."

He grinned over his tea, a child delighted by a new game. "I, for one, can't wait."

The two High Councilors were silent, looking to Shera. They had already known all this, she realized. This whole presentation was for Shera's sake.

Bareius noticed her staring at his coins. "You like these? Had 'em made special. I'll get you a set. Furman, make a note."

"This seems like...a *lot* of work," Shera said honestly.

The alchemist's expression firmed, "I wish there were another choice," he said, in a surprisingly sincere tone. "Sadly, other avenues are closed to us. Perhaps we've been headed for this ever since the Emperor died."

He certainly didn't mean that as a jab at Shera, but she heard it as one. No matter what she did, she always created more work for herself.

She needed a nap.

"From what I've heard, Shera, you're going to be very important in your Guild from now on. You worked for the Emperor personally, and now they say you're a *Soulbound.* Killing one of Nakothi's Handmaidens, how does that feel?" With a visible gesture, he pushed the question aside. "Never mind. I invited you here today because I need to know. Can I count on your support?"

Shera looked from Yala, who seemed irritated, to Tyril—napping in his chair—to Kerian. Her mentor smiled a little, in what she thought was sympathy.

In the end, there was only one answer she could give.

"Ask me in the morning," she said, and left the room.

CHAPTER TWENTY-SEVEN

TEN YEARS AGO

When Shera returned to her room on the Gray Island, Kerian was waiting for her.

In spite of herself, Shera groaned. Not only was Kerian possibly the *last* person she wanted to talk to at that exact moment, the woman was sitting on her bed. After the night she'd had, Shera would have murdered someone for a full eight hours of sleep.

Shera let the door close behind her, peeling off her knife-belt. "*Please* move."

Kerian folded her hands in her lap, leaning back against the headboard. "I need to speak with you, and I suspect you may try to sleep before I get the chance. I'm here to remove temptation from your path."

"Then the joke's on you. I can sleep on the floor."

"Did he take you to Nakothi?"

Shera's breath caught. "I think that's confidential."

The older Consultant sighed, rubbing the scar that split her face in two. "There's usually one Consultant or another around the Emperor, either working for him or defending him. Over the years, we've pieced enough together."

There was a chair against the wall, but Shera felt too tired even to walk that far. She simply collapsed onto the wooden floor. "He had a mission for us. We had to stop *someone* from doing *something*, and I'm still not completely sure what."

Kerian nodded. "And is the former Watchman buried at sea?"

Shera didn't even pretend surprise at Kerian's knowledge. "Worse. The Emperor put him to sleep and left him there."

"That seems needlessly cruel. Tie a cannonball to his ankles and push him overboard. It's simple, humane, and it removes questions."

Shera wasn't entirely sure that Lucan would call drowning someone 'humane,' but she couldn't care less what happened to the Blackwatch traitor.

Finally, Kerian stood up from the bed. Shera drifted up as though pulled to her pillow by invisible strings, but the older woman put a hand on her shoulder. With the other, she reached into her satchel.

"I think I might be able to fill in some of those blanks." From within the leather satchel, she pulled forth a sheaf of paper, bound in string. "Removed from the Miners' archives, with the blessing of the Council.

"The Watchman and his crew were headed to that island to harvest a heart from Nakothi's corpse, in the hopes of attaining eternal life. I'm sure the Emperor told you that much. What he didn't tell you was *why.*"

She tossed the bundle of papers onto the bed. "Some light reading for you, whenever you wake up. It pertains to a group of men and women who call themselves 'The Sleepless.' Their goals, their methods, everything we've gathered about them for the past few centuries."

Shera picked up the papers and moved them off the bed. "I look forward to that. In the morning."

"That which sleeps will soon wake," Kerian said.

Shera froze.

"It's their motto," she continued. "According to them, the Great Elders are not dead. They are merely sleeping, and soon they will rise to reclaim the world that was once theirs."

"Is that true?" Shera asked, her mind filled with a wind that whispered of *rebirth.*

Kerian shrugged. "Probably. But the Emperor defeated them once. We'll have to trust him to do it again."

If he was still around...but he didn't think he would be.

"From the very stones I will strip all memory of your existence," he'd promised. And he could Read the truth in anything he touched.

But she had to tell someone.

"He wants us to kill him," Shera whispered. "He thinks he's being corrupted by the Dead Mother."

Kerian stopped while reaching for the doorknob; the only sign of motion her braids swinging against each other. "Our client is Emperor," she said at last.

That night, Shera's sleep was plagued by nightmares.

PRESENT DAY

Meia woke with her arms tied behind her back, lashed to the mast of a ship. Waves splashed all around her, sending fresh ocean water crashing across the deck.

She recognized this dark green wood, the sail above her that looked as though it was made from stretched Elder skin. Calder Marten's ship. *The Testament.*

An old man bent over to look at her, his beard sweeping the deck. Two pairs of glasses hung from his neck, and he placed one of them on his nose. When her eyes focused on his, he grinned.

"Morning, Princess," he said. "We're real—"

He didn't get another word before she butted him in the lip with her forehead, then ground her teeth against the pain and *shifted* her hands. They felt as though she'd crushed them in a vice, and they made an unhealthy crackling noise, but they slipped straight through the ropes.

A second later, when her hands had returned to normal, she pulled a stretch of rope apart with her bare hands.

Another man, a Heartlander in a white suit and hat, raised a pistol. She bunched the muscles in her legs, leaping up to the stern deck. She landed inches in front of him, holding his pistol in a firm grip and keeping it firmly pointed away from herself.

He seemed to remember her, his eyes widening. "It's you. I thought you looked familiar, but I didn't think Calder could capture *you.*"

Meia had to rack her brain for a moment before she recognized him.

That's right. The dead island.

Back on Nakothi's island, she had run into some trouble locating Shera. Shortly before her fight with Urzaia, she'd rescued a few Watchmen from the Children of Nakothi.

At least, she'd *assumed* they were Watchmen.

She released his pistol. He'd seen her dodge gunmen and kill a giant Elderspawn with her bare hands. He wouldn't pick a fight.

As soon as his pistol was free, he shoved it into the holster at his side. She looked around the deck, surveying the horizon. No land in sight.

"How long was I unconscious, sir?" she asked.

He cleared his throat uncomfortably. "A day or so, I'd say."

"Hm." There was a ship anchored next to them, only a few yards away. Its wood was an unnatural burnt red, and flames licked up where its hull met the water. It must be an alchemist's trick, but the effect was quite impressive: it made the boat look as though it floated on waves of fire.

The old man was furtively signaling the crewmen on the other deck, trying to get them to send over a boat for him. As though he could keep it a secret with her standing right here.

"I'll be heading back to the Gray Island," Meia said at last.

The man in white hesitated a moment before speaking. "The Captain intends to head for the Capital, ma'am."

She met his eyes. "I'll be heading back to the Gray Island on this ship. Either *with* a crew, or *without* one."

He sighed. "I'd thought it would be something like that. The Captain left a ransom note for you, you know."

She closed her eyes, hoping that she could will away these last few days as a bad dream. "What did it say?"

The Waverider scout handed Shera a small scroll, tied with a green ribbon. She unfurled the message.

Shera, it began.

You took my wife from me, so I'm taking someone from you. Your yellow-haired Consultant friend, the one who defended you so enthusiastically on Nakothi's island.

Don't follow me, or she dies. Don't attack, or she dies. Certainly don't try and contact the Navigators. They can't do anything for her.

If you want her back, you must

Shera didn't read the rest. She crumpled the paper and tossed it over her shoulder.

The scout looked at her nervously. "Well? Are we going to negotiate?"

Shera still hadn't caught up on her rest; she yawned. "Send a team out to pick her up and dispose of the bodies. On second thought, wait a few days.

Let's give her a chance to try and sail back on her own."

If Meia had been careless enough to get herself captured in the first place, she deserved a day or two of consequences. If Shera thought that Meia would end up with her throat slit and her body in the ocean, then a team of Gardeners would be headed out to sea right now. They would depopulate *The Testament* and send it down to Kelarac.

But Calder wouldn't do that, and he certainly wouldn't send a ransom note afterwards, which meant that Meia had been captured *alive.* There was nothing more embarrassing. Even if Shera had wanted to send someone, Meia's pride wouldn't allow her to accept help.

She would have to rescue herself.

THE END

OF THE ELDER EMPIRE: FIRST SHADOW

Next time, follow Shera in…

Coming Soon!

For updates, visit *www.WillWight.com*

turn the page for a glossary and
excerpts from The Guild Guide

AM'HARANAI The ancient order of spies and assassins that would eventually become the Consultant's Guild. Some formal documents still refer to the Consultant's Guild in this way.

ARCHITECT One type of Consultant. The Architects mostly stay in one place, ruling over Guild business and deciding general strategy. They include alchemists, surgeons, Readers, strategists, and specialists of all types.

AWAKEN A Reader can Awaken an object by bringing out its latent powers of Intent. An Awakened object is very powerful, but it gains a measure of self-awareness. Also, it can never be invested again.

Jarelys Teach, the Head of the Imperial Guard, carries an ancient executioner's blade that has been Awakened. It now bears the power of all the lives it took, and is lethal even at a distance.

All Soulbound Vessels are Awakened.

CHILDREN OF THE DEAD MOTHER Elderspawn created by the power of Nakothi out of human corpses.

CONSULTANT A member of the Consultants Guild, also known as the Am'haranai. Mercenary spies and covert agents that specialize in gathering and manipulating information for their clients.

Consultants come in five basic varieties: Architects, Gardeners, Masons, Miners, and Shepherds.

For more, see the Guild Guide.

DEAD MOTHER, THE *See: Nakothi.*

ELDER Any member of the various races that ruled the world in ancient days, keeping humanity as slaves. The most powerful among them are known as Great Elders, and their lesser are often called Elderspawn.

GARDENER One type of Consultant. The Gardeners kill people for hire.

Intent The power of focused will that all humans possess. Whenever you use an object *intentionally,* for a *specific purpose,* you are investing your Intent into that object. The power of your Intent builds up in that object over time, making it better at a given task.

Every human being uses their Intent, but most people do so blindly; only Readers can sense what they're doing.

See also: Invest, Reader.

Invest Besides its usual financial implications, to "invest" means to imbue an object with one's Intent. By intentionally using an object, you *invest* that object with a measure of your Intent, which makes it better at performing that specific task.

So a pair of scissors used by a barber every day for years become progressively better and better at cutting hair. After a few years, the scissors will cut cleanly through even the thickest strands of tangled hair, slicing through with practically no effort. A razor used by a serial killer will become more and more lethal with time. A razor used by a serial-killing barber will be very confused.

Kameira A collective term for any natural creature with unexplainable powers. Cloudseeker Hydras can move objects without touching them, Windwatchers can change and detect air currents, and Deepstriders control water. There are many different types of Kameira…though, seemingly, not as many as in the past. The Guild of Greenwardens is dedicated to studying and restoring Kameira populations.

Humans can borrow the miraculous powers of Kameira by creating Vessels from their body parts, and then bonding with those Vessels to become Soulbound.

Mason One type of Consultant. Masons are craftsmen and professionals in a particular trade, covertly sending back information to their Guild. There are Masons undercover in every industry and business throughout the Empire.

Miner One type of Consultant. This secretive order is in charge of the Consultants' vast library, sorting and disseminating information to serve the Guild's various clients.

Nakothi, the Dead Mother A Great Elder who died in the Aion Sea. Her power kills humans and remakes their bodies into hideous servants.

Navigator A member of the Navigator's Guild. The Navigators are the only ones capable of sailing the deadly Aion Sea, delivering goods and passengers from one continent to the other.

For more, see the Guild Guide.

Reader A person who can read and manipulate the Intent of objects. Every human being invests their Intent subconsciously, simply by using ordinary objects. However, Readers can do so with a greater degree of focus and clarity, thanks to their special senses.

Readers often receive visions of an object's past.

Shepherd One type of Consultant. The Shepherds are observers, thieves, and saboteurs that specialize in infiltrating a location and leaving unnoticed.

Soulbound A human who can channel the power of an Elder or a Kameira. These powers are contained in a Vessel, which is *bound* to a person during the Awakening process. Soulbound are rare and powerful because they combine the focus of human Intent with the miraculous power of inhuman beings.

Bliss, the Guild Head of the Blackwatch, is a Soulbound with the Spear of Tharlos as her Vessel. Therefore, she can borrow the reality-warping powers of the Great Elder known as Tharlos, the Formless Legion.

A person becomes a Soulbound by having a personally significant object Awakened. If the object has a strong connection to an Elder or Kameira, and if it is significant *enough,* then it can become a Soulbound Vessel.

See also: Vessel.

Vessel An Awakened object that becomes the source of a Soulbound's power. Not all Awakened items become Soulbound Vessels, but all Vessels are Awakened.

In order to become a person's Vessel, an item must fulfill two criteria: it must be *personally linked* to the individual, and it must be invested with the power of a Kameira or an Elder.

1.) Personal link: A ring that you bought at a pawnshop three weeks ago could not become your Soulbound Vessel. It has not absorbed enough of your Intent, it is not significant to you, and it is not *bound* to you in any way. A wedding ring that you've worn for fifteen years and is significant to you for some reason—perhaps you pried it off your spouse's bloody corpse—could indeed become your Vessel, assuming it fulfills the second criteria as well.

2.) Power: A spear made of an Elder's bone could allow one to use that Elder's power of illusion and madness. If you bonded with a necklace of Deepstrider scales, you might be able to sense and control the ocean's currents as that Kameira does.

See also: Soulbound.

Watchman A member of the Blackwatch Guild.

For more, see the Guild Guide.

THE GUILD GUIDE

A brief guide to the Ten Imperial Guilds of the Aurelian Empire, written by a licensed Witness for your edification and betterment!

The Am'haranai

Also known as Consultants, the members of this mysterious brotherhood work behind the scenes for the good of the Empire...or for anyone with enough gold to pay them. Consultants are more than willing to provide strategic advice, tactical support, and information to the Empire's rich and elite, so long as it doesn't destabilize the government they've worked so hard to build.

Believe it or not, the Am'haranai were the first Imperial Guild, having existed in one form or another since long before the birth of the Empire. The next time you walk by the local chapter house of the Consultants, know that you're in the presence of true Imperial History.

The Consultants' local Guild Representative would not give us a definitive response to the less savory rumors surrounding this particular Guild. Juicy speculation suggests that—for the right price—the Consultants will provide a number of darker services, including espionage, sabotage, and even assassination. We can neither confirm nor refute such rumors at this time.

Consultants in the field are known to refer to each other by code names, to conceal their true identities.

Shepherds are their expert scouts, trained to watch, remember, and report.

Architects are the leaders of the Am'haranai, and typically do not leave their island fortress. They're the strategists, alchemists, tacticians, and Readers that make the work of the Consultants possible.

Masons are a truly terrifying order, though once again the Guild Representative put off most of my questions. They go undercover as everyday folk like you or me, living ordinary lives for months or years, and then providing information to their Architect leaders. Your best friend, your neighbor, that street alchemist across from your house...any of them could be a Mason secretly watching you!

Other, less credible reports suggest the existence of a fourth brand of Consultant: the **Gardeners.** The job of a Gardener is to "remove weeds."

They are the black operatives, the pure assassins, the knives in the dark.

The Guild Representative had this to say on the matter: "There is not now, and never has been, an order of the Am'haranai known as the Gardeners. That's simple speculation based on our Guild crest, which is actually derived from our origin as humble farmers. Having said that, if you do have someone interfering with your business, it is possible that we could help you bring the situation to a satisfactory conclusion...for an appropriate level of compensation, of course."

Since the Emperor's death (may his soul fly free), I have no doubt that business has been very good indeed for this particular Guild.

Guild Head: **The Council of Architects.** No one knows much about the leadership of the Consultants, but it seems that the Architects collectively vote on Guild policy, coming to decisions through careful deliberation and long experience.

Crest: Gardening Shears

The Blackwatch

Thanks to generations of legends and misinformation perpetuated by the Luminians, many of you have certain preconceived notions about the Blackwatch. They're hated by many, feared by all, and I urge you not to heed the rumors. Every Watchman I've ever met has been professional, focused, and inquisitive--very few of them actually worship the Elders.

Let me put a few of your unfounded fears to rest: no, they do not eat human flesh for power. No, they do not conduct dark rituals involving blood sacrifice. No, they do not kidnap babies from their cradles.

Yes, they do use certain powers and techniques of the Elders. That's no reason to treat them like cultists.

The Blackwatch was originally founded by the Emperor for two purposes: watching over the graves of the Great Elders, and studying the Elder Races to twist their great powers for the good of the Empire. It is thanks to the Blackwatch that Urg'Naut or the Dead Mother have not risen and devoured our living world.

Members of this Guild are known as **Watchmen.** They respond to calls for help and reports of Elder activity. Each Watchman carries seven long, black nails invested with the power to bind Lesser Elders for vivisection and study.

The goals of the Blackwatch often bring them into conflict with Knights and Pilgrims of the Luminian Order, who hunt down Lesser Elders with the goal of destroying them completely.

If the two would only work together, it's possible that Aurelian lands would never be troubled by Elder attacks again.

Guild Head: The current head of the Blackwatch is a young-seeming woman known only as **Bliss.** Her origins are shrouded in mystery, though tenuous evidence suggests that she was born in a Kanatalia research facility.

Like every Blackwatch Head before her, she carries the **Spear of Tharlos,** a weapon supposedly carved from the bone of a Great Elder. I have never interviewed anyone who witnessed the Spear in battle and survived with their sanity intact.

Crest: the Elder's Eyes (six eyes on a mass of tentacles)

The Champions

I doubt there is a single child in any corner of the Aurelian Empire who does not know some story of the Champion's Guild, but I will still labor to separate fact from romantic fiction.

The Champions as we know them today rose out of an old Izyrian tradition. In ancient days, before the Empire, the continent of Izyria was divided into a thousand clans. When two clans had a dispute, instead of going to war, they would send two representatives into a formal duel. The winner's clan, of course, won the dispute. These clan champions were often Soulbound, strengthened by some secret alchemical technique, and highly skilled fighters.

When the Emperor (may his soul fly free) originally crossed the Aion Sea with the aim of enfolding Izyria into his fledgling Empire, he created his own collection of duelists to defeat the natives at their own cultural game.

Thus, the Champions were born.

Champions became, as we have all seen, the best fighters in the Empire. They singlehandedly quell rebellions, reinforce Imperial troops in the field, and put down dangerous Kameira. And sometimes, when the Empire still needed to fight its own duels, the existence of this Guild ensured that the Emperor never lost.

Since the death of the Emperor, this Guild has become—dare I say it—a dangerous liability. Each Champion has largely gone his or her own way. The Guild still trains initiates according to the old traditions, but it doesn't have the organizational stability or control it once did.

Guild Head: **Baldezar Kern,** an undefeated duelist and the man who singlehandedly pacified the South Sea Revolutionary Army. Though he is known as a gentle man with an easy sense of humor, when he straps on his trademark horned helmet, he becomes a force of carnage on the battlefield like none I have ever seen. I had the opportunity to witness Kern on the warpath almost fifteen years ago, and the sight of this man in battle will haunt me until the day of my death.

Crest: the Golden Crown

The Greenwardens

While the Greenwardens do protect us from wild Kameira and keep the Imperial Parks that we all know and enjoy, you may not be aware that they were originally intended to save the world.

The Guild of Greenwardens was founded at a time in our history when alchemy was first coming into its own, and we were afraid that a combination of alchemy, then-modern weaponry such as the cannon, and unregulated human Intent would tear the world apart.

Greenwardens were created to preserve Kameira, preventing us from driving them extinct, and to monitor and repair the effects of alchemical and gunpowder weapons on the environment. They each carry an Awakened talisman, which for some has become their Soulbound Vessel: a shining green jewel that they use to heal wounds and promote the growth of plants.

Guild Head: **Tomas Stillwell** is a practicing physician and a fully inducted Magister of the Vey Illai as well as the Guild Head of the Greenwardens, proving that no physical infirmity can prevent you from contributing to your Empire. Though he lost his legs in a childhood encounter with a wild Kameira, he never let that experience make him bitter. Instead, it drove him to study Kameira, their habits, and how they function. He is now one of the most famous natural scientists in the Empire, and he has done much to prevent the extinction of species such as the stormwing and the shadowrider.

Crest: the Emerald

The Imperial Guard

I trust that all of you understand the purpose of the Imperial Guard: to protect the Emperor's person, and to shield him from attack and unwanted attention. Some suggest that they failed, that the death of the Emperor proves that the Guard were unequal to their task.

I can assure you that this is not the case.

Through a secret alchemical process known only to the Guild of Alchemists, the Imperial Guard replaces some of their original body parts with those of Kameira. Some Guardsmen have patches of armored Nightwyrm hide grafted onto their skin, or their eyes substituted with those of a Cloud Eagle. The process is said to be long and unbearably painful, and it results in guardians with the appearance of monsters.

However, in the twelve hundred years that the Emperor reigned, not a single assassination attempt reached his person. We owe that fact solely to the power and extraordinary sensitivity of the Imperial Guard.

I know that many outside the Capital are wondering what the Guard are up to, now that they have no Emperor to guard. Well, in the words of their Guild Head, "We may no longer have an Emperor, but we have an Empire. That, we will preserve until the sun rises in the west."

The resolve of a true patriot, gentle readers.

Guild Head: **Jarelys Teach,** a General in the Emperor's military and Head of his Imperial Guard, does not at first strike you as an imposing woman. I have met her on many occasions, and found her to be singularly devoted to her job. Popular legend says that she swallowed the blood of a Nightwraith, thereby absorbing its powers, but that's little more than speculation. It's a matter of Imperial record that she carries Tyrfang, the Awakened blade used to execute the Emperor's rivals over a thousand years ago.

Crest: the Aurelian Shield (a shield bearing the sun-and-moon symbol of the Aurelian Empire)

Kanatalia, the Guild of Alchemists

As I write this guide, I sip a glass of enhanced wine that slowly shifts flavor from cherry to apple to lemon. A cart rumbles by my house, with a hawker loudly announcing his remedies for sale. A quicklamp provides my light, glowing a steady blue, never smoking or flickering like a candle.

Truly, one cannot escape the advances of alchemy in our modern society.

Though alchemists have existed since long before the Empire, Kanatalia is one of the more recent additions to the Ten Guilds. It was the first organization to unify the previously contentious brotherhood of alchemists, allowing them to collectively achieve what they never could separately.

Matches, quicklamps, potions, invested alloys, healing salves, enhanced soldiers, vaccines...practically every scientific advance in the past century, including the advance of science itself, can be traced back to Kanatalia's door.

Just don't ask too many questions. A true Kanatalian alchemist can be very protective of his secrets, and you might find yourself a drooling vegetable if you get on the wrong side of an experienced potion-maker.

Guild Head: **Nathanael Bareius** did not become one of the richest men in the Empire by relaxing on his inheritance. After receiving a substantial fortune from his late father, Lord Bareius went on to receive a full education at the Aurelian National Academy. He graduated as a licensed Imperial alchemist and a member of Kanatalia. At that point, he wagered all of his capital on a single risky investment: alchemy. He opened his vaults, spending every bit he had to make sure that every corner and crevice of the Empire had a licensed Kanatalian alchemist there to provide illumination, potions, medical care, and Guild-approved recreational substances.

Lord Bareius has personally earned back triple his initial investment over the past ten years, and is now poised as the most prominent leader in the Capital. Even more significantly, he seems to have won the battle of public opinion—I haven't seen a street in the Capital unlit by alchemical lanterns, and no one has died of dysentery or plague since before the Emperor's death. No matter what you think of his politics, Nathanael Bareius has made great strides in moving our Empire forward into this new century.

Crest: the Bottled Flame

The Luminian Order

Ah, the Luminians. A more versatile Guild you won't find anywhere: they're responsible for building cathedrals, policing Imperial roads, hunting down Elders, and generally acting heroic.

Luminian Knights, the martial arm of the Order, march around in their powerfully invested steel armor, fighting deadly monsters chest-to-chest. Their swords are bound with light so that they reflect the sun even in the dead of night, burning through creatures of darkness.

The trademark representatives of the Luminian Order are **Pilgrims,** humble wanderers in simple robes. They are each Readers—some of them Soulbound—charged to remove harmful Intent and the maddening influence of the Elders.

The Luminian Order and the Blackwatch have each held a knife to the other's back for hundreds of years, arguing over the best way to protect the populace, to prevent the rise of the Great Elders, and to keep the Empire whole. Perhaps if one of them would learn to compromise, we would all feel safer after midnight.

Guild Head: **Father Jameson Allbright** is an old man, but his vigilance has never dimmed in the fight against darkness. He is one of the oldest Soulbound on record, wielding his shining Vessel to bring the purifying light to Elder worshipers and malicious Readers alike.

Crest: the White Sun (usually on a red banner)

The Magisters

Magisters are the most accomplished and educated Readers in the world. You probably grew up with a local Reader, who invested your knives and cleansed your graveyard of harmful Intent. Most small-town Readers are powerful and possibly even quite skilled.

But they aren't Magisters.

A Magister is a Reader who has received an extensive education inside the Vey Illai, an extensive forest in the Aurelian heartland, inside what was once the original Imperial Academy. They can use their Intent with a degree of focus, subtlety, and precision that an ordinary Reader could barely comprehend.

Magisters are in charge of regulating Readers and the use of human Intent, in much the same way that a father is in charge of preventing his children from misbehaving.

It's impossible for all Readers to study at the Vey Illai and become Magisters, because there are simply too many people with a talent for Reading. And of course everyone invests their Intent into objects, to one degree or another.

But the best and most powerful are called Magisters.

Guild Head: **Professor Mekendi Maxeus,** one of the most distinguished researchers at the Aurelian National Academy, retired from his lecture tour to the "relaxing" position as head of one of the largest Imperial Guilds. He isn't seen outside much these days, having received several disfiguring facial scars in the Inheritance Conflict five years ago, but he still lends his overwhelming power of Intent to the construction of new public monuments in the Capital. He carries a black staff, and I have personally witnessed him use it to blast a collapsed building off a pair of trapped children. I have met few heroes in my career, but this man is among them.

Crest: the Open Book

The Navigators

When I call the Navigators a Guild, I use the term loosely.

Navigators are the only sailors who can cross the deadly, shifting ocean at the heart of our Empire: the Aion Sea. We therefore rely on them for communication, trade, exploration, and transport between the eastern continent of Aurelia and the western continent, Izyria.

It's too bad that they're the most shifty and unreliable collection of pirates, confidence artists, mercenaries, and outright criminals the Empire has ever seen.

No one knows how they cross the Aion, with its hundreds of deadly Kameira, its disappearing islands, its unpredictable weather, and its host of lurking Elders, but anyone else who sails far enough out into the ocean either vanishes or returns insane.

The best way to recognize a real Navigator from a faker is to ask to see their Guild license, which is unmistakable and cannot be reproduced. Unfortunately, that only tells you which sailor is truly able to cross the Aion: not whether he can be trusted.

Guild Head: **Captain Cheska Bennett** is one of the few reliable Navigators left in this world. She owns *The Eternal,* a most striking ship with billowing red sails and a wake that trails flame. She commands truly shocking prices for her services, but if you hire her, you can be certain that every splinter of your cargo will remain secure between one continent and the other.

Crest: the Navigator's Wheel (a ship's wheel with a single eye at the center)

The Witnesses

I am proud to count myself among the honorable Guild of Witnesses, the final entry on this written tour of Imperial history. Witnesses are the official record-keepers of the Empire, having chronicled the entirety of the Empire's history since our inception. We also observe momentous events, record battles, produce educational reading materials for the general public, and notarize official documents.

As Sadesthenes once said, *"The Witnesses are the grease that allow the wheels of Empire to turn."*

Generally speaking, Witnesses travel in pairs:

As a **Chronicler,** I am a Reader with the ability to store my memories inside a special alchemically created candle. I burn the candle while I write, and as the memories flow out, I can record my thoughts without any margin of error even years after the events I have witnessed.

Always, I am accompanied by my **Silent One,** a trained warrior and my bodyguard. Silent Ones bind their mouths to symbolize their inability to betray secret or sensitive events, but contrary to popular belief, we do *not* remove their tongues. We're not barbarians. They are capable of speech, they are simply discouraged from doing so in the presence of outsiders.

Guild Head: The Heads of my own Guild are the twin sisters **Azea and Calazan Farstrider,** natives of exotic Izyria. Though they are young, having risen to prominence after the Emperor's untimely demise, I have never met anyone so dedicated to accuracy and neutrality. Azea works as a Chronicler, and Calazan as her attendant Silent One, though I can personally confirm that either sister can perform either role. Azea is a remarkable fighter in her own right, and Calazan a skilled Reader and clerk.

Crest: the Quill and Candle

And now…

A preview for the parallel novel,

OF SEA & SHADOW

Follow Calder as he hunts the Heart of Nakothi, trying to save the Empire by raising a new Emperor.

CHAPTER ONE

Calder Marten stood on the deck of his ship, sailing into the wall of black clouds and rain. He clamped his hat down, holding it tight against the slashing grip of the storm.

"No more need for sails, Andel!" Calder shouted. "We go against the wind!"

Quartermaster Andel Petronus stood next to him, clutching his own hat. "What do you expect me to do about that, sir?"

"Nothing! I simply enjoy shouting!"

Calder gripped the wheel, Reading the Intent bound into the wood. His mind flowed through the bones of the ship, sensing every inch of The Testament as though it were his own body.

He sent a simple, silent order to his Vessel. Behind him, the sails furled.

They looked more like a bat's wings than ordinary canvas sheets; *The Testament's* sails were nothing more than stretches of membranous green skin that seemed to grow from the mast and yard. When they folded, the ship resembled a Nightwyrm bunching its wings to dive.

As the ship began to slow, Calder sent another mental command. After a moment they continued moving, jerking forward a few dozen yards at a stretch, as though an invisible giant tugged them along behind.

"Is my wife secure?"

The Quartermaster shook his head. "I'm afraid she's dead, sir. A fever took her in the night."

Calder spared a glance from the upcoming storm wall to catch a look at Andel's face. Andel Petronus was a Heartlander, dark-skinned, and his white suit and hat stood out against the black wood of the deck.

The man, as usual, wore no expression. He pressed his hat down with one hand and clung to the railing with the other.

"One day you're actually going to have bad news for me, Andel."

"Then I'll try to smile, so you know something's wrong." The man in white strode off across the deck, shouting orders. "Raise the thunderlights! Ready the cannons!"

Calder silently persuaded the ship to release its four captives: thunderlights, huge alchemical lanterns with copper spikes that unfolded almost as high as the mast. Thick ropes hauled the devices out of the hold through a hatch on deck, until a glass lantern big enough to hold a man rested on each of the four corners of the ship.

The lines tightened themselves, tying each thunderlight to the deck, but

Andel had to release the copper spike by hand. As the first drops of rain began to slap the ship, Andel turned a crank on the lantern, slowly raising a copper limb into the sky.

An Imperial Navigator could sail the Aion Sea with a light crew thanks to the Captain's control over the ship, but even Calder couldn't handle everything. The storm was a dark slice of night in front of them now, flashing with lightning and rolling with wind-tossed waves. As the ship slammed down into a valley between two waves, sending spray rolling over the deck, Calder looked to his gunner.

Dalton Foster straddled one of the cannons, a hammer in one hand and an alchemist's spray-bottle in the other. He was leaning out over the railing, his head practically stuck inside the cannon's mouth.

"How's it coming with those cannons, Foster?" Calder shouted.

Foster pulled his head out and turned. His wild hair and beard were soaked through until he looked like a cat that had escaped the bath. He tore one pair of spectacles off, letting them dangle from a cord around his neck, and lifted a second pair to his eyes.

"That depends, Captain! Do you want to *hit* our quarry, or do you want a face full of shrapnel when the cannon explodes?"

"Must I choose, or can I have it all?"

Calder squinted up through the rain, scanning the ceiling of dark clouds and jagged light. The Kameira they hunted wasn't particularly dangerous on its own, but it only flew during lightning-storms. They'd been tracking this one for weeks, and if it got away this time, he might decide to mutiny against himself. Those thunderlights had cost him a hundred goldmarks apiece.

Andel finally finished setting the lights, their copper poles stabbing into the storm.

Normally they would be risking their mast in a storm like this, but those copper poles were invested to attract lightning. Calder had Read them himself, checking and strengthening their Intent. He only hoped they would work soon, so they didn't spend any more time in this weather than necessary.

Even as the thought occurred to him, a spear of lightning stabbed one of the copper spikes. There came a blinding flash from the starboard thunderlight, and then the liquid in the glass container ignited, glowing with the bright yellow of a cheery summer noon.

In essence, thunderlights worked the same as quicklamps: they were glass containers of alchemical formula that produced bright, steady light. But unlike quicklamps, which glowed for a few years and had to be replaced, these thunderlights would work as long as they had lightning to recharge them.

They were essential equipment for any Navigator that meant to hunt Stormwings, but Calder was missing something even more critical.

Namely, his prey. Normally a Stormwing would show itself on the storm wall, drifting over the tops of the choppy waves, but *The Testament* was still charging through air thick with slashing rain. All with no sight of the Kameira.

Calder was about to call for more drastic measures, but then a song drifted over the detonations of thunder and the crash of waves against the hull. It sounded something like a pod of whales singing in chorus, somehow keeping harmony with the percussion of the storm.

"Port side, Andel!" Calder shouted as the Stormwing blasted through a wave.

He caught sight of it in flight. The Kameira soared over their ship, a line of pure white lightning with wings of shadow stretching off to the sides. It sang in triumph and exultation as it passed over, its volume piercing even through the storm.

The wheel fought him as he forced the ship to starboard, lining up with the Stormwing as it vanished behind a wave. A bright detonation marked the creature's passage, sending up a towering spray.

Andel's white suit was already soaked through, but he didn't let that affect his dignity as he marched across the deck. "We have a shot, Mister Foster. Load the redshot."

Foster clung to the cannon like a monkey to a tree branch, furiously working on something that Calder couldn't make out through the rain. "What do you think I'm trying to do? Hmm? You think I've picked just this moment to polish the iron?"

The Quartermaster's response remained as even as ever. "I don't care what you're polishing. I want a red ball in that cannon *right now*."

The Stormwing passed in front, and by the creature's own luminescence, Calder caught a better look. It resembled nothing so much as a manta ray the size of their ship, with a bright rippling luminescence rolling up the tip of its tail and all the way through its spine. It glided on the wind, lashing the peak of a wave with its tail. A bright flash of light exploded from the point of contact, sending up another plume of water.

Calder leaned forward, trying to angle his three-cornered hat so that it kept more water out of his eyes. It didn't help. A second bolt of lightning lit up the thunderlight on the bow, giving them a better glimpse of the Stormwing as it vanished behind another wave.

He shoved the wheel to one side, sliding past the wave in the Kameira's wake. "Where's that shot, Foster?"

Foster shouted something that was swallowed up by the thunder, jamming a red ball into the cannon. He fumbled around on the end of the cannon as Calder tried to keep the ship as steady as possible, working as much through Reading and his Intent as through any manipulation of the wheel.

Finally, a flare of light came from the back of the cannon. The gunner yelled in triumph, hauling his weapon around to point at the storm-chopped horizon.

At that moment the Stormwing blasted up from the waves, exposing its belly to the ship, the core of its body rippling with luminescence. It howled a song of triumph.

Calder forced his Intent down into the wood. *Hold steady.*

But there was nothing the ship could do against the forces of nature. *The Testament* began to slip down the other side of a wave.

When the cannon fired, its shot tore a strip of skin from the edge of the Kameira's wing instead of taking the creature in the head.

Redshot, a special ammunition used by Kameira hunters, was designed by the Alchemist's Guild to prevent the powerful creatures from striking back when injured or dying. Simple tranquilizers had been used since time immemorial, but Stormwings were among those Kameira breeds that managed to escape as soon as they felt the pain of the shot. They would simply dive beneath the waves to flee from the pain.

With that in mind, a round of redshot was actually a hollow ball containing an alchemical paralytic, tranquilizer, and hallucinogen. The compound was designed to work in concert, confusing and subduing the Stormwing before putting it to sleep.

In its confusion, the creature would settle down and float on the surface of the waves to get its bearings. The paralytic meant it couldn't get far, and as it rested, the tranquilizer would have its time to set in. Calder and his crew would catch the Kameira in their invested steel nets, hauling it back to port to sell fresh.

But if the shot wasn't a direct hit, the whole plan died a fiery death. Now they had a confused, pain-enraged, *hallucinating* monster striking at them with a tail that caused explosions. And they had to fight it in the middle of a storm.

If they made it back to port, drinks were on Foster.

The Stormwing screamed, lashing its tail at the ship. The deck exploded in a blinding flash of light, sending splinters, torn rope, and one of the spare cannons hurtling into the storm. Calder felt the broken wood like a physical pain, and through the smoking hole he could see a slice of his hold.

He couldn't help worrying about his wife—she was supposed to be in a different part of the ship, but what if fate was unkind, and she had found herself impaled on a piece of debris? Then again, he was relieved that the Stormwing's strike hadn't shattered any of the thunderlights. They had enough to worry about without adding an alchemically fueled fire on top of everything else.

Foster clung to the back of his cannon, trying to swing it around for a clear shot as the Stormwing banked around for another pass, screaming as it thrashed its deadly tail in the air. Andel hurried over to the hole in the deck, kneeling and gazing into the hold as though he could fix it in the middle of the storm.

"Look what it's doing to my ship!" Andel shouted.

As he watched the Stormwing come back around, Calder realized that he was wasting his time. If they kept at it, they would be flopping around until they got in a lucky shot or the Kameira tore them apart.

He abandoned the wheel, hopping down to stand beside Andel. He unbuttoned his sleeve, rolling it up to the elbow.

It was about time for extreme measures.

Calder knelt beside his Quartermaster. "Pardon me, Andel, but this is *my* ship."

Then he pressed his palm to the deck and Read the ship. Visions flashed through his mind—*Calder nails one plank to another, begging them to stick; Calder's mother places her own hands on the wood, persuading them to repel water.*

He called on the bond between him and *The Testament*...and the bond between the ship and something far older.

A six-fingered hand rose up from the ocean.

The hand—webbed, dark blue, and big enough to rip the belly out of the ship—lifted out of the waves like a sunken tower cresting the surface. Dull, algae-spotted metal encircled the wrist: a manacle made of enough iron to recast every cannon onboard. Links of chain, each thicker than an anchor, trailed from the creature's arm to vanish in the dark water beneath *The Testament.*

Reaching up from the storm-tossed surface, the hand closed in a giant fist around the Stormwing's tail, jerking the Kameira to a halt in the air. The Stormwing screamed, thrashing and beating its wings, even turning in on itself to sink its fangs into the scaled hand.

From the shadows beneath *The Testament*, a cloud of bubbles rose. A hiss of pain sliced through the storm, and the giant arm flexed. It whipped the Stormwing against the water with a crack that deafened the thunder itself. Water rose in a rolling wave away from the impact, a wall of the ocean rising for them.

"Brace yourselves!" Calder shouted, and the Quartermaster echoed him.

Calder dove for the lines, wrapping himself in fistfuls of coarse rope. When he saw Foster still scrambling to control the loose cannon, he sent a simple mental signal to the ship. Ropes snaked over to Foster, grabbing him by the wrists and ankles and holding him fast.

"Light and life protect us," he muttered to himself, as the wave loomed over them.

A weight settled onto his right shoulder as if a cat had suddenly landed there. Something tickled his cheek, and a deep baritone echoed him. "PROTECT US," it chuckled.

Calder turned to glare at the creature perched on his shoulder. It was a squat little monster with a dark green, leathery hide and stubby little bat wings. Its eyes were solid black orbs, its mouth hidden behind a mass of squirming tentacles.

"Shuffles, what are you—"

Then the icy water of the Aion Sea crashed down on them both.

Darkness and cold rushed over Calder, trying to tear his eyes open, drowning his ears in a rush of sound. The water clawed at his body, trying to pull him out and away. His wrists burned where the ropes cut into him, but he didn't dare loosen his grip.

Finally, the wave subsided. Before the water had completely washed over the ship, Calder was untangling himself from the lines, hurrying back to the wheel.

The Stormwing was still alive, but it wouldn't be for long. Each of its wings was caught in the grip of a giant hand, and it struggled uselessly to escape.

As the Kameira writhed, a true monster rose from beneath *The Testament.*

Both of its arms were bound in shackles that terminated beneath Calder's ship, but the rest of its body was unbound. It stood like a man, with a row of ridges running down its spine like sails. Its head belonged to a predatory fish, though it bore three black eyes on either side of its face.

It drew the Stormwing closer as though to get a better look at its meal. The Kameira still struggled, but the towering monster's grip was unbreakable.

The blue lips parted, revealing a mouth full of shark's teeth. It hissed, a sound sharper than a knife's blade, and gills flapped on either side of its neck.

Then the Lyathatan, the Elderspawn bound to the bottom of *The Testament*, tore its prey apart.

One wing came off in each hand, spattering the ship's deck with droplets of luminescent blood.

Calder's heart sank even as Foster fought his way free of the lines, sending a futile kick at his own cannon. "You couldn't wait? You could not wait *one* more second for me to line up another shot?"

Calder sent his Intent through the ship, running down the invested chains, to the Lyathatan itself. The Elderspawn was old beyond imagining, but it did tend to listen to its captor. Most of the time.

Into his Reading, Calder poured his need for the Stormwing, his desperation to bring back something to sell, and his determination to extract the Kameira's precious fluid.

Usually that worked, though sometimes he had to throw in a bribe.

Andel walked below deck, presumably to check on the rest of the crew, but Foster was still going. "Now we're locked in the middle of a storm with nothing to show for it, and we won't find another one this late in the season—"

He was cut off when the severed tail and spine of the Stormwing landed on the deck, leaking glowing yellow-white fluid. It was big enough that it crossed *The Testament* from stem to stern, and bright enough to drown out the illumination of the thunderlights.

Calder heaved a sigh and let his whole weight rest against the wheel. "Foster, get Petal and Urzaia up here. We need to preserve as much as possible."

Foster marched down the ladder. "Petal! Woodsman! Get your buckets and get on deck before I make you bleed!"

Shuffles chuckled in Calder's ear, tentacles waving. "BLEEEED."

Calder ignored it. The Bellowing Horror liked to imitate the most disturbing words it heard, but the creature was entirely harmless. He'd begun to treat the thing like a parrot. Ship captains were supposed to have parrots.

It didn't look like they'd get the full payoff they'd hoped for, but they could probably retain sixty or seventy percent of the Stormwing's luminescent liquid. Two-thirds of a fortune was still a fortune; the Alchemist's Guild would pay in hundreds of goldmarks for vials of this fluid.

He grinned, settling his hat back on his head, and bowed in the Lyathatan's direction.

The giant was slowly settling beneath the waves, hissing as it disappeared under the water.

Disconcerting and reassuring at the same time. As Sadesthenes said, "*The worst enemies make the best allies.*"

Calder wasn't sure he could count the Lyathatan as an ally, exactly, but certainly as an asset. It had agreed to serve him for a short time, but 'a short time' to the ancient Elderspawn could extend into the lives of Calder's grandchildren.

He turned the wheel, sending his Intent down, and the Lyathatan obediently dragged the ship along. Away from the flashes of lightning. After weeks of chasing this Kameira, they could finally leave storms behind them, and Calder had never before looked so forward to sunshine.

Boots pounded back up the ladder, and Urzaia Woodsman appeared, a bucket dangling from each of his huge hands. He gave his gap-toothed smile when he emerged, staring up into the rain with his one remaining eye. "I never get tired of the rain. No matter how often I feel it, you hear me?"

"Well, I've felt it *too* often," Calder called down. "We're heading out to smoother seas."

"That is a shame. The monsters here are much bigger."

Petal slid out behind Urzaia without a word, her frizzy hair hiding her face. She sank onto the deck beside the severed Stormwing spine, crooning as she milked glowing liquid into her bucket.

Calder didn't bother saying anything. When the ship's alchemist was lost in her own world, nothing so mundane as human speech would get her attention.

The next person onto the deck was a surprise: his wife, Jyrine Tessella Marten.

Jerri wore a bright green raincoat that matched her emerald earrings. Bracelets flashed on her wrists as she hurriedly pulled her hair back, tucking it under her waterproof hood. She wore a wide, eager smile that instantly worried him.

It had taken him days of pleading to get her to stay below during the confrontation with the Kameira. There was nothing she could do to help, and the more people they had on deck, the greater the risk. She had finally agreed, but she wasn't happy about it.

If she thought there was something in the hold more interesting than two giant monsters fighting, he needed to see it.

She rushed up to him, pecking him on the cheek and wrapping him in tanned arms.

Alarm bells sounded in his head.

"You would not *believe* what I found down in the hold!" Her eyes sparkled as though she had heard wonderful news.

Calder leaned back, examining her expression from arm's length. "What did you find?"

She pulled on his wrist, tugging him away from the wheel. "You'll have to come see!"

The last time she'd had a surprise for him, it had ended up being a clawed Elderspawn that he'd been forced to nail to the inside of the hull. "Should I bring my pistol?"

"Only if you plan on shooting Andel, which I would wholeheartedly support. It's not a monster this time, but I would have sworn it was *impossible.* Maybe a Reader could tell me how they did it."

That was entirely too intriguing to pass up, so he let her guide him down into the belly of the ship.

The hold had been packed with barrels, crates, and packets of gear, though most of the space was unoccupied. They had planned to return with a new load of cargo, after all. Now, raindrops and thin rivers of luminescence flowed in from the fractured deck above, through the hole that the Stormwing had blasted. Some of the crates had cracked open, leaking salt or wine, and a loose barrel rolled around on the wood.

Calder stopped the wild barrel with one foot, looking around for anything unusual.

Jyrine picked up a quicklamp, shook it, and raised it to one side.

In the splash of yellow light, Calder saw a message burned into the inside of the hull, as though someone had scorched a letter onto his ship. Thin wisps of smoke still rose from the charred wood.

Calder kicked the barrel aside, walking up to examine the lettering. "Petal didn't do this?"

"I came in here after the explosion to survey the damage, and I saw it being written. It burned itself into the wood as though someone was writing with an invisible pen." She clapped her hands eagerly, like a child at a show. "Now read it!"

He did, his own excitement growing by the word.

Calder,

Hope this mysterious message finds you well! I just learned how to do this, and it's going to blow the pants off certain people back in the Capital. If you see it first, show it to Jyrine. She appreciates a good touch of theater.

The Guild has a new client. A pair of Witnesses wants to hire you to take them to a certain island, and withdraw a certain relic.

This could be huge, Calder. Not just for you, but for the Empire. And for the Emperor.

Calder stopped reading for a moment, shooting a glance at his wife. "The Emperor?"

Jerri's smile widened. "Keep reading. It gets better."

Whatever else this letter said, the Emperor had been dead for over five years. What did the Witnesses hope to find on the island? A way to bring him back from the dead?

With the Emperor, they might even be able to do it. That was a disturbing thought.

And by the way, this will be big for you. This was the Chronicler in charge of finance in the Imperial Palace. He wants me to tell you that if you're successful, you will "sleep under sheets of golden silk in the cabin of your flagship. At the head of your brand-new fleet." His words.

So I suggest you get your leaky tub and your flea-bitten crew back to port before he comes to his senses and hires somebody else.

-Cheska

Captain Cheska Bennett, Head of the Navigator's Guild, was prone to exaggeration. But if she'd taken the effort to burn an entire letter onto the wood of his ship to get his attention, then this must be big. And if the reward was half as generous as promised...

He felt his mouth go dry. Sadesthenes once said, "*The wise man is not blinded by gold, but only a fool turns it down.*"

Calder rushed back up to the deck, Jerri following close behind him. "Andel! I'm raising the sails! I find myself suddenly homesick."

The story continues in...

OF SEA & SHADOW

Available now on Amazon!

WILL WIGHT lives in Florida, among the citrus fruits and slithering sea creatures. He graduated from the University of Central Florida in 2013, earning a Master's of Fine Arts in Creative Writing and a flute of dragon's bone.

Whosoever visits his website, *www.WillWight.com*, shall possess the power of Thor.

If you'd like to contact him, say his name three times into a candle-lit mirror at midnight. Or you could just send him an email at *will@willwight.com*.

(This paperback is made from 100% recycled troll-hide, for a sturdier finish.)

Made in the USA
Charleston, SC
26 May 2015